PENGUIN (

AMERICAN INDIAN STORIES, LEGENDS,
AND OTHER WRITINGS

ZITKALA-ŠA, known also as Gertrude Simmons Bonnin, was born on the Yankton Sioux reservation in South Dakota in 1876. A lifelong writer and activist, she is best known for a series of semiautobiographical stories about her childhood and schooling in Eastern boarding schools. Zitkala-Ša was a teacher, a student at the New England Conservatory of Music, coauthor of an opera entitled *The Sun Dance*, secretary-treasurer of the first pan-Indian political organization, the Society of American Indians, and editor of its quarterly magazine, *American Indian Magazine*. She wrote fiction, manifestos, speeches, poetry, and musical scores, retold Sioux legends, and was a prolific letter writer. She was founder and president of the National Council of American Indians, the Washington-based tribal advocacy group that she led until her death in 1938.

CATHY N. DAVIDSON, Ruth F. DeVarney Professor of English and vice provost for interdisciplinary studies at Duke University, is past president of the American Studies Association and former editor of the journal *American Literature*. She has written or edited more than fifteen books, including *Revolution and the Word: The Rise of the Novel in America*, *Reading in America*, *The Oxford Companion to Women's Writing in the United States* (with Linda Wagner-Martin), *Closing: The Life and Death of an American Factory* (with photographer Bill Bamberger), and *Thirty-Six Views of Mt. Fuji: On Finding Myself in Japan*.

ADA NORRIS is a Ph.D. candidate in the English Department at Duke University completing a dissertation on Zitkala-Ša's pedagogical stories and cultural contexts.

ZITKALA-ŠA

American Indian Stories, Legends, and Other Writings

Edited with an Introduction and Notes by

CATHY N. DAVIDSON *and* ADA NORRIS

PENGUIN BOOKS

PENGUIN BOOKS

Published by the Penguin Group

Penguin Group (USA) Inc., 375 Hudson Street, New York, New York 10014, U.S.A.
Penguin Group (Canada), 90 Eglinton Avenue East, Suite 700, Toronto, Ontario,
Canada M4P 2Y3 (a division of Pearson Penguin Canada Inc.)
Penguin Books Ltd, 80 Strand, London WC2R 0RL, England
Penguin Ireland, 25 St Stephen's Green, Dublin 2, Ireland
(a division of Penguin Books Ltd)
Penguin Group (Australia), 250 Camberwell Road, Camberwell, Victoria 3124,
Australia (a division of Pearson Australia Group Pty Ltd)
Penguin Books India Pvt Ltd, 11 Community Centre, Panchsheel Park,
New Delhi – 110 017, India
Penguin Group (NZ), 67 Apollo Drive, Rosedale, North Shore 0632, New Zealand
(a division of Pearson New Zealand Ltd)
Penguin Books (South Africa) (Pty) Ltd, 24 Sturdee Avenue,
Rosebank, Johannesburg 2196, South Africa

Penguin Books Ltd, Registered Offices: 80 Strand, London WC2R 0RL, England

First published in Penguin Books 2003

LIBRARY OF CONGRESS CATALOGING-IN-PUBLICATION DATA
Zitkala-Sa, 1876–1938.
American Indian stories, legends, and other writings / Zitkala-Sa ; edited with an
introduction and notes by Cathy N. Davidson and Ada Norris.
p. cm. — (Penguin classics)
Includes bibliographical references.
ISBN 978-0-14-243709-4
1. Indians of North America—Folklore.   2. Indians of North America—Social conditions.
3. Legends—United States.   4. Speeches, addresses, etc., Indian—United States.
I. Davidson, Cathy N., 1949–   II. Norris, Ada.   III. Title.   IV. Series.

E98.F6 Z58 2003
398.2'089'97—dc21   2002032268

Printed in the United States of America
Set in Sabon

Contents

I
Old Indian Legends

II
American Indian Stories

III
Selections from American Indian Magazine

IV
Poetry, Pamphlets, Essays, and Speeches

Acknowledgments

The editors would like to thank the Special Collections and Manuscripts staff at Brigham Young University for their solicitous attention and generous access to their well-managed and organized collection. Ada Norris visited this archive to look at Zitkala-Ša's papers as well as manuscripts of the score and libretto of *The Sun Dance* opera in July 2001. David Whittaker, Russ Taylor, and the students at Special Collections were tremendously helpful. We also thank the Interlibrary Loan staff of Duke University Library for filling many, often time-consuming, requests over the past couple of years without which this would have been a much more difficult endeavor.

Ada Norris: Thanks to Caroline White and everyone at Penguin Classics for their commitment to this project. For funding, thanks to the Graduate School of Duke University for support for a trip to Utah, the Department of English for an Ashbel Brice Award for some of the key research, and the John Hope Franklin Institute for Interdisciplinary Studies in the Humanities for a fellowship giving intellectual and financial support in the final stages of this project. Special thanks to Cathy N. Davidson for bringing me onto the project, and for her unparalleled generosity as a coeditor, coteacher, mentor, and scholar. Also, my deepest thanks to Dana Seitler for all her help, editorial and otherwise.

Cathy N. Davidson: I would like to thank the editors at Penguin Classics, and especially Caroline White, who aggressively pursued this project for several years in order to make Zitkala-Ša's work available to the widest possible general readership. I also thank Ada Norris, without whose historical and archival research this would have been a far more ordinary book. In two years of team-teaching and another two years of discussing Zitkala-Ša's writing, Ada Norris has been the best possible interlocutor, collaborator, and intellectual partner. I wish to thank Ken Wissoker for his editorial insights and loving support. Finally, I thank the many Native American and Canadian First People scholars, writers, and activists who, for the past two decades, have illuminated our thinking, teaching, and research. In particular, this volume was partly inspired by my brother-in-law, the late Roy "Sykes" Cunningham—Métis activist and advocate and human being extraordinaire.

Durham, North Carolina
May 2002

Introduction

As writer, teacher, and activist, Zitkala-Ša played a major part in articulating the role of Native Americans in an era of westward expansion, settlement, and conquest. Born in 1876, Zitkala-Ša was a witness, survivor, and trenchant chronicler of major events in white-Indian relations of the nineteenth and early twentieth centuries. The year of her birth coincided with the Battle of Little Big Horn (also called the battle of Greasy Grass), and with the beginning of the systematic violation by the U.S. government of the 1868 Treaty of Laramie. This treaty had established Native rights and control over the "Great Sioux Reservation," which included parts of present-day South Dakota, North Dakota, Montana, and Wyoming. But with the discovery of gold in 1873, the land suddenly became desirable for U.S. interests. By 1876 the aggressive assault by the U.S. Army against the Sioux reached its climax. George Custer, with the Seventh Cavalry, attacked Sitting Bull's alliance of Sioux and Cheyenne at Little Big Horn Creek, but was surrounded by Crazy Horse and his warriors and killed. By 1877 all Sioux, except for some Hunkpapas led by Sitting Bull and Oglalas led by Crazy Horse, had surrendered. Crazy Horse was tricked and summarily assassinated in September. That same year, Congress passed a law that shrunk the Great Sioux Reservation from 134 million acres to 15 million. After this period of aggression, the United States shifted strategies, replacing violence with a massive assimilation policy: the Dawes Act of 1887 began the work of dissolving communal and tribal land rights, and government-run Indian boarding schools systematically broke apart families and installed curriculums and disciplinary

structures intended to eradicate traditional tribal culture. To
say that Zitkala-Ša was born into a transitional era in white-
Indian relations seems a stark understatement.

Some of these events form the backdrop for Zitkala-Ša's
stories, particularly the three major works published in the
Atlantic Monthly in 1900. Unspoken in Zitkala-Ša's powerful
semiautobiographical story cycle is the fact that another Indian
massacre, the massacre at Wounded Knee and the murder of
Sitting Bull, occurred while she was at home on the Yankton
reservation on a school break. At this time, the popularity of
the messianic Ghost Dance religion had risen among the Sioux.
A peaceful spiritual practice that integrated Lakota and Christian beliefs, the Ghost Dance was based on the idea that,
through dance and ritual, the decimated buffalo population
and massacred Indians would come back to life again, Indian
lands would be returned, and the U.S. Army and other white
aggressors would disappear. In the face of overwhelming violence, it is not surprising that this apocalyptic religion found so
many adherents. Fearful that the Ghost Dance would mobilize
the Sioux politically, on December 15, 1890, a special unit of
the Indian police was sent to murder the great Sioux leader
Sitting Bull. On December 28, at least three hundred Sioux
men, women, and children were killed at Wounded Knee
Creek, and the Ghost Dance religion, in essence, died. Thus
Zitkala-Ša's tales are survivor stories on the most profound and
compelling level.

A writer creatively responding to Native American events
and a political activist, Zitkala-Ša has enjoyed a varying reputation over the last hundred years. At the beginning of the
twentieth century she was the toast of literary society, chosen
by *Harper's Bazaar* as one of the "Persons Who Interest Us"
(1900). As was typical of popular characterizations of the period, the article tracked her progress from a "veritable little
savage" "running wild" to an Indian girl of "beauty and many
talents" with a "rare command of English and much artistic
feeling." Her work was published in both prestigious and popular magazines, was read widely and had critical success. In the

1920s, stories from her first book, *Old Indian Legends* (1901), appeared in textbooks and school readers intended for schoolchildren in New York, Washington, D.C., Virginia, and other Eastern states.

Although her work garnered respect during her lifetime, it lay in some obscurity after her death in 1938 before being rediscovered and reassessed in the 1970s and 1980s. She was a superb writer, but her work is not easily characterized by one or another political position; Zitkala-Ša trod the unstable terrain between radicalism, separatism, assimilationism, and intermittent conservatism. No wonder then that biographical accounts tend to be confusing or even mythological, often grasping one part of her story to the neglect or even suppression of others. Zitkala-Ša challenges easy categorization, suggesting that we don't have ready access to the critical language needed to talk about the contradictions, multiplicity, or chaos—to use Zitkala-Ša's own term—that may exist within the work of a single author or the course of an individual life history. She did not live a dual or fractured life. Rather, she moved in, out, around, and between worlds: from her Yankton reservation to a federal boarding school and back again; from Ute reservations to the halls of power in Washington, D.C.; from the position of secretary-treasurer of the Society of American Indians to membership in the League of American Penwomen. With each move came shifting interpretive contexts and a range of allegations or misattributions by both her allies and her enemies. This presents a challenge to contemporary readers attempting to make some sense of her complex story. Her writing urges us to put American Indian identity, culture, and history into our ongoing conversations about authenticity, integration, education, nationality, assimilation, and civil rights and antiracism struggles.

Zitkala-Ša moved in and out of community centers among the Utes, her son Ohiya's Benedictine boarding school, meetings with the General Federation of Women's Clubs, talks by her Christian Science friends, violin performances, congressional committees, legal meetings, gala New York affairs, and tribal lodge meetings. Not surprisingly, her life played out in an array of spheres and on the public record in numerous ways. For example, that Zitkala-Ša was a "direct descendent of Sitting Bull" was one of the favorite biographical items that the mainstream press reprinted—from the *New York Times* and the *Washington Times* to political journals like *Indian Truth*. Zitkala Ša herself was implicated in propagating this myth. It became one of her favorite autobiographical stories; she had a picture of herself at the Sitting Bull monument dedication ceremony displayed prominently in her home and sent copies of it to friends. But the intent behind the reference to herself as the "granddaughter of Sitting Bull" was not that she was part of the literal line of genealogical descent, as the popular press assumed. Rather, she had a different idea about what counted as family in Indian culture, based more on cultural and historical ties than on blood, and she was savvy to the popular Anglo stories about Native American culture and their favorite and prototypical heroes, such as Sitting Bull. In a short piece written in 1924, "Heart to Heart," Zitkala-Ša described her home in the Dakota Plains as a "big family circle," going on to explain that: "Either by marriage, by blood, or by adoption every member of the tribe bore some relation to the rest." Doreen Rappaport's 1997 biography, *The Flight of the Red Bird*, written primarily for young readers, calls the claim "ludicrous" on the basis that "Sitting Bull was a Hunkpapa and if she was his granddaughter she could not be of pure Yankton blood." Rappaport argues that Zitkala-Ša calculated that mainstream Americans "lumped all Indians together and did not distinguish among the various tribes in the Sioux federation." While interesting, this analysis is based on a literal notion of kinship that Zitkala-Ša (who, with a white father, was not of "pure Yankton blood" anyway) clearly disregarded.

We may never know if or how Zitkala-Ša was indeed "related" to Sitting Bull. We do not even know for certain who her father was. One possibility is that he was a man named Fechner, purportedly a white man who may have been abusive toward Zitkala-Ša's brother. Nor do we know much about her mother's previous husband, John Haysting Simmons, whose name the young Zitkala-Ša used until a falling out with her family prompted her to rename herself.

We can do little more than attempt to keep up with her rapid moves between Catholicism, paganism, Mormonism, and Christian Science. She is variously called a full-blooded Sioux, a "half-breed," and any number of things in between. More interesting is the continual proliferation of categories, names, and places that circulated around Zitkala-Ša during, and after, her lifetime. What we do know is pieced together from her stories, letters, editorials, the *Congressional Record*, and tribal histories, as well as critical readings of Zitkala-Ša's work itself.

1876–1899:
EARLY CHILDHOOD AND SCHOOLING

Zitkala-Ša was born Gertrude Simmons at South Dakota's Yankton Reservation in 1876. She lived there with her mother, Ellen Simmons, whose Yankton Nakota name was Taté I Yóhin Win (translated as Reaches for the Wind), and her brother David (who never took a non-Anglo name; Zitkala-Ša fictionalized him as Dawée), until he went east for school. Young Gertrude lived on the reservation until she was eight. In "Impressions of an Indian Childhood," first published in the *Atlantic Monthly* in 1900, Zitkala-Ša presents her mother and her extended tribal community as teachers, caretakers, and models. Education here came organically through the "wild freedom" of everyday life, with adults, children, animals, the spirits, and the land linked in a web of mutual sustenance and respect. In 1884 her Yankton life came to an abrupt end when missionaries arrived to recruit children from the reservation following official governmental policies of assimilation. Zitkala-Ša tells this story in paradigmatic terms in "School Days of an Indian Girl," in which she is tempted by the missionaries' promises of plentiful "red apples" to hop the "iron horse" and go east. She was shorn of her identity—made to cut her long hair, barred from speaking her own language—but still able to call upon a store of strategies learned while listening to the traditional tales with which she grew up. Resisting the pressures of assimilation in small ways, employing trickster strategies such as vandalizing the school's Bible, she was able to maintain a sense of herself.

Zitkala-Ša attended White's Manual Labor Institute, a Quaker boarding school for Indians in Wabash, Indiana, until 1887 when she returned to the reservation and lived with her mother for a difficult year and a half. For the first time she felt alienated from life at the reservation and especially from her own mother, who had been against her traveling east for school in the first place. For a brief period in 1889–90 Zitkala-Ša attended the Santee Technical School, which was nearby in Nebraska. Soon after that she went back to White's Manual, staying until 1895, when she enrolled at Earlham College in Richmond, Indiana. There she frequently published poems and articles in the school paper, *The Earlhamite*, and the next year went to the Indiana State Oratorical Contest as Earlham's representative to compete in a public debate. The audience was mostly white, and when it was her turn to speak, a few of them held up a "a large white flag, with a drawing of a most forlorn Indian girl on it," with the word "squaw" written underneath. In "The School Days of an Indian Girl," Zitkala-Ša describes this behavior as "worse than barbarian rudeness." Shaken but determined, she persevered and took second place in the contest. Though gratified to see the flag fall from sight, and "the hands which hurled it hung limp in defeat," she realized later in the night: "The little taste of victory did not satisfy a hunger in my heart." The experience was to be a formative one for Zitkala-Ša and echoed that of some of her contemporaries who also were grappling with what it meant to excel in a largely white institution of higher education. In the opening paragraphs of *The Souls of Black Folk*, W.E.B. DuBois recalls, "That sky was bluest when I could beat my mates at examination-time, or beat them at a foot-race, or even beat their stringy heads."

Leaving Earlham due to poor health in 1897, Zitkala-Ša went to teach at the infamous Carlisle Indian Industrial School. Carlisle, under the leadership of retired army general Richard Henry Pratt, was a Pennsylvania boarding school founded with the express purpose of separating Indians from their reservation and tribal contexts in order to assimilate them into white society. Famously, Pratt's slogan while running the Carlisle school was "Kill the Indian and save the man!" The methods employed by Pratt and his contemporaries ranged from forced and prolonged separation from family, beatings, and food deprivation to less overtly violent tactics, including a forced work system which farmed out students to area families to be immersed in everyday white culture and "labor." To qualify for federal funding, boarding schools were required to practice a strict English-only policy. Pratt wrote in the January–March 1915 issue of the *Quarterly Journal of the American Indians* of his educational policy: "Do not feed America to the Indian, which is tribalizing and not an Americanizing process, but feed the Indian to America, and America will do the assimilating and annihilate the problem."

During her first year as a teacher at Carlisle, Zitkala-Ša was sent west by Pratt to attract new Indian students—bringing upon others the same disruptive separation she herself had experienced thirteen years earlier. This paradox did not go unnoticed by Zitkala-Ša who, after teaching at Carlisle for two years, wrote: "In the process of my education I had lost all consciousness of the nature world about me. Thus, when a hidden rage took me to the small white-walled prison which I then called my room, I unknowingly turned away from my one salvation." In 1899, Zitkala-Ša left behind the restrictive white walls of the boarding school. She resigned from her teaching post in order to study music and violin at the New England Conservatory of Music in Boston, Massachusetts. Playing and studying music, writing an opera libretto and score, as well as working with various other performing musicians, would be a lifelong preoccupation and avocation.

1900–1902:
"LITTLE LITERARY SKY ROCKET"

While Zitkala-Ša was enrolled at the New England Conservatory of Music she experienced a flurry of literary publicity
and recognition. Between 1900 and 1902, her writings appeared in the most prestigious publications, such as *Harper's*
and the *Atlantic Monthly*. Her fiction and autobiographical
stories ran alongside the work of such notable writers as Stephen Crane, Theodore Dreiser, Henry James, Edith Wharton,
W.E.B. DuBois, and Kate Chopin. Her stories were illustrated
by Frederick Remington, one of the most renowned illustrators
of his day, famous for his depictions of stereotypically lean and
muscular Indian warriors. At the same time, her 1901 book,
Old Indian Legends, was illustrated by Angel De Cora, a well-
known Winnebago artist who also taught at the Carlisle School
and who sketched scenes of Indian families in everyday life.

Zitkala-Ša's series of three autobiographical short stories
(moving from childhood to student to teacher) appeared in the
Atlantic Monthly over a course of three months in 1900. In
1901 *Harper's Monthly Magazine* ran "The Soft-Hearted
Sioux" and "The Trial Path," and her collection of retold
Sioux tales, *Old Indian Legends*, was published by Ginn &
Co., a literary and textbook publisher. In 1902 "A Warrior's
Daughter" appeared in *Everybody's Magazine*, "Why I Am a
Pagan" in *Atlantic Monthly*, and "Iya, the Camp-Eater" in
Twin Territories. In 1904 she published the story "Shooting of
the Red Eagle" in *Indian Leader*. During this period she also
published essays arguing for the importance of Indian dance in
Carlisle's *Red Man and the Helper* and the Santee School's pa-
per, the *Word Carrier*.

Not only was Zitkala-Ša's fiction fueled by her desire to de-
pict and document American Indian culture and its mytholo-
gies, but it also displayed a political savvy that was as serious
as it was playful. Writing in 1901 to her then-fiancé, Carlos
Montezuma, an Apache doctor and renowned radical activist
against the reservation system and the Bureau of Indian Affairs

(who would ultimately align himself with Pratt-style rapid assimilation), Zitkala-Ša says in her typical wry fashion: "By the way, the *Atlantic Monthly* has just accepted a little scribble of mine—'Why I Am a Pagan.' I imagine Carlisle will rear up on its haunches at sight of the little sky rocket! ha ha!" She predicted correctly. The conservative General Pratt wrote in *Red Man and Helper* that the story was "trash" and its author "worse than a pagan."

It was one of the ironies of her career that Zitkala-Ša was vilified by the Indian school where she taught at the same time she was being lionized by high literary society. In another letter to Montezuma, in March of 1901, she writes:

> In contrast with Carlisle's opinion of my work—Boston pats me with no little pride. The "Atlantic Monthly" wrote me a note in praise of the story. An intelligent literary critic says my writing has a distinguished air about it—. Others say I am concerning myself with glory! Ah—but so many words! What do I care—I knew that all the world could not take a liberal view of my work—But in spite of other varied opinions I am bound to *live* my own life.

Here again we see the way she performed different cultural roles and won friends or enemies depending upon how closely she did or did not ascribe to certain ideologies about what might or might not be "good for the Indians."

1902–1919:
DANCING, PEYOTE WARS, AND
THE SOCIETY OF AMERICAN INDIANS

In August 1902, after juggling at least a couple of tragic and tempestuous relationships (one boyfriend died, her engagement to Carlos Montezuma exploded in a bitter lovers' quarrel), Zitkala-Ša married Raymond T. Bonnin, a childhood friend from the Yankton Reservation. Raymond Bonnin was anything but a fiery radical. Rather than protest the Bureau of Indian Affairs, he obtained a post in Utah working among the Ute Indians. In 1902, Zitkala-Ša moved to Utah with her husband, and shortly after reaching there she gave birth to her only son, Raymond Ohiya Bonnin.

Some scholars mark this move as the putative end of Zitkala-Ša's literary career. She never again published in *Atlantic Monthly* and *Harper's*. However, she continued to write and publish a wide variety of works—fiction and legends, poetry, political essays, sketches, an opera, and numerous letters—until the end of her life. In Utah, Zitkala-Ša taught school and developed a community center, significantly shifting the style of her teaching from General Pratt's coercive assimilation to a grassroots, communitarian practice. She started a sewing club, began a hot lunch program, and opened a free arts and crafts space for children. At the same time, she collaborated on *The Sun Dance*, an opera that melded Native American ritual with the standard European operatic tradition.

During most of Zitkala-Ša's life the federal government had tried repeatedly to quash the Sun Dance ritual. Missionaries and government officials opposed the ceremony, claiming it was "barbaric, wild and heathenish" and "torturous." As the ceremonies would attract as many as nine to fifteen thousand people, it was also, and perhaps primarily, seen as too great a threat to "allow" so many Indians to congregate in one place. In 1881, the Sioux Sun Dance was banned by authorities on the Pine Ridge Reservation in South Dakota. The commissioner of Indian affairs declared the ritual illegal in 1883. In 1884 a federal regulation made the practice of any Native American Indian religion illegal and the Department of Interior again banned the Sun Dance in 1904. The dance continued to be practiced covertly until the Indian Reorganization Act of 1934, which, in addition to providing for self-government of the reservations by the Indian residents, allowed the open practice of dance.

Despite the repeated attempts to eradicate the practice, in Zitkala-Ša's experience the Sun Dance was alive and flourishing among Plains tribes, from Utah to the Dakotas. The Sun Dance was a celebration that lasted as long as a week and was, in at least some of its forms, a highly organized and ritualized set of practices involving dancers and supporters gathered around a circular space, in the center of which stood a pole made of a sacred tree. Stages of the celebration included, but were not limited to, a capture, torture, and escape sequence that attracted the most attention from missionary and Christian groups who ultimately rallied for the ban. Zitkala-Ša became an advocate for the ritual and through the opera, which she wrote with William Hanson, translated its power for predominantly white audiences.

Hanson was a white Mormon music teacher living in Vernal, Utah, whom she met while working among the Utes. The two shared an interest in literature and music, and Hanson's own body of work reflects a pointed interest in Native customs and culture. Over the course of a couple of years, Zitkala-Ša and William Hanson composed a libretto that centered on the entanglements of a love triangle played out during the week-long Sun Dance ritual. They spent much time on the musical score, which incorporated oral musical Indian traditions into a highly organized and acculturated Western musical form.

The story of *The Sun Dance* could easily have come from the pages of *Old Indian Legends*. A Shoshone brave named Sweet Singer gets into some trouble with his home tribe: he foolishly has taken the medicine man's "love-leaves," causing a "Shoshone virgin whom he does not love" to fall in love with him. To extricate himself he follows an invitation from the chief of the Dakota Sioux to officiate as leader of their Sun Dance singers. As it happens, he also has a crush on the chieftain's daughter, Winona. A more upright young brave named Ohiya (the name also of Zitkala-Ša's son) has already pledged his love to Winona and must now prove himself in the annual Sun Dance ceremony—where the tricky Sweet Singer is master of ceremonies.

The Sun Dance was performed around Utah in 1913 and 1914 to enthusiastic response and rave reviews. One reviewer noted in Salt Lake City's *Deseret News* in March 1913: "There was more color and variety of movement, more vivid stage effects" than he had witnessed in an opera before, and it paid homage to "the inner spiritual life of this much wronged and misunderstood people." A critic writing in *Musical American* on April 26, 1913, admitted to "skepticism as to the success of this attempt to weld the various customs of Indian life into an opera, but the enthusiasm became so general that the following evenings the audience was augmented by persons from various reservation towns, some of whom had to travel over 40 miles." It was about twenty years before *The Sun Dance* was revived, brought to Broadway as the New York Light Opera Guild's "Opera of the Year" in 1938. This time, Hanson's name appeared by itself on most publicity and programs, while Zitkala-Ša was listed as a "collaborator," if at all, and the production's sensational exoticism was emphasized: one handbill promised a "tuneful and scintillating light opera" that depicted "the love-life, tenderness and nobility of a once savage tribe."

On the heels of this opera celebrating an embattled religion, Zitkala-Ša embarked on a campaign that may seem to some contemporary eyes as her most fraught, complicated, and at times reactionary. While working at the community center among the Utes, Zitkala-Ša started to see an increase of ceremonial peyote use and she denounced it. For Zitkala-Ša, there was a world of difference between peyote rituals and other Native spiritual practices. She saw the peyote use as nothing more than "debilitating and degenerating" drug use. Like the many nineteenth-century feminists who became strong temperance activists in response to what they perceived as a danger to both social and family welfare, Zitkala-Ša became an outspoken critic of peyote, especially as used by men. In some of her letters, she expresses her concern for public safety, particularly of women and children, but also for the moral and spiritual state of Native Americans. Yet her concerns put her in an uncomfortable alliance with some reactionary whites with whom she disagreed passionately about other Native American issues, including the Sun Dance ritual. Most notably, her anti-peyote stand in the years 1913–1918 drew both the admiration of her old Carlisle School critic, General Pratt, and the ire of a white, politically liberal ethnologist, James Mooney, who was em-

ployed by the Bureau of American Ethnology and had spent his
career in the field, studying first the Ghost Dance religion and
then religious practices involving peyote.

In one of the most oddly symbolic and confused moments in
white-Indian relations of the time, Mooney stood before
Congress and denounced Zitkala-Ša as a fraud, disparaging her
as someone who "claims to be a Sioux woman." In his testimony before the Senate subcommittee on peyote, Mooney
not only disagreed with Zitkala-Ša's stance on peyote use,
but at length derided the Indian dress Zitkala-Ša wore for a
photograph that ran in the February 17, 1918, issue of the
Washington Times: "She wore a fringed dress whose style
identified its provenance as a southern Plains tribe; her belt was
that of a Navajo man; and the fan she carried was, itself, a type
used by men in the peyote ceremony." In an attempt to discredit her politics about peyote regulation, he employed an old
trick typically used against women: he overemphasized her
physical appearance and thus drew attention away from the se-
riousness of her interest in the political issues at hand. In doing
so, he also discredited her racial authenticity, insinuating her
lack of knowledge of Indian culture and her haphazard affilia-
tion with different tribes.

Like a number of more recent critics, Mooney fell into the
logic of "racial purity" in judging Zitkala-Ša. All evidence suggests, however, that she was well aware that her "Indian cos-
tume" (as she called it) was a tribal mélange but wore it
nonetheless because she felt it would help further the cause of
Indian rights. While raising support for her anti-peyote movement, Zitkala-Ša turned to the Women's Temperance Society,
and in a letter written to Arthur Parker, then president of the
Society of American Indians, on March 2, 1917, Zitkala-Ša
mentions she had been asked to give a piano solo "all in Indian
dress." She explained, "I have agreed, for in this case the use of
Indian dress for a drawing card is for a good cause. No doubt,
there may be some, who may not wholly approve of the Indian
dress. I hope it does not displease you. Even a clown has to
dress differently from his usual citizen's suit. In News papers,
italics are resorted to, with good effect." Whether or not, from

a contemporary viewpoint, we agree with Zitkala-Ša's choice, what is clear is that she made it with political consciousness, understanding her identity as both deeply cultural and performative.

Like many other public intellectuals, Zitkala-Ša has been accused of "selling out" largely because of the difficult balancing act she attempted as a mediator between tribal, bureaucratic, and activist contexts. To speak her mind and her principles meant occasionally sharing beliefs with those whose other ideas she found repugnant. It also required alliances that were imperfect and unstable. Not only does politics make for the proverbial strange bedfellows, but different people, with different political affiliations, can oppose the same practice for very different reasons. In the slapdash world of actual political legislation, this can result in one being branded reactionary or radical when one is trying to voice a highly individualized (and thoughtful) opposition to a practice. Zitkala-Ša, with her characteristic wry humor, sums up her ambiguous and often uncomfortable status in another letter written to Arthur Parker after he expressed sympathy at the "horror" of continuing to live and work on a reservation:

> Every Indian who has attempted to do real uplift work for the tribes gets stung. No wonder that he quits trying, goes back to the blanket, and sits in the teepee like a boiled owl. I have not sense enough to stop. Wouldn't know until I was killed; and the chances are I wouldn't know then, being dead.

She understood the criticism and scrutiny that more often than not accompanied political work, but she did not let that modify her beliefs. Among Zitkala-Ša's papers, housed at Brigham Young University, is a scrap of paper on which she repeatedly scrawled the following quote by Abraham Lincoln: "I must stand with anybody that stands right; stand with him while he is right and part with him when he goes wrong."

In 1916, at roughly the same time that she was campaigning against peyote, Zitkala-Ša was elected secretary and treasurer of the Society of American Indians (SAI), the first national pan-

Indian political organization run entirely by Native people. By some accounts, Zitkala-Ša's understated, behind-the-scenes husband was a bit jealous of her literary activities, and possibly to salve this rift as well as to make a change from the difficult routine of life in Utah, they decided to move east to SAI's Washington, D.C., office and send their son to Catholic boarding school—an ironic decision considering Zitkala-Ša's own history with boarding schools.

While SAI was concerned with tribal self-determination and the abuses of the Bureau of Indian Affairs (BIA) in terms of land allotment, the organization focused a lot of its energy on issues of education, assimilation, and citizenship. Often tagged as "red progressives" working in the "assimilative era" of American Indian politics, SAI struggled with the impossible task of attending to many different tribal interests while dealing with an increasingly punitive federal education and social welfare system. Initially, SAI was a progressive and experimental political force that worked on both local and national levels— for example, it initiated a community center movement, aimed at improving reservation life. Zitkala-Ša's center at Fort Duchesne among the Utes was the inaugural site. SAI hoped the centers would provide social services to poor Indians living on reservations, and focused its efforts on better health and nutrition as well as education. But SAI's relationship with reservation life was unstable. Among the many conflicts that emerged were disagreements over peyote and the position on the BIA, the government agency in charge of Indian and reservation policy. Some wanted to cut all ties with the BIA, believing it turned Indians into dependent wards of the state. Others believed in preserving the space fostered by the reservation system.

The *Quarterly Journal of the Society of American Indians* changed its name to *American Indian Magazine* in 1916 so it might broaden its readership base and gain some autonomy from the organization it represented. Zitkala-Ša joined the contributing editors in the last issue of 1915 (the final issue before the name change). The new magazine announced its mission to make the publication "the medium of communication between students and friends of the American Indian, especially between those engaged in the uplift and advancement of the race." Articles about the "Perils of Peyote Poison," debates on assimilation and citizenship, essays about Indian support of the World War, along with poetry, drawings, public letters, memoirs, and historical pieces like "The Truth About the Massacre at Wounded Knee" were all published while Zitkala-Ša was involved with the magazine. There was also a range of regular columns such as "The Editorial Sanctum," "Men and Women Whose Lives Count," and "What the Papers Say About Indians," which effectively established new links between the editors and SAI, their readers, and the popular press more generally. In the 1916 edition, a photograph of Zitkala-Ša was featured as the magazine's frontispiece to mark her election as secretary of SAI; she was described as "a fountain of energy. . . . She lives for one great ideal, the complete liberty of her race and for this end she devotes every minute of her life without compensation. We believe that she is the most remarkable Indian woman living, and yet she is the most unassuming."

With the Autumn 1918 issue of the *American Indian Magazine,* Zitkala-Ša became its editor. She continued to write articles and stories in addition to regular editorials. Under her editorship, the magazine began publishing new columns like "The Funny Side of War Work" and "Chatter" (which ranged from news about increased circulation of the magazine to inspirational quotes like "Genius is two per cent talent and ninety-eight percent application"), as well as "Under the Sun," which expanded the scope of the magazine to include news from around the world.

1919–1938:
THE NATIONAL COUNCIL OF
AMERICAN INDIANS

Although the SAI dissolved under the pressures of internal disagreement in 1919, Zitkala-Ša and her husband continued to act as advocates and mediators for various tribal interests. As a part of her work for the "Indian cause," Zitkala-Ša collected her previously published fiction as well as some new material into *American Indian Stories*, brought out by Hayworth Publishing House in 1921. In personal letters from the time, she calls her new book the "blanket book" (the cover image was an image of a Navajo blanket). The significance of this cover and the references to it surely weren't accidental. For one thing, they demonstrate how she continued to pick and choose among tribal representations. For another, they stand in stark contrast to the assimilative efforts of Indian boarding schools' regulations—regulations which figure centrally in these stories—requiring all students to disavow their tribal customs (colloquially, students who rejected their boarding school education and returned to their reservation were said to be going "back to the blanket").

In the 1920s, Zitkala-Ša became involved with the General Federation of Women's Clubs (GFWC), an umbrella organization for mostly white women's advocacy and suffrage groups. In 1921 she urged the GFWC to establish an Indian Welfare Committee. And in 1924, in her capacity as a GFWC representative, she investigated land and oil abuses in Oklahoma (most of which had been Indian Territory until 1907) for a report commissioned by the Indian Rights Association. This report, *Oklahoma's Poor Rich Indians: An Orgy of Graft and Exploitation of the Five Civilized Tribes—Legalized Robbery*, called for immediate government action and redress, and would lead to the formation of the Meriam Commission, a group of government officials brought together to attend to a range of problems on reservations. The Meriam Report of 1928 laid the groundwork for fundamental changes in Indian policy.

During the same period, Zitkala-Ša also spent time in California and wrote a series of articles about the California Indians to increase their political voice in the state. Published in the *San Francisco Bulletin* and in the *California Indian Herald*, these reflective pieces brought together poetics and politics in what was a new style of writing for Zitkala-Ša. The elements found in all her work come together in these short pieces: her love for nature mingles with retold tales and the call for political change. The three "chapters" and a final piece entitled "Heart to Heart" were to Zitkala-Ša as much a literary endeavor as a political mission. In a familiar and engaging first-person voice, she weaves together fragments touching on violated treaties, the state of affairs for Indians in California and elsewhere in the United States, and the otherwise silent histories of Indian life held within the sacred redwood forests.

In 1926 Zitkala-Ša founded and was elected president of the National Council of American Indians (NCAI)—for which her husband, Raymond, served as secretary—an organization that she would continue to run until her death in 1938. Their motto was "Help Indians Help Themselves in Protecting Their Rights and Properties." The group would become a major presence and advocate for redressing tribal inequities and abuses. NCAI came to represent at least forty-nine tribes, as letters and briefs written by and to them affirm. During this period Zitkala-Ša handled an impressive range of work. She routinely went to congressional meetings and sessions where she addressed issues such as Ute land and monetary claims, specific land allotment settlements for Navajos, distribution of rations and supplies to Yankton Sioux, and benefits for Native American World War I veterans. She continually publicized her work, wrote letters informing people of upcoming legislation, stumped for candidates, raised funds, and educated tribal communities about their civic rights.

At sixty-one years old, and in failing health, Zitkala-Ša fell into a coma on January 25, 1938, and died the following day. In perhaps the greatest misrepresentation in a life often misrepresented, she was described in the hospital's postmortem report as "Gertrude Bonnin from South Dakota—Housewife." Because of Raymond Bonnin's service as a captain with the U.S. Army, she was buried in Arlington National Cemetery, with a headstone that reads "Gertrude Simmons Bonnin—'Zitkala-Ša' of the Sioux Indians—1876–1938." Memorial services were held at the Church of Jesus Christ of Latter-Day

Saints. One of those who talked was John Collier, Commissioner of Indian Affairs under Franklin D. Roosevelt, who memorialized her as the "last of the great Indian Orators."

READING *AMERICAN INDIAN STORIES* TODAY

This volume presents a selection of Zitkala-Ša's writings that are as urgent, variable, and fascinating as her dedicated and multifaceted life. Because her writing is powerful and her subject early childhood, *American Indian Stories*, in particular, resonates with contemporary readers. In their acuity and complexity, this volume's stories provide both intellectual substance and emotional power.

Thematically, the stories explore the ways young people grow up and are educated into the values of a culture. Zitkala-Ša takes some basic autobiographical material, melds it with stories of other Native Americans who have been sent away to boarding school, then shapes it into a narrative that reverses the assumptions of some of the most popular and esteemed forms of nineteenth-century American and European literature. For example, Nathaniel Hawthorne's *The Scarlet Letter* looks different when it is read alongside Zitkala-Ša, who approaches similar issues of sexuality, sin, and freedom from subtly or sometimes radically opposite points of view. The Indians in *The Scarlet Letter* are portrayed as shadowy background figures, representing mysterious powers, magic, and the unbridled and potentially sinister world of nature. They bear little resemblance to the Indians we see in Zitkala-Ša's rendering of a boarding school in "The School Days of an Indian Girl," or of a girl at home with her mother on the Yankton reservation.

"The School Days of an Indian Girl" and "Impressions of an Indian Childhood" make real and vivid the pain of cultural dislocation enacted on a young girl who is not only vulnerable to change but initially welcomes it. Despite her mother's opposition, the young narrator insists on going to an Eastern government boarding school, miles from home, because she is sure that this school represents the promise of the future. Or at least she believes the missionaries, who arrive at the reservation to recruit young Indian children by promising them delicious red apples. Zitkala-Ša gives this potent symbol of Western mythology new resonance. The apple is, of course, the instrument of seduction in the book of Genesis. In "School Days" it is the catalyst of the child's fall from prelapsarian grace (the unsullied reservation) to the harsh world of the boarding school. The apple also links her tale of temptation and seduction with the lure of assimilationism: the apple is red on the outside, white on the inside. Through this symbol, the young girl becomes the innocent exemplar of the myth of assimilation that is key to the ideology of America, the great "melting pot." Zitkala-Ša's journey from reservation to boarding school reverses geographically the European immigrant's journey from Europe to New England and then west across America that was happening at the same time. It echoes and yet differentiates itself from the impulse of the world's diverse (primarily white) populations to assimilate into a heterogeneous—but also homogenized—American culture.

The effectiveness of "Impressions of an Indian Childhood" and "The School Days of an Indian Girl" lies in their point of view. Zitkala-Ša lends the maturity of the adult author to the terrified perspective of the small child. After the seemingly interminable trip across the prairies, the eight-year-old girl is thrown into a new world where all of the rules are different. Zitkala-Ša shows us this new world through the child's fearful eyes, maintaining this perspective so skillfully that she defamiliarizes the reader's world. Having to sit in a chair is a kind of torture. The squeak of leather-soled shoes is harsh and jarring to the ears. The way white people stand close to the person to whom they are speaking is a form of trespass. And the school's mandatory cutting of her long braid is an assault akin to rape. With an anthropologist's acuity in dissecting a foreign culture, Zitkala-Ša documents the aberrations of white culture, putting her reader into the position of having to judge harshly the very culture of which the reader is a part. Our empathy is with the child, not the child's "educators." The violence of this initiation rite into white life is so primitive that we are forced to reconsider the norms not of Native American society but of white society. "Normal" behaviors become practices, rituals, or customs that, from a Sioux point of view, range from the inexplicable to the unsightly to the barbaric. In other words, the initiation this Indian child undergoes is more violent than the initiation rituals of the Sun Dance that white Americans reacted so strongly against.

What makes Zitkala-Ša such a unique and masterful writer is her ability to portray the perceptions, assumptions, experiences, and customs of the Sioux while also making the reader rethink the perceptions, assumptions, experiences, and customs of white, middle-class Americans. This double edge comes from her manipulation of one of the most important forms of nineteenth-century European and American literature, the bildungsroman. A bildungsroman charts the "building" or education of a main character counseled by others into more understanding and sophistication in the ways of the world. What is rarely questioned in the bildungsroman is the validity of that world.

In her stories, Zitkala-Ša introduces a familiar figure, the child, limited in experience and full of expectations, many of which will be proven false. Where Zitkala-Ša subverts the form is in showing that the ways of the world are the problem, not the solution. The boarding school is a place of disrespect, degradation, and violence. Although the child thinks she is resisting the worst lessons of this dehumanized and dehumanizing environment, she succumbs little by little to its values. Each time she accepts something of the white ways taught at the boarding school, she is renouncing some quintessential part of her Sioux upbringing. Zitkala-Ša puts the reader (putatively white and middle-class) in the position of knowledge: we see, long before the child herself, that she is failing to preserve her Sioux identity. Zitkala-Ša sets up a plot whereby the adult reader distinguishes herself or himself from the innocent, ignorant child basically by indicting a white system of values. That is, we understand that the child has been despoiled, even while the child feels herself to be brave, independent, and triumphant.

The reader's point of view and the child's come together in the scene in which she returns, after three years' absence, to her mother's house. There are few scenes more emotionally harrowing or perspicacious than the encounter of the mother and her unhappy daughter. Home again, the daughter vehemently renounces the white ways she has learned—exchanging her shoes for soft moccasins, refusing to read in the Indian Bible her mother (who cannot read) proffers her. Scornful of the Anglicized Indians who pass by, tearful to be in the "heart of chaos," neither "a wild Indian nor a tame one," the narrator feels close to her mother. Yet, as readers, we recognize the mother's hopeless attempt to do something—anything—to console her inconsolable child, and the despair that prompts her to throw a shawl over her head and shoulders, step into the night, and howl to her brothers' spirits, asking for support in her "helpless misery." The conclusion is shattering: "My fingers grew icy cold, as I realized that my unrestrained tears had betrayed my suffering to her, and she was grieving for me."

The mother dries her tears before returning to the house, lest she cause the troubled daughter more pain. The daughter, understanding now, pretends to be asleep to avoid another confrontation. Inevitably, the daughter succumbs to her fate—a white man's fate. "A few more moons of such a turmoil drove me away to the Eastern school. I rode on the white man's iron steed, thinking it would bring me back to my mother in a few winters, when I should be grown tall, and there would be congenial friends awaiting me."

The familiar transliterations of Indian language—many moons, the white man's iron steed—remind one of the stock Indian phrases and characters found in any number of typical Westerns of the time, especially those of popular writers such as Owen Wister and Zane Grey. Again, though, the reader knows clearly what the despairing child cannot: that another trip east will only seal her alienation. In going east to school again, the girl is fleeing from her own sense of failure and betrayal, her profound sense not only of alienation but of alienation from her own self and values. The terrible subjunctive in the sentence ("would . . . should . . . would") is less a promise of what might happen than a taunting reminder of the distance between desire and fulfillment, fantasy and reality.

The politics of this story reside in its affective register. It is impossible not to empathize with this child and her mother and the disenfranchisement each feels. Yet, to experience empathy requires that the reader be critical of the system of Indian education. It requires the reader to be suspicious of the lessons in white culture this child has mastered. "My mother had never gone inside of a schoolhouse," the child narrator says at one point, "and so she was not capable of comforting her daughter who could read and write." This is not the logic of the loving, if defiant, little girl before her schooling in Indiana. It is the logic of a child who has been miseducated to the pernicious principle that book learning counts more than the deepest emotional bond between mother and daughter. This bildungsroman, in other words, is designed not to show the reader how much this child has grown and developed, but rather to show how her education into the seductive norms of white culture has left her desolate.

Another powerful level is added to the story when we remember that it depicts the years when Zitkala-Ša was away at Indian school and then returned to South Dakota. Where the author is reticent is on one of the most horrific and shameful incidents in white-Indian relations: the massacre at Wounded Knee. Nowhere in these stories is there a reference to this historical act of genocide. And yet these stories, first published a decade after Wounded Knee, carry within them an unspoken history of devastation. They are an allegory of the powerful meting out judgment on the powerless—teachers to children, whites to Indians. Such elliptical political commentary makes for haunting and powerful literature.

Why would the *Atlantic Monthly* publish fiction by a Native American that seems, to contemporary eyes, so overtly to condemn white middle-class American culture? Literary scholar Patricia Okker notes that Zitkala-Ša's autobiographical stories appeared in the very same 1900 volume of the magazine in which Mary Johnston's historical novel *To Have and to Hold* was serialized. *To Have and to Hold* indulges in all the possible stereotypes of evil and devilish "savages." Americans were fascinated by Native Americans, and may not have worried all that much about the reliability, accuracy, racism, or even skill of popular authors bent on reproducing racial stereotypes. One reason for the publication of Zitkala-Ša, then, may be that the *Atlantic Monthly* editors deemed her and her material exotic, and of interest to their readers. Turn-of-the-century readers were able to hold on to both concepts of the Native American—the stereotypical "savage" as well as this individuated young and abused girl-child heading east by train—and the emotion of the stories made their critical politics more palatable. Indeed, Zitkala-Ša's autobiographical fictions, with their double perspectives, depend on her readers giving up their prejudices, at least for the duration of the reading experience, in order to make connections and assumptions that the youthful narrator cannot make for herself.

Kenneth Lincoln uses the term "bicultural play" to describe such techniques. By this, he means a cross-cultural exchange in which the "*seers* . . . are *seeing* the *seen*," in which the "native 'seers' peer back." As in her story "The Soft-Hearted Sioux," Zitkala-Ša is quick to turn a trope. In that story, an Indian boy is taught by Christians that it is evil to hunt and kill animals. By the end of the story, the same Indian is being executed by Christians. The turn is an indictment of piety and hypocrisy, especially the Christians' censorious attitude toward hunting but not when the spoil of the hunt is an Indian charged with killing a white man. Capital punishment is somehow exempt from Christian indictments of killing living creatures—especially when it is an Indian who is executed.

Zitkala-Ša's stories detail two cultures in struggle, documenting the gaps and fissures separating them. Her fiction is not only about bicultural play but also about the ways that one culture structures the interpretation of another. But her writing is much more than a piece of history or a comparative template between Native and white culture. The expansiveness and variedness of her writing, her creativity, and her political commitment might best be understood in the way that scholar, poet, and theorist Gerald Vizenor describes Native American literature: as "unstudied landscapes, wild and comic rather than tragic and representational, storied with narrative wisps and tribal discourse." By reading Zitkala-Ša's autobiographical fiction or the fictions of her storied life, one understands the costs and consequences of the life she led as well as the triumph of her accomplishments. Her life began the year of the Battle of Little Big Horn and ended the year the opera *The Sun Dance* was performed on the New York stage. Hers is truly a remarkable story, told best by the writer herself.

Suggestions for Further Reading

Since the 1970s there has been a burgeoning of excellent scholarship on Native American literature and culture. For historical contexts we especially recommend turning to Hazel Hertzberg and Frederick Hoxie; for Native literary studies we suggest the work of Paula Gunn Allen, Arnold Krupat, and Robert Warrior.

For work on Zitkala-Ša, we recommend the biographical essays by Dexter Fisher, P. Jane Hafen, and William Willard; the University of Nebraska Press editions of her writings; and the following examples of scholarship on Zitkala-Ša and relevant cultural and historical contexts.

Allen, Paula Gunn. *The Sacred Hoop: Recovering the Feminine in American Indian Traditions.* Boston: Beacon, 1986.

———, ed. *Spider Woman's Granddaughters: Traditional Tales and Contemporary Writing by Native American Women.* Boston: Beacon, 1989.

Bell, Betty Louise. " 'If This Is Paganism . . .': Zitkala-Ša and the Devil's Language." In *Native American Religious Identity: Unforgotten Gods,* Jace Weaver, ed. Maryknoll, N.Y.: Orbis, 1998. 61–68.

Bernardin, Susan. "The Lessons of a Sentimental Education: Zitkala-Ša's Autobiographical Narratives." *Western American Literature* 32.3 (November 1997): 212–38.

Brown, Dee. *Bury My Heart at Wounded Knee: An Indian History of the American West.* New York: Holt, Rinehart, & Winston, 1970.

Churchill, Ward. *Struggle for the Land: Native North American Resistance to Genocide, Ecocide, and Colonization.* Winnipeg: Arbeiter Ring Publishing, 1999.

———. "The Earth Is Our Mother: Struggles for American Indian Land and Liberation in the Contemporary United States." In *The State of Native America: Genocide, Colonization, and Resistance,* M. Annette Jaimes, ed. Boston: South End Press, 1992. 139–88.

Coleman, Michael C. *American Indian Children at School, 1850–1930.* Jackson: University Press of Mississippi, 1993.

Cutter, Martha J. "Zitkala-Ša's Autobiographical Writings: The Problems of a Canonical Search for Language and Identity." *MELUS* 19.1 (Spring 1994): 31–45.

Diana, Vanessa Holford. " 'Hanging in the Heart of Chaos': Bi-Cultural Limbo, Self-(Re)presentation, and the White Audience in Zitkala-Ša's *American Indian Stories.*" *Cimarron Review* 121 (October 1997): 154–73.

Edmunds, R. David. *The New Warriors: Native American Leaders Since 1900.* Lincoln: University of Nebraska Press, 2001.

Fisher, Dexter. "The Transformation of Tradition: A Study of Zitkala-Ša and Mourning Dove, Two Transitional American Indian Writers." In *Critical Essays on Native American Literature,* Andrew Wiget, ed. Boston: Hall, 1985. 202–11.

———. "Zitkala-Ša: The Evolution of a Writer." *American Indian Quarterly* 5.3 (1979): 229–38. Reprinted as Foreword to *American Indian Stories* by Zitkala-Ša. Lincoln: University of Nebraska Press, 1985.

Hafen, P. Jane. "A Cultural Duet: Zitkala-Ša and *The Sun Dance Opera.*" *Great Plains Quarterly* 18.2 (Spring 1998): 102–11.

———. "Zitkala-Ša: Sentimentality and Sovereignty." *Wicazo Sa Review* 12.2 (Fall 1997): 31–42.

Hanson, William F. *Sun Dance Land.* Provo: J. Grant Stevenson, 1967.

Heflin, Ruth J. *"I Remain Alive": The Sioux Literary Renaissance.* Syracuse: Syracuse University Press, 2000.

Hertzberg, Hazel. *The Search for an American Indian Identity: Modern Pan-Indian Movements.* Syracuse: Syracuse University Press, 1971.

Hoefel, Roseanne. "Writing, Performance, Activism: Zitkala-Ša and Pauline Johnson." In *Native American Women in Literature and Culture,* Susan Castillo and Victor M. P. DaRosa, eds. Porto, Portugal: Fernando Pessoa University Press, 1997. 107–18.

Hoxie, Frederick E. *A Final Promise: A Campaign to Assimilate the Indians. 1880–1920.* New York: Cambridge University Press, 1989.

Krupat, Arnold. *For Those Who Came After: A Study of Native Ameri-*

can *Autobiography*. Berkeley: University of California Press, 1989.

Lincoln, Kenneth. *Ind'in Humor: Bicultural Play in Native America*. New York: Oxford University Press, 1993.

Lukens, Margaret A. "The American Story of Zitkala-Ša." In *In Her Own Voice: Nineteenth-Century American Women Essayists,* Sherry Lee Linkon, ed. New York: Garland, 1997. 141–55.

Okker, Patricia. "Native American Literatures and the Canon: The Case of Zitkala-Ša." In *American Realism and the Canon*, Tom Quirk and Gary Scharnhorst, eds. Newark: University of Delaware Press, 1994. 87–101.

Rappaport, Doreen. *The Flight of Red Bird: The Life of Zitkala-Ša*. New York: Puffin, 1999.

Ruoff, A. Lavonne Brown. "Early Native American Women Authors: Jane Johnston Schoolcraft, Sarah Winnemucca, S. Alice Callahan, E. Pauline Johnson, and Zitkala-Ša." In *Nineteenth-Century American Women Writers: A Critical Reader*, Karen L. Kilcup, ed. Malden, Mass.: Blackwell, 1998.

Smith, Jeanne. " 'A Second Tongue': The Trickster's Voice in the Works of Zitkala-Ša." In *Tricksterism in Turn-of-the-Century American Literature: A Multicultural Perspective,* Elizabeth Ammons and Annette White-Parks, eds. Hanover, N.H.: University Press of New England, 1994. 46–60.

Smith, Sidonie. "Cheesecake, Nymphs, and 'We the People': Un/National Subjects about 1900." *Prose Studies* 17.1 (April 1994): 120–40.

Spack, Ruth. "Revisioning American Indian Women: Zitkala-Ša's Revolutionary *American Indian Stories*." *Legacy* 14.1 (1997): 25–43.

Vizenor, Gerald. *Narrative Chance: Postmodern Discourse on Native American Indian Literatures*. Albuquerque: University of New Mexico Press, 1989.

———. "Trickster Discourse." *American Indian Quarterly* 14 (1990): 277–88.

Warrior, Robert Allen. *Tribal Secrets: Recovering American Indian Intellectual Traditions*. Minneapolis: University of Minnesota Press, 1995.

Wexler, Laura. "Tender Violence: Literary Eavesdropping, Domestic Fiction, and Educational Reform." In *The Culture of Sentiment: Race, Gender, Sentimentality in Nineteenth-Century America*, Shirley Samuels, ed. New York: Oxford University Press, 1992.

Wiget, Andrew. *Native American Literature*. Boston: Twayne, 1985.

Willard, William. "The First Amendment, Anglo-Conformity, and American Indian Religious Freedom." *Wicazo Ša Review* 7 (Spring 1991): 25–42.

———. "Zitkala-Ša: A Woman Who Would Be Heard." *Wicazo Ša Review* 1 (Spring 1985): 11–16.

Zitkala-Ša. *American Indian Stories*. (1921), Foreword by Dexter Fisher. Lincoln: University of Nebraska Press, 1985.

———. *Dreams and Thunder: Stories, Poems, and* The Sun Dance Opera. P. Jane Hafen, ed. Lincoln: University of Nebraska Press, 2001.

———. *Old Indian Legends*. (1901), Foreword by Agnes Picotte. Lincoln: University of Nebraska Press, 1995.

Chronology

1868 The Treaty of Laramie establishes the "Great Sioux Reservation" along with measures for its protection—including a stipulation that changes to the treaty require the consent of three-fourths of all men living on the reservation.

1873 Gold is discovered by a nonnative on Sioux land.

1874 The Women's Christian Temperance Union is formed.

1876 Zitkala-Ša (Gertrude Simmons) is born on the Yankton Reservation in South Dakota.

1876 The Battle of Little Big Horn: General George Custer leads one famous and unsuccessful leg of a three-pronged offensive to take over Sioux land in Montana, and is killed.

1880s The U.S. government bans the Sun Dance and other tribal religious practices.

1881 The Tuskegee Normal and Industrial Institute is founded by Booker T. Washington.

1883 Buffalo Bill's Wild West Show begins touring.

1884 Missionaries come to the Yankton Reservation; Zitkala-Ša attends White's Manual Technical Institute in Wabash, Indiana, on and off through 1895.

1887 The Dawes Severalty Act or General Allotment Act is passed; the central legislative act inaugurating the assimilative era, it breaks up tribal lands and affiliations by allotting plots of land, in trust, to individuals.

1889 The Indian Territory is opened to white settlement (it will formally become Oklahoma in 1907).

1890 A prophet named Wovoka introduces a new religion based on the Ghost Dance, which sweeps across the Sioux reservation. Sitting Bull is killed on December 15. More than three hundred Sioux are massacred at Wounded Knee Creek on December 29.

1895–1897 Zitkala-Ša attends Earlham College in Richmond, Indiana.

1896 Zitkala-Ša wins second prize at the Indiana State Oratorical Contest.

1896 The U.S. Supreme Court's decision in *Plessy v. Ferguson* upholds the doctrine of "separate but equal," thus initiating the age of Jim Crow.

1897 Zitkala-Ša accepts a teaching position at the Carlisle Indian Industrial School in Pennsylvania.

1898 The Spanish-American War is waged from mid-April to mid-August. As a result, the United States gains the Hawaiian Islands, Puerto Rico, and the Philippine Islands.

1899 Zitkala-Ša goes to study at the New England Conservatory of Music in Boston.

1900 Zitkala-Ša travels with the Carlisle School to play violin at the Paris Exposition.

1901 Zitkala-Ša's *Old Indian Legends* is published.

1902 Zitkala-Ša marries Raymond Bonnin.

1903 Zitkala-Ša and Raymond Bonnin's son, Ohiya Bonnin, is born.

1903–1916 Zitkala-Ša and family live on the Uintah Reservation in Utah.

1906 The Burke Act makes it easier for white homesteaders to buy reservation land, while making it much more difficult for Native Americans to acquire American citizenship.

1909 The National Association for the Advancement of Colored People (NAACP) is founded.

1911 The Society of American Indians (the first pan-Indian political advocacy group run entirely by Indians) is founded.

1913 Ohiya is enrolled at a Catholic boarding school in Illinois.

1916 Peyote hearings are held in the U.S. Congress.

1916–1920 Zitkala-Ša is elected secretary of the Society of American Indians and becomes editor of *American Indian Magazine*. Raymond Bonnin enlists in the army and serves stateside. He is honorably discharged in August 1919.

1917 Antipeyote legislation is passed in Colorado, Nevada, and Utah. The United States enters the World War in April.

1919 The World War ends. The Eighteenth Amendment is passed, initiating the prohibition of alcohol.

1920 The Nineteenth Amendment is passed, giving women the right to vote. Indian veterans are permitted to apply for citizenship.

1921 Zitkala-Ša's *American Indian Stories* is published by Hayworth Publishing House.

1924 The Indian Citizenship Act naturalizes Indians born within U.S. territorial limits. *Oklahoma's Poor Rich Indians* —a study on graft and other abuses against Oklahoma Indians—is published, with Zitkala-Ša as co-author.

1926 Zitkala-Ša founds and presides over the National Council of American Indians, a nonprofit lobbying group for reform and Indian rights.

1929 The stock market crashes on October 19, beginning the Great Depression.

1934 The Indian Reorganization Act, part of Franklin Delano Roosevelt's New Deal policy, ends the allotment policy started with the Dawes Act, repeals bans on the Sun Dance and other spiritual practices, and recognizes tribal governments as sovereign nations.

1938 Zitkala-Ša dies on January 26. The opera *The Sun Dance* is performed by the New York City Light Opera Guild.

A Note on the Texts

We have tapped a full range of sources to put together this Penguin Classics edition of Zitkala-Ša's writing. Obvious typographical errors have been silently corrected. We have let stand the punctuation and grammatical conventions of the day, except in those cases where it might interfere with the reader's understanding.

Old Indian Legends and *American Indian Stories* are based on facsimiles of the 1901 Ginn & Co. edition and 1921 Hayworth edition respectively.

Zitkala-Ša's magazine writings have been culled from the original issues of the *Quarterly Journal of the Society of American Indians* and the *American Indian Magazine*.

The sources for the last section are varied. The three pieces from Zitkala-Ša's Earlham College days ("Side by Side," "A Ballad," and "Iris of Life") are taken from facsimiles from *The Earlhamite*. "A Protest Against the Abolition of the Indian Dance" appeared first in the August 1902 *Red Man and Helper*. "The Menace of Peyote" existed as a pamphlet distributed by the General Federation of Women's Clubs, date unknown, which we copied from the original housed at Brigham Young University's Special Collections. "Americanize the First American" and "Bureaucracy Versus Democracy" have been copied from their original pamphlet form. Some versions of the pamphlet included a stunning pictograph of Zitkala-Ša's argument in the form of an 11 × 17 handwritten circle chart, which proved too difficult to reproduce here. "A Dakota Ode to Washington" was published as a part of the *Congressional Record* for the "Proceedings Held in the Washington Monument," and we extracted this piece from a copy of that record. The four California Indian pieces are copied from a microfilm version of the *California Indian Herald*.

Much of Zitkala-Ša's work that we found in manuscript form was not available for this edition. For some of these works see P. Jane Hafen's collection of Zitkala-Ša's stories and a version of *The Sun Dance* libretto—*Dreams and Thunder: Stories, Poems, and* The Sun Dance Opera (University of Nebraska Press, 2001).

I

OLD INDIAN LEGENDS

The selections from *Old Indian Legends* fit into the category of the "retold tale," a traditional or oral legend passed down for generations—in this case, among various bands of the Sioux Indians. These retold tales feature a range of important figures common to the shared Sioux cosmology. Iktomi the shape-shifting trickster (who most often took the form of a spider), Iya the glutton, muskrats and badgers—all the "people," as the animals-spirits-tricksters are often called, of a traditional world of Native storytelling. Many of these legends center around Iktomi, who is as often a wily pest as a brave hero and, through his shape-shifting, teaches a lesson about social responsibility and behavior. In the first decades of the twentieth century, many important American Indian writers of Zitkala-Ša's generation were retelling and committing these stories to written text. Charles Eastman, a Santee Sioux, published a number of books of legends, including *Red Hunters and the Animal People* (1904), *Old Indian Days* (1906), and *Wigwam Evenings—Sioux Tales Retold* (1909); Chief Luther Standing Bear, a Teton Lakota, wrote a number of volumes of legends; and Ella Deloria, a Yankton Sioux, published *Dakota Texts* (1932). There is much to learn from a comparative approach: studying the changes among stories reveals the ways in which "retold" tales repeat and, in their repetition, profoundly alter understandings of historically embedded narratives.

Zitkala-Ša retells a popular story cycle in the three-part story of "The Badger and the Bear," "The Tree-Bound," and "Shooting of the Red Eagle." Literary critic Jeanne Smith notes how Zitkala-Ša makes significant changes to the traditional

tales in order to address key political and social issues in the
lives of American Indians in 1901—specifically, land infringe-
ments, challenges to tribal sovereignty, and the effects of missionary boarding schools on Yankton or Sioux culture more
generally. In her original Preface, included here, Zitkala-Ša recommended her book both for the "blue-eyed little patriot" as
well as the "black-haired aborigine." In other words, she saw
her purpose as both preserving these ancient Indian legends for
future generations of Native Americans and educating white
readers into an indigenous literary tradition.

Preface

These legends are relics of our country's once virgin soil. These and many others are the tales the little black-haired aborigine loved so much to hear beside the night fire.

For him the personified elements and other spirits played in a vast world right around the center fire of the wigwam.

Iktomi, the snare weaver, Iya, the Eater, and Old Double-Face are not wholly fanciful creatures.

There were other worlds of legendary folk for the young aborigine, such as "The Star-Men of the Sky," "The Thunder Birds Blinking Zigzag Lightning," and "The Mysterious Spirits of Trees and Flowers."

Under an open sky, nestling close to the earth, the old Dakota story-tellers have told me these legends. In both Dakotas, North and South, I have often listened to the same story told over again by a new story-teller.

While I recognized such a legend without the least difficulty, I found the renderings varying much in little incidents. Generally one helped the other in restoring some lost link in the original character of the tale. And now I have tried to transplant the native spirit of these tales—root and all—into the English language, since America in the last few centuries has acquired a second tongue.

The old legends of America belong quite as much to the blue-eyed little patriot as to the black-haired aborigine. And when they are grown tall like the wise grown-ups may they not lack interest in a further study of Indian folklore, a study which so strongly suggests our near kinship with the rest of humanity and points a steady finger toward the great brotherhood of

mankind, and by which one is so forcibly impressed with the
possible earnestness of life as seen through the teepee door! If it
be true that much lies "in the eye of the beholder," then in the
American aborigine as in any other race, sincerity of belief,
though it were based upon mere optical illusion, demands a little respect.

After all he seems at heart much like other peoples.

Iktomi and the Ducks

Iktomi is a spider fairy. He wears brown deerskin leggins with long soft fringes on either side, and tiny beaded moccasins on his feet. His long black hair is parted in the middle and wrapped with red, red bands. Each round braid hangs over a small brown ear and falls forward over his shoulders.

He even paints his funny face with red and yellow, and draws big black rings around his eyes. He wears a deerskin jacket, with bright colored beads sewed tightly on it. Iktomi dresses like a real Dakota brave. In truth, his paint and deerskins are the best part of him—if ever dress is part of man or fairy.

Iktomi is a wily fellow. His hands are always kept in mischief. He prefers to spread a snare rather than to earn the smallest thing with honest hunting. Why! he laughs outright with wide open mouth when some simple folk are caught in a trap, sure and fast.

He never dreams another lives so bright as he. Often his own conceit leads him hard against the common sense of simpler people.

Poor Iktomi cannot help being a little imp. And so long as he is a naughty fairy, he cannot find a single friend. No one helps him when he is in trouble. No one really loves him. Those who come to admire his handsome beaded jacket and long fringed leggins soon go away sick and tired of his vain, vain words and heartless laughter.

Thus Iktomi lives alone in a cone-shaped wigwam upon the plain. One day he sat hungry within his teepee. Suddenly he rushed out, dragging after him his blanket. Quickly spreading it on the ground, he tore up dry tall grass with both his hands and tossed it fast into the blanket.

Tying all the four corners together in a knot, he threw the light bundle of grass over his shoulder.

Snatching up a slender willow stick with his free left hand, he started off with a hop and a leap. From side to side bounced the bundle on his back, as he ran light-footed over the uneven ground. Soon he came to the edge of the great level land. On the hilltop he paused for breath. With wicked smacks of his dry parched lips, as if tasting some tender meat, he looked straight into space toward the marshy river bottom. With a thin palm shading his eyes from the western sun, he peered far away into the lowlands, munching his own cheeks all the while. "Ah-ha!" grunted he, satisfied with what he saw.

A group of wild ducks were dancing and feasting in the marshes. With wings outspread, tip to tip, they moved up and down in a large circle. Within the ring, around a small drum, sat the chosen singers, nodding their heads and blinking their eyes.

They sang in unison a merry dance-song, and beat a lively tattoo on the drum.

Following a winding footpath near by, came a bent figure of a Dakota brave. He bore on his back a very large bundle. With a willow cane he propped himself up as he staggered along beneath his burden.

"Ho! who is there?" called out a curious old duck, still bobbing up and down in the circular dance.

Hereupon the drummers stretched their necks till they strangled their song for a look at the stranger passing by.

"Ho, Iktomi! Old fellow, pray tell us what you carry in your blanket. Do not hurry off! Stop! halt!" urged one of the singers.

"Stop! stay! Show us what is in your blanket!" cried out other voices.

"My friends, I must not spoil your dance. Oh, you would not care to see if you only knew what is in my blanket. Sing on! dance on! I must not show you what I carry on my back," answered Iktomi, nudging his own sides with his elbows. This reply broke up the ring entirely. Now all the ducks crowded about Iktomi.

"We must see what you carry! We must know what is in your blanket!" they shouted in both his ears. Some even brushed their wings against the mysterious bundle. Nudging himself again, wily Iktomi said, "My friends, 'tis only a pack of songs I carry in my blanket."

"Oh, then let us hear your songs!" cried the curious ducks.

At length Iktomi consented to sing his songs. With delight all the ducks flapped their wings and cried together, "Hoye! hoye!"

Iktomi, with great care, laid down his bundle on the ground.

"I will build first a round straw house, for I never sing my songs in the open air," said he.

Quickly he bent green willow sticks, planting both ends of each pole into the earth. These he covered thick with reeds and grasses. Soon the straw hut was ready. One by one the fat ducks waddled in through a small opening, which was the only entrance way. Beside the door Iktomi stood smiling, as the ducks, eyeing his bundle of songs, strutted into the hut.

In a strange low voice Iktomi began his queer old tunes. All the ducks sat round-eyed in a circle about the mysterious singer. It was dim in that straw hut, for Iktomi had not forgot to cover up the small entrance way. All of a sudden his song burst into full voice. As the startled ducks sat uneasily on the ground, Iktomi changed his tune into a minor strain. These were the words he sang:

"Ištokmus wacipo, tuwayatunwanpi kinhan išta nišašapi kta," which is, "With eyes closed you must dance. He who dares to open his eyes, forever red eyes shall have."

Up rose the circle of seated ducks and holding their wings close against their sides began to dance to the rhythm of Iktomi's song and drum.

With eyes closed they did dance! Iktomi ceased to beat his drum. He began to sing louder and faster. He seemed to be moving about in the center of the ring. No duck dared blink a wink. Each one shut his eyes very tight and danced even harder. Up and down! Shifting to the right of them they hopped round and round in that blind dance. It was a difficult dance for the curious folk.

At length one of the dancers could close his eyes no longer! It was a Skiska who peeped the least tiny blink at Iktomi within the center of the circle. "Oh! oh!" squawked he in awful terror! "Run! fly! Iktomi is twisting your heads and breaking your necks! Run out and fly! fly!" he cried. Hereupon the ducks opened their eyes. There beside Iktomi's bundle of songs lay half of their crowd—flat on their backs.

Out they flew through the opening Skiska had made as he rushed forth with his alarm.

But as they soared high into the blue sky they cried to one another: "Oh! your eyes are red-red!" "And yours are red-red!" For the warning words of the magic minor strain had proven true. "Ah-ha!" laughed Iktomi, untying the four corners of his blanket, "I shall sit no more hungry within my dwelling." Homeward he trudged along with nice fat ducks in his blanket. He left the little straw hut for the rains and winds to pull down.

Having reached his own teepee on the high level lands, Iktomi kindled a large fire out of doors. He planted sharp-pointed sticks around the leaping flames. On each stake he fastened a duck to roast. A few he buried under the ashes to bake. Disappearing within his teepee, he came out again with some huge seashells. These were his dishes. Placing one under each roasting duck, he muttered, "The sweet fat oozing out will taste well with the hard-cooked breasts."

Heaping more willows upon the fire, Iktomi sat down on the ground with crossed shins. A long chin between his knees pointed toward the red flames, while his eyes were on the browning ducks.

Just above his ankles he clasped and unclasped his long bony fingers. Now and then he sniffed impatiently the savory odor.

The brisk wind which stirred the fire also played with a squeaky old tree beside Iktomi's wigwam.

From side to side the tree was swaying and crying in an old man's voice, "Help! I'll break! I'll fall!" Iktomi shrugged his great shoulders, but did not once take his eyes from the ducks. The dripping of amber oil into pearly dishes, drop by drop, pleased his hungry eyes. Still the old tree man called for help. "Hĕ! What sound is it that makes my ear ache!" exclaimed Iktomi, holding a hand on his ear.

He rose and looked around. The squeaking came from the tree. Then he began climbing the tree to find the disagreeable sound. He placed his foot right on a cracked limb without seeing it. Just then a whiff of wind came rushing by and pressed together the broken edges. There in a strong wooden hand Iktomi's foot was caught.

"Oh! my foot is crushed!" he howled like a coward. In vain he pulled and puffed to free himself.

While sitting a prisoner on the tree he spied, through his tears, a pack of gray wolves roaming over the level lands. Waving his hands toward them, he called in his loudest voice, "Hĕ! Gray wolves! Don't you come here! I'm caught fast in the tree so that my duck feast is getting cold. Don't you come to eat up my meal."

The leader of the pack upon hearing Iktomi's words turned to his comrades and said:

"Ah! hear the foolish fellow! He says he has a duck feast to be eaten! Let us hurry there for our share!" Away bounded the wolves toward Iktomi's lodge.

From the tree Iktomi watched the hungry wolves eat up his nicely browned fat ducks. His foot pained him more and more. He heard them crack the small round bones with their strong long teeth and eat out the oily marrow. Now severe pains shot up from his foot through his whole body. "Hin-hin-hin!" sobbed Iktomi. Real tears washed brown streaks across his red-painted cheeks. Smacking their lips, the wolves began to leave the place, when Iktomi cried out like a pouting child, "At least you have left my baking under the ashes!"

"Ho! po!" shouted the mischievous wolves; "he says more ducks are to be found under the ashes! Come! Let us have our fill this once!"

Running back to the dead fire, they pawed out the ducks

with such rude haste that a cloud of ashes rose like gray smoke over them.

"Hin-hin-hin!" moaned Iktomi, when the wolves had scampered off. All too late, the sturdy breeze returned, and, passing by, pulled apart the broken edges of the tree. Iktomi was released. But alas! he had no duck feast.

Iktomi's Blanket

Alone within his teepee sat Iktomi. The sun was but a hand's-breadth from the western edge of land.

"Those bad, bad gray wolves! They ate up all my nice fat ducks!" muttered he, rocking his body to and fro.

He was cuddling the evil memory he bore those hungry wolves. At last he ceased to sway his body backward and forward, but sat still and stiff as a stone image.

"Oh! I'll go to Inyan, the great-grandfather, and pray for food!" he exclaimed.

At once he hurried forth from his teepee and, with his blanket over one shoulder, drew nigh to a huge rock on a hillside.

With half-crouching, half-running strides, he fell upon Inyan with outspread hands.

"Grandfather! pity me. I am hungry. I am starving. Give me food. Great-grandfather, give me meat to eat!" he cried. All the while he stroked and caressed the face of the great stone god.

The all-powerful Great Spirit, who makes the trees and grass, can hear the voice of those who pray in many varied ways. The hearing of Inyan, the large hard stone, was the one most sought after. He was the great-grandfather, for he had sat upon the hillside many, many seasons. He had seen the prairie put on a snow-white blanket and then change it for a bright green robe more than a thousand times.

Still unaffected by the myriad moons, he rested on the everlasting hill, listening to the prayers of Indian warriors. Before the finding of the magic arrow he had sat there.

Now, as Iktomi prayed and wept before the great-grandfather, the sky in the west was red like a glowing face.

The sunset poured a soft mellow light upon the huge gray stone and the solitary figure beside it. It was the smile of the Great Spirit upon the grandfather and the wayward child.

The prayer was heard. Iktomi knew it. "Now, grandfather, accept my offering; 'tis all I have," said Iktomi as he spread his half-worn blanket upon Inyan's cold shoulders. Then Iktomi, happy with the smile of the sunset sky, followed a footpath leading toward a thicketed ravine. He had not gone many paces into the shrubbery when before him lay a freshly wounded deer!

"This is the answer from the red western sky!" cried Iktomi with hands uplifted.

Slipping a long thin blade from out his belt, he cut large chunks of choice meat. Sharpening some willow sticks, he planted them around a wood-pile he had ready to kindle. On these stakes he meant to roast the venison.

While he was rubbing briskly two long sticks to start a fire, the sun in the west fell out of the sky below the edge of land. Twilight was over all. Iktomi felt the cold night air upon his bare neck and shoulders. "Ough!" he shivered as he wiped his knife on the grass. Tucking it in a beaded case hanging from his belt, Iktomi stood erect, looking about. He shivered again. "Ough! Ah! I am cold. I wish I had my blanket!" whispered he, hovering over the pile of dry sticks and the sharp stakes round about it. Suddenly he paused and dropped his hands at his sides.

"The old great-grandfather does not feel the cold as I do. He does not need my old blanket as I do. I wish I had not given it to him. Oh! I think I'll run up there and take it back!" said he, pointing his long chin toward the large gray stone.

Iktomi, in the warm sunshine, had no need of his blanket, and it had been very easy to part with a thing which he could not miss. But the chilly night wind quite froze his ardent thank-offering.

Thus running up the hillside, his teeth chattering all the way, he drew near to Inyan, the sacred symbol. Seizing one corner of the half-worn blanket, Iktomi pulled it off with a jerk.

"Give my blanket back, old grandfather! You do not need it.

I do!" This was very wrong, yet Iktomi did it, for his wit was not wisdom. Drawing the blanket tight over his shoulders, he descended the hill with hurrying feet.

He was soon upon the edge of the ravine. A young moon, like a bright bent bow, climbed up from the southwest horizon a little way into the sky.

In this pale light Iktomi stood motionless as a ghost amid the thicket. His wood-pile was not yet kindled. His pointed stakes were still bare as he had left them. But where was the deer—the venison he had felt warm in his hands a moment ago? It was gone. Only the dry rib bones lay on the ground like giant fingers from an open grave. Iktomi was troubled. At length, stooping over the white dried bones, he took hold of one and shook it. The bones, loose in their sockets, rattled together at his touch. Iktomi let go his hold. He sprang back amazed. And though he wore a blanket his teeth chattered more than ever. Then his blunted sense will surprise you, little reader; for instead of being grieved that he had taken back his blanket, he cried aloud, "Hin-hin-hin! If only I had eaten the venison before going for my blanket!"

Those tears no longer moved the hand of the Generous Giver. They were selfish tears. The Great Spirit does not heed them ever.

Iktomi and the Muskrat

Beside a white lake, beneath a large grown willow tree, sat Iktomi on the bare ground. The heap of smouldering ashes told of a recent open fire. With ankles crossed together around a pot of soup, Iktomi bent over some delicious boiled fish.

Fast he dipped his black horn spoon into the soup, for he was ravenous. Iktomi had no regular meal times. Often when he was hungry he went without food.

Well hid between the lake and the wild rice, he looked nowhere save into the pot of fish. Not knowing when the next meal would be, he meant to eat enough now to last some time.

"How, how, my friend!" said a voice out of the wild rice. Iktomi started. He almost choked with his soup. He peered through the long reeds from where he sat with his long horn spoon in mid-air.

"How, my friend!" said the voice again, this time close at his side. Iktomi turned and there stood a dripping muskrat who had just come out of the lake.

"Oh, it is my friend who startled me. I wondered if among the wild rice some spirit voice was talking. How, how, my friend!" said Iktomi. The muskrat stood smiling. On his lips hung a ready "Yes, my friend," when Iktomi would ask, "My friend, will you sit down beside me and share my food?"

That was the custom of the plains people. Yet Iktomi sat silent. He hummed an old dance-song and beat gently on the edge of the pot with his buffalo-horn spoon. The muskrat began to feel awkward before such lack of hospitality and wished himself under water.

After many heart throbs Iktomi stopped drumming with his

horn ladle, and looking upward into the muskrat's face, he said:

"My friend, let us run a race to see who shall win this pot of fish. If I win, I shall not need to share it with you. If you win, you shall have half of it." Springing to his feet, Iktomi began at once to tighten the belt about his waist.

"My friend Ikto, I cannot run a race with you! I am not a swift runner, and you are nimble as a deer. We shall not run any race together," answered the hungry muskrat.

For a moment Iktomi stood with a hand on his long protruding chin. His eyes were fixed upon something in the air. The muskrat looked out of the corners of his eyes without moving his head. He watched the wily Iktomi concocting a plot.

"Yes, yes," said Iktomi, suddenly turning his gaze upon the unwelcome visitor; "I shall carry a large stone on my back. That will slacken my usual speed; and the race will be a fair one."

Saying this he laid a firm hand upon the muskrat's shoulder and started off along the edge of the lake. When they reached the opposite side Iktomi pried about in search of a heavy stone.

He found one half-buried in the shallow water. Pulling it out upon dry land, he wrapped it in his blanket.

"Now, my friend, you shall run on the left side of the lake, I on the other. The race is for the boiled fish in yonder kettle!" said Iktomi.

The muskrat helped to lift the heavy stone upon Iktomi's back. Then they parted. Each took a narrow path through the tall reeds fringing the shore. Iktomi found his load a heavy one. Perspiration hung like beads on his brow. His chest heaved hard and fast.

He looked across the lake to see how far the muskrat had gone, but nowhere did he see any sign of him. "Well, he is running low under the wild rice!" said he. Yet as he scanned the tall grasses on the lake shore, he saw not one stir as if to make way for the runner. "Ah, has he gone so fast ahead that the disturbed grasses in his trail have quieted again?" exclaimed Iktomi. With that thought he quickly dropped the heavy stone.

"No more of this!" said he, patting his chest with both hands.

Off with a springing bound, he ran swiftly toward the goal. Tufts of reeds and grass fell flat under his feet. Hardly had they raised their heads when Iktomi was many paces gone.

Soon he reached the heap of cold ashes. Iktomi halted stiff as if he had struck an invisible cliff. His black eyes showed a ring of white about them as he stared at the empty ground. There was no pot of boiled fish! There was no water-man in sight! "Oh, if only I had shared my food like a real Dakota, I would not have lost it all! Why did I not know the muskrat would run through the water? He swims faster than I could ever run! That is what he has done. He has laughed at me for carrying a weight on my back while he shot hither like an arrow!"

Crying thus to himself, Iktomi stepped to the water's brink. He stooped forward with a hand on each bent knee and peeped far into the deep water.

"There!" he exclaimed, "I see you, my friend, sitting with your ankles wound around my little pot of fish! My friend, I am hungry. Give me a bone!"

"Ha! ha! ha!" laughed the water-man, the muskrat. The sound did not rise up out of the lake, for it came down from overhead. With his hands still on his knees, Iktomi turned his face upward into the great willow tree. Opening wide his mouth he begged, "My friend, my friend, give me a bone to gnaw!"

"Ha! ha!" laughed the muskrat, and leaning over the limb he sat upon, he let fall a small sharp bone which dropped right into Iktomi's throat. Iktomi almost choked to death before he could get it out. In the tree the muskrat sat laughing loud. "Next time, say to a visiting friend, 'Be seated beside me, my friend. Let me share with you my food.' "

Iktomi and the Coyote

Afar off upon a large level land, a summer sun was shining bright. Here and there over the rolling green were tall bunches of coarse gray weeds. Iktomi in his fringed buckskins walked alone across the prairie with a black bare head glossy in the sunlight. He walked through the grass without following any well-worn footpath.

From one large bunch of coarse weeds to another he wound his way about the great plain. He lifted his foot lightly and placed it gently forward like a wildcat prowling noiselessly through the thick grass. He stopped a few steps away from a very large bunch of wild sage. From shoulder to shoulder he tilted his head. Still farther he bent from side to side, first low over one hip and then over the other. Far forward he stooped, stretching his long thin neck like a duck, to see what lay under a fur coat beyond the bunch of coarse grass.

A sleek gray-faced prairie wolf! his pointed black nose tucked in between his four feet drawn snugly together; his handsome bushy tail wound over his nose and feet; a coyote fast asleep in the shadow of a bunch of grass!—this is what Iktomi spied. Carefully he raised one foot and cautiously reached out with his toes. Gently, gently he lifted the foot behind and placed it before the other. Thus he came nearer and nearer to the round fur ball lying motionless under the sage grass.

Now Iktomi stood beside it, looking at the closed eyelids that did not quiver the least bit. Pressing his lips into straight lines and nodding his head slowly, he bent over the wolf. He held his ear close to the coyote's nose, but not a breath of air stirred from it.

"Dead!" said he at last. "Dead, but not long since he ran over these plains! See! there in his paw is caught a fresh feather. He is nice fat meat!" Taking hold of the paw with the bird feather fast on it, he exclaimed, "Why, he is still warm! I'll carry him to my dwelling and have a roast for my evening meal. Ah-ha!" he laughed, as he seized the coyote by its two fore paws and its two hind feet and swung him over head across his shoulders. The wolf was large and the teepee was far across the prairie. Iktomi trudged along with his burden, smacking his hungry lips together. He blinked his eyes hard to keep out the salty perspiration streaming down his face.

All the while the coyote on his back lay gazing into the sky with wide open eyes. His long white teeth fairly gleamed as he smiled and smiled.

"To ride on one's own feet is tiresome, but to be carried like a warrior from a brave fight is great fun!" said the coyote in his heart. He had never been borne on any one's back before and the new experience delighted him. He lay there lazily on Iktomi's shoulders, now and then blinking blue winks. Did you never see a birdie blink a blue wink? This is how it first became a saying among the plains people. When a bird stands aloof watching your strange ways, a thin bluish white tissue slips quickly over his eyes and as quickly off again; so quick that you think it was only a mysterious blue wink. Sometimes when children grow drowsy they blink blue winks, while others who are too proud to look with friendly eyes upon people blink in this cold bird-manner.

The coyote was affected by both sleepiness and pride. His winks were almost as blue as the sky. In the midst of his new pleasure the swaying motion ceased. Iktomi had reached his dwelling place. The coyote felt drowsy no longer, for in the next instant he was slipping out of Iktomi's hands. He was falling, falling through space, and then he struck the ground with such a bump he did not wish to breathe for a while. He wondered what Iktomi would do, thus he lay still where he fell. Humming a dance-song, one from his bundle of mystery songs,

Iktomi hopped and darted about at an imaginary dance and feast. He gathered dry willow sticks and broke them in two against his knee. He built a large fire out of doors. The flames leaped up high in red and yellow streaks. Now Iktomi returned to the coyote who had been looking on through his eyelashes.

Taking him again by his paws and hind feet, he swung him to and fro. Then as the wolf swung toward the red flames, Iktomi let him go. Once again the coyote fell through space. Hot air smote his nostrils. He saw red dancing fire, and now he struck a bed of cracking embers. With a quick turn he leaped out of the flames. From his heels were scattered a shower of red coals upon Iktomi's bare arms and shoulders. Dumfounded, Iktomi thought he saw a spirit walk out of his fire. His jaws fell apart. He thrust a palm to his face, hard over his mouth! He could scarce keep from shrieking.

Rolling over and over on the grass and rubbing the sides of his head against the ground, the coyote soon put out the fire on his fur. Iktomi's eyes were almost ready to jump out of his head as he stood cooling a burn on his brown arm with his breath.

Sitting on his haunches, on the opposite side of the fire from where Iktomi stood, the coyote began to laugh at him.

"Another day, my friend, do not take too much for granted. Make sure the enemy is stone dead before you make a fire!"

Then off he ran so swiftly that his long bushy tail hung out in a straight line with his back.

Iktomi and the Fawn

In one of his wanderings through the wooded lands, Iktomi saw a rare bird sitting high in a tree-top. Its long fan-like tail feathers had caught all the beautiful colors of the rainbow. Handsome in the glistening summer sun sat the bird of rainbow plumage. Iktomi hurried hither with his eyes fast on the bird.

He stood beneath the tree looking long and wistfully at the peacock's bright feathers. At length he heaved a sigh and began: "Oh, I wish I had such pretty feathers! How I wish I were not I! If only I were a handsome feathered creature how happy I would be! I'd be so glad to sit upon a very high tree and bask in the summer sun like you!" said he suddenly, pointing his bony finger up toward the peacock, who was eyeing the stranger below, turning his head from side to side.

"I beg of you make me into a bird with green and purple feathers like yours!" implored Iktomi, tired now of playing the brave in beaded buckskins. The peacock then spoke to Iktomi: "I have a magic power. My touch will change you in a moment into the most beautiful peacock if you can keep one condition."

"Yes! yes!" shouted Iktomi, jumping up and down, patting his lips with his palm, which caused his voice to vibrate in a peculiar fashion. "Yes! yes! I could keep ten conditions if only you would change me into a bird with long, bright tail feathers. Oh, I am so ugly! I am so tired of being myself! Change me! Do!"

Hereupon the peacock spread out both his wings, and scarce moving them, he sailed slowly down upon the ground. Right beside Iktomi he alighted. Very low in Iktomi's ear the peacock whispered, "Are you willing to keep one condition, though hard it be?"

"Yes! yes! I've told you ten of them if need be!" exclaimed Iktomi, with some impatience.

"Then I pronounce you a handsome feathered bird. No longer are you Iktomi the mischief-maker." Saying this the peacock touched Iktomi with the tips of his wings.

Iktomi vanished at the touch. There stood beneath the tree two handsome peacocks. While one of the pair strutted about with a head turned aside as if dazzled by his own bright-tinted tail feathers, the other bird soared slowly upward. He sat quiet and unconscious of his gay plumage. He seemed content to perch there on a large limb in the warm sunshine.

After a little while the vain peacock, dizzy with his bright colors, spread out his wings and lit on the same branch with the elder bird.

"Oh!" he exclaimed, "how hard to fly! Brightly tinted feathers are handsome, but I wish they were light enough to fly!" Just there the elder bird interrupted him. "That is the one condition. Never try to fly like other birds. Upon the day you try to fly you shall be changed into your former self."

"Oh, what a shame that bright feathers cannot fly into the sky!" cried the peacock. Already he grew restless. He longed to soar through space. He yearned to fly above the trees high upward to the sun.

"Oh, there I see a flock of birds flying thither! Oh! oh!" said he, flapping his wings, "I must try my wings! I am tired of bright tail feathers. I want to try my wings."

"No, no!" clucked the elder bird. The flock of chattering birds flew by with whirring wings. "Ōōp! ōōp!" called some to their mates.

Possessed by an irrepressible impulse the Iktomi peacock called out, "Hĕ! I want to come! Wait for me!" and with that he gave a lunge into the air. The flock of flying feathers wheeled about and lowered over the tree whence came the peacock's cry. Only one rare bird sat on the tree, and beneath, on the ground, stood a brave in brown buckskins.

"I am my old self again!" groaned Iktomi in a sad voice. "Make me over, pretty bird. Try me this once again!" he pleaded in vain.

"Old Iktomi wants to fly! Ah! We cannot wait for him!" sang the birds as they flew away.

Muttering unhappy vows to himself, Iktomi had not gone far when he chanced upon a bunch of long slender arrows. One by one they rose in the air and shot a straight line over the prairie. Others shot up into the blue sky and were soon lost to sight. Only one was left. He was making ready for his flight when Iktomi rushed upon him and wailed, "I want to be an arrow! Make me into an arrow! I want to pierce the blue Blue overhead. I want to strike yonder summer sun in its center. Make me into an arrow!"

"Can you keep a condition? One condition, though hard it be?" the arrow turned to ask.

"Yes! yes!" shouted Iktomi, delighted.

Hereupon the slender arrow tapped him gently with his sharp flint beak. There was no Iktomi, but two arrows stood ready to fly. "Now, young arrow, this is the one condition. Your flight must always be in a straight line. Never turn a curve nor jump about like a young fawn," said the arrow magician. He spoke slowly and sternly.

At once he set about to teach the new arrow how to shoot in a long straight line.

"This is the way to pierce the Blue overhead," said he; and off he spun high into the sky.

While he was gone a herd of deer came trotting by. Behind them played the young fawns together. They frolicked about like kittens. They bounced on all fours like balls. Then they pitched forward, kicking their heels in the air. The Iktomi arrow watched them so happy on the ground. Looking quickly up into the sky, he said in his heart, "The magician is out of sight. I'll just romp and frolic with these fawns until he returns. Fawns! Friends, do not fear me. I want to jump and leap with you. I long to be happy as you are," said he. The young fawns stopped with stiff legs and stared at the speaking arrow with large brown wondering eyes. "See! I can jump as well as you!" went on Iktomi. He gave one tiny leap like a fawn. All of a sudden the fawns snorted with extended nostrils at what they beheld. There among them stood Iktomi in brown buckskins, and the strange talking arrow was gone.

"Oh! I am myself. My old self!" cried Iktomi, pinching himself and plucking imaginary pieces out of his jacket.

"Hin-hin-hin! I wanted to fly!"

The real arrow now returned to the earth. He alighted very near Iktomi. From the high sky he had seen the fawns playing on the green. He had seen Iktomi make his one leap, and the charm was broken. Iktomi became his former self.

"Arrow, my friend, change me once more!" begged Iktomi.

"No, no more," replied the arrow. Then away he shot through the air in the direction his comrades had flown.

By this time the fawns gathered close around Iktomi. They poked their noses at him trying to know who he was.

Iktomi's tears were like a spring shower. A new desire dried them quickly away. Stepping boldly to the largest fawn, he looked closely at the little brown spots all over the furry face.

"Oh, fawn! What beautiful brown spots on your face! Fawn, dear little fawn, can you tell me how those brown spots were made on your face?"

"Yes," said the fawn. "When I was very, very small, my mother marked them on my face with a red hot fire. She dug a large hole in the ground and made a soft bed of grass and twigs in it. Then she placed me gently there. She covered me over with dry sweet grass and piled dry cedars on top. From a neighbor's fire she brought hither a red, red ember. This she tucked carefully in at my head. This is how the brown spots were made on my face."

"Now, fawn, my friend, will you do the same for me? Won't you mark my face with brown, brown spots just like yours?" asked Iktomi, always eager to be like other people.

"Yes. I can dig the ground and fill it with dry grass and sticks. If you will jump into the pit, I'll cover you with sweet smelling grass and cedar wood," answered the fawn.

"Say," interrupted Ikto, "will you be sure to cover me with a great deal of dry grass and twigs? You will make sure that the spots will be as brown as those you wear."

"Oh, yes. I'll pile up grass and willows once oftener than my mother did."

"Now let us dig the hole, pull the grass, and gather sticks," cried Iktomi in glee.

Thus with his own hands he aids in making his grave. After the hole was dug and cushioned with grass, Iktomi, muttering something about brown spots, leaped down into it. Lengthwise, flat on his back, he lay. While the fawn covered him over with cedars, a far-away voice came up through them, "Brown, brown spots to wear forever!" A red ember was tucked under the dry grass. Off scampered the fawns after their mothers; and when a great distance away they looked backward. They saw a blue smoke rising, writhing upward till it vanished in the blue ether.

"Is that Iktomi's spirit?" asked one fawn of another.

"No! I think he would jump out before he could burn into smoke and cinders," answered his comrade.

The Badger and the Bear

On the edge of a forest there lived a large family of badgers. In the ground their dwelling was made. Its walls and roof were covered with rocks and straw.

Old father badger was a great hunter. He knew well how to track the deer and buffalo. Every day he came home carrying on his back some wild game. This kept mother badger very busy, and the baby badgers very chubby. While the well-fed children played about, digging little make-believe dwellings, their mother hung thin sliced meats upon long willow racks. As fast as the meats were dried and seasoned by sun and wind, she packed them carefully away in a large thick bag.

This bag was like a huge stiff envelope, but far more beautiful to see, for it was painted all over with many bright colors. These firmly tied bags of dried meat were laid upon the rocks in the walls of the dwelling. In this way they were both useful and decorative.

One day father badger did not go off for a hunt. He stayed at home, making new arrows. His children sat about him on the ground floor. Their small black eyes danced with delight as they watched the gay colors painted upon the arrows.

All of a sudden there was heard a heavy footfall near the entrance way. The oval-shaped door-frame was pushed aside. In stepped a large black foot with great big claws. Then the other clumsy foot came next. All the while the baby badgers stared hard at the unexpected comer. After the second foot, in peeped the head of a big black bear! His black nose was dry and parched. Silently he entered the dwelling and sat down on the ground by the doorway. His black eyes never left the painted bags on the rocky walls. He guessed what was in them. He was a very hungry bear. Seeing the racks of red meat hanging in the yard, he had come to visit the badger family.

Though he was a stranger and his strong paws and jaws frightened the small badgers, the father said, "How, how, friend! Your lips and nose look feverish and hungry. Will you eat with us?"

"Yes, my friend," said the bear. "I am starved. I saw your racks of red fresh meat, and knowing your heart is kind, I came hither. Give me meat to eat, my friend."

Hereupon the mother badger took long strides across the room, and as she had to pass in front of the strange visitor, she said: "Ah han! Allow me to pass!" which was an apology.

"How, how!" replied the bear, drawing himself closer to the wall and crossing his shins together.

Mother badger chose the most tender red meat, and soon over a bed of coals she broiled the venison.

That day the bear had all he could eat. At nightfall he rose, and smacking his lips together,—that is the noisy way of saying "the food was very good!"—he left the badger dwelling. The baby badgers, peeping through the door-flap after the shaggy bear, saw him disappear into the woods near by.

Day after day the crackling of twigs in the forest told of heavy footsteps. Out would come the same black bear. He never lifted the door-flap, but thrusting it aside entered slowly in. Always in the same place by the entrance way he sat down with crossed shins.

His daily visits were so regular that mother badger placed a fur rug in his place. She did not wish a guest in her dwelling to sit upon the bare hard ground.

At last one time when the bear returned, his nose was bright and black. His coat was glossy. He had grown fat upon the badgers' hospitality.

As he entered the dwelling a pair of wicked gleams shot out of his shaggy head. Surprised by the strange behavior of the guest who remained standing upon the rug, leaning his round back against the wall, father badger queried: "How, my friend! What?"

The bear took one stride forward and shook his paw in the badger's face. He said: "I am strong, very strong!"

"Yes, yes, so you are," replied the badger. From the farther end of the room mother badger muttered over her bead work: "Yes, you grew strong from our well-filled bowls."

The bear smiled, showing a row of large sharp teeth.

"I have no dwelling. I have no bags of dried meat. I have no arrows. All these I have found here on this spot," said he, stamping his heavy foot. "I want them! See! I am strong!" repeated he, lifting both his terrible paws.

Quietly the father badger spoke: "I fed you. I called you friend, though you came here a stranger and a beggar. For the sake of my little ones leave us in peace."

Mother badger, in her excited way, had pierced hard through the buckskin and stuck her fingers repeatedly with her sharp awl until she had laid aside her work. Now, while her husband was talking to the bear, she motioned with her hands to the children. On tiptoe they hastened to her side.

For reply came a low growl. It grew louder and more fierce. "Wä-ough!" he roared, and by force hurled the badgers out. First the father badger; then the mother. The little badgers he tossed by pairs. He threw them hard upon the ground. Standing in the entrance way and showing his ugly teeth, he snarled, "Be gone!"

The father and mother badger, having gained their feet, picked up their kicking little babes, and, wailing aloud, drew the air into their flattened lungs till they could stand alone upon their feet. No sooner had the baby badgers caught their breath than they howled and shrieked with pain and fright. Ah! what a dismal cry was theirs as the whole badger family went forth wailing from out their own dwelling! A little distance away from their stolen house the father badger built a small round hut. He made it of bent willows and covered it with dry grass and twigs.

This was shelter for the night; but alas! it was empty of food and arrows. All day father badger prowled through the forest, but without his arrows he could not get food for his children. Upon his return, the cry of the little ones for meat, the sad quiet of the mother with bowed head, hurt him like a poisoned arrow wound.

"I'll beg meat for you!" said he in an unsteady voice. Covering his head and entire body in a long loose robe he halted beside the big black bear. The bear was slicing red meat to hang upon the rack. He did not pause for a look at the comer. As the badger stood there unrecognized, he saw that the bear had brought with him his whole family. Little cubs played under the high-hanging new meats. They laughed and pointed with their wee noses upward at the thin sliced meats upon the poles.

"Have you no heart, Black Bear? My children are starving. Give me a small piece of meat for them," begged the badger.

"Wä-ough!" growled the angry bear, and pounced upon the badger. "Be gone!" said he, and with his big hind foot he sent father badger sprawling on the ground.

All the little ruffian bears hooted and shouted "ha-ha!" to see the beggar fall upon his face. There was one, however, who did not even smile. He was the youngest cub. His fur coat was not as black and glossy as those his elders wore. The hair was dry and dingy. It looked much more like kinky wool. He was the ugly cub. Poor little baby bear! he had always been laughed at by his older brothers. He could not help being himself. He could not change the differences between himself and his brothers. Thus again, though the rest laughed aloud at the badger's fall, he did not see the joke. His face was long and earnest. In his heart he was sad to see the badgers crying and starving. In his breast spread a burning desire to share his food with them.

"I shall not ask my father for meat to give away. He would say 'No!' Then my brothers would laugh at me," said the ugly baby bear to himself.

In an instant, as if his good intention had passed from him, he was singing happily and skipping around his father at work. Singing in his small high voice and dragging his feet in long strides after him, as if a prankish spirit oozed out from his heels, he strayed off through the tall grass. He was ambling toward the small round hut. When directly in front of the entrance way, he made a quick side kick with his left hind leg. Lo! there fell into the badger's hut a piece of fresh meat. It was tough meat, full of sinews, yet it was the only piece he could take without his father's notice.

Thus having given meat to the hungry badgers, the ugly baby bear ran quickly away to his father again.

On the following day the father badger came back once more. He stood watching the big bear cutting thin slices of meat.

"Give—" he began, when the bear, turning upon him with a growl, thrust him cruelly aside. The badger fell on his hands. He fell where the grass was wet with the blood of the newly carved buffalo. His keen starving eyes caught sight of a little red clot lying bright upon the green. Looking fearfully toward the bear and seeing his head was turned away, he snatched up the small thick blood. Underneath his girdled blanket he hid it in his hand.

On his return to his family, he said within himself: "I'll pray the Great Spirit to bless it." Thus he built a small round lodge. Sprinkling water upon the heated heap of sacred stones within, he made ready to purge his body. "The buffalo blood, too, must be purified before I ask a blessing upon it," thought the badger. He carried it into the sacred vapor lodge. After placing it near the sacred stones, he sat down beside it. After a long silence, he muttered: "Great Spirit, bless this little buffalo blood." Then he arose, and with a quiet dignity stepped out of the lodge. Close behind him some one followed. The badger turned to look over his shoulder and to his great joy he beheld a Dakota brave in handsome buckskins. In his hand he carried a magic arrow. Across his back dangled a long fringed quiver. In answer to the badger's prayer, the avenger had sprung from out of the red globules.

"My son!" exclaimed the badger with extended right hand.

"How, father," replied the brave; "I am your avenger!"

Immediately the badger told the sad story of his hungry little ones and the stingy bear.

Listening closely, the young man stood looking steadily upon the ground.

At length the father badger moved away.

"Where?" queried the avenger.

"My son, we have no food. I am going again to beg for meat," answered the badger.

"Then I go with you," replied the young brave. This made the old badger happy. He was proud of his son. He was delighted to be called "father" by the first human creature.

The bear saw the badger coming in the distance. He narrowed his eyes at the tall stranger walking beside him. He spied the arrow. At once he guessed it was the avenger of whom he had heard long, long ago. As they approached, the bear stood erect with a hand on his thigh. He smiled upon them.

"How, badger, my friend! Here is my knife. Cut your favorite pieces from the deer," said he, holding out a long thin blade.

"How!" said the badger eagerly. He wondered what had inspired the big bear to such a generous deed. The young avenger waited till the badger took the long knife in his hand.

Gazing full into the black bear's face, he said: "I come to do justice. You have returned only a knife to my poor father. Now return to him his dwelling." His voice was deep and powerful. In his black eyes burned a steady fire.

The long strong teeth of the bear rattled against each other, and his shaggy body shook with fear. "Ahōw!" cried he, as if he had been shot. Running into the dwelling he gasped, breathless and trembling, "Come out, all of you! This is the badger's dwelling. We must flee to the forest for fear of the avenger who carries the magic arrow."

Out they hurried, all the bears, and disappeared into the woods.

Singing and laughing, the badgers returned to their own dwelling.

Then the avenger left them.

"I go," said he in parting, "over the earth."

The Tree-Bound

It was a clear summer day. The blue, blue sky dropped low over the edge of the green level land. A large yellow sun hung directly overhead.

The singing of birds filled the summer space between earth and sky with sweet music. Again and again sang a yellow-breasted birdie—"Koda Ni Dakota!" He insisted upon it. "Koda Ni Dakota!" which was "Friend, you're a Dakota! Friend, you're a Dakota!" Perchance the birdie meant the avenger with the magic arrow, for there across the plain he strode. He was handsome in his paint and feathers, proud with his great buckskin quiver on his back and a long bow in his hand. Afar to an eastern camp of cone-shaped teepees he was going. There over the Indian village hovered a large red eagle threatening the safety of the people. Every morning rose this terrible red bird out of a high chalk bluff and spreading out his gigantic wings soared slowly over the round camp ground. Then it was that the people, terror-stricken, ran screaming into their lodges. Covering their heads with their blankets, they sat trembling with fear. No one dared to venture out till the red eagle had disappeared beyond the west, where meet the blue and green.

In vain tried the chieftain of the tribe to find among his warriors a powerful marksman who could send a death arrow to the man-hungry bird. At last to urge his men to their utmost skill he bade his crier proclaim a new reward.

Of the chieftain's two beautiful daughters he would have his choice who brought the dreaded red eagle with an arrow in its breast.

Upon hearing these words, the men of the village, both young and old, both heroes and cowards, trimmed new arrows for the contest. At gray dawn there stood indistinct under the shadow of the bluff many human figures; silent as ghosts and wrapped in robes girdled tight about their waists, they waited with chosen bow and arrow.

Some cunning old warriors stayed not with the group. They crouched low upon the open ground. But all eyes alike were fixed upon the top of the high bluff. Breathless they watched for the soaring of the red eagle.

From within the dwellings many eyes peeped through the small holes in the front lapels of the teepee. With shaking knees and hard-set teeth, the women peered out upon the Dakota men prowling about with bows and arrows.

At length when the morning sun also peeped over the eastern horizon at the armed Dakotas, the red eagle walked out upon the edge of the cliff. Pluming his gorgeous feathers, he ruffled his neck and flapped his strong wings together. Then he dived into the air. Slowly he winged his way over the round camp ground; over the men with their strong bows and arrows! In an instant the long bows were bent. Strong straight arrows with red feathered tips sped upward to the blue sky. Ah! slowly moved those indifferent wings, untouched by the poison-beaked arrows. Off to the west beyond the reach of arrow, beyond the reach of eye, the red eagle flew away.

A sudden clamor of high-pitched voices broke the deadly stillness of the dawn. The women talked excitedly about the invulnerable red of the eagle's feathers, while the would-be heroes sulked within their wigwams. "Hĕ-hĕ-hĕ!" groaned the chieftain.

On the evening of the same day sat a group of hunters around a bright burning fire. They were talking of a strange young man whom they spied while out upon a hunt for deer beyond the bluffs. They saw the stranger taking aim. Following the point of his arrow with their eyes, they beheld a herd of buffalo. The arrow sprang from the bow! It darted into the skull of the foremost buffalo. But unlike other arrows it pierced through the head of the creature and spinning in the air lit into the next buffalo head. One by one the buffalo fell upon the sweet grass they were grazing. With straight quivering limbs they lay on their sides. The young man stood calmly by, counting on his fingers the buffalo as they dropped dead to the ground. When the last one fell, he ran thither and picking up his magic arrow wiped it carefully on the soft grass. He slipped it into his long fringed quiver.

"He is going to make a feast for some hungry tribe of men or beasts!" cried the hunters among themselves as they hastened away.

They were afraid of the stranger with the sacred arrow. When the hunter's tale of the stranger's arrow reached the ears of the chieftain, his face brightened with a smile. He sent forth fleet horsemen, to learn of him his birth, his name, and his deeds.

"If he is the avenger with the magic arrow, sprung up from the earth out of a clot of buffalo blood, bid him come hither. Let him kill the red eagle with his magic arrow. Let him win for himself one of my beautiful daughters," he had said to his messengers, for the old story of the badger's man-son was known all over the level lands.

After four days and nights the braves returned. "He is coming," they said. "We have seen him. He is straight and tall; handsome in face, with large black eyes. He paints his round cheeks with bright red, and wears the penciled lines of red over his temples like our men of honored rank. He carries on his back a long fringed quiver in which he keeps his magic arrow. His bow is long and strong. He is coming now to kill the big red eagle." All around the camp ground from mouth to ear passed those words of the returned messengers.

Now it chanced that immortal Iktomi, fully recovered from the brown burnt spots, overheard the people talking. At once he was filled with a new desire. "If only I had the magic arrow, I would kill the red eagle and win the chieftain's daughter for a wife," said he in his heart.

Back to his lonely wigwam he hastened. Beneath the tree in

front of his teepee he sat upon the ground with chin between his drawn-up knees. His keen eyes scanned the wide plain. He was watching for the avenger.

" 'He is coming!' said the people," muttered old Iktomi. All of a sudden he raised an open palm to his brow and peered afar into the west. The summer sun hung bright in the middle of a cloudless sky. There across the green prairie was a man walking bareheaded toward the east.

"Ha! ha! 'tis he! the man with the magic arrow!" laughed Iktomi. And when the bird with the yellow breast sang loud again—"Koda Ni Dakota! Friend, you're a Dakota!"—Iktomi put his hand over his mouth as he threw his head far backward, laughing at both the bird and man.

"He is your friend, but his arrow will kill one of your kind! He is a Dakota, but soon he'll grow into the bark on this tree! Ha! ha! ha!" he laughed again.

The young avenger walked with swaying strides nearer and nearer toward the lonely wigwam and tree. Iktomi heard the swish! swish! of the stranger's feet through the tall grass. He was passing now beyond the tree, when Iktomi, springing to his feet, called out: "How, how, my friend! I see you are dressed in handsome deerskins and have red paint on your cheeks. You are going to some feast or dance, may I ask?" Seeing the young man only smiled Iktomi went on: "I have not had a mouthful of food this day. Have pity on me, young brave, and shoot yonder bird for me!" With these words Iktomi pointed toward the tree-top, where sat a bird on the highest branch. The young avenger, always ready to help those in distress, sent an arrow upward and the bird fell. In the next branch it was caught between the forked prongs.

"My friend, climb the tree and get the bird. I cannot climb so high. I would get dizzy and fall," pleaded Iktomi. The avenger began to scale the tree, when Iktomi cried to him: "My friend, your beaded buckskins may be torn by the branches. Leave them safe upon the grass till you are down again."

"You are right," replied the young man, quickly slipping off his long fringed quiver. Together with his dangling pouches and tinkling ornaments, he placed it on the ground. Now he climbed the tree unhindered. Soon from the top he took the bird. "My friend, toss to me your arrow that I may have the honor of wiping it clean on soft deerskin!" exclaimed Iktomi.

"How!" said the brave, and threw the bird and arrow to the ground.

At once Iktomi seized the arrow. Rubbing it first on the grass and then on a piece of deerskin, he muttered indistinct words all the while. The young man, stepping downward from limb to limb, hearing the low muttering, said: "Iktomi, I cannot hear what you say!"

"Oh, my friend, I was only talking of your big heart."

Again stooping over the arrow Iktomi continued his repetition of charm words. "Grow fast, grow fast to the bark of the tree," he whispered. Still the young man moved slowly downward. Suddenly dropping the arrow and standing erect, Iktomi said aloud: "Grow fast to the bark of the tree!" Before the brave could leap from the tree he became tight-grown to the bark.

"Ah! ha!" laughed the bad Iktomi. "I have the magic arrow! I have the beaded buckskins of the great avenger!" Hooting and dancing beneath the tree, he said: "I shall kill the red eagle; I shall wed the chieftain's beautiful daughter!"

"Oh, Iktomi, set me free!" begged the tree-bound Dakota brave. But Iktomi's ears were like the fungus on a tree. He did not hear with them.

Wearing the handsome buckskins and carrying proudly the magic arrow in his right hand, he started off eastward. Imitating the swaying strides of the avenger, he walked away with a face turned slightly skyward.

"Oh, set me free! I am glued to the tree like its own bark! Cut me loose!" moaned the prisoner.

A young woman, carrying on her strong back a bundle of tightly bound willow sticks, passed near by the lonely teepee. She heard the wailing man's voice. She paused to listen to the sad words. Looking around she saw nowhere a human creature. "It may be a spirit," thought she.

"Oh! cut me loose! set me free! Iktomi has played me false! He has made me bark of his tree!" cried the voice again.

The young woman dropped her pack of firewood to the ground. With her stone axe she hurried to the tree. There before her astonished eyes clung a young brave close to the tree.

Too shy for words, yet too kind-hearted to leave the stranger tree-bound, she cut loose the whole bark. Like an open jacket she drew it to the ground. With it came the young man also. Free once more, he started away. Looking backward, a few paces from the young woman, he waved his hand, upward and downward, before her face. This was a sign of gratitude used when words failed to interpret strong emotion.

When the bewildered woman reached her dwelling, she mounted a pony and rode swiftly across the rolling land. To the camp ground in the east, to the chieftain troubled by the red eagle, she carried her story.

Shooting of the Red Eagle

A man in buckskins sat upon the top of a little hillock. The setting sun shone bright upon a strong bow in his hand. His face was turned toward the round camp ground at the foot of the hill. He had walked a long journey hither. He was waiting for the chieftain's men to spy him.

Soon four strong men ran forth from the center wigwam toward the hillock, where sat the man with the long bow.

"He is the avenger come to shoot the red eagle," cried the runners to each other as they bent forward swinging their elbows together.

They reached the side of the stranger, but he did not heed them. Proud and silent he gazed upon the cone-shaped wigwams beneath him. Spreading a handsomely decorated buffalo robe before the man, two of the warriors lifted him by each shoulder and placed him gently on it. Then the four men took, each, a corner of the blanket and carried the stranger, with long proud steps, toward the chieftain's teepee.

Ready to greet the stranger, the tall chieftain stood at the entrance way. "How, you are the avenger with the magic arrow!" said he, extending to him a smooth soft hand.

"How, great chieftain!" replied the man, holding long the chieftain's hand. Entering the teepee, the chieftain motioned the young man to the right side of the doorway, while he sat down opposite him with a center fire burning between them. Wordless, like a bashful Indian maid, the avenger ate in silence the food set before him on the ground in front of his crossed shins. When he had finished his meal he handed the empty bowl to the chieftain's wife, saying, "Mother-in-law, here is your dish!"

"Han, my son!" answered the woman, taking the bowl.

With the magic arrow in his quiver the stranger felt not in the least too presuming in addressing the woman as his mother-in-law.

Complaining of fatigue, he covered his face with his blanket and soon within the chieftain's teepee he lay fast asleep.

"The young man is not handsome after all!" whispered the woman in her husband's ear.

"Ah, but after he has killed the red eagle he will seem handsome enough!" answered the chieftain.

That night the star men in their burial procession in the sky reached the low northern horizon, before the center fires within the teepees had flickered out. The ringing laughter which had floated up through the smoke lapels was now hushed, and only the distant howling of wolves broke the quiet of the village. But the lull between midnight and dawn was short indeed. Very early the oval-shaped door-flaps were thrust aside and many brown faces peered out of the wigwams toward the top of the highest bluff.

Now the sun rose up out of the east. The red painted avenger stood ready within the camp ground for the flying of the red eagle. He appeared, that terrible bird! He hovered over the round village as if he could pounce down upon it and devour the whole tribe.

When the first arrow shot up into the sky the anxious watchers thrust a hand quickly over their half-uttered "hinnu!" The second and the third arrows flew upward but missed by a wide space the red eagle soaring with lazy indifference over the little man with the long bow. All his arrows he spent in vain. "Ah! my blanket brushed my elbow and shifted the course of my arrow!" said the stranger as the people gathered around him.

During this happening, a woman on horseback halted her pony at the chieftain's teepee. It was no other than the young woman who cut loose the tree-bound captive!

While she told the story the chieftain listened with downcast face. "I passed him on my way. He is near!" she ended.

Indignant at the bold impostor, the wrathful eyes of the chieftain snapped fire like red cinders in the night time. His lips were closed. At length to the woman he said: "How, you have done me a good deed." Then with quick decision he gave command to a fleet horseman to meet the avenger. "Clothe him in these my best buckskins," said he, pointing to a bundle within the wigwam.

In the meanwhile strong men seized Iktomi and dragged him by his long hair to the hilltop. There upon a mock-pillared grave they bound him hand and feet. Grown-ups and children sneered and hooted at Iktomi's disgrace. For a half-day he lay there, the laughing-stock of the people. Upon the arrival of the real avenger, Iktomi was released and chased away beyond the outer limits of the camp ground.

On the following morning at daybreak, peeped the people out of half-open door-flaps.

There again in the midst of the large camp ground was a man in beaded buckskins. In his hand was a strong bow and red-tipped arrow. Again the big red eagle appeared on the edge of the bluff. He plumed his feathers and flapped his huge wings.

The young man crouched low to the ground. He placed the arrow on the bow, drawing a poisoned flint for the eagle.

The bird rose into the air. He moved his outspread wings one, two, three times and lo! the eagle tumbled from the great height and fell heavily to the earth. An arrow stuck in his breast! He was dead!

So quick was the hand of the avenger, so sure his sight, that no one had seen the arrow fly from his long bent bow.

In awe and amazement the village was dumb. And when the avenger, plucking a red eagle feather, placed it in his black hair, a loud shout of the people went up to the sky. Then hither and thither ran singing men and women making a great feast for the avenger.

Thus he won the beautiful Indian princess who never tired of telling to her children the story of the big red eagle.

Iktomi and the Turtle

The huntsman Patkaša (turtle) stood bent over a newly slain deer.

The red-tipped arrow he drew from the wounded deer was unlike the arrows in his own quiver. Another's stray shot had killed the deer. Patkaša had hunted all the morning without so much as spying an ordinary blackbird.

At last returning homeward, tired and heavy-hearted that he had no meat for the hungry mouths in his wigwam, he walked slowly with downcast eyes. Kind ghosts pitied the unhappy hunter and led him to the newly slain deer, that his children should not cry for food.

When Patkaša stumbled upon the deer in his path, he exclaimed: "Good spirits have pushed me hither!"

Thus he leaned long over the gift of the friendly ghosts.

"How, my friend!" said a voice behind his ear, and a hand fell on his shoulder. It was not a spirit this time. It was old Iktomi.

"How, Iktomi!" answered Patkaša, still stooping over the deer.

"My friend, you are a skilled hunter," began Iktomi, smiling a thin smile which spread from one ear to the other.

Suddenly raising up his head Patkaša's black eyes twinkled as he asked: "Oh, you really say so?"

"Yes, my friend, you are a skillful fellow. Now let us have a little contest. Let us see who can jump over the deer without touching a hair on his hide," suggested Iktomi.

"Oh, I fear I cannot do it!" cried Patkaša, rubbing his funny, thick palms together.

"Have no coward's doubt, Patkaša. I say you are a skillful fellow who finds nothing hard to do." With these words Iktomi led Patkaša a short distance away. In little puffs Patkaša laughed uneasily.

"Now, you may jump first," said Iktomi.

Patkaša, with doubled fists, swung his fat arms to and fro, all the while biting hard his under lip.

Just before the run and leap Iktomi put in: "Let the winner have the deer to eat!"

It was too late now to say no. Patkaša was more afraid of being called a coward than of losing the deer. "Ho-wo," he replied, still working his short arms. At length he started off on the run. So quick and small were his steps that he seemed to be kicking the ground only. Then the leap! But Patkaša tripped upon a stick and fell hard against the side of the deer.

"Hě-hě-hě!" exclaimed Iktomi, pretending disappointment that his friend had fallen.

Lifting him to his feet, he said: "Now it is my turn to try the high jump!" Hardly was the last word spoken than Iktomi gave a leap high above the deer.

"The game is mine!" laughed he, patting the sullen Patkaša on the back. "My friend, watch the deer while I go to bring my children," said Iktomi, darting lightly through the tall grass.

Patkaša was always ready to believe the words of scheming people and to do the little favors any one asked of him. However, on this occasion, he did not answer "Yes, my friend." He realized that Iktomi's flattering tongue had made him foolish.

He turned up his nose at Iktomi, now almost out of sight, as much as to say: "Oh, no, Ikto; I do not hear your words!"

Soon there came a murmur of voices. The sound of laughter grew louder and louder. All of a sudden it became hushed. Old Iktomi led his young Iktomi brood to the place where he had left the turtle, but it was vacant. Nowhere was there any sign of Patkaša or the deer. Then the babes did howl!

"Be still!" said father Iktomi to his children. "I know where Patkaša lives. Follow me. I shall take you to the turtle's dwelling." He ran along a narrow footpath toward the creek near by. Close upon his heels came his children with tear-streaked faces.

"There!" said Iktomi in a loud whisper as he gathered his little ones on the bank. "There is Patkaša broiling venison! There is his teepee, and the savory fire is in his front yard!"

The young Iktomis stretched their necks and rolled their round black eyes like newly hatched birds. They peered into the water.

"Now, I will cool Patkaša's fire. I shall bring you the broiled venison. Watch closely. When you see the black coals rise to the surface of the water, clap your hands and shout aloud, for soon after that sign I shall return to you with some tender meat."

Thus saying Iktomi plunged into the creek. Splash! splash! the water leaped upward into spray. Scarcely had it become leveled and smooth than there bubbled up many black spots. The creek was seething with the dancing of round black things.

"The cooled fire! The coals!" laughed the brood of Iktomis. Clapping together their little hands, they chased one another along the edge of the creek. They shouted and hooted with great glee.

"Āhäš!" said a gruff voice across the water. It was Patkaša. In a large willow tree leaning far over the water he sat upon a large limb. On the very same branch was a bright burning fire over which Patkaša broiled the venison. By this time the water was calm again. No more danced those black spots on its surface, for they were the toes of old Iktomi. He was drowned.

The Iktomi children hurried away from the creek, crying and calling for their water-dead father.

Dance in a Buffalo Skull

It was night upon the prairie. Overhead the stars were twinkling bright their red and yellow lights. The moon was young. A silvery thread among the stars, it soon drifted low beneath the horizon.

Upon the ground the land was pitchy black. There are night people on the plain who love the dark. Amid the black level land they meet to frolic under the stars. Then when their sharp ears hear any strange footfalls nigh, they scamper away into the deep shadows of night. There they are safely hid from all dangers, they think.

Thus it was that one very black night, afar off from the edge of the level land, out of the wooded river bottom glided forth two balls of fire. They came farther and farther into the level land. They grew larger and brighter. The dark hid the body of the creature with those fiery eyes. They came on and on, just over the tops of the prairie grass. It might have been a wildcat prowling low on soft, stealthy feet. Slowly but surely the terrible eyes drew nearer and nearer to the heart of the level land.

There in a huge old buffalo skull was a gay feast and dance! Tiny little field mice were singing and dancing in a circle to the boom-boom of a wee, wee drum. They were laughing and talking among themselves while their chosen singers sang loud a merry tune.

They built a small open fire within the center of their queer dance house. The light streamed out of the buffalo skull through all the curious sockets and holes.

A light on the plain in the middle of the night was an unusual thing. But so merry were the mice they did not hear the "kinš, kinš" of sleepy birds, disturbed by the unaccustomed fire.

A pack of wolves, fearing to come nigh this night fire, stood together a little distance away, and, turning their pointed noses to the stars, howled and yelped most dismally. Even the cry of the wolves was unheeded by the mice within the lighted buffalo skull.

They were feasting and dancing; they were singing and laughing—those funny little furry fellows.

All the while across the dark from out of the low river bottom came that pair of fiery eyes.

Now closer and more swift, now fiercer and glaring, the eyes moved toward the buffalo skull. All unconscious of those fearful eyes, the happy mice nibbled at dried roots and venison. The singers had started another song. The drummers beat the time, turning their heads from side to side in rhythm. In a ring around the fire hopped the mice, each bouncing hard on his two hind feet. Some carried their tails over their arms, while others trailed them proudly along.

Ah, very near are those round yellow eyes! Very low to the ground they seem to creep—creep toward the buffalo skull. All of a sudden they slide into the eye-sockets of the old skull.

"Spirit of the buffalo!" squeaked a frightened mouse as he jumped out from a hole in the back part of the skull.

"A cat! a cat!" cried other mice as they scrambled out of holes both large and snug. Noiseless they ran away into the dark.

The Toad and the Boy

The water-fowls were flying over the marshy lakes. It was now the hunting season. Indian men, with bows and arrows, were wading waist deep amid the wild rice. Near by, within their wigwams, the wives were roasting wild duck and making down pillows.

In the largest teepee sat a young mother wrapping red porcupine quills about the long fringes of a buckskin cushion. Beside her lay a black-eyed baby boy cooing and laughing. Reaching and kicking upward with his tiny hands and feet, he played with the dangling strings of his heavy-beaded bonnet hanging empty on a tent pole above him.

At length the mother laid aside her red quills and white sinew-threads. The babe fell fast asleep. Leaning on one hand and softly whispering a little lullaby, she threw a light cover over her baby. It was almost time for the return of her husband.

Remembering there were no willow sticks for the fire, she quickly girdled her blanket tight about her waist, and with a short-handled ax slipped through her belt, she hurried away toward the wooded ravine. She was strong and swung an ax as skillfully as any man. Her loose buckskin dress was made for such freedom. Soon carrying easily a bundle of long willows on her back, with a loop of rope over both her shoulders, she came striding homeward.

Near the entrance way she stooped low, at once shifting the bundle to the right and with both hands lifting the noose from over her head. Having thus dropped the wood to the ground, she disappeared into her teepee. In a moment she came running

out again, crying, "My son! My little son is gone!" Her keen
eyes swept east and west and all around her. There was
nowhere any sign of the child.

Running with clinched fists to the nearest teepees, she called:
"Has any one seen my baby? He is gone! My little son is
gone!"

"Hinnú! Hinnú!" exclaimed the women, rising to their feet
and rushing out of their wigwams.

"We have not seen your child! What has happened?" queried
the women.

With great tears in her eyes the mother told her story.

"We will search with you," they said to her as she started
off.

They met the returning husbands, who turned about and
joined in the hunt for the missing child. Along the shore of the
lakes, among the high-grown reeds, they looked in vain. He
was nowhere to be found. After many days and nights the
search was given up. It was sad, indeed, to hear the mother
wailing aloud for her little son.

It was growing late in the autumn. The birds were flying high
toward the south. The teepees around the lakes were gone, save
one lonely dwelling.

Till the winter snow covered the ground and ice covered the
lakes, the wailing woman's voice was heard from that solitary
wigwam. From some far distance was also the sound of the father's voice singing a sad song.

Thus ten summers and as many winters have come and gone
since the strange disappearance of the little child. Every autumn
with the hunters came the unhappy parents of the lost baby to
search again for him.

Toward the latter part of the tenth season when, one by one,
the teepees were folded and the families went away from the
lake region, the mother walked again along the lake shore
weeping. One evening, across the lake from where the crying
woman stood, a pair of bright black eyes peered at her through
the tall reeds and wild rice. A little wild boy stopped his play
among the tall grasses. His long, loose hair hanging down his
brown back and shoulders was carelessly tossed from his round

face. He wore a loin cloth of woven sweet grass. Crouching low to the marshly ground, he listened to the wailing voice. As the voice grew hoarse and only sobs shook the slender figure of the woman, the eyes of the wild boy grew dim and wet.

At length, when the moaning ceased, he sprang to his feet and ran like a nymph with swift outstretched toes. He rushed into a small hut of reeds and grasses.

"Mother! Mother! Tell me what voice it was I heard which pleased my ears, but made my eyes grow wet!" said he, breathless.

"Han, my son," grunted a big, ugly toad. "It was the voice of a weeping woman you heard. My son, do not say you like it. Do not tell me it brought tears to your eyes. You have never heard me weep. I can please your ear and break your heart. Listen!" replied the great old toad.

Stepping outside, she stood by the entrance way. She was old and badly puffed out. She had reared a large family of little toads, but none of them had aroused her love, nor ever grieved her. She had heard the wailing human voice and marveled at the throat which produced the strange sound. Now, in her great desire to keep the stolen boy awhile longer, she ventured to cry as the Dakota woman does. In a gruff, coarse voice she broke forth:

"Hin-hin, doe-skin! Hin-hin, Ermine, Ermine! Hin-hin, red blanket, with white border!"

Not knowing that the syllables of a Dakota's cry are the names of loved ones gone, the ugly toad mother sought to please the boy's ear with the names of valuable articles. Having shrieked in a torturing voice and mouthed extravagant names, the old toad rolled her tearless eyes with great satisfaction. Hopping back into her dwelling, she asked:

"My son, did my voice bring tears to your eyes? Did my words bring gladness to your ears? Do you not like my wailing better?"

"No, no!" pouted the boy with some impatience. "I want to hear the woman's voice! Tell me, mother, why the human voice stirs all my feelings!"

The toad mother said within her breast, "The human child

has heard and seen his real mother. I cannot keep him longer, I fear. Oh, no, I cannot give away the pretty creature I have taught to call me 'mother' all these many winters."

"Mother," went on the child voice, "tell me one thing. Tell me why my little brothers and sisters are all unlike me."

The big, ugly toad, looking at her pudgy children, said: "The eldest is always best."

This reply quieted the boy for a while. Very closely watched the old toad mother her stolen human son. When by chance he started off alone, she shoved out one of her own children after him, saying: "Do not come back without your big brother."

Thus the wild boy with the long, loose hair sits every day on a marshy island hid among the tall reeds. But he is not alone. Always at his feet hops a little toad brother. One day an Indian hunter, wading in the deep waters, spied the boy. He had heard of the baby stolen long ago.

"This is he!" murmured the hunter to himself as he ran to his wigwam. "I saw among the tall reeds a black-haired boy at play!" shouted he to the people.

At once the unhappy father and mother cried out, " 'Tis he, our boy!" Quickly he led them to the lake. Peeping through the wild rice, he pointed with unsteady finger toward the boy playing all unawares.

" 'Tis he! 'tis he!" cried the mother, for she knew him.

In silence the hunter stood aside, while the happy father and mother caressed their baby boy grown tall.

Iya, the Camp-Eater

From the tall grass came the voice of a crying babe. The hunts-men who were passing nigh heard and halted.

The tallest one among them hastened toward the high grass with long, cautious strides. He waded through the growth of green with just a head above it all. Suddenly exclaiming "Hunhe!" he dropped out of sight. In another instant he held up in both his hands a tiny little baby, wrapped in soft brown buckskins.

"Oh ho, a wood-child!" cried the men, for they were hunt-ing along the wooded river bottom where this babe was found.

While the hunters were questioning whether or no they should carry it home, the wee Indian baby kept up his little howl.

"His voice is strong!" said one.

"At times it sounds like an old man's voice!" whispered a su-perstitious fellow, who feared some bad spirit hid in the small child to cheat them by and by.

"Let us take it to our wise chieftain," at length they said; and the moment they started toward the camp ground the strange wood-child ceased to cry.

Beside the chieftain's teepee waited the hunters while the tall man entered with the child.

"How! how!" nodded the kind-faced chieftain, listening to the queer story. Then rising, he took the infant in his strong arms; gently he laid the black-eyed babe in his daughter's lap. "This is to be your little son!" said he, smiling.

"Yes, father," she replied. Pleased with the child, she smoothed the long black hair fringing his round brown face.

"Tell the people that I give a feast and dance this day for the naming of my daughter's little son," bade the chieftain.

In the meanwhile among the men waiting by the entrance way, one said in a low voice: "I have heard that bad spirits come as little children into a camp which they mean to destroy."

"No! no! Let us not be overcautious. It would be cowardly to leave a baby in the wild wood where prowl the hungry wolves!" answered an elderly man.

The tall man now came out of the chieftain's teepee. With a word he sent them to their dwellings half running with joy.

"A feast! a dance for the naming of the chieftain's grandchild!" cried he in a loud voice to the village people.

"What? what?" asked they in great surprise,—holding a hand to the ear to catch the words of the crier.

There was a momentary silence among the people while they listened to the ringing voice of the man walking in the center ground. Then broke forth a rippling, laughing babble among the cone-shaped teepees. All were glad to hear of the chieftain's grandson. They were happy to attend the feast and dance for its naming. With excited fingers they twisted their hair into glossy braids and painted their cheeks with bright red paint. To and fro hurried the women, handsome in their gala-day dress. Men in loose deerskins, with long tinkling metal fringes, strode in small numbers toward the center of the round camp ground.

Here underneath a temporary shade-house of green leaves they were to dance and feast. The children in deerskins and paints, just like their elders, were jolly little men and women. Beside their eager parents they skipped along toward the green dance house.

Here seated in a large circle, the people were assembled, the proud chieftain rose with the little baby in his arms. The noisy hum of voices was hushed. Not a tinkling of a metal fringe broke the silence. The crier came forward to greet the chieftain, then bent attentively over the small babe, listening to the words of the chieftain. When he paused the crier spoke aloud to the people:

"This woodland child is adopted by the chieftain's eldest daughter. His name is Chaske. He wears the title of the eldest son. In honor of Chaske the chieftain gives this feast and dance! These are the words of him you see holding a baby in his arms."

"Yes! Yes! Hinnu! How!" came from the circle. At once the drummers beat softly and slowly their drum while the chosen singers hummed together to find the common pitch. The beat of the drum grew louder and faster. The singers burst forth in a lively tune. Then the drumbeats subsided and faintly marked the rhythm of the singing. Here and there bounced up men and women, both young and old. They danced and sang with merry light hearts. Then came the hour of feasting.

Late into the night the air of the camp ground was alive with the laughing voices of women and the singing in unison of young men. Within her father's teepee sat the chieftain's daughter. Proud of her little one, she watched over him asleep in her lap.

Gradually a deep quiet stole over the camp ground, as one by one the people fell into pleasant dreams. Now all the village was still. Alone sat the beautiful young mother watching the babe in her lap, asleep with a gaping little mouth. Amid the quiet of the night, her ear heard the far-off hum of many voices. The faint sound of murmuring people was in the air. Upward she glanced at the smoke hole of the wigwam and saw a bright star peeping down upon her. "Spirits in the air above?" she wondered. Yet there was no sign to tell her of their nearness. The fine small sound of voices grew larger and nearer.

"Father! rise! I hear the coming of some tribe. Hostile or friendly—I cannot tell. Rise and see!" whispered the young woman.

"Yes, my daughter!" answered the chieftain, springing to his feet.

Though asleep, his ear was ever alert. Thus rushing out into the open, he listened for strange sounds. With an eagle eye he scanned the camp ground for some sign.

Returning he said: "My daughter, I hear nothing and see no sign of evil nigh."

"Oh! the sound of many voices comes up from the earth about me!" exclaimed the young mother.

Bending low over her babe she gave ear to the ground. Horrified was she to find the mysterious sound came out of the open mouth of her sleeping child!

"Why so unlike other babes!" she cried within her heart as she slipped him gently from her lap to the ground. "Mother, listen and tell me if this child is an evil spirit come to destroy our camp!" she whispered loud.

Placing an ear close to the open baby mouth, the chieftain and his wife, each in turn heard the voices of a great camp. The singing of men and women, the beating of the drum, the rattling of deer-hoofs strung like bells on a string, these were the sounds they heard.

"We must go away," said the chieftain, leading them into the night. Out in the open he whispered to the frightened young woman: "Iya, the camp-eater, has come in the guise of a babe. Had you gone to sleep, he would have jumped out into his own shape and would have devoured our camp. He is a giant with spindling legs. He cannot fight, for he cannot run. He is powerful only in the night with his tricks. We are safe as soon as day breaks." Then moving closer to the woman, he whispered: "If he wakes now, he will swallow the whole tribe with one hideous gulp! Come, we must flee with our people."

Thus creeping from teepee to teepee a secret alarm signal was given. At midnight the teepees were gone and there was left no sign of the village save heaps of dead ashes. So quietly had the people folded their wigwams and bundled their tent poles that they slipped away unheard by the sleeping Iya babe.

When the morning sun arose, the babe awoke. Seeing himself deserted, he threw off his baby form in a hot rage.

Wearing his own ugly shape, his huge body toppled to and fro, from side to side, on a pair of thin legs far too small for their burden. Though with every move he came dangerously nigh to falling, he followed in the trail of the fleeing people.

"I shall eat you in the sight of a noonday sun!" cried Iya in his vain rage, when he spied them encamped beyond a river.

By some unknown cunning he swam the river and sought his way toward the teepees.

"Hin! hin!" he grunted and growled. With perspiration beading his brow he strove to wiggle his slender legs beneath his giant form.

"Ha! ha!" laughed all the village people to see Iya made foolish with anger. "Such spindle legs cannot stand to fight by daylight!" shouted the brave ones who were terror-struck the night before by the name "Iya."

Warriors with long knives rushed forth and slew the camp-eater.

Lo! there rose out of the giant a whole Indian tribe: their camp ground, their teepees in a large circle, and the people laughing and dancing.

"We are glad to be free!" said these strange people.

Thus Iya was killed; and no more are the camp grounds in danger of being swallowed up in a single night time.

Manśtin, the Rabbit

Manśtin was an adventurous brave, but very kind-hearted. Stamping a moccasined foot as he drew on his buckskin leggins, he said: "Grandmother, beware of Iktomi! Do not let him lure you into some cunning trap. I am going to the North country on a long hunt."

With these words of caution to the bent old rabbit grandmother with whom he had lived since he was a tiny babe, Manśtin started off toward the north. He was scarce over the great high hills when he heard the shrieking of a human child.

"Wän!" he ejaculated, pointing his long ears toward the direction of the sound; "Wän! that is the work of cruel Double-Face. Shameless coward! he delights in torturing helpless creatures!"

Muttering indistinct words, Manśtin ran up the last hill and lo! in the ravine beyond stood the terrible monster with a face in front and one in the back of his head!

This brown giant was without clothes save for a wild-cat-skin about his loins. With a wicked gleaming eye, he watched the little black-haired baby he held in his strong arm. In a laughing voice he hummed an Indian mother's lullaby, "Ä-bōō! Äbōō!" and at the same time he switched the naked baby with a thorny wild-rose bush.

Quickly Manśtin jumped behind a large sage bush on the brow of the hill. He bent his bow and the sinewy string twanged. Now an arrow stuck above the ear of Double-Face. It was a poisoned arrow, and the giant fell dead. Then Manśtin took the little brown baby and hurried away from the ravine. Soon he came to a teepee from whence loud wailing voices broke. It was the teepee of the stolen baby and the mourners were its heart-broken parents.

When gallant Manstin returned the child to the eager arms of the mother there came a sudden terror into the eyes of both the Dakotas. They feared lest it was Double-Face come in a new guise to torture them. The rabbit understood their fear and said: "I am Manstin, the kind-hearted,—Manstin, the noted huntsman. I am your friend. Do not fear."

That night a strange thing happened. While the father and mother slept, Manstin took the wee baby. With his feet placed gently yet firmly upon the tiny toes of the little child, he drew upward by each small hand the sleeping child till he was a full-grown man. With a forefinger he traced a slit in the upper lip; and when on the morrow the man and woman awoke they could not distinguish their own son from Manstin, so much alike were the braves.

"Henceforth we are friends, to help each other," said Manstin, shaking a right hand in farewell. "The earth is our common ear, to carry from its uttermost extremes one's slightest wish for the other!"

"Ho! Be it so!" answered the newly made man.

Upon leaving his friend, Manstin hurried away toward the North country whither he was bound for a long hunt. Suddenly he came upon the edge of a wide brook. His alert eye caught sight of a rawhide rope staked to the water's brink, which led away toward a small round hut in the distance. The ground was trodden into a deep groove beneath the loosely drawn rawhide rope.

"Hun-hĕ!" exclaimed Manstin, bending over the freshly made footprints in the moist bank of the brook. "A man's footprints!" he said to himself. "A blind man lives in yonder hut! This rope is his guide by which he comes for his daily water!" surmised Manstin, who knew all the peculiar contrivances of the people. At once his eyes became fixed upon the solitary dwelling and hither he followed his curiosity,—a real blind man's rope.

Quietly he lifted the door-flap and entered in. An old toothless grandfather, blind and shaky with age, sat upon the

ground. He was not deaf however. He heard the entrance and
felt the presence of some stranger.

"How, grandchild," he mumbled, for he was old enough to
be grandparent to every living thing, "how! I cannot see you.
Pray, speak your name!"

"Grandfather, I am Manštin," answered the rabbit, all the
while looking with curious eyes about the wigwam.

"Grandfather, what is it so tightly packed in all these buckskin bags placed against the tent poles?" he asked.

"My grandchild, those are dried buffalo meat and venison.
These are magic bags which never grow empty. I am blind and
cannot go on a hunt. Hence a kind Maker has given me these
magic bags of choicest foods."

Then the old, bent man pulled at a rope which lay by his
right hand. "This leads me to the brook where I drink! and
this," said he, turning to the one on his left, "and this takes me
into the forest, where I feel about for dry sticks for my fire."

"Grandfather, I wish I lived in such sure luxury! I would lean
back against a tent pole, and with crossed feet I would smoke
sweet willow bark the rest of my days," sighed Manštin.

"My grandchild, your eyes are your luxury! you would be
unhappy without them!" the old man replied.

"Grandfather, I would give you my two eyes for your place!"
cried Manštin.

"How! you have said it. Arise. Take out your eyes and give
them to me. Henceforth you are at home here in my stead."

At once Manštin took out both his eyes and the old man put
them on! Rejoicing, the old grandfather started away with his
young eyes while the blind rabbit filled his dream pipe, leaning
lazily against the tent pole. For a short time it was a most
pleasant pastime to smoke willow bark and to eat from the
magic bags.

Manštin grew thirsty, but there was no water in the small
dwelling. Taking one of the rawhide ropes he started toward
the brook to quench his thirst. He was young and unwilling
to trudge slowly in the old man's footpath. He was full of glee,
for it had been many long moons since he had tasted such
good food. Thus he skipped confidently along, jerking the old

weather-eaten rawhide spasmodically till all of a sudden it gave way and Manstin fell head-long into the water.

"Ĕn! Ĕn!" he grunted, kicking frantically amid stream. All along the slippery bank he vainly tried to climb, till at last he chanced upon the old stake and the deeply worn footpath. Exhausted and inwardly disgusted with his mishaps, he crawled more cautiously on all fours to his wigwam door. Dripping with his recent plunge, he sat with chattering teeth within his unfired wigwam.

The sun had set and the night air was chilly, but there was no fire-wood in the dwelling. "Hin!" murmured Manstin and bravely tried the other rope. "I go for some fire-wood!" he said, following the rawhide rope which led into the forest. Soon he stumbled upon thickly strewn dry willow sticks. Eagerly with both hands he gathered the wood into his out-spread blanket. Manstin was naturally an energetic fellow.

When he had a large heap, he tied two opposite ends of blanket together and lifted the bundle of wood upon his back, but alas! he had unconsciously dropped the end of the rope and now he was lost in the wood!

"Hin! hin!" he groaned. Then pausing a moment, he set his fan-like ears to catch any sound of approaching footsteps. There was none. Not even a night bird twittered to help him out of his predicament.

With a bold face, he made a start at random.

He fell into some tangled wood where he was held fast. Manstin let go his bundle and began to lament having given away his two eyes.

"Friend, my friend, I have need of you! The old oak tree grandfather has gone off with my eyes and I am lost in the woods!" he cried with his lips close to the earth.

Scarcely had he spoken when the sound of voices was audible on the outer edge of the forest. Nearer and louder grew the voices—one was the clear flute tones of a young brave and the other the tremulous squeaks of an old grandfather.

It was Manstin's friend with the Earth Ear and the old grandfather. "Here Manstin, take back your eyes," said the old man, "I knew you would not be content in my stead, but I wanted you to learn your lesson. I have had pleasure seeing with your eyes and trying your bow and arrows, but since I am old and feeble I much prefer my own teepee and my magic bags!"

Thus talking the three returned to the hut. The old grandfather crept into his wigwam, which is often mistaken for a mere oak tree by little Indian girls and boys.

Manstin, with his own bright eyes fitted into his head again, went on happily to hunt in the North country.

The Warlike Seven

Once seven people went out to make war,—the Ashes, the Fire, the Bladder, the Grasshopper, the Dragon Fly, the Fish, and the Turtle. As they were talking excitedly, waving their fists in violent gestures, a wind came and blew the Ashes away. "Ho!" cried the others, "he could not fight, this one!"

The six went on running to make war more quickly. They descended a deep valley, the Fire going foremost until they came to a river. The Fire said "Hsss—tchu!" and was gone. "Ho!" hooted the others, "he could not fight, this one!"

Therefore the five went on the more quickly to make war. They came to a great wood. While they were going through it, the Bladder was heard to sneer and to say, "Hĕ! you should rise above these, brothers." With these words he went upward among the tree-tops; and the thorn apple pricked him. He fell through the branches and was nothing! "You see this!" said the four, "this one could not fight."

Still the remaining warriors would not turn back. The four went boldly on to make war. The Grasshopper with his cousin, the Dragon Fly, went foremost. They reached a marshy place, and the mire was very deep. As they waded through the mud, the Grasshopper's legs stuck, and he pulled them off! He crawled upon a log and wept, "You see me, brothers, I cannot go!"

The Dragon Fly went on, weeping for his cousin. He would not be comforted, for he loved his cousin dearly. The more he grieved, the louder he cried, till his body shook with great violence. He blew his red swollen nose with a loud noise so that his head came off his slender neck, and he was fallen upon the grass.

"You see how it is," said the Fish, lashing his tail impatiently, "these people were not warriors!" "Come!" he said, "let us go on to make war."

Thus the Fish and the Turtle came to a large camp ground.

"Ho!" exclaimed the people of this round village of teepees, "Who are these little ones? What do they seek?"

Neither of the warriors carried weapons with them, and their unimposing stature misled the curious people.

The Fish was spokesman. With a peculiar omission of syllables, he said: "Shu . . . hi pi!"

"Wän! what? what?" clamored eager voices of men and women.

Again the Fish said: "Shu . . . hi pi!" Everywhere stood young and old with a palm to an ear. Still no one guessed what the Fish had mumbled!

From the bewildered crowd witty old Iktomi came forward. "Hĕ, listen!" he shouted, rubbing his mischievous palms together, for where there was any trouble brewing, he was always in the midst of it.

"This little strange man says, 'Zuya unhipi! We come to make war!' "

"Ūun!" resented the people, suddenly stricken glum. "Let us kill the silly pair! They can do nothing! They do not know the meaning of the phrase. Let us build a fire and boil them both!"

"If you put us on to boil," said the Fish, "there will be trouble."

"Ho ho!" laughed the village folk. "We shall see."

And so they made a fire.

"I have never been so angered!" said the Fish. The Turtle in a whispered reply said: "We shall die!"

When a pair of strong hands lifted the Fish over the sputtering water, he put his mouth downward. "Whssh!" he said. He blew the water all over the people, so that many were burned and could not see. Screaming with pain, they ran away.

"Oh, what shall we do with these dreadful ones?" they said.

Others exclaimed: "Let us carry them to the lake of muddy water and drown them!"

Instantly they ran with them. They threw the Fish and the Turtle into the lake. Toward the center of the large lake the Turtle dived. There he peeped up out of the water and, waving a hand at the crowd, sang out, "This is where I live!"

The Fish swam hither and thither with such frolicsome darts that his back fin made the water fly. "Ě han!" whooped the Fish, "this is where I live!"

"Oh, what have we done!" said the frightened people, "this will be our undoing."

Then a wise chief said: "Iya, the Eater, shall come and swallow the lake!"

So one went running. He brought Iya, the Eater; and Iya drank all day at the lake till his belly was like the earth. Then the Fish and the Turtle dived into the mud; and Iya said: "They are not in me." Hearing this the people cried greatly.

Iktomi wading in the lake had been swallowed like a gnat in the water. Within the great Iya he was looking skyward. So deep was the water in the Eater's stomach that the surface of the swallowed lake almost touched the sky.

"I will go that way," said Iktomi, looking at the concave within arm's reach.

He struck his knife upward in the Eater's stomach, and the water falling out drowned those people of the village.

Now when the great water fell into its own bed, the Fish and the Turtle came to the shore. They went home painted victors and loud-voiced singers.

II

AMERICAN INDIAN
STORIES

Most of the stories in *American Indian Stories*, Zitkala-Ša's most acclaimed literary work, were originally published between 1900 and 1902. Zitkala-Ša collected these published and a few unpublished stories together in one volume in 1921, including two new pieces, "A Dream of Her Grandfather" and "The Widespread Enigma Concerning Blue-Star Woman." Zitkala-Ša concluded this edition with "America's Indian Problem," parts of which were culled from an article she wrote for *Edict Magazine*, with her own added commentary.

American Indian Stories can be read as separate pieces, but gains in its power and intensity by being read as a continuous (if nonlinear) narrative. The book starts with an autobiographical narrative that moves from the child to the student to the teacher, and then opens up to a series of stories centered around a female hero. In "A Warrior's Daughter," Tusee rescues her captured lover by sneaking into an enemy camp disguised as a "bent old woman," while "Blue-Star Woman" reads as both a cautionary warning against the strategies of land grafters and a utopian vision of feminist solidarity. In the middle of this cycle is Zitkala-Ša's profound exploration of spirituality, originally published as "Why I Am a Pagan" (and reprinted in *American Indian Stories* as "The Great Spirit"). She ended the collection by moving to her own political present tense. "America's Indian Problem" pulls the collection into focus, both continuing the cycle (we know now it's child-student-teacher-*activist*), but also suggesting we reread all of *American Indian Stories* as a literary manifesto.

Impressions of an
Indian Childhood

I
MY MOTHER

A wigwam of weather-stained canvas stood at the base of some irregularly ascending hills. A footpath wound its way gently down the sloping land till it reached the broad river bottom; creeping through the long swamp grasses that bent over it on either side, it came out on the edge of the Missouri.

Here, morning, noon, and evening, my mother came to draw water from the muddy stream for our household use. Always, when my mother started for the river, I stopped my play to run along with her. She was only of medium height. Often she was sad and silent, at which times her full arched lips were compressed into hard and bitter lines, and shadows fell under her black eyes. Then I clung to her hand and begged to know what made the tears fall.

"Hush; my little daughter must never talk about my tears"; and smiling through them, she patted my head and said, "Now let me see how fast you can run today." Whereupon I tore away at my highest possible speed, with my long black hair blowing in the breeze.

I was a wild little girl of seven. Loosely clad in a slip of brown buckskin, and light-footed with a pair of soft moccasins on my feet, I was as free as the wind that blew my hair, and no less spirited than a bounding deer. These were my mother's pride,—my wild freedom and overflowing spirits. She taught me no fear save that of intruding myself upon others.

Having gone many paces ahead I stopped, panting for

breath, and laughing with glee as my mother watched my every movement. I was not wholly conscious of myself, but was more keenly alive to the fire within. It was as if I were the activity, and my hands and feet were only experiments for my spirit to work upon.

Returning from the river, I tugged beside my mother, with my hand upon the bucket I believed I was carrying. One time, on such a return, I remember a bit of conversation we had. My grown-up cousin, Warca-Ziwin (Sunflower), who was then seventeen, always went to the river alone for water for her mother. Their wigwam was not far from ours; and I saw her daily going to and from the river. I admired my cousin greatly. So I said: "Mother, when I am tall as my cousin Warca-Ziwin, you shall not have to come for water. I will do it for you."

With a strange tremor in her voice which I could not understand, she answered, "If the paleface does not take away from us the river we drink."

"Mother, who is this bad paleface?" I asked.

"My little daughter, he is a sham,—a sickly sham! The bronzed Dakota is the only real man."

I looked up into my mother's face while she spoke; and seeing her bite her lips, I knew she was unhappy. This aroused revenge in my small soul. Stamping my foot on the earth, I cried aloud, "I hate the paleface that makes my mother cry!"

Setting the pail of water on the ground, my mother stooped, and stretching her left hand out on the level with my eyes, she placed her other arm about me; she pointed to the hill where my uncle and my only sister lay buried.

"There is what the paleface has done! Since then your father too has been buried in a hill nearer the rising sun. We were once very happy. But the paleface has stolen our lands and driven us hither. Having defrauded us of our land, the paleface forced us away.

"Well, it happened on the day we moved camp that your sister and uncle were both very sick. Many others were ailing, but there seemed to be no help. We traveled many days and nights; not in the grand, happy way that we moved camp when I was a little girl, but we were driven, my child, driven like a herd of buffalo. With every step, your sister, who was not as large as you are now, shrieked with the painful jar until she was hoarse with crying. She grew more and more feverish. Her little hands and cheeks were burning hot. Her little lips were parched and dry, but she would not drink the water I gave her. Then I discovered that her throat was swollen and red. My poor child, how I cried with her because the Great Spirit had forgotten us!

"At last, when we reached this western country, on the first weary night your sister died. And soon your uncle died also, leaving a widow and an orphan daughter, your cousin Warca-Ziwin. Both your sister and uncle might have been happy with us today, had it not been for the heartless paleface."

My mother was silent the rest of the way to our wigwam. Though I saw no tears in her eyes, I knew that was because I was with her. She seldom wept before me.

II

THE LEGENDS

During the summer days my mother built her fire in the shadow of our wigwam.

In the early morning our simple breakfast was spread upon the grass west of our tepee. At the farthest point of the shade my mother sat beside her fire, toasting a savory piece of dried meat. Near her, I sat upon my feet, eating my dried meat with unleavened bread, and drinking strong black coffee.

The morning meal was our quiet hour, when we two were entirely alone. At noon, several who chanced to be passing by stopped to rest, and to share our luncheon with us, for they were sure of our hospitality.

My uncle, whose death my mother ever lamented, was one of our nation's bravest warriors. His name was on the lips of old men when talking of the proud feats of valor; and it was mentioned by younger men, too, in connection with deeds of gallantry. Old women praised him for his kindness toward

them; young women held him up as an ideal to their sweet-
hearts. Every one loved him, and my mother worshiped his
memory. Thus it happened that even strangers were sure of
welcome in our lodge, if they but asked a favor in my uncle's
name.

Though I heard many strange experiences related by these
wayfarers, I loved best the evening meal, for that was the time
old legends were told. I was always glad when the sun hung
low in the west, for then my mother sent me to invite the
neighboring old men and women to eat supper with us.
Running all the way to the wigwams, I halted shyly at the en-
trances. Sometimes I stood long moments without saying a
word. It was not any fear that made me so dumb when out
upon such a happy errand; nor was it that I wished to withhold
the invitation, for it was all I could do to observe this very
proper silence. But it was a sensing of the atmosphere, to assure myself that I should not hinder other plans. My mother
used to say to me, as I was almost bounding away for the old
people: "Wait a moment before you invite any one. If other
plans are being discussed, do not interfere, but go elsewhere."

The old folks knew the meaning of my pauses; and often
they coaxed my confidence by asking, "What do you seek, little
granddaughter?"

"My mother says you are to come to our tepee this evening,"
I instantly exploded, and breathed the freer afterwards.

"Yes, yes, gladly, gladly I shall come!" each replied. Rising at
once and carrying their blankets across one shoulder, they
flocked leisurely from their various wigwams toward our
dwelling.

My mission done, I ran back, skipping and jumping with delight. All out of breath, I told my mother almost the exact
words of the answers to my invitation. Frequently she asked,
"What were they doing when you entered their tepee?" This
taught me to remember all I saw at a single glance. Often I told
my mother my impressions without being questioned.

While in the neighboring wigwams sometimes an old Indian
woman asked me, "What is your mother doing?" Unless my

mother had cautioned me not to tell, I generally answered her questions without reserve.

At the arrival of our guests I sat close to my mother, and did not leave her side without first asking her consent. I ate my supper in quiet, listening patiently to the talk of the old people, wishing all the time that they would begin the stories I loved best. At last, when I could not wait any longer, I whispered in my mother's ear, "Ask them to tell an Iktomi story, mother."

Soothing my impatience, my mother said aloud, "My little daughter is anxious to hear your legends." By this time all were through eating, and the evening was fast deepening into twilight.

As each in turn began to tell a legend, I pillowed my head in my mother's lap; and lying flat upon my back, I watched the stars as they peeped down upon me, one by one. The increasing interest of the tale aroused me, and I sat up eagerly listening to every word. The old women made funny remarks, and laughed so heartily that I could not help joining them.

The distant howling of a pack of wolves or the hooting of an owl in the river bottom frightened me, and I nestled into my mother's lap. She added some dry sticks to the open fire, and the bright flames leaped up into the faces of the old folks as they sat around in a great circle.

On such an evening, I remember the glare of the fire shone on a tattooed star upon the brow of the old warrior who was telling a story. I watched him curiously as he made his unconscious gestures. The blue star upon his bronzed forehead was a puzzle to me. Looking about, I saw two parallel lines on the chin of one of the old women. The rest had none. I examined my mother's face, but found no sign there.

After the warrior's story was finished, I asked the old woman the meaning of the blue lines on her chin, looking all the while out of the corners of my eyes at the warrior with the star on his forehead. I was a little afraid that he would rebuke me for my boldness.

Here the old woman began: "Why, my grandchild, they are signs,—secret signs I dare not tell you. I shall, however, tell you a wonderful story about a woman who had a cross tattooed upon each of her cheeks."

It was a long story of a woman whose magic power lay hidden behind the marks upon her face. I fell asleep before the story was completed.

Ever after that night I felt suspicious of tattooed people. Wherever I saw one I glanced furtively at the mark and round about it, wondering what terrible magic power was covered there.

It was rarely that such a fearful story as this one was told by the camp fire. Its impression was so acute that the picture still remains vividly clear and pronounced.

III
THE BEADWORK

Soon after breakfast mother sometimes began her beadwork. On a bright, clear day, she pulled out the wooden pegs that pinned the skirt of our wigwam to the ground, and rolled the canvas part way up on its frame of slender poles. Then the cool morning breezes swept freely through our dwelling, now and then wafting the perfume of sweet grasses from newly burnt prairie.

Untying the long tasseled strings that bound a small brown buckskin bag, my mother spread upon a mat beside her bunches of colored beads, just as an artist arranges the paints upon his palette. On a lapboard she smoothed out a double sheet of soft white buckskin; and drawing from a beaded case that hung on the left of her wide belt a long, narrow blade, she trimmed the buckskin into shape. Often she worked upon small moccasins for her small daughter. Then I became intensely interested in her designing. With a proud, beaming face, I watched her work. In imagination, I saw myself walking in a new pair of snugly fitting moccasins. I felt the envious eyes of my playmates upon the pretty red beads decorating my feet.

Close beside my mother I sat on a rug, with a scrap of buckskin in one hand and an awl in the other. This was the beginning of my practical observation lessons in the art of beadwork. From a skein of finely twisted threads of silvery sinews my mother pulled out a single one. With an awl she pierced the buckskin, and skillfully threaded it with the white sinew. Picking up the tiny beads one by one, she strung them with the point of her thread, always twisting it carefully after every stitch.

It took many trials before I learned how to knot my sinew thread on the point of my finger, as I saw her do. Then the next difficulty was in keeping my thread stiffly twisted, so that I could easily string my beads upon it. My mother required of me original designs for my lessons in beading. At first I frequently ensnared many a sunny hour into working a long design. Soon I learned from self-inflicted punishment to refrain from drawing complex patterns, for I had to finish whatever I began.

After some experience I usually drew easy and simple crosses and squares. These were some of the set forms. My original designs were not always symmetrical nor sufficiently characteristic, two faults with which my mother had little patience. The quietness of her oversight made me feel strongly responsible and dependent upon my own judgment. She treated me as a dignified little individual as long as I was on my good behavior; and how humiliated I was when some boldness of mine drew forth a rebuke from her!

In the choice of colors she left me to my own taste. I was pleased with an outline of yellow upon a background of dark blue, or a combination of red and myrtle-green. There was another of red with a bluish-gray that was more conventionally used. When I became a little familiar with designing and the various pleasing combinations of color, a harder lesson was given me. It was the sewing on, instead of beads, some tinted porcupine quills, moistened and flattened between the nails of the thumb and forefinger. My mother cut off the prickly ends and burned them at once in the center fire. These sharp points were poisonous, and worked into the flesh wherever they lodged. For this reason, my mother said, I should not do much alone in quills until I was as tall as my cousin Warca-Ziwin.

Always after these confining lessons I was wild with surplus spirits, and found joyous relief in running loose in the open again. Many a summer afternoon a party of four or five of my playmates roamed over the hills with me. We each carried a light sharpened rod about four feet long, with which we pried up certain sweet roots. When we had eaten all the choice roots we chanced upon, we shouldered our rods and strayed off into patches of a stalky plant under whose yellow blossoms we found little crystal drops of gum. Drop by drop we gathered this nature's rock-candy, until each of us could boast of a lump the size of a small bird's egg. Soon satiated with its woody flavor, we tossed away our gum, to return again to the sweet roots.

I remember well how we used to exchange our necklaces, beaded belts, and sometimes even our moccasins. We pretended to offer them as gifts to one another. We delighted in impersonating our own mothers. We talked of things we had heard them say in their conversations. We imitated their various manners, even to the inflection of their voices. In the lap of the prairie we seated ourselves upon our feet, and leaning our painted cheeks in the palms of our hands, we rested our elbows on our knees, and bent forward as old women were most accustomed to do.

While one was telling of some heroic deed recently done by a near relative, the rest of us listened attentively, and exclaimed in undertones, "Han! han!" (yes! yes!) whenever the speaker paused for breath, or sometimes for our sympathy. As the discourse became more thrilling, according to our ideas, we raised our voices in these interjections. In these impersonations our parents were led to say only those things that were in common favor.

No matter how exciting a tale we might be rehearsing, the mere shifting of a cloud shadow in the landscape near by was sufficient to change our impulses; and soon we were all chasing the great shadows that played among the hills. We shouted and whooped in the chase; laughing and calling to one another, we were like little sportive nymphs on that Dakota sea of rolling green.

On one occasion I forgot the cloud shadow in a strange notion to catch up with my own shadow. Standing straight and still, I began to glide after it, putting out one foot cautiously. When, with the greatest care, I set my foot in advance of myself, my shadow crept onward too. Then again I tried it; this time with the other foot. Still again my shadow escaped me. I began to run; and away flew my shadow, always just a step beyond me. Faster and faster I ran, setting my teeth and clenching my fists, determined to overtake my own fleet shadow. But ever swifter it glided before me, while I was growing breathless and hot. Slackening my speed, I was greatly vexed that my shadow should check its pace also. Daring it to the utmost, as I thought, I sat down upon a rock imbedded in the hillside.

So! my shadow had the impudence to sit down beside me!

Now my comrades caught up with me, and began to ask why I was running away so fast.

"Oh, I was chasing my shadow! Didn't you ever do that?" I inquired, surprised that they should not understand.

They planted their moccasined feet firmly upon my shadow to stay it, and I arose. Again my shadow slipped away, and moved as often as I did. Then we gave up trying to catch my shadow.

Before this peculiar experience I have no distinct memory of having recognized any vital bond between myself and my own shadow. I never gave it an afterthought.

Returning our borrowed belts and trinkets, we rambled homeward. That evening, as on other evenings, I went to sleep over my legends.

IV
THE COFFEE-MAKING

One summer afternoon my mother left me alone in our wigwam while she went across the way to my aunt's dwelling.

I did not much like to stay alone in our tepee for I feared a tall, broad-shouldered crazy man, some forty years old, who walked loose among the hills. Wiyaka-Napbina (Wearer of a Feather Necklace) was harmless, and whenever he came into a wigwam he was driven there by extreme hunger. He went nude except for the half of a red blanket he girdled around his waist. In one tawny arm he used to carry a heavy bunch of wild sunflowers that he gathered in his aimless ramblings. His black hair was matted by the winds, and scorched into a dry red by the constant summer sun. As he took great strides, placing one brown bare foot directly in front of the other, he swung his long lean arm to and fro.

Frequently he paused in his walk and gazed far backward, shading his eyes with his hand. He was under the belief that an evil spirit was haunting his steps. This was what my mother told me once, when I sneered at such a silly big man. I was brave when my mother was near by, and Wiyaka-Napbina walking farther and farther away.

"Pity the man, my child. I knew him when he was a brave and handsome youth. He was overtaken by a malicious spirit among the hills, one day, when he went hither and thither after his ponies. Since then he can not stay away from the hills," she said.

I felt so sorry for the man in his misfortune that I prayed to the Great Spirit to restore him. But though I pitied him at a distance, I was still afraid of him when he appeared near our wigwam.

Thus, when my mother left me by myself that afternoon I sat in a fearful mood within our tepee. I recalled all I had ever heard about Wiyaka-Napbina; and I tried to assure myself that though he might pass near by, he would not come to our wigwam because there was no little girl around our grounds.

Just then, from without a hand lifted the canvas covering of the entrance; the shadow of a man fell within the wigwam, and a large roughly moccasined foot was planted inside.

For a moment I did not dare to breathe or stir, for I thought that could be no other than Wiyaka-Napbina. The next instant I sighed aloud in relief. It was an old grandfather who had often told me Iktomi legends.

"Where is your mother, my little grandchild?" were his first words.

"My mother is soon coming back from my aunt's tepee," I replied.

"Then I shall wait awhile for her return," he said, crossing his feet and seating himself upon a mat.

At once I began to play the part of a generous hostess. I turned to my mother's coffeepot.

Lifting the lid, I found nothing but coffee grounds in the bottom. I set the pot on a heap of cold ashes in the center, and filled it half full of warm Missouri River water. During this performance I felt conscious of being watched. Then breaking off a small piece of our unleavened bread, I placed it in a bowl. Turning soon to the coffeepot, which would never have boiled on a dead fire had I waited forever, I poured out a cup of worse than muddy warm water. Carrying the bowl in one hand and cup in the other, I handed the light luncheon to the old warrior. I offered them to him with the air of bestowing generous hospitality.

"How! how!" he said, and placed the dishes on the ground in front of his crossed feet. He nibbled at the bread and sipped from the cup. I sat back against a pole watching him. I was proud to have succeeded so well in serving refreshments to a guest all by myself. Before the old warrior had finished eating, my mother entered. Immediately she wondered where I had found coffee, for she knew I had never made any, and that she had left the coffeepot empty. Answering the question in my mother's eyes, the warrior remarked, "My granddaughter made coffee on a heap of dead ashes, and served me the moment I came."

They both laughed, and mother said, "Wait a little longer, and I shall build a fire." She meant to make some real coffee. But neither she nor the warrior, whom the law of our custom had compelled to partake of my insipid hospitality, said anything to embarrass me. They treated my best judgment, poor as it was, with the utmost respect. It was not till long years afterward that I learned how ridiculous a thing I had done.

V

THE DEAD MAN'S PLUM BUSH

One autumn afternoon many people came streaming toward the dwelling of our near neighbor. With painted faces, and wearing broad white bosoms of elk's teeth, they hurried down the narrow footpath to Haraka Wambdi's wigwam. Young mothers held their children by the hand, and half pulled them along in their haste. They overtook and passed by the bent old grandmothers who were trudging along with crooked canes toward the center of excitement. Most of the young braves galloped hither on their ponies. Toothless warriors, like the old women, came more slowly, though mounted on lively ponies. They sat proudly erect on their horses. They wore their eagle plumes, and waved their various trophies of former wars.

In front of the wigwam a great fire was built, and several large black kettles of venison were suspended over it. The crowd were seated about it on the grass in a great circle. Behind them some of the braves stood leaning against the necks of their ponies, their tall figures draped in loose robes which were well drawn over their eyes.

Young girls, with their faces glowing like bright red autumn leaves, their glossy braids falling over each ear, sat coquettishly beside their chaperons. It was a custom for young Indian women to invite some older relative to escort them to the public feasts. Though it was not an iron law, it was generally observed.

Haraka Wambdi was a strong young brave, who had just

returned from his first battle, a warrior. His near relatives, to celebrate his new rank, were spreading a feast to which the whole of the Indian village was invited.

Holding my pretty striped blanket in readiness to throw over my shoulders, I grew more and more restless as I watched the gay throng assembling. My mother was busily broiling a wild duck that my aunt had that morning brought over.

"Mother, mother, why do you stop to cook a small meal when we are invited to a feast?" I asked, with a snarl in my voice.

"My child, learn to wait. On our way to the celebration we are going to stop at Chanyu's wigwam. His aged mother-in-law is lying very ill, and I think she would like a taste of this small game."

Having once seen the suffering on the thin, pinched features of this dying woman, I felt a momentary shame that I had not remembered her before.

On our way I ran ahead of my mother and was reaching out my hand to pick some purple plums that grew on a small bush, when I was checked by a low "Sh!" from my mother.

"Why, mother, I want to taste the plums!" I exclaimed, as I dropped my hand to my side in disappointment.

"Never pluck a single plum from this brush, my child, for its roots are wrapped around an Indian's skeleton. A brave is buried here. While he lived he was so fond of playing the game of striped plum seeds that, at his death, his set of plum seeds were buried in his hands. From them sprang up this little bush."

Eyeing the forbidden fruit, I trod lightly on the sacred ground, and dared to speak only in whispers until we had gone many paces from it. After that time I halted in my ramblings whenever I came in sight of the plum bush. I grew sober with awe, and was alert to hear a long-drawn-out whistle rise from the roots of it. Though I had never heard with my own ears this strange whistle of departed spirits, yet I had listened so frequently to hear the old folks describe it that I knew I should recognize it at once.

The lasting impression of that day, as I recall it now, is what my mother told me about the dead man's plum bush.

VI
THE GROUND SQUIRREL

In the busy autumn days my cousin Warca-Ziwin's mother came to our wigwam to help my mother preserve foods for our winter use. I was very fond of my aunt, because she was not so quiet as my mother. Though she was older, she was more jovial and less reserved. She was slender and remarkably erect. While my mother's hair was heavy and black, my aunt had unusually thin locks.

Ever since I knew her she wore a string of large blue beads around her neck,—beads that were precious because my uncle had given them to her when she was a younger woman. She had a peculiar swing in her gait, caused by a long stride rarely natural to so slight a figure. It was during my aunt's visit with us that my mother forgot her accustomed quietness, often laughing heartily at some of my aunt's witty remarks.

I loved my aunt threefold: for her hearty laughter, for the cheerfulness she caused my mother, and most of all for the times she dried my tears and held me in her lap, when my mother had reproved me.

Early in the cool mornings, just as the yellow rim of the sun rose above the hills, we were up and eating our breakfast. We awoke so early that we saw the sacred hour when a misty smoke hung over a pit surrounded by an impassable sinking mire. This strange smoke appeared every morning, both winter and summer; but most visibly in midwinter it rose immediately above the marshy spot. By the time the full face of the sun appeared above the eastern horizon, the smoke vanished. Even very old men, who had known this country the longest, said that the smoke from this pit had never failed a single day to rise heavenward.

As I frolicked about our dwelling I used to stop suddenly, and with a fearful awe watch the smoking of the unknown fires. While the vapor was visible I was afraid to go very far from our wigwam unless I went with my mother.

From a field in the fertile river bottom my mother and aunt gathered an abundant supply of corn. Near our tepee they spread a large canvas upon the grass, and dried their sweet corn in it. I was left to watch the corn, that nothing should disturb it. I played around it with dolls made of ears of corn. I braided their soft fine silk for hair, and gave them blankets as various as the scraps I found in my mother's workbag.

There was a little stranger with a black-and-yellow-striped coat that used to come to the drying corn. It was a little ground squirrel, who was so fearless of me that he came to one corner of the canvas and carried away as much of the sweet corn as he could hold. I wanted very much to catch him and rub his pretty fur back, but my mother said he would be so frightened if I caught him that he would bite my fingers. So I was as content as he to keep the corn between us. Every morning he came for more corn. Some evenings I have seen him creeping about our grounds; and when I gave a sudden whoop of recognition he ran quickly out of sight.

When mother had dried all the corn she wished, then she sliced great pumpkins into thin rings; and these she doubled and linked together into long chains. She hung them on a pole that stretched between two forked posts. The wind and sun soon thoroughly dried the chains of pumpkin. Then she packed them away in a case of thick and stiff buckskin.

In the sun and wind she also dried many wild fruits,—cherries, berries, and plums. But chiefest among my early recollections of autumn is that one of the corn drying and the ground squirrel.

I have few memories of winter days at this period of my life, though many of the summer. There is one only which I can recall.

Some missionaries gave me a little bag of marbles. They were all sizes and colors. Among them were some of colored glass. Walking with my mother to the river, on a late winter day, we found great chunks of ice piled all along the bank. The ice on the river was floating in huge pieces. As I stood beside one large block, I noticed for the first time the colors of the rainbow in the crystal ice. Immediately I thought of my glass marbles at home. With my bare fingers I tried to pick out some of the colors, for they seemed so near the surface. But my fingers began to sting with the intense cold, and I had to bite them hard to keep from crying.

From that day on, for many a moon, I believed that glass marbles had river ice inside of them.

VII

THE BIG RED APPLES

The first turning away from the easy, natural flow of my life occurred in an early spring. It was in my eighth year; in the month of March, I afterward learned. At this age I knew but one language, and that was my mother's native tongue.

From some of my playmates I heard that two paleface missionaries were in our village. They were from that class of white men who wore big hats and carried large hearts, they said. Running direct to my mother, I began to question her why these two strangers were among us. She told me, after I had teased much, that they had come to take away Indian boys and girls to the East. My mother did not seem to want me to talk about them. But in a day or two, I gleaned many wonderful stories from my playfellows concerning the strangers.

"Mother, my friend Judéwin is going home with the missionaries. She is going to a more beautiful country than ours; the palefaces told her so!" I said wistfully, wishing in my heart that I too might go.

Mother sat in a chair, and I was hanging on her knee. Within the last two seasons my big brother Dawée had returned from a three years' education in the East, and his coming back influenced my mother to take a farther step from her native way of living. First it was a change from the buffalo skin to the white

man's canvas that covered our wigwam. Now she had given up
her wigwam of slender poles, to live, a foreigner, in a home of
clumsy logs.

"Yes, my child, several others besides Judéwin are going
away with the palefaces. Your brother said the missionaries
had inquired about his little sister," she said, watching my face
very closely.

My heart thumped so hard against my breast, I wondered if
she could hear it.

"Did he tell them to take me, mother?" I asked, fearing lest
Dawée had forbidden the palefaces to see me, and that my
hope of going to the Wonderland would be entirely blighted.

With a sad, slow smile, she answered: "There! I knew you
were wishing to go, because Judéwin has filled your ears with
the white man's lies. Don't believe a word they say! Their
words are sweet, but, my child, their deeds are bitter. You will
cry for me, but they will not even soothe you. Stay with me,
my little one! Your brother Dawée says that going East, away
from your mother, is too hard an experience for his baby
sister."

Thus my mother discouraged my curiosity about the lands
beyond our eastern horizon; for it was not yet an ambition for
Letters that was stirring me. But on the following day the missionaries did come to our very house. I spied them coming up
the footpath leading to our cottage. A third man was with
them, but he was not my brother Dawée. It was another, a
young interpreter, a paleface who had a smattering of the
Indian language. I was ready to run out to meet them, but I did
not dare to displease my mother. With great glee, I jumped up
and down on our ground floor. I begged my mother to open
the door, that they would be sure to come to us. Alas! They
came, they saw, and they conquered!

Judéwin had told me of the great tree where grew red, red
apples; and how we could reach out our hands and pick all the
red apples we could eat. I had never seen apple trees. I had
never tasted more than a dozen red apples in my life; and when
I heard of the orchards of the East, I was eager to roam among
them. The missionaries smiled into my eyes and patted my

head. I wondered how mother could say such hard words against him.

"Mother, ask them if little girls may have all the red apples they want, when they go East," I whispered aloud, in my excitement.

The interpreter heard me, and answered: "Yes, little girl, the nice red apples are for those who pick them; and you will have a ride on the iron horse if you go with these good people."

I had never seen a train, and he knew it.

"Mother, I am going East! I like big red apples, and I want to ride on the iron horse! Mother, say yes!" I pleaded.

My mother said nothing. The missionaries waited in silence; and my eyes began to blur with tears, though I struggled to choke them back. The corners of my mouth twitched, and my mother saw me.

"I am not ready to give you any word," she said to them. "Tomorrow I shall send you my answer by my son."

With this they left us. Alone with my mother, I yielded to my tears, and cried aloud, shaking my head so as not to hear what she was saying to me. This was the first time I had ever been so unwilling to give up my own desire that I refused to hearken to my mother's voice.

There was a solemn silence in our home that night. Before I went to bed I begged the Great Spirit to make my mother willing I should go with the missionaries.

The next morning came, and my mother called me to her side. "My daughter, do you still persist in wishing to leave your mother?" she asked.

"Oh, mother, it is not that I wish to leave you, but I want to see the wonderful Eastern land," I answered.

My dear old aunt came to our house that morning, and I heard her say, "Let her try it."

I hoped that, as usual, my aunt was pleading on my side. My brother Dawée came for mother's decision. I dropped my play, and crept close to my aunt.

"Yes, Dawée, my daughter, though she does not understand what it all means, is anxious to go. She will need an education when she is grown, for then there will be fewer real Dakotas, and many more palefaces. This tearing her away, so young, from her mother is necessary, if I would have her an educated woman. The palefaces, who owe us a large debt for stolen lands, have begun to pay a tardy justice in offering some education to our children. But I know my daughter must suffer keenly in this experiment. For her sake, I dread to tell you my reply to the missionaries. Go, tell them that they may take my little daughter, and that the Great Spirit shall not fail to reward them according to their hearts."

Wrapped in my heavy blanket, I walked with my mother to the carriage that was soon to take us to the iron horse. I was happy. I met my playmates, who were also wearing their best thick blankets. We showed one another our new beaded moccasins, and the width of the belts that girdled our new dresses. Soon we were being drawn rapidly away by the white man's horses. When I saw the lonely figure of my mother vanish in the distance, a sense of regret settled heavily upon me. I felt suddenly weak, as if I might fall limp to the ground. I was in the hands of strangers whom my mother did not fully trust. I no longer felt free to be myself, or to voice my own feelings. The tears trickled down my cheeks, and I buried my face in the folds of my blanket. Now the first step, parting me from my mother, was taken, and all my belated tears availed nothing.

Having driven thirty miles to the ferryboat, we crossed the Missouri in the evening. Then riding again a few miles eastward, we stopped before a massive brick building. I looked at it in amazement, and with a vague misgiving, for in our village I had never seen so large a house. Trembling with fear and distrust of the palefaces, my teeth chattering from the chilly ride, I crept noiselessly in my soft moccasins along the narrow hall, keeping very close to the bare wall. I was as frightened and bewildered as the captured young of a wild creature.

The School Days of an Indian Girl

I

THE LAND OF RED APPLES

There were eight in our party of bronzed children who were going East with the missionaries. Among us were three young braves, two tall girls, and we three little ones, Judéwin, Thowin, and I.

We had been very impatient to start on our journey to the Red Apple Country, which, we were told, lay a little beyond the great circular horizon of the Western prairie. Under a sky of rosy apples we dreamt of roaming as freely and happily as we had chased the cloud shadows on the Dakota plains. We had anticipated much pleasure from a ride on the iron horse, but the throngs of staring palefaces disturbed and troubled us.

On the train, fair women, with tottering babies on each arm, stopped their haste and scrutinized the children of absent mothers. Large men, with heavy bundles in their hands, halted near by, and riveted their glassy blue eyes upon us.

I sank deep into the corner of my seat, for I resented being watched. Directly in front of me, children who were no larger than I hung themselves upon the backs of their seats, with their bold white faces toward me. Sometimes they took their forefingers out of their mouths and pointed at my moccasined feet. Their mothers, instead of reproving such rude curiosity, looked closely at me, and attracted their children's further notice to my blanket. This embarrassed me, and kept me constantly on the verge of tears.

I sat perfectly still, with my eyes downcast, daring only now and then to shoot long glances around me. Chancing to turn to the window at my side, I was quite breathless upon seeing one familiar object. It was the telegraph pole which strode by at short paces. Very near my mother's dwelling, along the edge of a road thickly bordered with wild sunflowers, some poles like these had been planted by white men. Often I had stopped, on my way down the road, to hold my ear against the pole, and, hearing its low moaning, I used to wonder what the paleface had done to hurt it. Now I sat watching for each pole that glided by to be the last one.

In this way I had forgotten my uncomfortable surroundings, when I heard one of my comrades call out my name. I saw the missionary standing very near, tossing candies and gums into our midst. This amused us all, and we tried to see who could catch the most of the sweetmeats.

Though we rode several days inside of the iron horse, I do not recall a single thing about our luncheons.

It was night when we reached the school grounds. The lights from the windows of the large buildings fell upon some of the icicled trees that stood beneath them. We were led toward an open door, where the brightness of the lights within flooded out over the heads of the excited palefaces who blocked our way. My body trembled more from fear than from the snow I trod upon.

Entering the house, I stood close against the wall. The strong glaring light in the large whitewashed room dazzled my eyes. The noisy hurrying of hard shoes upon a bare wooden floor increased the whirring in my ears. My only safety seemed to be in keeping next to the wall. As I was wondering in which direction to escape from all this confusion, two warm hands grasped me firmly, and in the same moment I was tossed high in midair. A rosy-cheeked paleface woman caught me in her arms. I was both frightened and insulted by such trifling. I stared into her eyes, wishing her to let me stand on my own feet, but she jumped me up and down with increasing enthusiasm. My mother had never made a plaything of her wee daughter. Remembering this I began to cry aloud.

They misunderstood the cause of my tears, and placed me at

a white table loaded with food. There our party were united again. As I did not hush my crying, one of the older ones whispered to me, "Wait until you are alone in the night."

It was very little I could swallow besides my sobs, that evening.

"Oh, I want my mother and my brother Dawée! I want to go to my aunt!" I pleaded; but the ears of the palefaces could not hear me.

From the table we were taken along an upward incline of wooden boxes, which I learned afterward to call a stairway. At the top was a quiet hall, dimly lighted. Many narrow beds were in one straight line down the entire length of the wall. In them lay sleeping brown faces, which peeped just out of the coverings. I was tucked into bed with one of the tall girls, because she talked to me in my mother tongue and seemed to soothe me.

I had arrived in the wonderful land of rosy skies, but I was not happy, as I had thought I should be. My long travel and the bewildering sights had exhausted me. I fell asleep, heaving deep, tired sobs. My tears were left to dry themselves in streaks, because neither my aunt nor my mother was near to wipe them away.

II
THE CUTTING OF MY LONG HAIR

The first day in the land of apples was a bitter-cold one; for the snow still covered the ground, and the trees were bare. A large bell rang for breakfast, its loud metallic voice crashing through the belfry overhead and into our sensitive ears. The annoying clatter of shoes on bare floors gave us no peace. The constant clash of harsh noises, with an undercurrent of many voices murmuring an unknown tongue, made a bedlam within which I was securely tied. And though my spirit tore itself in struggling for its lost freedom, all was useless.

A paleface woman, with white hair, came up after us. We

were placed in a line of girls who were marching into the din-
ing room. These were Indian girls, in stiff shoes and closely
clinging dresses. The small girls wore sleeved aprons and shingled hair. As I walked noiselessly in my soft moccasins, I felt
like sinking to the floor, for my blanket had been stripped from
my shoulders. I looked hard at the Indian girls, who seemed
not to care that they were even more immodestly dressed than
I, in their tightly fitting clothes. While we marched in, the boys
entered at an opposite door. I watched for the three young
braves who came in our party. I spied them in the rear ranks,
looking as uncomfortable as I felt.

A small bell was tapped, and each of the pupils drew a chair
from under the table. Supposing this act meant they were to be
seated, I pulled out mine and at once slipped into it from one
side. But when I turned my head, I saw that I was the only one
seated, and all the rest at our table remained standing. Just as I
began to rise, looking shyly around to see how chairs were to
be used, a second bell was sounded. All were seated at last, and
I had to crawl back into my chair again. I heard a man's voice
at one end of the hall, and I looked around to see him. But all
the others hung their heads over their plates. As I glanced at
the long chain of tables, I caught the eyes of a paleface woman
upon me. Immediately I dropped my eyes, wondering why I
was so keenly watched by the strange woman. The man ceased
his mutterings, and then a third bell was tapped. Every one
picked up his knife and fork and began eating. I began crying
instead, for by this time I was afraid to venture anything more.

But this eating by formula was not the hardest trial in that
first day. Late in the morning, my friend Judéwin gave me a terrible warning. Judéwin knew a few words of English; and she
had overheard the paleface woman talk about cutting our long,
heavy hair. Our mothers had taught us that only unskilled warriors who were captured had their hair shingled by the enemy.
Among our people, short hair was worn by mourners, and
shingled hair by cowards!

We discussed our fate some moments, and when Judéwin
said, "We have to submit, because they are strong," I rebelled.

"No, I will not submit! I will struggle first!" I answered.

I watched for my chance, and when no one noticed I disappeared. I crept up the stairs as quietly as I could in my squeaking shoes,—my moccasins had been exchanged for shoes. Along the hall I passed, without knowing whither I was going. Turning aside to an open door, I found a large room with three white beds in it. The windows were covered with dark green curtains, which made the room very dim. Thankful that no one was there, I directed my steps toward the corner farthest from the door. On my hands and knees I crawled under the bed, and cuddled myself in the dark corner.

From my hiding place I peered out, shuddering with fear whenever I heard footsteps near by. Though in the hall loud voices were calling my name, and I knew that even Judéwin was searching for me, I did not open my mouth to answer. Then the steps were quickened and the voices became excited. The sounds came nearer and nearer. Women and girls entered the room. I held my breath and watched them open closet doors and peep behind large trunks. Some one threw up the curtains, and the room was filled with sudden light. What caused them to stoop and look under the bed I do not know. I remember being dragged out, though I resisted by kicking and scratching wildly. In spite of myself, I was carried downstairs and tied fast in a chair.

I cried aloud, shaking my head all the while until I felt the cold blades of the scissors against my neck, and heard them gnaw off one of my thick braids. Then I lost my spirit. Since the day I was taken from my mother I had suffered extreme indignities. People had stared at me. I had been tossed about in the air like a wooden puppet. And now my long hair was shingled like a coward's! In my anguish I moaned for my mother, but no one came to comfort me. Not a soul reasoned quietly with me, as my own mother used to do; for now I was only one of many little animals driven by a herder.

III

THE SNOW EPISODE

A short time after our arrival we three Dakotas were playing in the snowdrift. We were all still deaf to the English language, excepting Judéwin, who always heard such puzzling things. One morning we learned through her ears that we were forbidden to fall lengthwise in the snow, as we had been doing, to see our own impressions. However, before many hours we had forgotten the order, and were having great sport in the snow, when a shrill voice called us. Looking up, we saw an imperative hand beckoning us into the house. We shook the snow off ourselves, and started toward the woman as slowly as we dared.

Judéwin said: "Now the paleface is angry with us. She is going to punish us for falling into the snow. If she looks straight into your eyes and talks loudly, you must wait until she stops. Then, after a tiny pause, say, 'No.'" The rest of the way we practiced upon the little word "no."

As it happened, Thowin was summoned to judgment first. The door shut behind her with a click.

Judéwin and I stood silently listening at the keyhole. The paleface woman talked in very severe tones. Her words fell from her lips like crackling embers, and her inflection ran up like the small end of a switch. I understood her voice better than the things she was saying. I was certain we had made her very impatient with us. Judéwin heard enough of the words to realize all too late that she had taught us the wrong reply.

"Oh, poor Thowin!" she gasped, as she put both hands over her ears.

Just then I heard Thowin's tremulous answer, "No."

With an angry exclamation, the woman gave her a hard spanking. Then she stopped to say something. Judéwin said it was this: "Are you going to obey my word the next time?"

Thowin answered again with the only word at her command, "No."

This time the woman meant her blows to smart, for the poor frightened girl shrieked at the top of her voice. In the midst of the whipping the blows ceased abruptly, and the woman asked another question: "Are you going to fall in the snow again?"

Thowin gave her bad passwood another trial. We heard her say feebly, "No! No!"

With this the woman hid away her half-worn slipper, and led the child out, stroking her black shorn head. Perhaps it occurred to her that brute force is not the solution for such a problem. She did nothing to Judéwin nor to me. She only returned to us our unhappy comrade, and left us alone in the room.

During the first two or three seasons misunderstandings as ridiculous as this one of the snow episode frequently took place, bringing unjustifiable frights and punishments into our little lives.

Within a year I was able to express myself somewhat in broken English. As soon as I comprehended a part of what was said and done, a mischievous spirit of revenge possessed me. One day I was called in from my play for some misconduct. I had disregarded a rule which seemed to me very needlessly binding. I was sent into the kitchen to mash the turnips for dinner. It was noon, and steaming dishes were hastily carried into the dining-room. I hated turnips, and their odor which came from the brown jar was offensive to me. With fire in my heart, I took the wooden tool that the paleface woman held out to me. I stood upon a step, and, grasping the handle with both hands, I bent in hot rage over the turnips. I worked my vengeance upon them. All were so busily occupied that no one noticed me. I saw that the turnips were in a pulp, and that further beating could not improve them; but the order was, "Mash these turnips," and mash them I would! I renewed my energy; and as I sent the masher into the bottom of the jar, I felt a satisfying sensation that the weight of my body had gone into it.

Just here a paleface woman came up to my table. As she looked into the jar, she shoved my hands roughly aside. I stood fearless and angry. She placed her red hands upon the rim of the jar. Then she gave one lift and strode away from the table.

But lo! the pulpy contents fell through the crumbled bottom to the floor! She spared me no scolding phrases that I had earned. I did not heed them. I felt triumphant in my revenge, though deep within me I was a wee bit sorry to have broken the jar.

As I sat eating my dinner, and saw that no turnips were served, I whooped in my heart for having once asserted the rebellion within me.

IV

THE DEVIL

Among the legends the old warriors used to tell me were many stories of evil spirits. But I was taught to fear them no more than those who stalked about in material guise. I never knew there was an insolent chieftain among the bad spirits, who dared to array his forces against the Great Spirit, until I heard this white man's legend from a paleface woman.

Out of a large book she showed me a picture of the white man's devil. I looked in horror upon the strong claws that grew out of his fur-covered fingers. His feet were like his hands. Trailing at his heels was a scaly tail tipped with a serpent's open jaws. His face was a patchwork: he had bearded cheeks, like some I had seen palefaces wear; his nose was an eagle's bill, and his sharp-pointed ears were pricked up like those of a sly fox. Above them a pair of cow's horns curved upward. I trembled with awe, and my heart throbbed in my throat, as I looked at the king of evil spirits. Then I heard the paleface woman say that this terrible creature roamed loose in the world, and that little girls who disobeyed school regulations were to be tortured by him.

That night I dreamt about this evil divinity. Once again I seemed to be in my mother's cottage. An Indian woman had come to visit my mother. On opposite sides of the kitchen stove, which stood in the center of the small house, my mother and her guest were seated in straight-backed chairs. I played with a train of empty spools hitched together on a string. It was night, and the wick burned feebly. Suddenly I heard some one turn our door-knob from without.

My mother and the woman hushed their talk, and both looked toward the door. It opened gradually. I waited behind the stove. The hinges squeaked as the door was slowly, very slowly pushed inward.

Then in rushed the devil! He was tall! He looked exactly like the picture I had seen of him in the white man's papers. He did not speak to my mother, because he did not know the Indian language, but his glittering yellow eyes were fastened upon me. He took long strides around the stove, passing behind the woman's chair. I threw down my spools, and ran to my mother. He did not fear her, but followed closely after me. Then I ran round and round the stove, crying aloud for help. But my mother and the woman seemed not to know my danger. They sat still, looking quietly upon the devil's chase after me. At last I grew dizzy. My head revolved as on a hidden pivot. My knees became numb, and doubled under my weight like a pair of knife blades without a spring. Beside my mother's chair I fell in a heap. Just as the devil stooped over me with outstretched claws my mother awoke from her quiet indifference, and lifted me on her lap. Whereupon the devil vanished, and I was awake.

On the following morning I took my revenge upon the devil. Stealing into the room where a wall of shelves was filled with books, I drew forth The Stories of the Bible. With a broken slate pencil I carried in my apron pocket, I began by scratching out his wicked eyes. A few moments later, when I was ready to leave the room, there was a ragged hole in the page where the picture of the devil had once been.

V

IRON ROUTINE

A loud-clamoring bell awakened us at half-past six in the cold winter mornings. From happy dreams of Western rolling lands and unlassoed freedom we tumbled out upon chilly bare floors back again into a paleface day. We had short time to jump into our shoes and clothes, and wet our eyes with icy water, before a small hand bell was vigorously rung for roll call.

There were too many drowsy children and too numerous orders for the day to waste a moment in any apology to nature for giving her children such a shock in the early morning. We rushed downstairs, bounding over two high steps at a time, to land in the assembly room.

A paleface woman, with a yellow-covered roll book open on her arm and a gnawed pencil in her hand, appeared at the door. Her small, tired face was coldly lighted with a pair of large gray eyes.

She stood still in a halo of authority, while over the rim of her spectacles her eyes pried nervously about the room. Having glanced at her long list of names and called out the first one, she tossed up her chin and peered through the crystals of her spectacles to make sure of the answer "Here."

Relentlessly her pencil black-marked our daily records if we were not present to respond to our names, and no chum of ours had done it successfully for us. No matter if a dull headache or the painful cough of slow consumption had delayed the absentee, there was only time enough to mark the tardiness. It was next to impossible to leave the iron routine after the civilizing machine had once begun its day's buzzing; and as it was inbred in me to suffer in silence rather than to appeal to the ears of one whose open eyes could not see my pain, I have many times trudged in the day's harness heavy-footed, like a dumb sick brute.

Once I lost a dear classmate. I remember well how she used to mope along at my side, until one morning she could not raise her head from her pillow. At her deathbed I stood weeping, as the paleface woman sat near her moistening the dry lips. Among the folds of the bedclothes I saw the open pages of the white man's Bible. The dying Indian girl talked disconnectedly of Jesus the Christ and the paleface who was cooling her swollen hands and feet.

I grew bitter, and censured the woman for cruel neglect of

our physical ills. I despised the pencils that moved automatically, and the one teaspoon which dealt out, from a large bottle, healing to a row of variously ailing Indian children. I blamed the hard-working, well-meaning, ignorant woman who was inculcating in our hearts her superstitious ideas. Though I was sullen in all my little troubles, as soon as I felt better I was ready again to smile upon the cruel woman. Within a week I was again actively testing the chains which tightly bound my individuality like a mummy for burial.

The melancholy of those black days has left so long a shadow that it darkens the path of years that have since gone by. These sad memories rise above those of smoothly grinding school days. Perhaps my Indian nature is the moaning wind which stirs them now for their present record. But, however tempestuous this is within me, it comes out as the low voice of a curiously colored seashell, which is only for those ears that are bent with compassion to hear it.

VI

FOUR STRANGE SUMMERS

After my first three years of school, I roamed again in the Western country through four strange summers.

During this time I seemed to hang in the heart of chaos, beyond the touch or voice of human aid. My brother, being almost ten years my senior, did not quite understand my feelings. My mother had never gone inside of a schoolhouse, and so she was not capable of comforting her daughter who could read and write. Even nature seemed to have no place for me. I was neither a wee girl nor a tall one; neither a wild Indian nor a tame one. This deporable situation was the effect of my brief course in the East, and the unsatisfactory "teenth" in a girl's years.

It was under these trying conditions that, one bright afternoon, as I sat restless and unhappy in my mother's cabin, I caught the sound of the spirited step of my brother's pony on

the road which passed by our dwelling. Soon I heard the
wheels of a light buckboard, and Dawée's familiar "Ho!" to his
pony. He alighted upon the bare ground in front of our house.
Tying his pony to one of the projecting corner logs of the low-
roofed cottage, he stepped upon the wooden doorstep.

I met him there with a hurried greeting, and, as I passed by,
he looked a quiet "What?" into my eyes.

When he began talking with my mother, I slipped the rope
from the pony's bridle. Seizing the reins and bracing my feet
against the dashboard, I wheeled around in an instant. The
pony was ever ready to try his speed. Looking backward, I saw
Dawée waving his hand to me. I turned with the curve in the
road and disappeared. I followed the winding road which
crawled upward between the bases of little hillocks. Deep
water-worn ditches ran parallel on either side. A strong wind
blew against my cheeks and fluttered my sleeves. The pony
reached the top of the highest hill, and began an even race on
the level lands. There was nothing moving within that great circular horizon of the Dakota prairies save the tall grasses, over
which the wind blew and rolled off in long, shadowy waves.

Within this vast wigwam of blue and green I rode reckless
and insignificant. It satisfied my small consciousness to see the
white foam fly from the pony's mouth.

Suddenly, out of the earth a coyote came forth at a swinging
trot that was taking the cunning thief toward the hills and the
village beyond. Upon the moment's impulse, I gave him a long
chase and a wholesome fright. As I turned away to go back to
the village, the wolf sank down upon his haunches for rest, for
it was a hot summer day; and as I drove slowly homeward, I
saw his sharp nose still pointed at me, until I vanished below
the margin of the hilltops.

In a little while I came in sight of my mother's house. Dawée
stood in the yard, laughing at an old warrior who was pointing
his forefinger, and again waving his whole hand, toward the
hills. With his blanket drawn over one shoulder, he talked and
motioned excitedly. Dawée turned the old man by the shoulder
and pointed me out to him.

"Oh, han!" (Oh, yes) the warrior muttered, and went his

way. He had climbed the top of his favorite barren hill to survey the surrounding prairies, when he spied my chase after the coyote. His keen eyes recognized the pony and driver. At once uneasy for my safety, he had come running to my mother's cabin to give her warning. I did not appreciate his kindly interest, for there was an unrest gnawing at my heart.

As soon as he went away, I asked Dawée about something else.

"No, my baby sister, I cannot take you with me to the party tonight," he replied. Though I was not far from fifteen, and I felt that before long I should enjoy all the privileges of my tall cousin, Dawée persisted in calling me his baby sister.

That moonlight night, I cried in my mother's presence when I heard the jolly young people pass by our cottage. They were no more young braves in blankets and eagle plumes, nor Indian maids with prettily painted cheeks. They had gone three years to school in the East, and had become civilized. The young men wore the white man's coat and trousers, with bright neckties. The girls wore tight muslin dresses, with ribbons at neck and waist. At these gatherings they talked English. I could speak English almost as well as my brother, but I was not properly dressed to be taken along. I had no hat, no ribbons, and no close-fitting gown. Since my return from school I had thrown away my shoes, and wore again the soft moccasins.

While Dawée was busily preparing to go I controlled my tears. But when I heard him bounding away on his pony, I buried my face in my arms and cried hot tears.

My mother was troubled by my unhappiness. Coming to my side, she offered me the only printed matter we had in our home. It was an Indian Bible, given her some years ago by a missionary. She tried to console me. "Here, my child, are the white man's papers. Read a little from them," she said most piously.

I took it from her hand, for her sake; but my enraged spirit felt more like burning the book, which afforded me no help, and was a perfect delusion to my mother. I did not read it, but laid it unopened on the floor, where I sat on my feet. The dim yellow light of the braided muslin burning in a small vessel of oil flickered and sizzled in the awful silent storm which followed my rejection of the Bible.

Now my wrath against the fates consumed my tears before they reached my eyes. I sat stony, with a bowed head. My mother threw a shawl over her head and shoulders, and stepped out into the night.

After an uncertain solitude, I was suddenly aroused by a loud cry piercing the night. It was my mother's voice wailing among the barren hills which held the bones of buried warriors. She called aloud for her brothers' spirits to support her in her helpless misery. My fingers grew icy cold, as I realized that my unrestrained tears had betrayed my suffering to her, and she was grieving for me.

Before she returned, though I knew she was on her way, for she had ceased her weeping, I extinguished the light, and leaned my head on the window sill.

Many schemes of running away from my surroundings hovered about in my mind. A few more moons of such a turmoil drove me away to the Eastern school. I rode on the white man's iron steed, thinking it would bring me back to my mother in a few winters, when I should be grown tall, and there would be congenial friends awaiting me.

VII

INCURRING MY MOTHER'S DISPLEASURE

In the second journey to the East I had not come without some precautions. I had a secret interview with one of our best medicine men, and when I left his wigwam I carried securely in my sleeve a tiny bunch of magic roots. This possession assured me of friends wherever I should go. So absolutely did I believe in its charms that I wore it through all the school routine for more than a year. Then, before I lost my faith in the dead roots, I lost the little buckskin bag containing all my good luck.

At the close of this second term of three years I was the

proud owner of my first diploma.[1] The following autumn I ventured upon a college career against my mother's will.

I had written for her approval, but in her reply I found no encouragement. She called my notice to her neighbors' children, who had completed their education in three years. They had returned to their homes, and were then talking English with the frontier settlers. Her few words hinted that I had better give up my slow attempt to learn the white man's ways, and be content to roam over the prairies and find my living upon wild roots. I silenced her by deliberate disobedience.

Thus, homeless and heavy-hearted, I began anew my life among strangers.

As I hid myself in my little room in the college dormitory, away from the scornful and yet curious eyes of the students, I pined for sympathy. Often I wept in secret, wishing I had gone West, to be nourished by my mother's love, instead of remaining among a cold race whose hearts were frozen hard with prejudice.

During the fall and winter seasons I scarcely had a real friend, though by that time several of my classmates were courteous to me at a safe distance.

My mother had not yet forgiven my rudeness to her, and I had no moment for letter-writing. By daylight and lamplight, I spun with reeds and thistles, until my hands were tired from their weaving, the magic design which promised me the white man's respect.

At length, in the spring term, I entered an oratorical contest among the various classes. As the day of competition approached, it did not seem possible that the event was so near at hand, but it came. In the chapel the classes assembled together, with their invited guests. The high platform was carpeted, and gaily festooned with college colors. A bright white light illumined the room, and outlined clearly the great polished beams that arched the domed ceiling. The assembled crowds filled the air with pulsating murmurs. When the hour for speaking arrived all were hushed. But on the wall the old clock which pointed out the trying moment ticked calmly on.

One after another I saw and heard the orators. Still, I could not realize that they longed for the favorable decision of the judges as much as I did. Each contestant received a loud burst of applause, and some were cheered heartily. Too soon my turn came, and I paused a moment behind the curtains for a deep breath. After my concluding words, I heard the same applause that the others had called out.

Upon my retreating steps, I was astounded to receive from my fellow-students a large bouquet of roses tied with flowing ribbons. With the lovely flowers I fled from the stage. This friendly token was a rebuke to me for the hard feelings I had borne them.

Later, the decision of the judges awarded me the first place. Then there was a mad uproar in the hall, where my classmates sang and shouted my name at the top of their lungs; and the disappointed students howled and brayed in fearfully dissonant tin trumpets. In this excitement, happy students rushed forward to offer their congratulations. And I could not conceal a smile when they wished to escort me in a procession to the students' parlor, where all were going to calm themselves. Thanking them for the kind spirit which prompted them to make such a proposition, I walked alone with the night to my own little room.

A few weeks afterward, I appeared as the college representative in another contest. This time the competition was among orators from different colleges in our State. It was held at the State capital, in one of the largest opera houses.

Here again was a strong prejudice against my people. In the evening, as the great audience filled the house, the student bodies began warring among themselves. Fortunately, I was spared witnessing any of the noisy wrangling before the contest began. The slurs against the Indian that stained the lips of our opponents were already burning like a dry fever within my breast.

But after the orations were delivered a deeper burn awaited me. There, before that vast ocean of eyes, some college rowdies threw out a large white flag, with a drawing of a most forlorn Indian girl on it. Under this they had printed in bold black letters words that ridiculed the college which was represented by a "squaw." Such worse than barbarian rudeness embittered me. While we waited for the verdict of the judges, I gleamed fiercely upon the throngs of palefaces. My teeth were hard set, as I saw the white flag still floating insolently in the air.

Then anxiously we watched the man carry toward the stage the envelope containing the final decision.

There were two prizes given, that night, and one of them was mine!

The evil spirit laughed within me when the white flag dropped out of sight, and the hands which hurled it hung limp in defeat.

Leaving the crowd as quickly as possible, I was soon in my room. The rest of the night I sat in an armchair and gazed into the crackling fire. I laughed no more in triumph when thus alone. The little taste of victory did not satisfy a hunger in my heart. In my mind I saw my mother far away on the Western plains, and she was holding a charge against me.

An Indian Teacher Among Indians

I

MY FIRST DAY

Though an illness left me unable to continue my college course, my pride kept me from returning to my mother. Had she known of my worn condition, she would have said the white man's papers were not worth the freedom and health I had lost by them. Such a rebuke from my mother would have been unbearable, and as I felt then it would be far too true to be comfortable.

Since the winter when I had my first dreams about red apples I had been traveling slowly toward the morning horizon. There had been no doubt about the direction in which I wished to go to spend my energies in a work for the Indian race. Thus I had written my mother briefly, saying my plan for the year was to teach in an Eastern Indian school.[2] Sending this message to her in the West, I started at once eastward.

Thus I found myself, tired and hot, in a black veiling of car smoke, as I stood wearily on a street corner of an old-fashioned town, waiting for a car. In a few moments more I should be on the school grounds, where a new work was ready for my inexperienced hands.

Upon entering the school campus, I was surprised at the thickly clustered buildings which made it a quaint little village, much more interesting than the town itself. The large trees among the houses gave the place a cool, refreshing shade, and the grass a deeper green. Within this large court of grass and trees stood a low green pump. The queer boxlike case had a revolving handle on its side, which clanked and creaked constantly.

I made myself known, and was shown to my room,—a small, carpeted room, with ghastly walls and ceiling. The two windows, both on the same side, were curtained with heavy muslin yellowed with age. A clean white bed was in one corner of the room, and opposite it was a square pine table covered with a black woolen blanket.

Without removing my hat from my head, I seated myself in one of the two stiff-backed chairs that were placed beside the table. For several heart throbs I sat still looking from ceiling to floor, from wall to wall, trying hard to imagine years of contentment there. Even while I was wondering if my exhausted strength would sustain me through this undertaking, I heard a heavy tread stop at my door. Opening it, I met the imposing figure of a stately gray-haired man. With a light straw hat in one hand, and the right hand extended for greeting, he smiled kindly upon me. For some reason I was awed by his wondrous height and his strong square shoulders, which I felt were a finger's length above my head.

I was always slight, and my serious illness in the early spring had made me look rather frail and languid. His quick eye measured my height and breadth. Then he looked into my face. I imagined that a visible shadow flitted across his countenance as he let my hand fall. I knew he was no other than my employer.

"Ah ha! so you are the little Indian girl who created the excitement among the college orators!" he said, more to himself than to me. I thought I heard a subtle note of disappointment in his voice. Looking in from where he stood, with one sweeping glance, he asked if I lacked anything for my room.

After he turned to go, I listened to his step until it grew faint and was lost in the distance. I was aware that my car-smoked appearance had not concealed the lines of pain on my face.

For a short moment my spirit laughed at my ill fortune, and I entertained the idea of exerting myself to make an improvement. But as I tossed my hat off a leaden weakness came over me, and I felt as if years of weariness lay like water-soaked logs upon me. I threw myself upon the bed, and, closing my eyes, forgot my good intention.

II
A TRIP WESTWARD

One sultry month I sat at a desk heaped up with work. Now, as I recall it, I wonder how I could have dared to disregard nature's warning with such recklessness. Fortunately, my inheritance of a marvelous endurance enabled me to bend without breaking.

Though I had gone to and fro, from my room to the office, in an unhappy silence, I was watched by those around me. On an early morning I was summoned to the superintendent's office. For a half-hour I listened to his words, and when I returned to my room I remembered one sentence above the rest. It was this: "I am going to turn you loose to pasture!" He was sending me West to gather Indian pupils for the school, and this was his way of expressing it.

I needed nourishment, but the midsummer's travel across the continent to search the hot prairies for overconfident parents who would intrust their children to strangers was a lean pasturage. However, I dwelt on the hope of seeing my mother. I tried to reason that a change was a rest. Within a couple of days I started toward my mother's home.

The intense heat and the sticky car smoke that followed my homeward trail did not noticeably restore my vitality. Hour after hour I gazed upon the country which was receding rapidly from me. I noticed the gradual expansion of the horizon as we emerged out of the forests into the plains. The great high buildings, whose towers overlooked the dense woodlands, and whose gigantic clusters formed large cities, diminished, together with the groves, until only little log cabins lay snugly in the bosom of the vast prairie. The cloud shadows which drifted about on the waving yellow of long-dried grasses thrilled me like the meeting of old friends.

At a small station, consisting of a single frame house with a rickety board walk around it, I alighted from the iron horse, just thirty miles from my mother and my brother Dawée. A strong hot wind seemed determined to blow my hat off, and return me to olden days when I roamed bareheaded over the hills. After the puffing engine of my train was gone, I stood on the platform in deep solitude. In the distance I saw the gently rolling land leap up into bare hills. At their bases a broad gray road was winding itself round about them until it came by the station. Among these hills I rode in a light conveyance, with a trusty driver, whose unkempt flaxen hair hung shaggy about his ears and his leather neck of reddish tan. From accident or decay he had lost one of his long front teeth.

Though I call him a paleface, his cheeks were of a brick red. His moist blue eyes, blurred and bloodshot, twitched involuntarily. For a long time he had driven through grass and snow from this solitary station to the Indian village. His weather-stained clothes fitted badly his warped shoulders. He was stooped, and his protruding chin, with its tuft of dry flax, nodded as monotonously as did the head of his faithful beast.

All the morning I looked about me, recognizing old familiar sky lines of rugged bluffs and round-topped hills. By the roadside I caught glimpses of various plants whose sweet roots were delicacies among my people. When I saw the first cone-shaped wigwam, I could not help uttering an exclamation which caused my driver a sudden jump out of his drowsy nodding.

At noon, as we drove through the eastern edge of the reservation, I grew very impatient and restless. Constantly I wondered what my mother would say upon seeing her little daughter grown tall. I had not written her the day of my arrival, thinking I would surprise her. Crossing a ravine thicketed with low shrubs and plum bushes, we approached a large yellow acre of wild sunflowers. Just beyond this nature's garden we drew near to my mother's cottage. Close by the log cabin stood a little canvas-covered wigwam. The driver stopped in front of the open door, and in a long moment my mother appeared at the threshold.

I had expected her to run out to greet me, but she stood still, all the while staring at the weather-beaten man at my side. At length, when her loftiness became unbearable, I called to her, "Mother, why do you stop?"

This seemed to break the evil moment, and she hastened out to hold my head against her cheek.

"My daughter, what madness possessed you to bring home such a fellow?" she asked, pointing at the driver, who was fumbling in his pockets for change while he held the bill I gave him between his jagged teeth.

"Bring him! Why, no, mother, he has brought me! He is a driver!" I exclaimed.

Upon this revelation, my mother threw her arms about me and apologized for her mistaken inference. We laughed away the momentary hurt. Then she built a brisk fire on the ground in the tepee, and hung a blackened coffeepot on one of the prongs of a forked pole which leaned over the flames. Placing a pan on a heap of red embers, she baked some unleavened bread. This light luncheon she brought into the cabin, and arranged on a table covered with a checkered oilcloth.

My mother had never gone to school, and though she meant always to give up her own customs for such of the white man's ways as pleased her, she made only compromises. Her two windows, directly opposite each other, she curtained with a pink-flowered print. The naked logs were unstained, and rudely carved with the axe so as to fit into one another. The sod roof was trying to boast of tiny sunflowers, the seeds of which had probably been planted by the constant wind. As I leaned my head against the logs, I discovered the peculiar odor that I could not forget. The rains had soaked the earth and roof so that the smell of damp clay was but the natural breath of such a dwelling.

"Mother, why is not your house cemented? Do you have no interest in a more comfortable shelter?" I asked, when the apparent inconveniences of her home seemed to suggest indifference on her part.

"You forget, my child, that I am now old, and I do not work with beads any more. Your brother Dawée, too, has lost his position, and we are left without means to buy even a morsel of food," she replied.

Dawée was a government clerk in our reservation when I last heard from him. I was surprised upon hearing what my mother said concerning his lack of employment. Seeing the puzzled expression on my face, she continued: "Dawée! Oh, has he not told you that the Great Father at Washington sent a white son to take your brother's pen from him? Since then Dawée has not been able to make use of the education the Eastern school has given him."

I found no words with which to answer satisfactorily. I found no reason with which to cool my inflamed feelings.

Dawée was a whole day's journey off on the prairie, and my mother did not expect him until the next day. We were silent.

When, at length, I raised my head to hear more clearly the moaning of the wind in the corner logs, I noticed the daylight streaming into the dingy room through several places where the logs fitted unevenly. Turning to my mother, I urged her to tell me more about Dawée's trouble, but she only said: "Well, my daughter, this village has been these many winters a refuge for white robbers. The Indian cannot complain to the Great Father in Washington without suffering outrage for it here. Dawée tried to secure justice for our tribe in a small matter, and today you see the folly of it."

Again, though she stopped to hear what I might say, I was silent.

"My child, there is only one source of justice, and I have been praying steadfastly to the Great Spirit to avenge our wrongs," she said, seeing I did not move my lips.

My shattered energy was unable to hold longer any faith, and I cried out desperately: "Mother, don't pray again! The Great Spirit does not care if we live or die! Let us not look for good or justice: then we shall not be disappointed!"

"Sh! my child, do not talk so madly. There is Taku Iyotan Wasaka,[3] to which I pray," she answered, as she stroked my head again as she used to do when I was a smaller child.

III
MY MOTHER'S CURSE UPON
WHITE SETTLERS

One black night mother and I sat alone in the dim starlight, in front of our wigwam. We were facing the river, as we talked about the shrinking limits of the village. She told me about the poverty-stricken white settlers, who lived in caves dug in the long ravines of the high hills across the river.

A whole tribe of broad-footed white beggars had rushed hither to make claims on those wild lands. Even as she was telling this I spied a small glimmering light in the bluffs.

"That is a white man's lodge where you see the burning fire," she said. Then, a short distance from it, only a little lower than the first, was another light. As I became accustomed to the night, I saw more and more twinkling lights, here and there, scattered all along the wide black margin of the river.

Still looking toward the distant firelight, my mother continued: "My daughter, beware of the paleface. It was the cruel paleface who caused the death of your sister and your uncle, my brave brother. It is this same paleface who offers in one palm the holy papers, and with the other gives a holy baptism of firewater. He is the hypocrite who reads with one eye, 'Thou shalt not kill,' and with the other gloats upon the sufferings of the Indian race." Then suddenly discovering a new fire in the bluffs, she exclaimed, "Well, well, my daughter, there is the light of another white rascal!"

She sprang to her feet, and, standing firm beside her wigwam, she sent a curse upon those who sat around the hated white man's light. Raising her right arm forcibly into line with her eye, she threw her whole might into her doubled fist as she shot it vehemently at the strangers. Long she held her outstretched fingers toward the settler's lodge, as if an invisible power passed from them to the evil at which she aimed.

IV

RETROSPECTION

Leaving my mother, I returned to the school in the East. As months passed over me, I slowly comprehended that the large army of white teachers in Indian schools had a larger missionary creed than I had suspected.

It was one which included self-preservation quite as much as Indian education. When I saw an opium-eater holding a position as teacher of Indians, I did not understand what good was expected, until a Christian in power replied that this pumpkin-colored creature had a feeble mother to support. An inebriate paleface sat stupid in a doctor's chair, while Indian patients carried their ailments to untimely graves, because his fair wife was dependent upon him for her daily food.

I find it hard to count that white man a teacher who tortured an ambitious Indian youth by frequently reminding the brave changeling that he was nothing but a "government pauper."

Though I burned with indignation upon discovering on every side instances no less shameful than those I have mentioned, there was no present help. Even the few rare ones who have worked nobly for my race were powerless to choose workmen like themselves. To be sure, a man was sent from the Great Father to inspect Indian schools, but what he saw was usually the students' sample work *made* for exhibition. I was nettled by this sly cunning of the workmen who hoodwinked the Indian's pale Father at Washington.

My illness, which prevented the conclusion of my college course, together with my mother's stories of the encroaching frontier settlers, left me in no mood to strain my eyes in searching for latent good in my white co-workers.

At this stage of my own evolution, I was ready to curse men of small capacity for being the dwarfs their God had made them. In the process of my education I had lost all consciousness of the nature world about me. Thus, when a hidden rage took me to the small white-walled prison which I then

called my room, I unknowingly turned away from my one salvation.

Alone in my room, I sat like the petrified Indian woman of
whom my mother used to tell me. I wished my heart's burdens
would turn me to unfeeling stone. But alive, in my tomb, I was
destitute!

For the white man's papers I had given up my faith in the
Great Spirit. For these same papers I had forgotten the healing
in trees and brooks. On account of my mother's simple view of
life, and my lack of any, I gave her up, also. I made no friends
among the race of people I loathed. Like a slender tree, I had
been uprooted from my mother, nature, and God. I was shorn
of my branches, which had waved in sympathy and love for
home and friends. The natural coat of bark which had pro-
tected my oversenstive nature was scraped off to the very
quick.

Now a cold bare pole I seemed to be, planted in a strange
earth. Still, I seemed to hope a day would come when my mute
aching head, reared upward to the sky, would flash a zigzag
lightning across the heavens. With this dream of vent for a
long-pent consciousness, I walked again amid the crowds.

At last, one weary day in the schoolroom, a new idea presented itself to me. It was a new way of solving the problem of
my inner self. I liked it. Thus I resigned my position as teacher;
and now I am in an Eastern city, following the long course of
study I have set for myself. Now, as I look back upon the recent past, I see it from a distance, as a whole. I remember how,
from morning till evening, many specimens of civilized peoples
visited the Indian school. The city folks with canes and eye-
glasses, the countrymen with sunburnt cheeks and clumsy feet,
forgot their relative social ranks in an ignorant curiosity. Both
sorts of these Christian palefaces were alike astounded at seeing
the children of savage warriors so docile and industrious.

As answers to their shallow inquiries they received the students' sample work to look upon. Examining the neatly figured
pages, and gazing upon the Indian girls and boys bending over
their books, the white visitors walked out of the schoolhouse
well satisfied: they were educating the children of the red man!

They were paying a liberal fee to the government employees in whose able hands lay the small forest of Indian timber.

In this fashion many have passed idly through the Indian schools during the last decade, afterward to boast of their charity to the North American Indian. But few there are who have paused to question whether real life or long-lasting death lies beneath this semblance of civilization.

The Great Spirit[4]

When the spirit swells my breast I love to roam leisurely among the green hills; or sometimes, sitting on the brink of the murmuring Missouri, I marvel at the great blue overhead. With half-closed eyes I watch the huge cloud shadows in their noiseless play upon the high bluffs opposite me, while into my ear ripple the sweet, soft cadences of the river's song. Folded hands lie in my lap, for the time forgot. My heart and I lie small upon the earth like a grain of throbbing sand. Drifting clouds and tinkling waters, together with the warmth of a genial summer day, bespeak with eloquence the loving Mystery round about us. During the idle while I sat upon the sunny river brink, I grew somewhat, though my response be not so clearly manifest as in the green grass fringing the edge of the high bluff back of me.

At length retracing the uncertain footpath scaling the precipitous embankment, I seek the level lands where grow the wild prairie flowers. And they, the lovely little folk, soothe my soul with their perfumed breath.

Their quaint round faces of varied hue convince the heart which leaps with glad surprise that they, too, are living symbols of omnipotent thought. With a child's eager eye I drink in the myriad star shapes wrought in luxuriant color upon the green. Beautiful is the spiritual essence they embody.

I leave them nodding in the breeze, but take along with me their impress upon my heart. I pause to rest me upon a rock embedded on the side of a foothill facing the low river bottom. Here the Stone-Boy,[5] of whom the American aborigine tells, frolics about, shooting his baby arrows and shouting aloud with glee at the tiny shafts of lightning that flash from the flying arrow-beaks. What an ideal warrior he became, baffling the siege of the pests of all the land till he triumphed over their united attack. And here he lay,—Inyan our great-great-grandfather, older than the hill he rested on, older than the race of men who love to tell of his wonderful career.

Interwoven with the thread of this Indian legend of the rock, I fain would trace a subtle knowledge of the native folk which enabled them to recognize a kinship to any and all parts of this vast universe. By the leading of an ancient trail I move toward the Indian village.

With the strong, happy sense that both great and small are so surely enfolded in His magnitude that, without a miss, each has his allotted individual ground of opportunities, I am buoyant with good nature.

Yellow Breast, swaying upon the slender stem of a wild sunflower, warbles a sweet assurance of this as I pass near by. Breaking off the clear crystal song, he turns his wee head from side to side eyeing me wisely as slowly I plod with moccasined feet. Then again he yields himself to his song of joy. Flit, flit hither and yon, he fills the summer sky with his swift, sweet melody. And truly does it seem his vigorous freedom lies more in his little spirit than in his wing.

With these thoughts I reach the log cabin whither I am strongly drawn by the tie of a child to an aged mother. Out bounds my four-footed friend to meet me, frisking about my path with unmistakable delight. Chän is a black shaggy dog, "a thoroughbred little mongrel" of whom I am very fond. Chän seems to understand many words in Sioux, and will go to her mat even when I whisper the word, though generally I think she is guided by the tone of the voice. Often she tries to imitate the sliding inflection and long-drawn-out voice to the amusement of our guests, but her articulation is quite beyond my ear. In both my hands I hold her shaggy head and gaze into her large brown eyes. At once the dilated pupils contract into tiny black dots, as if the roguish spirit within would evade my questioning.

Finally resuming the chair at my desk I feel in keen sympathy

with my fellow-creatures, for I seem to see clearly again that all
are akin. The racial lines, which once were bitterly real, now
serve nothing more than marking out a living mosaic of human
beings. And even here men of the same color are like the ivory
keys of one instrument where each resembles all the rest, yet
varies from them in pitch and quality of voice. And those creatures who are for a time mere echoes of another's note are not
unlike the fable of the thin sick man whose distorted shadow,
dressed like a real creature, came to the old master to make
him follow as a shadow. Thus with a compassion for all echoes
in human guise, I greet the solemn-faced "native preacher"
whom I find awaiting me. I listen with respect for God's creature, though he mouth most strangely the jangling phrases of a
bigoted creed.

As our tribe is one large family, where every person is related
to all the others, he addressed me:—

"Cousin, I came from the morning church service to talk
with you."

"Yes?" I said interrogatively, as he paused for some word
from me.

Shifting uneasily about in the straight-backed chair he sat
upon, he began: "Every holy day (Sunday) I look about our little God's house, and not seeing you there, I am disappointed.
This is why I come today. Cousin, as I watch you from afar, I
see no unbecoming behavior and hear only good reports of
you, which all the more burns me with the wish that you were
a church member. Cousin, I was taught long years ago by kind
missionaries to read the holy book. These godly men taught me
also the folly of our old beliefs.

"There is one God who gives reward or punishment to the
race of dead men. In the upper region the Christian dead are
gathered in unceasing song and prayer. In the deep pit below,
the sinful ones dance in torturing flames.

"Think upon these things, my cousin, and choose now to
avoid the after-doom of hell fire!" Then followed a long silence
in which he clasped tighter and unclasped again his interlocked
fingers.

Like instantaneous lightning flashes came pictures of my own

mother's making, for she, too, is now a follower of the new superstition.

"Knocking out the chinking of our log cabin, some evil hand
thrust in a burning taper of braided dry grass, but failed of his
intent, for the fire died out and the half-burned brand fell inward to the floor. Directly above it, on a shelf, lay the holy
book. This is what we found after our return from a several
days' visit. Surely some great power is hid in the sacred book!"

Brushing away from my eyes many like pictures, I offered
midday meal to the converted Indian sitting wordless and with
downcast face. No sooner had he risen from the table with
"Cousin, I have relished it," than the church bell rang.

Thither he hurried forth with his afternoon sermon. I
watched him as he hastened along, his eyes bent fast upon the
dusty road till he disappeared at the end of a quarter of a mile.

The little incident recalled to mind the copy of a missionary
paper brought to my notice a few days ago, in which a
"Christian" pugilist[6] commented upon a recent article of mine,
grossly perverting the spirit of my pen. Still I would not forget
that the pale-faced missionary and the hoodooed aborigine are
both God's creatures, though small indeed their own concep-
tions of Infinite Love. A wee child toddling in a wonder world,
I prefer to their dogma my excursions into the natural gardens
where the voice of the Great Spirit is heard in the twittering of
birds, the rippling of mighty waters, and the sweet breathing of
flowers.[7]

Here, in a fleeting quiet, I am awakened by the fluttering
robe of the Great Spirit. To my innermost consciousness the
phenomenal universe is a royal mantle, vibrating with His divine breath. Caught in its flowing fringes are the spangles and
oscillating brilliants of sun, moon, and stars.

The Soft-Hearted Sioux

I

Beside the open fire I sat within our tepee. With my red blanket wrapped tightly about my crossed legs, I was thinking of the coming season, my sixteenth winter. On either side of the wig-wam were my parents. My father was whistling a tune between his teeth while polishing with his bare hand a red stone pipe he had recently carved. Almost in front of me, beyond the center fire, my old grandmother sat near the entranceway.

She turned her face toward her right and addressed most of her words to my mother. Now and then she spoke to me, but never did she allow her eyes to rest upon her daughter's husband, my father. It was only upon rare occasions that my grandmother said anything to him. Thus his ears were open and ready to catch the smallest wish she might express. Sometimes when my grandmother had been saying things which pleased him, my father used to comment upon them. At other times, when he could not approve of what was spoken, he used to work or smoke silently.

On this night my old grandmother began her talk about me. Filling the bowl of her red stone pipe with dry willow bark, she looked across at me.

"My grandchild, you are tall and are no longer a little boy." Narrowing her old eyes, she asked, "My grandchild, when are you going to bring here a handsome young woman?" I stared into the fire rather than meet her gaze. Waiting for my answer, she stooped forward and through the long stem drew a flame into the red stone pipe.

I smiled while my eyes were still fixed upon the bright fire, but I said nothing in reply. Turning to my mother, she offered her the pipe. I glanced at my grandmother. The loose buckskin sleeve fell off at her elbow and showed a wrist covered with silver bracelets. Holding up the fingers of her left hand, she named off the desirable young women of our village.

"Which one, my grandchild, which one?" she questioned.

"Hoh!" I said, pulling at my blanket in confusion. "Not yet!" Here my mother passed the pipe over the fire to my father. Then she, too, began speaking of what I should do.

"My son, be always active. Do not dislike a long hunt. Learn to provide much buffalo meat and many buckskins before you bring home a wife." Presently my father gave the pipe to my grandmother, and he took his turn in the exhortations.

"Ho, my son, I have been counting in my heart the bravest warriors of our people. There is not one of them who won his title in his sixteenth winter. My son, it is a great thing for some brave of sixteen winters to do."

Not a word had I to give in answer. I knew well the fame of my warrior father. He had earned the right of speaking such words, though even he himself was a brave only at my age. Refusing to smoke my grandmother's pipe because my heart was too much stirred by their words, and sorely troubled with a fear lest I should disappoint them, I arose to go. Drawing my blanket over my shoulders, I said, as I stepped toward the entranceway: "I go to hobble my pony. It is now late in the night."

II

Nine winters' snows had buried deep that night when my old grandmother, together with my father and mother, designed my future with the glow of a camp fire upon it.

Yet I did not grow up the warrior, huntsman, and husband I was to have been. At the mission school I learned it was wrong to kill. Nine winters I hunted for the soft heart of Christ, and prayed for the huntsmen who chased the buffalo on the plains.

In the autumn of the tenth year I was sent back to my tribe
to preach Christianity to them. With the white man's Bible in
my hand, and the white man's tender heart in my breast, I returned to my own people.

Wearing a foreigner's dress, I walked, a stranger, into my father's village.

Asking my way, for I had not forgotten my native tongue, an
old man led me toward the tepee where my father lay. From
my old companion I learned that my father had been sick many
moons. As we drew near the tepee, I heard the chanting of a
medicine-man within it. At once I wished to enter in and drive
from my home the sorcerer of the plains, but the old warrior
checked me. "Ho, wait outside until the medicine-man leaves
your father," he said. While talking he scanned me from head
to feet. Then he retraced his steps toward the heart of the
camping-ground.

My father's dwelling was on the outer limits of the round-
faced village. With every heart-throb I grew more impatient to
enter the wigwam.

While I turned the leaves of my Bible with nervous fingers,
the medicine-man came forth from the dwelling and walked
hurriedly away. His head and face were closely covered with
the loose robe which draped his entire figure.

He was tall and large. His long strides I have never forgot.
They seemed to me then the uncanny gait of eternal death.
Quickly pocketing my Bible, I went into the tepee.

Upon a mat lay my father, with furrowed face and gray
hair. His eyes and cheeks were sunken far into his head. His
sallow skin lay thin upon his pinched nose and high cheek-
bones. Stooping over him, I took his fevered hand. How,
Ate?" I greeted him. A light flashed from his listless eyes and
his dried lips parted. "My son!" he murmured, in a feeble
voice. Then again the wave of joy and recognition receded. He
closed his eyes, and his hand dropped from my open palm to
the ground.

Looking about, I saw an old woman sitting with bowed
head. Shaking hands with her, I recognized my mother. I sat
down between my father and mother as I used to do, but I did

not feel at home. The place where my old grandmother used to sit was now unoccupied. With my mother I bowed my head. Alike our throats were choked and tears were streaming from our eyes; but far apart in spirit our ideas and faiths separated us. My grief was for the soul unsaved; and I thought my mother wept to see a brave man's body broken by sickness.

Useless was my attempt to change the faith in the medicine-man to that abstract power named God. Then one day I became righteously mad with anger that the medicine-man should thus ensnare my father's soul. And when he came to chant his sacred songs I pointed toward the door and bade him go! The man's eyes glared upon me for an instant. Slowly gathering his robe about him, he turned his back upon the sick man and stepped out of our wigwam. "Ha, ha, ha! my son, I can not live without the medicine-man!" I heard my father cry when the sacred man was gone.

III

On a bright day, when the winged seeds of the prairie-grass were flying hither and thither, I walked solemnly toward the center of the camping-ground. My heart beat hard and irregularly at my side. Tighter I grasped the sacred book I carried under my arm. Now was the beginning of life's work.

Though I knew it would be hard, I did not once feel that failure was to be my reward. As I stepped unevenly on the rolling ground, I thought of the warriors soon to wash off their warpaints and follow me.

At length I reached the place where the people had assembled to hear me preach. In a large circle men and women sat upon the dry red grass. Within the ring I stood, with the white man's Bible in my hand. I tried to tell them of the soft heart of Christ.

In silence the vast circle of bareheaded warriors sat under an afternoon sun. At last, wiping the wet from my brow, I took my place in the ring. The hush of the assembly filled me with great hope.

I was turning my thoughts upward to the sky in gratitude, when a stir called me to earth again.

A tall, strong man arose. His loose robe hung in folds over his right shoulder. A pair of snapping black eyes fastened themselves like the poisonous fangs of a serpent upon me. He was the medicine-man. A tremor played about my heart and a chill cooled the fire in my veins.

Scornfully he pointed a long forefinger in my direction and asked:

"What loyal son is he who, returning to his father's people, wears a foreigner's dress?" He paused a moment, and then continued: "The dress of that foreigner of whom a story says he bound a native of our land, and heaping dry sticks around him, kindled a fire at his feet!" Waving his hand toward me, he exclaimed, "Here is the traitor to his people!"

I was helpless. Before the eyes of the crowd the cunning magician turned my honest heart into a vile nest of treachery. Alas! the people frowned as they looked upon me.

"Listen!" he went on. "Which one of you who have eyed the young man can see through his bosom and warn the people of the nest of young snakes hatching there? Whose ear was so acute that he caught the hissing of snakes whenever the young man opened his mouth? This one has not only proven false to you, but even to the Great Spirit who made him. He is a fool! Why do you sit here giving ear to a foolish man who could not defend his people because he fears to kill, who could not bring venison to renew the life of his sick father? With his prayers, let him drive away the enemy! With his soft heart, let him keep off starvation! We shall go elsewhere to dwell upon an untainted ground."

With this he disbanded the people. When the sun lowered in the west and the winds were quiet, the village of cone-shaped tepees was gone. The medicine-man had won the hearts of the people.

Only my father's dwelling was left to mark the fighting-ground.

IV

From a long night at my father's bedside I came out to look upon the morning. The yellow sun hung equally between the snow-covered land and the cloudless blue sky. The light of the new day was cold. The strong breath of winter crusted the snow and fitted crystal shells over the rivers and lakes. As I stood in front of the tepee, thinking of the vast prairies which separated us from our tribe, and wondering if the high sky like-wise separated the soft-hearted Son of God from us, the icy blast from the North blew through my hair and skull. My ne-glected hair had grown long and fell upon my neck.

My father had not risen from his bed since the day the medicine-man led the people away. Though I read from the Bible and prayed beside him upon my knees, my father would not listen. Yet I believed my prayers were not unheeded in heaven.

"Ha, ha, ha! my son," my father groaned upon the first snowfall. "My son, our food is gone. There is no one to bring me meat! My son, your soft heart has unfitted you for every-thing!" Then covering his face with the buffalo-robe, he said no more. Now while I stood out in that cold winter morning, I was starving. For two days I had not seen any food. But my own cold and hunger did not harass my soul as did the whin-ing cry of the sick old man.

Stepping again into the tepee, I untied my snow-shoes, which were fastened to the tentpoles.

My poor mother, watching by the sick one, and faithfully heaping wood upon the center fire, spoke to me:

"My son, do not fail again to bring your father meat, or he will starve to death."

"How, Ina," I answered, sorrowfully. From the tepee I started forth again to hunt food for my aged parents. All day I tracked the white level lands in vain. Nowhere, nowhere were there any other footprints but my own! In the evening of this third fast-day I came back without meat. Only a bundle of sticks for the fire I brought on my back. Dropping the wood outside, I lifted the door-flap and set one foot within the tepee.

There I grew dizzy and numb. My eyes swam in tears. Before me lay my old gray-haired father sobbing like a child. In his horny hands he clutched the buffalo-robe, and with his teeth he was gnawing off the edges. Chewing the dry stiff hair and buffalo-skin, my father's eyes sought my hands. Upon seeing them empty, he cried out:

"My son, your soft heart will let me starve before you bring me meat! Two hills eastward stand a herd of cattle. Yet you will see me die before you bring me food!"

Leaving my mother lying with covered head upon her mat, I rushed out into the night.

With a strange warmth in my heart and swiftness in my feet, I climbed over the first hill, and soon the second one. The moonlight upon the white country showed me a clear path to the white man's cattle. With my hand upon the knife in my belt, I leaned heavily against the fence while counting the herd.

Twenty in all I numbered. From among them I chose the best-fattened creature. Leaping over the fence, I plunged my knife into it.

My long knife was sharp, and my hands, no more fearful and slow, slashed off choice chunks of warm flesh. Bending under the meat I had taken for my starving father, I hurried across the prairie.

Toward home I fairly ran with the life-giving food I carried upon my back. Hardly had I climbed the second hill when I heard sounds coming after me. Faster and faster I ran with my load for my father, but the sounds were gaining upon me. I heard the clicking of snowshoes and the squeaking of the leather straps at my heels; yet I did not turn to see what pursued me, for I was intent upon reaching my father. Suddenly like thunder an angry voice shouted curses and threats into my ear! A rough hand wrenched my shoulder and took the meat from me! I stopped struggling to run. A deafening whir filled my head. The moon and stars began to move. Now the white prairie was sky, and the stars lay under my feet. Now again they were turning. At last the starry blue rose up into place. The noise in my ears was still. A great quiet filled the air. In my hand I found my long knife dripping with blood. At my feet a man's figure lay prone in blood-red snow. The horrible scene about me seemed a trick of my senses, for I could not understand it was real. Looking long upon the blood-stained snow, the load of meat for my starving father reached my recognition at last. Quickly I tossed it over my shoulder and started again homeward.

Tired and haunted I reached the door of the wigwam. Carrying the food before me, I entered with it into the tepee.

"Father, here is food!" I cried, as I dropped the meat near my mother. No answer came. Turning about, I beheld my gray-haired father dead! I saw by the unsteady firelight an old gray-haired skeleton lying rigid and stiff.

Out into the open I started, but the snow at my feet became bloody.

V

On the day after my father's death, having led my mother to the camp of the medicine-man, I gave myself up to those who were searching for the murderer of the paleface.

They bound me hand and foot. Here in this cell I was placed four days ago.

The shrieking winter winds have followed me hither. Rattling the bars, they howl unceasingly: "Your soft heart! your soft heart will see me die before you bring me food!" Hark! something is clanking the chain on the door. It is being opened. From the dark night without a black figure crosses the threshold . . . It is the guard. He comes to warn me of my fate. He tells me that tomorrow I must die. In his stern face I laugh aloud. I do not fear death.

Yet I wonder who shall come to welcome me in the realm of strange sight. Will the loving Jesus grant me pardon and give my soul a soothing sleep? or will my warrior father greet me and receive me as his son? Will my spirit fly upward to a happy heaven? or shall I sink into the bottomless pit, an outcast from a God of infinite love?

Soon, soon I shall know, for now I see the east is growing red. My heart is strong. My face is calm. My eyes are dry and eager for new scenes. My hands hang quietly at my side. Serene and brave, my soul awaits the men to perch me on the gallows for another flight. I go.

The Trial Path

It was an autumn night on the plain. The smoke-lapels of the cone-shaped tepee flapped gently in the breeze. From the low night sky, with its myriad fire points, a large bright star peeped in at the smoke-hole of the wigwam between its fluttering lapels, down upon two Dakotas talking in the dark. The mellow stream from the star above, a maid of twenty summers, on a bed of sweetgrass, drank in with her wakeful eyes. On the opposite side of the tepee, beyond the center fireplace, the grandmother spread her rug. Though once she had lain down, the telling of a story has aroused her to a sitting posture.

Her eyes are tight closed. With a thin palm she strokes her wind-shorn hair.

"Yes, my grandchild, the legend says the large bright stars are wise old warriors, and the small dim ones are handsome young braves," she reiterates, in a high, tremulous voice.

"Then this one peeping in at the smoke-hole yonder is my dear old grandfather," muses the young woman, in long-drawn-out words.

Her soft rich voice floats through the darkness within the tepee, over the cold ashes heaped on the center fire, and passes into the ear of the toothless old woman, who sits dumb in silent reverie. Thence it flies on swifter wing over many winter snows, till at last it cleaves the warm light atmosphere of her grandfather's youth. From there her grandmother made answer:

"Listen! I am young again. It is the day of your grandfather's death. The elder one, I mean, for there were two of them. They were like twins, though they were not brothers. They were

friends, inseparable! All things, good and bad, they shared together, save one, which made them mad. In that heated frenzy
the younger man slew his most intimate friend. He killed his
elder brother, for long had their affection made them kin."

The voice of the old woman broke. Swaying her stooped
shoulders to and fro as she sat upon her feet, she muttered vain
exclamations beneath her breath. Her eyes, closed tight against
the night, beheld behind them the light of bygone days. They
saw again a rolling black cloud spread itself over the land. Her
ear heard the deep rumbling of a tempest in the west. She bent
low a cowering head, while angry thunder-birds shrieked
across the sky. "Heyä! heyä!" (No! no!) groaned the toothless
grandmother at the fury she had awakened. But the glorious
peace afterward, when yellow sunshine made the people glad,
now lured her memory onward through the storm.

"How fast, how loud my heart beats as I listen to the messenger's horrible tale!" she ejaculates. "From the fresh grave of
the murdered man he hurried to our wigwam. Deliberately
crossing his bare shins, he sat down unbidden beside my father,
smoking a long-stemmed pipe. He had scarce caught his breath
when, panting, he began:

" 'He was an only son, and a much-adored brother.'

"With wild, suspecting eyes he glanced at me as if I were in
league with the man-killer, my lover. My father, exhaling sweet-
scented smoke, assented—'How.' Then interrupting the 'Eya'
on the lips of the round-eyed tale-bearer, he asked, 'My friend,
will you smoke?' He took the pipe by its red-stone bowl, and
pointed the long slender stem toward the man. 'Yes, yes, my
friend,' replied he, and reached out a long brown arm.

"For many heart-throbs he puffed out the blue smoke, which
hung like a cloud between us. But even through the smoke-mist
I saw his sharp black eyes glittering toward me. I longed to ask
what doom awaited the young murderer, but dared not open
my lips, lest I burst forth into screams instead. My father plied
the question. Returning the pipe, the man replied: 'Oh, the
chieftain and his chosen men have had counsel together. They
have agreed it is not safe to allow a man-killer loose in our

midst. He who kills one of our tribe is an enemy, and must suffer the fate of a foe.'

"My temples throbbed like a pair of hearts!

"While I listened, a crier passed by my father's tepee. Mounted, and swaying with his pony's steps, he proclaimed in a loud voice these words (hark! I hear them now!): 'Ho-po! Give ear, all you people. A terrible deed is done. Two friends—ay, brothers in heart—have quarreled together. Now one lies buried on the hill, while the other sits, a dreaded man-killer, within his dwelling. Says our chieftain: "He who kills one of our tribe commits the offense of an enemy. As such he must be tried. Let the father of the dead man choose the mode of torture or taking of life. He has suffered livid pain, and he alone can judge how great the punishment must be to avenge his wrong." It is done.

" 'Come, every one, to witness the judgment of a father upon him who was once his son's best friend. A wild pony is now lassoed. The man-killer must mount and ride the ranting beast. Stand you all in two parallel lines from the center tepee of the bereaved family to the wigwam opposite in the great outer ring. Between you, in the wide space, is the given trialway. From the outer circle the rider must mount and guide his pony toward the center tepee. If, having gone the entire distance, the man-killer gains the center tepee still sitting on the pony's back, his life is spared and pardon given. But should he fall, then he himself has chosen death.'

"The crier's words now cease. A lull holds the village breathless. Then hurrying feet tear along, swish, swish, through the tall grass. Sobbing women hasten toward the trialway. The muffled groan of the round camp-ground is unbearable. With my face hid in the folds of my blanket, I run with the crowd toward the open place in the outer circle of our village. In a moment the two long files of solemn-faced people mark the path of the public trial. Ah! I see strong men trying to lead the lassoed pony, pitching and rearing, with white foam flying from his mouth. I choke with pain as I recognize my handsome lover desolately alone, striding with set face toward the lassoed pony.

'Do not fall! Choose life and me!' I cry in my breast, but over my lips I hold my thick blanket.

"In an instant he has leaped astride the frightened beast, and the men have let go their hold. Like an arrow sprung from a strong bow, the pony, with extended nostrils, plunges halfway to the center tepee. With all his might the rider draws the strong reins in. The pony halts with wooden legs. The rider is thrown forward by force, but does not fall. Now the maddened creature pitches, with flying heels. The line of men and women sways outward. Now it is back in place, safe from the kicking, snorting thing.

"The pony is fierce, with its large black eyes bulging out of their sockets. With humped back and nose to the ground, it leaps into the air. I shut my eyes. I can not see him fall.

"A loud shout goes up from the hoarse throats of men and women. I look. So! The wild horse is conquered. My lover dismounts at the doorway of the center wigwam. The pony, wet with sweat and shaking with exhaustion, stands like a guilty dog at his master's side. Here at the entranceway of the tepee sit the bereaved father, mother, and sister. The old warrior father rises. Stepping forward two long strides, he grasps the hand of the murderer of his only son. Holding it so the people can see, he cries, with compassionate voice, 'My son!' A murmur of surprise sweeps like a puff of sudden wind along the lines.

"The mother, with swollen eyes, with her hair cut square with her shoulders, now rises. Hurrying to the young man, she takes his right hand. 'My son!' she greets him. But on the second word her voice shook, and she turned away in sobs.

"The young people rivet their eyes upon the young woman. She does not stir. With bowed head, she sits motionless. The old warrior speaks to her. 'Shake hands with the young brave, my little daughter. He was your brother's friend for many years. Now he must be both friend and brother to you.'

"Hereupon the girl rises. Slowly reaching out her slender hand, she cries, with twitching lips, 'My brother!' The trial ends."

"Grandmother!" exploded the girl on the bed of sweet-grass. "Is this true?"

"Tosh!" answered the grandmother, with a warmth in her voice. "It is all true. During the fifteen winters of our wedded life many ponies passed from our hands, but this little winner, Ohiyesa, was a constant member of our family. At length, on that sad day your grandfather died, Ohiyesa was killed at the grave."

Though the various groups of stars which move across the sky, marking the passing of time, told how the night was in its zenith, the old Dakota woman ventured an explanation of the burial ceremony.

"My grandchild, I have scarce ever breathed the sacred knowledge in my heart. Tonight I must tell you one of them. Surely you are old enough to understand.

"Our wise medicine-man said I did well to hasten Ohiyesa after his master. Perchance on the journey along the ghostpath your grandfather will weary, and in his heart wish for his pony. The creature, already bound on the spirit-trail, will be drawn by that subtle wish. Together master and beast will enter the next camp-ground."

The woman ceased her talking. But only the deep breathing of the girl broke the quiet, for now the night wind had lulled itself to sleep.

"Hinnu! hinnu! Asleep! I have been talking in the dark, unheard. I did wish the girl would plant in her heart this sacred tale," muttered she, in a querulous voice.

Nestling into her bed of sweet-scented grass, she dozed away into another dream. Still the guardian star in the night sky beamed compassionately down upon the little tepee on the plain.

A Warrior's Daughter

In the afternoon shadow of a large tepee, with red-painted smoke lapels, sat a warrior father with crossed shins. His head was so poised that his eye swept easily the vast level land to the eastern horizon line.

He was the chieftain's bravest warrior. He had won by heroic deeds the privilege of staking his wigwam within the great circle of tepees.

He was also one of the most generous gift givers to the toothless old people. For this he was entitled to the red-painted smoke lapels on his cone-shaped dwelling. He was proud of his honors. He never wearied of rehearsing nightly his own brave deeds. Though by wigwam fires he prated much of his high rank and widespread fame, his great joy was a wee black-eyed daughter of eight sturdy winters. Thus as he sat upon the soft grass, with his wife at his side, bent over her bead work, he was singing a dance song, and beat lightly the rhythm with his slender hands.

His shrewd eyes softened with pleasure as he watched the easy movements of the small body dancing on the green before him.

Tusee is taking her first dancing lesson. Her tightly-braided hair curves over both brown ears like a pair of crooked little horns which glisten in the summer sun.

With her snugly moccasined feet close together, and a wee hand at her belt to stay the long string of beads which hang from her bare neck, she bends her knees gently to the rhythm of her father's voice.

Now she ventures upon the earnest movement, slightly upward and sidewise, in a circle. At length the song drops into a closing cadence, and the little woman, clad in beaded deerskin, sits down beside the elder one. Like her mother, she sits upon her feet. In a brief moment the warrior repeats the last refrain. Again Tusee springs to her feet and dances to the swing of the few final measures.

Just as the dance was finished, an elderly man, with short, thick hair loose about his square shoulders, rode into their presence from the rear, and leaped lightly from his pony's back. Dropping the rawhide rein to the ground, he tossed himself lazily on the grass. "Hunhe, you have returned soon," said the warrior, while extending a hand to his little daughter.

Quickly the child ran to her father's side and cuddled close to him, while he tenderly placed a strong arm about her. Both father and child, eyeing the figure on the grass, waited to hear the man's report.

"It is true," began the man, with a stranger's accent. "This is the night of the dance."

"Hunha!" muttered the warrior with some surprise.

Propping himself upon his elbows, the man raised his face. His features were of the Southern type. From an enemy's camp he was taken captive long years ago by Tusee's father. But the unusual qualities of the slave had won the Sioux warrior's heart, and for the last three winters the man had had his freedom. He was made real man again. His hair was allowed to grow. However, he himself had chosen to stay in the warrior's family.

"Hunha!" again ejaculated the warrior father. Then turning to his little daughter, he asked, "Tusee, do you hear that?"

"Yes, father, and I am going to dance tonight!"

With these words she bounded out of his arm and frolicked about in glee. Hereupon the proud mother's voice rang out in a chiding laugh.

"My child, in honor of your first dance your father must give a generous gift. His ponies are wild, and roam beyond the great hill. Pray, what has he fit to offer?" she questioned, the pair of puzzled eyes fixed upon her.

"A pony from the herd, mother, a fleet-footed pony from the herd!" Tusee shouted with sudden inspiration.

Pointing a small forefinger toward the man lying on the grass, she cried, "Uncle, you will go after the pony tomorrow!" And pleased with her solution of the problem, she skipped wildly about. Her childish faith in her elders was not conditioned by a knowledge of human limitations, but thought all things possible to grown-ups.

"Hähob!" exclaimed the mother, with a rising inflection, implying by the expletive that her child's buoyant spirit be not weighted with a denial.

Quickly to the hard request the man replied, "How! I go if Tusee tells me so!"

This delighted the little one, whose black eyes brimmed over with light. Standing in front of the strong man, she clapped her small, brown hands with joy.

"That makes me glad! My heart is good! Go, uncle, and bring a handsome pony!" she cried. In an instant she would have frisked away, but an impulse held her tilting where she stood. In the man's own tongue, for he had taught her many words and phrases, she exploded, "Thank you, good uncle, thank you!" then tore away from sheer excess of glee.

The proud warrior father, smiling and narrowing his eyes, muttered approval, "Howo! Hechetu!"

Like her mother, Tusee has finely pencilled eyebrows and slightly extended nostrils; but in her sturdiness of form she resembles her father.

A loyal daughter, she sits within her tepee making beaded deerskins for her father, while he longs to stave off her every suitor as all unworthy of his old heart's pride. But Tusee is not alone in her dwelling. Near the entranceway a young brave is half reclining on a mat. In silence he watches the petals of a wild rose growing on the soft buckskin. Quickly the young woman slips the beads on the silvery sinew thread, and works them into the pretty flower design. Finally, in a low, deep voice, the young man begins:

"The sun is far past the zenith. It is now only a man's height above the western edge of land. I hurried hither to tell you tomorrow I join the war party."

He pauses for reply, but the maid's head drops lower over her deerskin, and her lips are more firmly drawn together. He continues:

"Last night in the moonlight I met your warrior father. He seemed to know I had just stepped forth from your tepee. I fear he did not like it, for though I greeted him, he was silent. I halted in his pathway. With what boldness I dared, while my heart was beating hard and fast, I asked him for his only daughter.

"Drawing himself erect to his tallest height, and gathering his loose robe more closely about his proud figure, he flashed a pair of piercing eyes upon me.

" 'Young man,' said he, with a cold, slow voice that chilled me to the marrow of my bones, 'hear me. Naught but an enemy's scalp-lock, plucked fresh with your own hand, will buy Tusee for your wife.' Then he turned on his heel and stalked away."

Tusee thrusts her work aside. With earnest eyes she scans her lover's face.

"My father's heart is really kind. He would know if you are brave and true," murmured the daughter, who wished no ill-will between her two loved ones.

Then rising to go, the youth holds out a right hand. "Grasp my hand once firmly before I go, Hoye. Pray tell me, will you wait and watch for my return?"

Tusee only nods assent, for mere words are vain.

At early dawn the round camp-ground awakes into song. Men and women sing of bravery and of triumph. They inspire the swelling breasts of the painted warriors mounted on prancing ponies bedecked with the green branches of trees.

Riding slowly around the great ring of cone-shaped tepees, here and there, a loud-singing warrior swears to avenge a former wrong, and thrusts a bare brown arm against the purple east, calling the Great Spirit to hear his vow. All having made the circuit, the singing war party gallops away southward.

Astride their ponies laden with food and deerskins, brave elderly women follow after their warriors. Among the foremost rides a young woman in elaborately beaded buckskin dress.

Proudly mounted, she curbs with the single rawhide loop a wild-eyed pony.

It is Tusee on her father's warhorse. Thus the war party of Indian men and their faithful women vanish beyond the southern skyline.

A day's journey brings them very near the enemy's borderland. Nightfall finds a pair of twin tepees nestled in a deep ravine. Within one lounge the painted warriors, smoking their pipes and telling weird stories by the firelight, while in the other watchful women crouch uneasily about their center fire.

By the first gray light in the east the tepees are banished. They are gone. The warriors are in the enemy's camp, breaking dreams with their tomahawks. The women are hid away in secret places in the long thicketed ravine.

The day is far spent, the red sun is low over the west.

At length straggling warriors return, one by one, to the deep hollow. In the twilight they number their men. Three are missing. Of these absent ones two are dead; but the third one, a young man, is a captive to the foe.

"He-he!" lament the warriors, taking food in haste.

In silence each woman, with long strides, hurries to and fro, tying large bundles on her pony's back. Under cover of night the war party must hasten homeward. Motionless, with bowed head, sits a woman in her hiding-place. She grieves for her lover.

In bitterness of spirit she hears the warriors' murmuring words. With set teeth she plans to cheat the hated enemy of their captive. In the meanwhile low signals are given, and the war party, unaware of Tusee's absence, steal quietly away. The soft thud of pony-hoofs grows fainter and fainter. The gradual hush of the empty ravine whirrs noisily in the ear of the young woman. Alert for any sound of footfalls nigh, she holds her breath to listen. Her right hand rests on a long knife in her belt. Ah, yes, she knows where her pony is hid, but not yet has she need of him. Satisfied that no danger is nigh, she prowls forth from her place of hiding. With a panther's tread and pace she climbs the high ridge beyond the low ravine. From thence she spies the enemy's camp-fires.

Rooted to the barren bluff the slender woman's figure stands on the pinnacle of night, outlined against a starry sky. The cool night breeze wafts to her burning ear snatches of song and drum. With desperate hate she bites her teeth.

Tusee beckons the stars to witness. With impassioned voice and uplifted face she pleads:

"Great Spirit, speed me to my lover's rescue! Give me swift cunning for a weapon this night! All-powerful Spirit, grant me my warrior-father's heart, strong to slay a foe and mighty to save a friend!"

In the midst of the enemy's camp-ground, underneath a temporary dance-house, are men and women in gala-day dress. It is late in the night, but the merry warriors bend and bow their nude, painted bodies before a bright center fire. To the lusty men's voices and the rhythmic throbbing drum, they leap and rebound with feathered headgears waving.

Women with red-painted cheeks and long, braided hair sit in a large half-circle against the willow railing. They, too, join in the singing, and rise to dance with their victorious warriors.

Amid this circular dance arena stands a prisoner bound to a post, haggard with shame and sorrow. He hangs his disheveled head.

He stares with unseeing eyes upon the bare earth at his feet. With jeers and smirking faces the dancers mock the Dakota captive. Rowdy braves and small boys hoot and yell in derision.

Silent among the noisy mob, a tall woman, leaning both elbows on the round willow railing, peers into the lighted arena. The dancing center fire shines bright into her handsome face, intensifying the night in her dark eyes. It breaks into myriad points upon her beaded dress. Unmindful of the surging throng jostling her at either side, she glares in upon the hateful, scoffing men. Suddenly she turns her head. Tittering maids whisper near her ear:

"There! There! See him now, sneering in the captive's face. 'Tis he who sprang upon the young man and dragged him by his long hair to yonder post. See! He is handsome! How gracefully he dances!"

The silent young woman looks toward the bound captive.
She sees a warrior, scarce older than the captive, flourishing a
tomahawk in the Dakota's face. A burning rage darts forth
from her eyes and brands him for a victim of revenge. Her
heart mutters within her breast, "Come, I wish to meet you,
vile foe, who captured my lover and tortures him now with a
living death."

Here the singers hush their voices, and the dancers scatter to
their various resting-places along the willow ring. The victor
gives a reluctant last twirl of his tomahawk, then, like the
others, he leaves the center ground. With head and shoulders
swaying from side to side, he carries a high-pointing chin toward the willow railing. Sitting down upon the ground with
crossed legs, he fans himself with an outspread turkey wing.

Now and then he stops his haughty blinking to peep out of
the corners of his eyes. He hears some one clearing her throat
gently. It is unmistakably for his ear. The wing-fan swings irregularly to and fro. At length he turns a proud face over a
bare shoulder and beholds a handsome woman smiling.

"Ah, she would speak to a hero!" thumps his heart wildly.

The singers raise their voices in unison. The music is irresistible. Again lunges the victor into the open arena. Again he
leers into the captive's face. At every interval between the songs
he returns to his resting-place. Here the young woman awaits
him. As he approaches she smiles boldly into his eyes. He is
pleased with her face and her smile.

Waving his wing-fan spasmodically in front of his face, he
sits with his ears pricked up. He catches a low whisper. A hand
taps him lightly on the shoulder. The handsome woman speaks
to him in his own tongue. "Come out into the night. I wish to
tell you who I am."

He must know what sweet words of praise the handsome
woman has for him. With both hands he spreads the meshes of
the loosely woven willows, and crawls out unnoticed into the
dark.

Before him stands the young woman. Beckoning him with a
slender hand, she steps backward, away from the light and the
restless throng of onlookers. He follows with impatient strides.

She quickens her pace. He lengthens his strides. Then suddenly the woman turns from him and darts away with amazing speed. Clinching his fists and biting his lower lip, the young man runs after the fleeing woman. In his maddened pursuit he forgets the dance arena.

Beside a cluster of low bushes the woman halts. The young man, panting for breath and plunging headlong forward, whispers loud, "Pray tell me, are you a woman or an evil spirit to lure me away?"

Turning on heels firmly planted in the earth, the woman gives a wild spring forward, like a panther for its prey. In a husky voice she hissed between her teeth, "I am a Dakota woman!"

From her unerring long knife the enemy falls heavily at her feet. The Great Spirit heard Tusee's prayer on the hilltop. He gave her a warrior's strong heart to lessen the foe by one.

A bent old woman's figure, with a bundle like a grandchild slung on her back, walks round and round the dance-house. The wearied onlookers are leaving in twos and threes. The tired dancers creep out of the willow railing, and some go out at the entrance way, till the singers, too, rise from the drum and are trudging drowsily homeward. Within the arena the center fire lies broken in red embers. The night no longer lingers about the willow railing, but, hovering into the dance-house, covers here and there a snoring man whom sleep has overpowered where he sat.

The captive in his tight-binding rawhide ropes hangs in hopeless despair. Close about him the gloom of night is slowly crouching. Yet the last red, crackling embers cast a faint light upon his long black hair, and, shining through the thick mats, caress his wan face with undying hope.

Still about the dance-house the old woman prowls. Now the embers are gray with ashes.

The old bent woman appears at the entrance way. With a cautious, groping foot she enters. Whispering between her teeth a lullaby for her sleeping child in her blanket, she searches for something forgotten.

Noisily snored the dreaming men in the darkest parts. As the lisping old woman draws nigh, the captive again opens his eyes.

A forefinger she presses to her lip. The young man arouses himself from his stupor. His senses belie him. Before his wide-open eyes the old bent figure straightens into its youthful stature. Tusee herself is beside him. With a stroke upward and downward she severs the cruel cords with her sharp blade. Dropping her blanket from her shoulders, so that it hangs from her girdled waist like a skirt, she shakes the large bundle into a light shawl for her lover. Quickly she spreads it over his bare back.

"Come!" she whispers, and turns to go; but the young man, numb and helpless, staggers nigh to falling.

The sight of his weakness makes her strong. A mighty power thrills her body. Stooping beneath his outstretched arms grasping at the air for support, Tusee lifts him upon her broad shoulders. With half-running, triumphant steps she carries him away into the open night.

A Dream of Her Grandfather

Her grandfather was a Dakota "medicine man." Among the Indians of his day he was widely known for his successful healing work. He was one of the leading men of the tribe and came to Washington, D.C., with one of the first delegations relative to affairs concerning the Indian people and the United States government.

His was the first band of the Great Sioux Nation to make treaties with the government in the hope of bringing about an amicable arrangement between the red and white Americans. The journey to the nation's capital was made almost entirely on pony-back, there being no railroads, and the Sioux delegation was beset with many hardships on the trail. His visit to Washington, in behalf of peace among men, proved to be his last earthly mission. From a sudden illness, he died and was buried here.

When his small granddaughter grew up she learned the white man's tongue, and followed in the footsteps of her grandfather to the very seat of government to carry on his humanitarian work. Though her days were filled with problems for welfare work among her people, she had a strange dream one night during her stay in Washington. The dream was this: Returning from an afternoon out, she found a large cedar chest had been delivered to her home in her absence. She sniffed the sweet perfume of the red wood, which reminded her of the breath of the forest,—and admired the box so neatly made, without trimmings. It looked so clean, strong and durable in its native genuineness. With elation, she took the tag in her hand and read her name aloud. "Who sent me this cedar chest?" she asked, and was told it came from her grandfather.

Wondering what gift it could be her grandfather wished now to confer upon her, wholly disregarding his death years ago, she was all eagerness to open the mystery chest.

She remembered her childhood days and the stories she loved to hear about the unusual powers of her grandfather,—recalled how she, the wee girl, had coveted the medicine bags, beaded and embroidered in porcupine quills, in symbols designed by the great "medicine man," her grandfather. Well did she remember her merited rebuke that such things were never made for relics. Treasures came in due time to those ready to receive them.

In great expectancy, she lifted the heavy lid of the cedar chest. "Oh!" she exclaimed, with a note of disappointment, seeing no beaded Indian regalia or trinkets. "Why does my grandfather send such a light gift in a heavy, large box?" She was mystified and much perplexed.

The gift was a fantastic thing, of texture far more delicate than a spider's filmy web. It was a vision! A picture of an Indian camp, not painted on canvas nor yet written. It was dream-stuff, suspended in the thin air, filling the inclosure of the cedar wood container. As she looked upon it, the picture grew more and more real, exceeding the proportions of the chest. It was all so illusive a breath might have blown it away; yet there it was, real as life,—a circular camp of white cone-shaped tepees, astir with Indian people. The village crier, with flowing head-dress of eagle plumes, mounted on a prancing white pony, rode within the arena. Indian men, women and children stopped in groups and clusters, while bright painted faces peered out of tepee doors, to listen to the chieftain's crier.

At this point, she, too, heard the full melodious voice. She heard distinctly the Dakota words he proclaimed to the people. "Be glad! Rejoice! Look up, and see the new day dawning! Help is near! Hear me, every one."

She caught the glad tidings and was thrilled with new hope for her people.

The Widespread Enigma Concerning
Blue-Star Woman

It was summer on the western plains. Fields of golden sunflowers, facing eastward, greeted the rising sun. Blue-Star Woman, with windshorn braids of white hair over each ear, sat in the shade of her log hut before an open fire. Lonely but unmolested she dwelt here like the ground squirrel that took its abode nearby,—both through the easy tolerance of the land owner. The Indian woman held a skillet over the burning embers. A large round cake, with long slashes in its center, was baking and crowding the capacity of the frying pan.

In deep abstraction Blue-Star Woman prepared her morning meal. "Who am I?" had become the obsessing riddle of her life. She was no longer a young woman, being in her fifty-third year. In the eyes of the white man's law, it was required of her to give proof of her membership in the Sioux tribe. The unwritten law of heart prompted her naturally to say, "I am a being. I am Blue-Star Woman. A piece of earth is my birthright."

It was taught for reasons now forgot that an Indian should never pronounce his or her name in answer to any inquiry. It was probably a means of protection in the days of black magic. Be this as it may, Blue-Star Woman lived in times when this teaching was disregarded. It gained her nothing, however, to pronounce her name to the government official to whom she applied for her share of tribal land. His persistent question was always, "Who were your parents?"

Blue-Star Woman was left an orphan at a tender age. She did not remember them. They were long gone to the spirit-land,—and she could not understand why they should be recalled to earth on her account. It was another one of the old, old teachings of her race that the names of the dead should not be idly spoken. It had become a sacrilege to mention carelessly the name of any departed one, especially in matters of disputes over worldy possessions. The unfortunate circumstances of her early childhood, together with the lack of written records of a roving people, placed a formidable barrier between her and her heritage. The fact was events of far greater importance to the tribe than her reincarnation had passed unrecorded in books. The verbal reports of the old-time men and women of the tribe were varied,—some were actually contradictory. Blue-Star Woman was unable to find even a twig of her family tree.

She sharpened one end of a long stick and with it speared the fried bread when it was browned. Heedless of the hot bread's "Tsing!" in a high treble as it was lifted from the fire, she added it to the six others which had preceded it. It had been many a moon since she had had a meal of fried bread, for she was too poor to buy at any one time all the necessary ingredients, particularly the fat in which to fry it. During the bread-making, the smoke-blackened coffeepot boiled over. The aroma of freshly made coffee smote her nostrils and roused her from the tantalizing memories.

The day before, friendly spirits, the unseen ones, had guided her aimless footsteps to her Indian neighbor's house. No sooner had she entered than she saw on the table some grocery bundles. "Iye-que, fortunate one!" she exclaimed as she took the straight-backed chair offered her. At once the Indian hostess untied the bundles and measured out a cupful of green coffee beans and a pound of lard. She gave them to Blue-Star Woman, saying, "I want to share my good fortune. Take these home with you." Thus it was that Blue-Star Woman had come into unexpected possession of the materials which now contributed richly to her breakfast.

The generosity of her friend had often saved her from starvation. Generosity is said to be a fault of Indian people, but neither the Pilgrim Fathers nor Blue-Star Woman ever held it seriously against them. Blue-Star Woman was even grateful for this gift of food. She was fond of coffee,—that black drink brought hither by those daring voyagers of long ago. The coffee habit was one of the signs of her progress in the white man's civilization, also had she emerged from the tepee into a log hut, another achievement. She had learned to read the primer and to write her name. Little Blue-Star attended school unhindered by a fond mother's fears that a foreign teacher might not spare the rod with her darling.

Blue-Star Woman was her individual name. For untold ages the Indian race had not used family names. A new-born child was given a brand-new name. Blue-Star Woman was proud to write her name for which she would not be required to substitute another's upon her marriage, as is the custom of civilized peoples.

"The times are changed now," she muttered under her breath. "My individual name seems to mean nothing." Looking out into space, she saw the nodding sunflowers, and they acquiesced with her. Their drying leaves reminded her of the near approach of autumn. Then soon, very soon, the ice would freeze along the banks of the muddy river. The day of the first ice was her birthday. She would be fifty-four winters old. How futile had been all these winters to secure her a share in tribal lands. A weary smile flickered across her face as she sat there on the ground like a bronze figure of patience and long-suffering.

The breadmaking was finished. The skillet was set aside to cool. She poured the appetizing coffee into her tin cup. With fried bread and black coffee she regaled herself. Again her mind reverted to her riddle. "The missionary preacher said he could not explain the white man's law to me. He who reads daily from the Holy Bible, which he tells me is God's book, cannot understand mere man's laws. This also puzzles me," thought she to herself. "Once a wise leader of our people, addressing a president of this country, said: 'I am a man. You are another. The Great Spirit is our witness!' This is simple and easy to understand, but the times are changed. The white man's laws are strange."

Blue-Star Woman broke off a piece of fried bread between a thumb and forefinger. She ate it hungrily, and sipped from her cup of fragrant coffee. "I do not understand the white man's law. It's like walking in the dark. In this darkness, I am growing fearful of everything."

Oblivious to the world, she had not heard the footfall of two Indian men who now stood before her.

Their short-cropped hair looked blue-black in contrast to the faded civilian clothes they wore. Their white man's shoes were rusty and unpolished. To the unconventional eyes of the old Indian woman, their celluloid collars appeared like shining marks of civilization. Blue-Star Woman looked up from the lap of mother earth without rising. "Hinnu, hinnu!" she ejaculated in undisguised surprise. "Pray, who are these would-be white men?" she inquired.

In one voice and by an assumed relationship the two Indian men addressed her. "Aunt, I shake hands with you." Again Blue-Star Woman remarked, "Oh, indeed! these near white men speak my native tongue and shake hands according to our custom." Did she guess the truth, she would have known they were simply deluded mortals, deceiving others and themselves most of all. Boisterously laughing and making conversation, they each in turn gripped her withered hand.

Like a sudden flurry of wind, tossing loose ends of things, they broke into her quiet morning hour and threw her groping thoughts into greater chaos. Masking their real errand with long-drawn faces, they feigned a concern for her welfare only. "We come to ask how you are living. We heard you were slowly starving to death. We heard you are one of those Indians who have been cheated out of their share in tribal lands by the government officials."

Blue-Star Woman became intensely interested.

"You see we are educated in the white man's ways," they said with protruding chests. One unconsciously thrust his thumbs into the armholes of his ill-fitting coat and strutted about in his pride. "We can help you get your land. We want to help our aunt. All old people like you ought to be helped before the younger ones. The old will die soon, and they may never get the benefit of their land unless some one like us helps them to get their rights, without further delay."

Blue-Star Woman listened attentively.

Motioning to the mats she spread upon the ground, she said: "Be seated, my nephews." She accepted the relationship assumed for the occasion. "I will give you some breakfast." Quickly she set before them a generous helping of fried bread and cups of coffee. Resuming her own meal, she continued, "You are wonderfully kind. It is true, my nephews, that I have grown old trying to secure my share of land. It may not be long till I shall pass under the sod."

The two men responded with "How, how," which meant, "Go on with your story. We are all ears." Blue-Star Woman had not yet detected any particular sharpness about their ears, but by an impulse she looked up into their faces and scrutinized them. They were busily engaged in eating. Their eyes were fast upon the food on the mat in front of their crossed shins. Inwardly she made a passing observation how, like ravenous wolves, her nephews devoured their food. Coyotes in midwinter could not have been more starved. Without comment she offered them the remaining fried cakes, and between them they took it all. She offered the second helping of coffee, which they accepted without hesitancy. Filling their cups, she placed her empty coffeepot on the dead ashes.

To them she rehearsed her many hardships. It had become a habit now to tell her long story of disappointments with all its petty details. It was only another instance of good intentions gone awry. It was a paradox upon a land of prophecy that its path to future glory be stained with the blood of its aborigines. Incongruous as it is, the two nephews, with their white associates, were glad of a condition so profitable to them. Their solicitation for Blue-Star Woman was not at all altruistic. They thrived in their grafting business. They and their occupation were the by-product of an unwieldly bureaucracy over the nation's wards.

"Dear aunt, you failed to establish the facts of your identity," they told her. Hereupon Blue-Star Woman's countenance fell. It was ever the same old words. It was the old song of the government official she loathed to hear. The next remark restored her courage. "If any one can discover evidence, it's us! I

tell you, aunt, we'll fix it all up for you." It was a great relief to
the old Indian woman to be thus unburdened of her riddle,
with a prospect of possessing land. "There is one thing you will
have to do,—that is, to pay us half of your land and money
when you get them." Here was a pause, and Blue-Star Woman
answered slowly, "Y-e-s," in an uncertain frame of mind.

The shrewd schemers noted her behavior. "Wouldn't you
rather have a half of a crust of bread than none at all?" they
asked. She was duly impressed with the force of their argument. In her heart she agreed, "A little something to eat is better than nothing!" The two men talked in regular relays. The
flow of smooth words was continuous and so much like
purring that all the woman's suspicions were put soundly to
sleep. "Look here, aunt, you know very well that prairie fire is
met with a back-fire." Blue-Star Woman, recalling her experiences in fire-fighting, quickly responded, "Yes, oh, yes."

"In just the same way, we fight crooks with crooks. We have
clever white lawyers working with us. They are the back-fire."
Then, as if remembering some particular incident, they both
laughed aloud and said, "Yes, and sometimes they use us as the
back-fire! We trade fifty-fifty."

Blue-Star Woman sat with her chin in the palm of one hand
with elbow resting in the other. She rocked herself slightly
forward and backward. At length she answered, "Yes, I will
pay you half of my share in tribal land and money when I get
them. In bygone days, brave young men of the order of the
White-Horse-Riders sought out the aged, the poor, the widows
and orphans to aid them, but they did their good work without pay. The White-Horse-Riders are gone. The times are
changed. I am a poor old Indian woman. I need warm clothing
before winter begins to blow its icicles through us. I need fire
wood. I need food. As you have said, a little help is better than
none."

Hereupon the two pretenders scored another success.

They rose to their feet. They had eaten up all the fried
bread and drained the coffeepot. They shook hands with Blue-
Star Woman and departed. In the quiet that followed their de-

parture she sat munching her small piece of bread, which, by a lucky chance, she had taken on her plate before the hungry wolves had come. Very slowly she ate the fragment of fried bread as if to increase it by diligent mastication. A self-condemning sense of guilt disturbed her. In her dire need she had become involved with tricksters. Her nephews laughingly told her, "We use crooks, and crooks use us in the skirmish over Indian lands."

The friendly shade of the house shrank away from her and hid itself under the narrow eaves of the dirt-covered roof. She shrugged her shoulders. The sun high in the sky had witnessed the affair and now glared down upon her white head. Gathering upon her arm the mats and cooking utensils, she hobbled into her log hut.

Under the brooding wilderness silence, on the Sioux Indian Reservation, the superintendent summoned together the leading Indian men of the tribe. He read a letter which he had received from headquarters in Washington, D.C. It announced the enrollment of Blue-Star Woman on their tribal roll of members and the approval of allotting land to her.

It came as a great shock to the tribesmen. Without their knowledge and consent their property was given to a strange woman. They protested in vain. The superintendent said, "I received this letter from Washington. I have read it to you for your information. I have fulfilled my duty. I can do no more." With these fateful words he dismissed the assembly.

Heavy hearted, Chief High Flier returned to his dwelling. Smoking his long-stemmed pipe he pondered over the case of Blue-Star Woman. The Indian's guardian had got into a way of usurping autocratic power in disposing of the wards' property. It was growing intolerable. "No doubt this Indian woman is entitled to allotment, but where? Certainly not here," he thought to himself.

Laying down his pipe, he called his little granddaughter from her play. "You are my interpreter and scribe," he said. "Bring your paper and pencil." A letter was written in the child's sprawling hand, and signed by the old chieftain. It read:

"My Friend:

"I make letter to you. My heart is sad. Washington give my tribe's land to a woman called Blue-Star. We do not know her. We were not asked to give land, but our land is taken from us to give to another Indian. This is not right. Lots of little children of my tribe have no land. Why this strange woman get our land which belongs to our children? Go to Washington and ask if our treaties tell him to give our property away without asking us. Tell him I thought we made good treaties on paper, but now our children cry for food. We are too poor. We cannot give even to our own little children. Washington is very rich. Washington now owns our country. If he wants to help this poor Indian woman, Blue-Star, let him give her some of his land and his money. This is all I will say until you answer me. I shake hands with you with my heart. The Great Spirit hears my words. They are true.

     Your friend,
      CHIEF HIGH FLIER
       X (his mark)

The letter was addressed to a prominent American woman. A stamp was carefully placed on the envelope.

Early the next morning, before the dew was off the grass, the chieftain's riding pony was caught from the pasture and brought to his log house. It was saddled and bridled by a younger man, his son with whom he made his home. The old chieftain came out, carrying in one hand his long-stemmed pipe and tobacco pouch. His blanket was loosely girdled about his waist. Tightly holding the saddle horn, he placed a moccasined foot carefully into the stirrup and pulled himself up awkwardly into the saddle, muttering to himself, "Alas, I can no more leap into my saddle. I now must crawl about in my helplessness." He was past eighty years of age, and no longer agile.

He set upon his ten-mile trip to the only post office for hundreds of miles around. In his shirt pocket, he carried the letter destined, in due season, to reach the heart of American people. His pony, grown old in service, jogged along the dusty road. Memories of other days thronged the wayside, and for the lonely rider transformed all the country. Those days were gone when the Indian youths were taught to be truthful,—to be merciful to the poor. Those days were gone when moral cleanliness was a chief virtue; when public feasts were given in honor of the virtuous girls and young men of the tribe. Untold mischief is now possible through these broken ancient laws. The younger generation were not being properly trained in the high virtues. A slowly starving race was growing mad, and the pitifully weak sold their lands for a pot of porridge.

"He, he, he! He, he, he!" he lamented. "Small Voice Woman, my own relative is being represented as the mother of this strange Blue-Star—the papers were made by two young Indian men who have learned the white man's ways. Why must I be forced to accept the mischief of children? My memory is clear. My reputation for veracity is well known.

"Small Voice Woman lived in my house until her death. She had only one child and it was a *boy*!" He held his hand over this thumping heart, and was reminded of the letter in his pocket. "This letter,—what will happen when it reaches my good friend?" he asked himself. The chieftain rubbed his dim eyes and groaned, "If only my good friend knew the folly of turning my letter into the hands of bureaucrats! In face of repeated defeat, I am daring once more to send this one letter." An inner voice said in his ear, "And this one letter will share the same fate of the other letters."

Startled by the unexpected voice, he jerked upon the bridle reins and brought the drowsy pony to a sudden halt. There was no one near. He found himself a mile from the post office, for the cluster of government buildings, where lived the superintendent, were now in plain sight. His thin frame shook with emotion. He could not go there with his letter.

He dismounted from his pony. His quavering voice chanted a bravery song as he gathered dry grasses and the dead stalks of last year's sunflowers. He built a fire, and crying aloud, for his sorrow was greater than he could bear, he cast the letter into the flames. The fire consumed it. He sent his message on the wings of fire and he believed she would get it. He yet trusted that help would come to his people before it was too late. The pony tossed his head in a readiness to go. He knew he was on the return trip and he was glad to travel.

The wind which blew so gently at dawn was now increased into a gale as the sun approached the zenith. The chieftain, on his way home, sensed a coming storm. He looked upward to the sky and around in every direction. Behind him, in the distance, he saw a cloud of dust. He saw several horsemen whipping their ponies and riding at great speed. Occasionally he heard their shouts, as if calling after some one. He slackened his pony's pace and frequently looked over his shoulder to see who the riders were advancing in hot haste upon him. He was growing curious. In a short time the riders surrounded him. On their coats shone brass buttons, and on their hats were gold cords and tassels. They were Indian police.

"Wan!" he exclaimed, finding himself the object of their chase. It was their foolish ilk who had murdered the great leader, Sitting Bull. "Pray, what is the joke? Why do young men surround an old man quietly riding home?"

"Uncle," said the spokesman, "we are hirelings, as you know. We are sent by the government superintendent to arrest you and take you back with us. The superintendent says you are one of the bad Indians, singing war songs and opposing the government all the time; this morning you were seen trying to set fire to the government agency."

"Hunhunhe!" replied the old chief, placing the palm of his hand over his mouth agape in astonishment. "All this is unbelievable!"

The policeman took hold of the pony's bridle and turned the reluctant little beast around. They led it back with them and the old chieftain set unresisting in the saddle. High Flier was taken before the superintendent, who charged him with setting fires to destroy government buildings and found him guilty. Thus Chief High Flier was sent to jail. He had already suffered much during his life. He was the voiceless man of America. And now in his old age he was cast into prison. The chagrin of it all, together with his utter helplessness to defend his own or his people's human rights, weighed heavily upon his spirit.

The foul air of the dingy cell nauseated him who loved the

open. He sat wearily down upon the tattered mattress, which lay on the rough board floor. He drew his robe closely about his tall figure, holding it partially over his face, his hands covered within the folds. In profound gloom the gray-haired prisoner sat there without a stir for long hours and knew not when the day ended and night began. He sat buried in his desperation. His eyes were closed, but he could not sleep. Bread and water in tin receptacles set upon the floor beside him untouched. He was not hungry. Venturesome mice crept out upon the floor and scampered in the dim starlight streaming through the iron bars of the cell window. They squeaked as they dared each other to run across his moccasined feet, but the chieftain neither saw nor heard them.

A terrific struggle was waged within his being. He fought as he never fought before. Tenaciously he hung upon hope for the day of salvation—that hope hoary with age. Defying all odds against him, he refused to surrender faith in good people.

Underneath his blanket, wrapped so closely about him, stole a luminous light. Before his stricken consciousness appeared a vision. Lo, his good friend, the American woman to whom he had sent his messages by fire, now stood there a legion! A vast multitude of women, with uplifted hands, gazed upon a huge stone image. Their upturned faces were eager and very earnest. The stone figure was that of a woman upon the brink of the Great Waters, facing eastward. The myriad living hands remained uplifted till the stone woman began to show signs of life. Very magestically she turned around, and, lo, she smiled upon this great galaxy of American women. She was the Statue of Liberty! It was she, who, though representing human liberty, formerly turned her back upon the American aborigine. Her face was aglow with compassion. Her eyes swept across the outspread continent of America, the home of the red man.

At this moment her torch flamed brighter and whiter till its radiance reached into the obscure and remote places of the land. Her light of liberty penetrated Indian reservations. A loud shout of joy rose up from the Indians of the earth, everywhere!

All too soon the picture was gone. Chief High Flier awoke. He lay prostrate on the floor where during the night he had fallen. He rose and took his seat again upon the mattress. Another day was ushered into his life. In his heart lay the secret vision of hope born in the midnight of his sorrows. It enabled him to serve his jail sentence with a mute dignity which baffled those who saw him.

Finally came the day of his release. There was rejoicing over all the land. The desolate hills that harbored wailing voices nightly now were hushed and still. Only gladness filled the air. A crowd gathered around the jail to greet the chieftain. His son stood at the entrance way, while the guard unlocked the prison door. Serenely quiet, the old Indian chief stepped forth. An unseen stone in his path caused him to stumble slightly, but his son grasped him by the hand and steadied his tottering steps. He led him to a heavy lumber wagon drawn by a small pony team which he had brought to take him home. The people thronged about him—hundreds shook hands with him and went away singing native songs of joy for the safe return to them of their absent one.

Among the happy people came Blue-Star Woman's two nephews. Each shook the chieftain's hand. One of them held out an ink pad saying, "We are glad we were able to get you out of jail. We have great influence with the Indian Bureau in Washington, D.C. When you need help, let us know. Here press your thumb in this pad." His companion took from his pocket a document prepared for the old chief's signature, and held it on the wagon wheel for the thumb mark. The chieftain was taken by surprise. He looked into his son's eyes to know the meaning of these two men. "It is our agreement," he explained to his old father. "I pledged to pay them half of your land if they got you out of jail."

The old chieftain sighed, but made no comment. Words were vain. He pressed his indelible thumb mark, his signature it was, upon the deed, and drove home with his son.

America's Indian Problem

The hospitality of the American aborigine, it is told, saved the early settlers from starvation during the first bleak winters. In commemoration of having been so well received, Newport erected "a cross as a sign of English dominion." With sweet words he quieted the suspicions of Chief Powhatan,[8] his friend. He "told him that the arms (of the cross) represented Powhatan and himself, and the middle their united league."

DeSoto and his Spaniards were graciously received by the Indian Princess Cofachiqui in the South. While on a sight-seeing tour they entered the ancestral tombs of those Indians. DeSoto "dipped into the pearls and gave his two joined hands full to each cavalier to make rosaries of, he said, to say prayers for their sins on. We imagine if their prayers were in proportion to their sins they must have spent the most of their time at their devotions."

It was in this fashion that the old world snatched away the fee in the land of the new. It was in this fashion that America was divided between the powers of Europe and the aborigines were dispossessed of their country. The barbaric rule of might from which the paleface had fled hither for refuge caught up with him again, and in the melee the hospitable native suffered "legal disability."

History tells that it was from the English and the Spanish our government inherited its legal victims, the American Indians, whom to this day we hold as wards and not as citizens of their own freedom loving land. A long century of dishonor followed this inheritance of somebody's loot. Now the time is at hand when the American Indian shall have his day in court through the help of the women of America. The stain upon America's fair name is to be removed, and the remnant of the Indian nation, suffering from malnutrition, is to number among the invited invisible guests at your dinner tables.

In this undertaking there must be cooperation of head, heart and hand. We serve both our own government and a voiceless people within our midst. We would open the door of American opportunity to the red man and encourage him to find his rightful place in our American life. We would remove the barriers that hinder his normal development.

Wardship is no substitute for American citizenship, therefore we seek his enfranchisement. The many treaties made in good faith with the Indian by our government we would like to see equitably settled. By a constructive program we hope to do away with the "piecemeal legislation" affecting Indians here and there which has proven an exceedingly expensive and disappointing method.

Do you know what *your* Bureau of Indian Affairs, in Washington, D.C., really is? How it is organized and how it deals with wards of the nation? This is our first study. Let us be informed of facts and then we may formulate our opinions. In the remaining space allowed me I shall quote from the report of the Bureau of Municipal Research, in their investigation of the Indian Bureau, published by them in the September issue, 1915, No. 65, "Municipal Research," 261 Broadway, New York City. This report is just as good for our use today as when it was first made, for very little, if any, change has been made in the administration of Indian Affairs since then.

PREFATORY NOTE

While this report was printed for the information of members of Congress, it was not made a part of the report of the Joint Commission of Congress, at whose request it was prepared, and is not available for distribution.

UNPUBLISHED DIGEST OF STATUTORY AND
TREATY PROVISIONS GOVERNING INDIAN FUNDS

When in 1913 inquiry was made into the accounting and reporting methods of the Indian Office by the President's Commission on Economy and Efficiency, it was found there was no digest of the provisions of statutes and treaties with Indian tribes governing Indian funds and the trust obligations of the government. Such a digest was therefore prepared. It was not completed, however, until after Congress adjourned March 4, 1913. Then, instead of being published, it found its way into the pigeon-holes in the Interior Department and the Civil Service Commission, where the working papers and unpublished reports of the commission were ordered stored. The digest itself would make a document of about three hundred pages.

UNPUBLISHED OUTLINE OF ORGANIZATION

By order of the President, the commission, in cooperation with various persons assigned to this work, also prepared at great pains a complete analysis of the organization of every department, office and commission of the federal government as of July 1, 1912. This represented a complete picture of the government as a whole in summary outline; it also represented an accurate picture of every administrative bureau, office, and of every operative or field station, and showed in his working relation each of the 500,000 officers and employes in the public service. The report in typewritten form was one of the working documents used in the preparation of the "budget" submitted by President Taft to Congress in February, 1913. The "budget" was ordered printed by Congress, but the cost thereof was to be charged against the President's appropriation. There was not enough money remaining in this appropriation to warrant the printing of the report on organization. It, therefore, also found repose in a dark closet.

TOO VOLUMINOUS TO BE MADE PART OF THIS SERIES

Congress alone could make the necessary provision for the publication of these materials; the documents are too voluminous to be printed as a part of this series, even if official permission were granted. It is again suggested, however, that the data might be made readily accessible and available to students by placing in manuscript division of the Library of Congress one copy of the unpublished reports and working papers of the President's Commission on Economy and Efficiency. This action was recommended by the commission, but the only official action taken was to order that the materials be placed under lock and key in the Civil Service Commission.

NEED FOR SPECIAL CARE IN MANAGEMENT

The need for special care in the management of Indian Affairs lies in the fact that in theory of law the Indian has not the rights of a citizen. He has not even the rights of a foreign resident. The Indian individually does not have access to the courts; he can not individually appeal to the administrative and judicial branches of the public service for the enforcement of his rights. He himself is considered as a ward of the United States. His property and funds are held in trust. . . . The Indian Office is the agency of the government for administering both the guardianship of the Indian and the trusteeship of his properties.

CONDITIONS ADVERSE TO GOOD ADMINISTRATION

The legal status of the Indian and his property is the condition which makes it incumbent on the government to assume the obligation of protector. What is of special interest in this inquiry is to note the conditions under which the Indian Office has been required to conduct its business. In no other relation are the agents of the government under conditions more adverse to efficient administration. The influence which make for the infidelity to trusteeship, for subversion of properties and funds, for the violation of physical and moral welfare have been powerful. The opportunities and inducements are much greater than those which have operated with ruinous effect on other branches of public service and on the trustees and officers of our great private corporations. In many instances, the integrity of these have been broken down.

GOVERNMENT MACHINERY INADEQUATE

. . . Behind the sham protection, which operated largely as a blind to publicity, have been at all times great wealth in the form of Indian funds to be subverted; valuable lands, mines, oil fields, and other natural resources to be despoiled or appropriated to the use of the trader; and large profits to be made by those dealing with trustees who were animated by motives of gain. This has been the situation in which the Indian Service has been for more than a century—the Indian during all this time having his rights and properties to greater or less extent neglected; the guardian, the government, in many instances, passive to conditions which have contributed to his undoing.

OPPORTUNITIES STILL PRESENT

And still, due to the increasing value of his remaining estate, there is left an inducement to fraud, corruption, and institutional incompetence almost beyond the possibility of comprehension. The properties and funds of the Indians today are estimated at not less than one thousand millions of dollars. There is still a great obligation to be discharged, which must run through many years. The government itself owes many millions of dollars for Indian moneys which it has converted to its own use, and it is of interest to note that it does not know and the officers do not know what is the present condition of the Indian funds in their keeping.

PRIMARY DEFECTS

. . . The story of the mismanagement of Indian Affairs is only a chapter in the history of the mismanagement of corporate trusts. The Indian has been the victim of the same kind of neglect, the same abortive processes, the same malpractices as have the life insurance policyholders, the bank depositor, the industrial and transportation shareholder. The form of organization of the trusteeship has been one which does not provide for independent audit and supervision. The institutional methods and practices have been such that they do not provide either a fact basis for official judgment or publicity of facts which, if made available, would supply evidence of infidelity. In the operation of this machinery, there has not been the means provided for effective official scrutiny and the public conscience could not be reached.

AMPLE PRECEDENTS TO BE FOLLOWED

Precedents to be followed are ample. In private corporate trusts that have been mismanaged a basis of appeal has been found only when some favorable circumstance has brought to light conditions so shocking as to cause those people who have possessed political power, as a matter of self-protection, to demand a thorough reorganization and revision of methods. The same motive has lain back of legislation for the Indian. But the motive to political action has been less effective, for the reason that in the past the Indians who have acted in self-protection have either been killed or placed in confinement. All the machinery of government has been set to work to repress rather than to provide adequate means for justly dealing with a large population which had no political rights.

III

SELECTIONS FROM
AMERICAN INDIAN
MAGAZINE

The editorials, public letters, narratives, essays, poems, and political pieces in this section were all published in the quarterly journal of the Society of American Indians, the *American Indian Magazine*. The magazine was distributed to all full members of the society (its Indian members and leadership) as well as "associate members" (non-Native friends of the Society), and was available, to some degree, to the public. Zitkala-Ša was on the editorial board from 1916 to 1918 and was the journal's editor from 1918 through 1920. Under her influence the magazine was beautifully produced, often featuring fine photography and artwork of and by Native Americans, as well as a wide variety of literary materials almost exclusively produced by Native Americans, with a few by high-profile scholars, politicians, and friends of the Society (Theodore Roosevelt, Walt Whitman, and Richard Henry Pratt all contributed to the journal). Zitkala-Ša's writings for the magazine varied widely: they include "The Indian's Awakening," a poem which takes up many of the issues in "School Days" and "Indian Teacher"; "The Red Man's America," a parody of "My Country 'Tis of Thee"; and the exhortatory "Letter to the Chiefs and Headmen of Tribes," advising Indians to keep hold of their tribal lands while at the same time participating in education programs and learning English. Soon after Zitkala-Ša stepped down as editor, the magazine folded.

The Indian's Awakening

(January–March 1916)

I snatch at my eagle plumes and long hair.
A hand cut my hair; my robes did deplete.
Left heart all unchanged; the work incomplete.
These favors unsought, I've paid since with care.
Dear teacher, you wished so much good to me,
That though I was blind, I strove hard to see.
Had you then, no courage frankly to tell
Old race-problems, Christ e'en failed to expel?

My light has grown dim, and black the abyss
That yawns at my feet. No bordering shore;
No bottom e'er found by hopes sunk before.
Despair I of good from deeds gone amiss.
My people, may God have pity on you!
The learning I hoped in you to imbue
Turns bitterly vain to meet both our needs.
No Sun for the flowers, vain planting seeds.

I've lost my long hair; my eagle plumes too.
From you my own people, I've gone astray.
A wanderer now, with no where to stay.
The Will-o-the-wisp learning, it brought me rue.
It brings no admittance. Where I have knocked
Some evil imps, hearts, have bolted and locked.
Alone with the night and fearful Abyss
I stand isolated, life gone amiss.

Intensified hush chills all my proud soul.
Oh, what am I? Whither bound thus and why?
Is there not a God on whom to rely?
A part of His Plan, the atoms enroll?
In answer, there comes a sweet Voice and clear,
My loneliness soothes with sounding so near.
A drink to my thirst, each vibrating note.
My vexing old burdens fall far remote

"Then close your sad eyes. Your spirit regain.
Behold what fantastic symbols abound,
What wondrous host of cosmos around.
From silvery sand, the tiniest grain
To man and the planet, God's at the heart.
In shifting mosaic, souls doth impart.
His spirits who pass through multiformed earth
Some lesson of life must learn in each birth."

Divinely the Voice sang. I felt refreshed.
And vanished the night, abyss and despair.
Harmonious kinship made all things fair.
I yearned with my soul to venture unleased.
Sweet Freedom. These stood in waiting, a steed
All prancing, well bridled, saddled for speed.
A foot in the stirrup! Off with a bound!
As light as a feather, making no sound.

Through ether, long leagues we galloped away.
An angry red river, we shyed in dismay,
For here were men sacrificed (cruel deed)
To reptiles and monsters, war, graft, and greed.
A jungle of discord drops in the rear.
By silence is quelled suspicious old fear,
And spite-gnats' low buzz is muffled at last.
Exploring the spirit, I must ride fast.

Away from these worldly ones, let us go,
Along a worn trail, much traveled and, Lo!
Familiar the scenes that come rushing by.
Now billowy sea and now azure sky.
Amid that enchanted shade, as they spun
Sun, moon, and the stars, their own orbits run!
Great Spirit, in realms so infinite reigns;
And wonderful wide are all His domains.

Hark! Here is the Spirit-world, He doth hold
A village of Indians, camped as of old.
Earth-legends by their fires, some did review,
While flowers and trees more radiant grew.
"Oh, You were all dead! In Lethe you were tossed!"
I cried, "Every where 'twas told you were lost!
Forsooth, they did scan your footprints on sand.
Bereaved, I did mourn your fearful sad end."

Then spoke One of the Spirit Space, so sedate.
"My child, We are souls, forever and aye.
The signs in our orbits point us the way.
Like planets, we do not tarry nor wait.
Those memories dim, from Dust to the Man,
Called Instincts, are trophies won while we ran.
Now various stars where loved ones remain
Are linked to our hearts with Memory-chain.

"In journeying here, the Aeons we've spent
Are countless and strange. How well I recall
Old Earth trails: the River Red; above all
The Desert sands burning us with intent.
All these we have passed to learn some new thing.
Oh hear me! Your dead doth lustily sing!
'Rejoice! Gift of Life pray waste not in wails!
The maker of Souls forever prevails!' "

Direct from the Spirit-world came my steed.
The phantom has place in what was all planned.
He carried me back to God and the land
Where all harmony, peace and love are the creed.
In triumph, I cite my joyous return.
The smallest wee creature I dare not spurn.
I sing "Gift of Life, pray waste not in wails!
The Maker of Souls forever prevails!"

A Year's Experience in Community
Service Work Among the
Ute Tribe of Indians
(October–December 1916)

We began our Community Center[1] work in the fall of 1915, by starting sewing classes among the women. There was no time to consult the fashion books. We met one day each week, devoting it to charity work for the aged members of the tribe. Plain, warm garments cut in the loose style they are accustomed to wear, were made for those who could neither see to sew nor buy their clothing ready made, with money they did not have. Sometimes members of the sewing classes helped one another with their necessary sewing. Later they learned very rapidly to crochet little caps, jackets and bootees for their babies. Old comforters were repaired; new quilts were pieced and quilted quite creditably by the women.

Many funny little stories were told at these sewing classes. With laughter they stitched away upon the article in hand. As the autumn advanced into winter and snow, we found new work to do in addition to our weekly sewing.

Every Monday, Indians from far and near came to the Government office. Some came to receive their monthly subsistence checks, others to sign papers or to give testimony in an heirship hearing. There was no rest-room to accommodate these "Monday Indians." All day the mothers with their babies, stood outdoors in the snow. There is nothing so tiresome as waiting. At noon the "Monday Indians" flocked by the tens and twenties to the homes of the Indian employees. Now the salaries of the Indian police, Indian interpreter, janitor and stableman are the smallest in the Government service—scarcely enough to support the families of these employees. This enforced hospitality of the Indian employees was very unfair. The longer an Indian employee stayed in the Government service, the deeper into debt he got. Yet since there is no employment by which ready money may be earned, they are tempted to try the Government jobs, thinking to get a few dollars thereby.

The wives of these Indian employees agreed with me that by locking up their homes and donating their services to prepare and serve a simple, wholesome lunch to these "Monday Indians," a mutual benefit would be gained to all concerned. The Monday lunch and rest-room were started. The soup, pies and coffee were prepared by the Indian women under my supervision. This was really a practical demonstration in domestic science. The women learned improved methods of preparing food in their own homes. The Indian men hauled the wood and cut it up for us. They were good enough to carry buckets of water for us, too.

At the close of the day enough provision had been saved in the homes of the Indian employees to last them a whole week. Moreover, the visiting Indians had been provided a legitimate accommodation. They had a comfortable place to rest without imposing upon any one.

We are grateful to Superintendent Kneale for his kindness in allowing us the use of a Government building, and encouraging us by sometimes coming to our lunches. Mrs. Kneale was always there to help us serve the lunches. There was a great rush at the noon hour and each of us wished we had more than a single pair of hands.

With the coming of springtime, when the Indians were busy with their farming, their trips to the Agency being less regular, we changed our plan. Then we ceased our sewing classes and lunch and rest-room work. We organized a local branch of the Society of American Indians which met once a month.

Our programs were both instructive and social. We spent part of the evening in a study of local conditions. We read papers upon selected subjects. We argued in favor of sending all Indian children to school. We talked also of the innumerable benefits to

a tribe that held its annual fairs. We mentioned here the good
work started by the Commissioner of Indian Affairs in empha-
sizing the vital importance to the future race, by the saving of
the babies. We encouraged co-operation in this, for it was so unmistakably in the right direction. The evening's discussions were
interspersed with music and readings in a lighter vein.

Throughout the entire year I made regular visits to the Indians at their camps. The territory is great and much time and
energy is lost on the road.

During the year, three donations were made to the Community Center work by members of the Society of American
Indians, which totaled $23.00. I wish to submit this itemized
account:

$ 5.00   Sewing materials, needles, thimbles,
              thread, scissors, easy patterns for
              children's dresses and aprons.
$ 8.00   Subscriptions to newspapers used in
              lunch and rest-room.
$10.00   Applied on purchase of dishes for
              lunch-room.
_____

$23.00

Dishes purchased for the Community Center work were:

4 doz. tablespoons
4 doz. teaspoons
4 doz. cups and saucers . . . $9.20
50 soup bowls 7.00
25 yds. oilcloth 5.50
Carpenter hire 2.00
                                              _____

                                              $23.70
                                              10.00 pd. by donation
                                              _____

                                              $13.70 pd. by lunches

There remains on hand a credit balance of $1.30.

During the summer the Community Center property was carefully packed away. With our acquired wealth of dishes and experience the first year, we are better prepared for the second year's work.

The lunch and rest room should operate in such a way as to furnish wholesome lunch to the Indians at a minimum cost, allowing only a small margin of gain, that the work may sustain itself.

Under the direct supervision of the Society of American Indians, I made my effort in Community Center work. There were no funds to carry on this experimental work; nor was there any salary attached to my assignment of duty.

I mention these merely as interesting items though they are only incidentals after all. "Where there is a will there is a way."

The field chosen for my work was not a new one. There were others who had already devoted years to the uplift of the race. They were not lacking in time-tested experience nor means either.

The Government had its salaried employees here. The Church had also provided for its self-sacrificing missionaries too.

The question naturally arose as to the advisability of the National organization of Indians diverting their energy upon a line of work already taken care of by able bodies. And perhaps there would be some to whom such an endeavor might appear as an interference with the workers in the field, more especially, since there were phases of our problem that urgently demanded our undivided attention.

The thought of interference with any good work is wholly foreign to our high motive; nor do we presume any superiority to those already in the field.

We have awakened, in the midst of a bewildering transition, to a divine obligation calling us to love, to honor our parents. No matter how ably, how well others of God's creatures perform their duties, they never can do our duty for us; nor can we hope for forgiveness, were we to stand idly by, satisfied to see others laboring for the uplift of our kinsmen. Our aged grandparents hunger for tenderness, kindness and sympathy from their own offspring. It is our first duty, it is our great privilege to be permitted to administer with our own hands, this gentle affection to our people. There is no more urgent call upon us; for all too soon these old ones will have passed on. It is possible, indeed, to combine with practical systematic effort, a bit of kindness and true sympathy.

Our Community Center work is non-sectarian and non-partisan. For this reason we are in a position to lend unobtrusively, very beneficial aid toward uniting and welding together the earnest endeavors of various groups of educators and missionaries.

Our chief thought is co-operation with all constructive uplift work for humanity. Therefore, in our attempt to do our very own duty to our race, we so with a full appreciation of all kindness and gratitude for all that good people have done and are still doing in behalf of our race.

The Red Man's America[2]
(January–March 1917)

My country! 'tis to thee,
Sweet land of Liberty,
My pleas I bring.
    Land where OUR fathers died,
    Whose offspring are denied
    The Franchise given wide,
    Hark, while I sing.

My native country, thee,
Thy Red man is not free,
Knows not thy love.
    Political bred ills,
    Peyote in temple hills,
    His heart with sorrow fills,
    Knows not thy love.

Let Lane's Bill swell the breeze,
And ring from all the trees,
Sweet freedom's song.
    Let Gandy's Bill awake
    All people, till they quake,
    Let Congress, silence break,
    The sound prolong.

Great Mystery, to thee,
Life of humanity,
To thee, we cling.
 Grant our home-land be bright,
 Grant us just human right,
 Protect us by Thy might,
 Great God, our king.

Chipeta, Widow of Chief Ouray[3]
with a Word About a
Deal in Blankets
(July–September 1917)

A year ago this fall it was my special privilege to be the guest of
Chipeta. I had gone to her for a heart to heart talk about the
use of peyote, a powerful narcotic, used by the Ute people.
Within her nephew's tepee where she gave me audience were
gathered friends, relatives and neighbors—for word had gone
out that I was coming to talk about matters of large importance with Chipeta. And Chipeta is an honored woman for she
is the widow of Chief Ouray, a red patriot who had many
times saved the lives of white settlers and who had in many an
emergency saved his tribe from disaster.

Our conversation drifted pleasantly to the days of Chipeta's
girlhood. It is an old time custom among Indians to enter upon
a subject slowly and not rush to discussion at once, nor try to
say all one desired to voice in one breath.

Chipeta was not boastful. More often she sat silently smiling
and nodding her assent to the stories one related of her wild
rides through the hills, risking her own personal safety to give
warning to her white friends of impending raids. With these
stories told, came the plunge into the talk about present day
conditions. I told of the rumors that she and her brother
McCook had been deceived into the use of a dangerous drug
and that they were being fleeced by the mercenary traffickers in
peyote buttons.

Earnestly she scanned my face as I told them of the inevitable degeneration that follows the habitual and indiscriminate

use of narcotics. Frankly she told me that peyote eased her brother's rheumatism and hers. Admitting the truth of my statements she said, "I have noticed that the pains return when I stop the use of the drug."

McCook then spoke. Terse and deeply significant was his reply: "When the Great White Father in Washington sent a letter to me telling me that whiskey was bad, I stopped our people from its use. When the Great White Father sent a letter to me telling me that gambling was bad, I forbade our people to play cards." There was a momentary pause. I wondered what he would say next. I hoped he would say, he now decided to give up the drug peyote and stop its use among his people. He concluded briefly:

"Now the Great White Father has sent me no letter telling me peyote is bad. Therefore, as long as he permits its use, we will continue to use it."

It was with a sad heart that I returned to the Agency. All along the journey questions presented themselves to my mind. Did you ever try giving a serious talk or lecture to an audience that was more or less under the influence of a drug? In such a case what results may you expect? Did you ever hear of an evangelist addressing a class of drug users who in their abnormal condition were helplessly unable to receive his message? What do civilized communities do with their drug victims? Do not they legislate for the protection of society and for the protection of the drug user? A great longing filled me for some message from the Great White Father telling his red children that peyote was bad for them and asking them to refuse to use or sell it. Federal action is needed. Chief Ouray, friend of the white man, would that your old friends might befriend your aged widow and the people whom you loved. Would that federal action might be taken before it is to late. These were the burden of my thoughts as I rode back from my visit with Chipeta.

Some time later, while conversing with a friend who had been interested in my visit I heard an amazing story. It was about my friend Chipeta. It was like a tale in a night-mare and

I could scarcely believe it. For Chipeta, for Chief Ouray and his people my indignation arose but I could not speak. This is what I heard told:

"In some way the idea was started that the Government ought to give a gift to Chipeta in grateful memory to Chief Ouray, faithful friend of the border settlers and loyal advocate of obedience to Federal orders. It was to be a token of regard also to Chipeta for the valuable service she, too, had rendered. The plan was presented to the Great White Father in Washington and was approved.

"The questions then came up as to the kind of gift that would be useful to Chipeta and at the same time suitable as a memento."

I heard the story of the discussion and light streamed into my heart. My fancy moved ahead of the story and I thought of the kind of gifts that were within range of possibility. What if the gift should be a genuine guarantee of water rights to the Ute Indians, or the title to their 250,000 acres of grazing lands to be held intact for the future unallotted children, or a message from the Great White Father giving news of Federal action against the peyote drug? All these things and more were needed and any one would have been a royal gift to the royal Chipeta. Then dimly in my ears the story went on.

With a sudden shock I heard that the gift chosen was a pair of trading store shawls. Scarcely could I believe my ears, for was this a suitable gift with which to honor loyal service through a period of many years?

"The shawls were purchased at a little trading station and sent to Washington where they were tagged as a gift from the Great White Father, in honor of the past friendship of Chief Ouray and of Chipeta to the white people. Then the shawls were reshipped to their starting point in Utah.

"With what innocent joy Chipeta received them. At once she returned the compliment by sending the donor a large and expensive Navajo blanket. It was a free will offering, paid for by personal money and given out of the gratitude of her heart for the little token that someone in Washington had given her.

"Little did Chipeta realize that she had never really received a gift, but that without her consent she had been made to pay for the 'gift shawls.'

"The bill for the shawls was sent to the Government office at Utah and Ouray Agency and the money in settlement was paid out of Ute money known as 'Interest on the Ute 5% Funds.' "

If the spirit eyes of Chief Ouray can see, his heart must be made sad. His widow has given away a beautiful blanket rug to reciprocate what she thinks a gift of tender sentiment.

Poor unsuspecting Chipeta, loyal friend of the whites in the days when Indian friendship counted! Your shawls derived even so cover your head like a royal mantle and it is not for you to bow your head in shame. Your reward for faithful service is the recollection of your husband's integrity and the consciousness of having within your light always done well. No shawl is big enough to obscure or to cover the gifts you have given freely and for which no material thing will ever repay you.

A Sioux Woman's Love
for Her Grandchild[4]
(October–December 1917)

Loosely clad in deerskin, dress of flying fringes,
Played a little black-haired maiden of the prairies;
Plunged amid the rolling green of grasses waving,
Brimming o'er with laughter, round face all aglowing.
Thru the oval teepee doorway, grandma watched her,
Narrowed aged eyes reflecting love most tender.

Seven summers since a new-born babe was left her.
Death had taken from her teepee, her own daughter.
Tireless love bestowed she on the little Bright Eyes,—
Eagerly attended her with great devotion.
Seven summers grew affection intertwining.
Bent old age adorned once more with hopes all budding.

Bright Eyes spied some "gaudy-wings" and chased them wildly.
Sipping dew and honey from the flowers, gaily
Flit the pretty butterflies, here now, then yonder.
"These, the green, wee babes," old grandma mused in wonder.
"One time snug in winter slumber, now in season
Leave their silken cradles; fly with gauzy pinion."

Shouting gleefully, the child roamed on fearlessly.
Glossy, her long hair, hung in two braids o'er each ear,
Zephyrs whispered to the flowers, at her passing,
Fragrant blossoms gave assent with gracious nodding.
Conscious lay the crystal dew, on bud and leaflet,
Iridescent joys emitting 'till the sun set.

Monster clouds crept in the sky; fell shadows in the prairie.
Grandma, on her cane, leaned breathless, sad and weary.
Listened vainly for the laughter of her darling.
"Where, Oh where, in sudden desert's endless rolling,
Could the wee girl still be playing?" cried she hoarsely,
Shaking as with ague in that silence somber.

Sobbing bitterly, she saw not men approaching.
Over wrought by sorrow, scarcely heard them talking.
Gusts of wind rushed by; cooled her fever;
Loosed her wisps of hair befitting to a mourner.
"In God's infinitude, where, Oh where is the grandchild?"
Winds caught up her moaning, shrieked and shook the teepee.

"Dry your tears, old grandma, cease excessive wailing."
(Empty words addressed they to an image standing.)
"Chieftain's word of sympathy and warning, hear you!
Moving dust-cloud of an army is on coming;
Though you've lost your grandchild, tempt no useless danger.
In the twilight, we must flee hence." This the order.

Duty done, they paused with heads bowed sadly.
These strong men were used to meeting battles bravely,
Yet the anguish of the woman smote them helpless.
Setting of the sun made further searching fruitless,
Darkness, rife with evil omens surging tempest
Came, obliterating hope's last ray for rescue.

Fleeing from the soldiers startled Red Men hurried
Riding travois, ponies faced the lightnings, lurid
'Gainst the sudden flashing, angry fires, a figure
Stood, propped by a cane. A soul in torture
Sacrificing life than leave behind her lost one.
Greater love hath no man; love surpassing reason.

Editorial Comment

(July–September 1918)

The Pierre, South Dakota, Conference is an accomplished fact. In these trying war times it was a privileged sacrifice to journey there.

Three of the S.A.I. Officers absent are in military service. Arthur C. Parker, President, is on military duty "Somewhere in America"; John M. Oskison, First Vice-President, is serving "Somewhere in France"; Margaret Frazier, Vice-President on Membership, is a trained nurse in the Red Cross work at Camp Bowie, Texas.

The Honorary President, Rev. Sherman Coolidge, presided over the meetings.

The delegation of members though numerically small, was strikingly representative. There were gathered together in behalf of Indian welfare work—Arapahoe, Apache, Oklahoman, Ojibway, Ute, Pottowatomie, Sioux from different tribes and others.

It was gratifying and significant that in the face of the Conference dates having been designated for country fairs on all reservations under Indian Bureau management, a successful conference was possible. Faithful Associate members crossed the continent to attend the American Indian Conference. Many new members were added to the rolls during the meeting.

The hospitality of the citizens of Pierre will ever be cherished in memory.

The spirit of a great united American brotherhood fighting in a common cause, the defense of world democracy, pervaded the whole affair. American Indians are watching democracy, baptized in fire and blood overseas. They are watching the chris-

tening with mingled feelings of deepest concern,—the thing lies
so close to their hearts it is difficult to give it expression. Indian
soldiers lie dead on European battlefields, having intermingled
their blood with that of every other race in the supreme sacrifice for an ideal.

Surely, the flaming shafts of light typifying political and legal
equality and justice,—government by the people, now pene-
trating the dark cloud of Europe are a continuous revelation.
The light grows more effulgent, emanating as it does from the
greatest of democracies,—America. The sunburst of democratic
ideals cannot bring new hope and courage to the small peoples of the earth without reaching the remotest corners within
America's own bounds.

Frank discussions are apt to call forth suppressed emotions
of the American Indian but need not thereby create ruffled feeling. The Society of American Indians is compelled by the stress
of the times to consider and discuss higher education for the
Red Man and the rights of small peoples at its Annual Conference.

It is needful to thrash out the truth about Indian matters.
Truth and justice are inseparable component parts of American
ideals. As America has declared democracy abroad, so must we
consistently practice it at home.

The American government is one where the voice of the people is heard. It is therefore not a radical step nor a presumption
for the native Red Man today to raise his voice about the welfare of his race. The Red Man has been mute too long. He
must speak for himself as no other can, nor should he be afraid
to speak the truth and to insist upon a hearing for the utterance
of truth can harm no one but must bless all mankind.

The future success of the Indian as a full-fledged American
citizen depends largely upon what he does for himself today. If
he is good enough to fight for American ideals he is good
enough for American citizenship now.

Our Conference was honored by the presence of an Indian
Bureau official, Mrs. Wilma R. Rhodes, Field Supervisor. This
representative of our government repeatedly took the floor of
the Conference to differ from the expressed opinions of the

Indian members. These debates were marked with intense feeling. The difference seemed to be the natural result of a difference of viewpoint and interest.

The Indian Bureau system was naturally defended by its representative. The members of the Conference expressed a decided preference for Public Schools and American institutions. The Bureau representative advocated the alleged sweet oil of Government Schools under the Bureau System, while the Conference members protested against what they believed to be the fat fly of paternalism in this particular brand of ointment.

The Society of American Indians appreciates every true friend but were the organization to begin naming them it would be an undertaking. The great object and purpose of the Conference is to study the interest of the race as a whole and to devise means and methods for its practical advancement and the attainment of its rightful position among the peoples of the world.

Indian Gifts to Civilized Man[5]

(July–September 1918)

Changing Woman, according to American Indian mythology, has once more rejuvenated herself. Out of old age she springs up in her former youthful beauty. In a royal robe of green, she adorns herself with gorgeous flowers. Changing Woman is the personification of the seasons.

This Indian Mother-Nature has ever been much adored by the red men. In turn she has loved her black-eyed children well. Many secrets she has told them in her secret bowers. Centuries of communion with her, in Indian gardens under primeval forests, have brought forth from insignificant plants, the acclimated and perfected corn and potato. Today they are important food for the people of the earth. They are a contribution from the Red Man of America. He does not crave any praise for the benefits we derive from his labors. It is for our own soul's good that we would give him due credit at this acceptable time.

Food conservation of the hour is our immediate duty. Mr. Hoover clearly points out how we may very materially aid our allies in saving wheat for them by our own usage of more corn and potatoes. For a brief moment thought reverts to the Red Man who gave us his corn and potato. Our real appreciation may not find expression in words. We are so absorbed and busily engaged in urgent war activities. We have scarcely a minute to spare for anything else. Notwithstanding these circumstances, our gratitude to the Indian for these gifts is demonstrated by our vast fields, so eloquent in their abundant annual crops. Truly, these speak louder than words.

The patriotic farmer, planting his garden and his field, may wonder as he toils in the blistering sun what service, if any, the American Indian is giving to America in her defense of world democracy. The Red Man, citizen or non-citizen of our United States, is a loyal son of America. Five thousand Indian men are in our army. Some have already spilled their life blood in the trenches. Others have won military medals "Over There." Indian women are courageously knitting sweaters, helmets and socks for our brave soldiers. The Indian has subscribed about ten million dollars in Liberty Bonds.

The Commissioner of Indian Affairs, Hon. Cato Sells, visiting four army camps in Texas, found 1,500 Indian soldiers there. Eighty-five per cent of this number are volunteers. Of the remaining fifteen per cent, some there are who did not claim their exemption, so eager were they to serve their country. Notwithstanding the difficulties that arise from the complicated system of classifying the government's wards, the Indian is in the front ranks of American patriotism. For absolute loyalty to the Stars and Stripes, the Indian has no peer.

It is especially gratifying that our great government did not segregate our Indian soldiers into Indian units, but permitted them to serve as Americans, shoulder to shoulder with their white brothers in khaki. Such a close companionship promises mutual benefits. The Indian is an adept at finding natural protection and hiding places. He inherits from his forefathers a wonderfully fine sense of direction which enables him to return to his starting point. Being thus so much at home in the out-of-doors, he may be an invaluable guide to our boys born and bred indoors. On the other hand the Indian may learn much practical white man's knowledge from first-hand experience; and, in their united struggle, will be gained a bond of sympathy that never was found in any book of learning.

The Indian race, once numbering about a million and a half, has dwindled to about three hundred thousand. Yet in proportion to his numbers, he is unexcelled in his response to the country's call for fighting men. Were a patriotism like his to sweep through our entire population of millions, we would have in a day, an invincible army of twelve and a half million men. When we realize that the only future hope of the Red

Man is in his educated, physically strong men, we marvel at his heroic response. This undaunted self-sacrifice of America's aboriginal son challenges your patriotism and mine. The sterling quality of his devotion to America is his most inspiring gift to the world. Well may we strive to cultivate in our hearts a better acquaintance with the Indian in our midst. He is just as worth while as the potato patch we are weeding and the cornfield we are plowing.

Secretary's Report in Brief

(July–September 1918)

Thousands of letters were issued from the office of the Secretary during the past two years. These letters went over-the-top of difficulties in the way of insufficient clerical assistance in the S.A.I. office owing to the great demand for clerks and stenographers in war activities, and the increased cost of mailing because of the higher postal rate. Letters are necessary to keep us in touch with our people on the various isolated reservations but the mere receiving and answering of letters, though a task in itself, is only the very beginning of the Society's real work in the Indian cause.

The Society of American Indians, by its activities, is in a position to give information about conditions now existing in Indian communities. Its duty is to convey its intimate knowledge of Indian matters to the American public for their information. The American people are interested since they are responsible for the final fulfillment of government treaties with Indians. They must be thoroughly informed to enable them to act justly, and impartially with all parties concerned. The Secretary continued her lectures throughout her term of office; and is glad to report that everywhere from coast to coast, she found large sympathetic audiences.

The American press has also responded to the special effort of the Society of American Indians to place items of Indian interest before the millions of readers. For this favor, we are most grateful to the editors and the writers upon Indian subjects.

The Pictorial Publicity Bureau of the government expressed a willingness to get out a poster depicting Indian patriotism in this war. It will be an invaluable source of encouragement to the Indians and a real enlightenment to that large part of our public that is ignorant of the real American in our midst. Public attention to the sterling patriotism of the Indians was invited by the first lady of the land when Mrs. Woodrow Wilson gave Indian names to some of our new warships. It will be a fitting and appropriate act of the Pictorial Publicity Bureau to contribute a picture at this time portraying Indian heroism in the war for democracy.

With reference to the discontinuance of the Carlisle school, the Secretary read the following two letters:

September 6, 1918

Hon. F. P. Keppell,
Third Assistant Secretary of War
War Department, Washington, D.C.

My Dear Mr. Keppell,

I have the honor, in behalf of a small body of Americans, to beg your forbearance in this request for a reconsideration of the non-continuance of the Carlisle Indian School. It is understood that the law of 1882 provides for the reversion of this property for military purposes.

Congress could not know thirty-six years ago that out of the old Carlisle barracks there was to stand today the Red Man's University. This fact bears directly upon Indian education and civilization to which our Government pledged itself in good faith. For the speedy fulfillment of this pledge the need is for more schools like Carlisle.

There must be a greater need for our Government to preserve, for purely economic reasons, the elaborately equipped machinery of the Carlisle School plant, for its honor bound obligation to educate the Indian. The transfer of Carlisle students to other Indian schools, inferior schools (for Carlisle is leading all the other schools) does not make up to the race the loss of educational opportunities only Carlisle can give. This is a serious loss, in the face of the sad fact that approximately 20,000 Indian children eligible for schools are still without schools in our America.

Realizing that old laws are amended to meet the needs of new conditions; and that our constitution is amended from time to time, I humbly beg to suggest that a reconsideration of the Carlisle matter be made with a view to taking necessary steps by which some other Indian school plant less vital to Indian education be accepted in lieu of Carlisle for military purposes.

Very earnestly,
(Signed) Gertrude Bonnin,
Secretary

September 16, 1918

My Dear Miss Bonnin:

I beg to acknowledge your letter of September 6th and regret that during this present emergency Carlisle Indian School may not be continued in its former capacity. As you are aware, every effort is being made to win the war in the shortest time and nearly every institution in the country has been asked to contribute in a greater or less degree to this end.

I sincerely trust that this change will not work a hardship upon your people and that they will find in other institutions the goal towards which they are aiming.

Very sincerely,
(Signed) F. P. Keppell
Third Assistant Secretary

"In other institutions," such as the public schools and American colleges, the American Indian must seek education. Under rules promulgated by the Hon. Secretary of the Interior, contracts are made with public schools for a few Indian students. This is truly a great stride in the right direction. May it not be carried further by contracting with high schools and colleges for the education of American Indians?

This war has emphasized in many ways the need of higher education for the Indians, and that the Indians themselves must make the effort upon their own initiative. They must have a voice in the manner in which their funds shall be used for their education and civilization.

In the olden days, the Indian hunter went forth in search of game that the family be fed and clothed. He did not sit in his tent waiting for some one to bring him food and raiment. Neither can the Indians today wait for some one else to bring to their door the indulgence of human rights. The Indians must go forth in search of the new game,—higher education, that they may enjoy equal rights with all American citizens.

In conclusion the Secretary reports that in the main the Society's plan to work for those large principles which benefit the many has been adhered to, exceptions being made in the cases where those concerned appeared to be pitifully helpless and suffering in distress. Never a penny has been received for remuneration from those who received aid in the name of the Society of American Indians.

Editorial Comment

(Winter 1919)

The eyes of the world are upon the Peace Conference sitting at Paris.[6]

Under the sun a new epoch is being staged!

Little peoples are to be granted the right of self determination!

Small nations and remnants of nations are to sit beside their great allies at the Peace Table; and their just claims are to be duly incorporated in the terms of a righteous peace.

Paris, for the moment, has become the center of the world's thought. Divers human petitions daily ascend to its Peace Table through foreign emissaries, people's representatives and the interest's lobbyists. From all parts of the earth, claims for adjustments equitable and otherwise are cabled and wirelessed. What patience and wisdom is needed now to render final decisions upon these highly involved and delicate enigmas reeking with inhumanities! The task may be difficult and the exposures of wrongs innumerable, still we believe—yes, we know, the world is to be made better as a result of these stirring times.

Immortal justice is the vortex around which swing the whirl of human events!

We are seeking to know justice, not as a fable but as a living, active, practical force in all that concerns our welfare!

Actions of the wise leaders assembled in Paris may be guided ostensibly by temporary man-made laws and aims, dividing human interests into domestic and international affairs, but even so those leaders cannot forget the eternal fact that humanity is essentially one undivided, closely intertwined fabric through which spiritual truth will shine with increasing brightness until it is fully understood and its requirements fulfilled. The universal cry for freedom from injustice is the voice of a multitude united by afflictions. To appease this human cry the application of democratic principles must be flexible enough to be universal.

Belgium is leading a historic procession of little peoples seeking freedom!

From the very folds of the great allied nations are many classes of men and women clamoring for a hearing. Their fathers, sons, brothers and husbands fought and died for democracy. Each is eager to receive the reward for which supreme sacrifice was made. Surely will the blood-soaked fields of No-Man's Land unceasingly cry out until the high principles for which blood spilled itself, are established in the governments of men.

Thus in this vast procession to Paris, we recognize and read the flying banners.

Labor organizations are seeking representation at the Peace Conference. Women of the world, mothers of the human race, are pressing forward for recognition. The Japanese are taking up the perplexing problem of race discrimination.

The Black man of America is offering his urgent petition for representation at the Conference; and already President Wilson has taken some action in his behalf by sending to Paris, Dr. Moton, of Tuskegee Institute, accompanied by Dr. DuBois.

A large New York assembly of American men and women wirelessed, it is reported, to President Wilson while he was in mid-ocean, enroute to Paris, requesting his aid in behalf of self-government for the Irish people.

The Red man asks for a very simple thing—citizenship in the land that was once his own—America. Who shall represent his cause at the World's Peace Conference? The American Indian, too, made the supreme sacrifice for liberty's sake. He loves democratic ideals. What shall world democracy mean to his race?

There never was a time more opportune than now for American to enfranchise the Red man!

America, Home of the Red Man
(Winter 1919)

To keep the home fires burning, the Society of American Indians held its annual conference this fall at Pierre, South Dakota. While en route to the West, the Secretary was accosted by a traveler whose eyes fairly gleamed under the little service pin she wore. At length curiosity spoke. The only preliminary introduction was a clearing of the throat. "You have a relative in the war?" asked the voice. "Yes, indeed," was the quick reply. "I have many cousins and nephews, somewhere in France. This star I am wearing is for my husband, a member of the great Sioux Nation, who is a volunteer in Uncle Sam's Army." A light spread over the countenance of the pale-faced stranger. "Oh! Yes! You are an Indian! Well, I knew when I first saw you that you must be a foreigner."

The amazing speech dropped like a sudden curtain behind which the speaker faded instantly from vision. In figures of fire, I saw, with the mind's eye, ten thousand Indian soldiers swaying to and fro on European battle-fields—finally mingling their precious blood with the blood of all other peoples of the earth, that democracy might live. Three-fourths of these Indian soldiers were volunteers and there were those also who did not claim exemption, so eager were they to defend their country and its democratic ideals. The Red Man of America loves democracy and hates mutilated treaties.

Twelve million dollars had been subscribed by the American Indians to the Liberty Loans. Generous donations they made to war funds of the Red Cross, Y.M.C.A. and other organizations.

I beheld rapidly shifting pictures of individual sacrifices of Indians both young and old.

An old grandmother, whom someone dubbed a "Utah squaw" now appeared wonderously glorified. Her furrowed face was aglow with radiance. Her bent form, clad in pitiful rags, changed in a twinkle of an eye to strength and grace. Her spirit shining through earth's misfortunes, revealed an angel in disguise. She donated five hundred dollars to the Red Cross and had left only thirteen dollars. "Thirteen dollars left? That is enough for me," the toothless old grandmother lisped in her own native tongue. It was her mite in this cause of world democracy.

Beside her stood an Indian brave in the Army uniform. Earlier he went overseas for active service at the front. A treasured file of his letters filled the air like white-winged pigeons, telling a story stranger than fiction.

He was a machine gunner. It was his duty to stand by his gun till he should drop. One day he fell, but the wound was not fatal. After his recovery he served as an infantryman. A Hun shrapnel found him again. His time, apparently, had not yet come to die. He recovered. Undaunted, he was glad when he was re-assigned to the Remount Station. "I have nothing to do now," his letters read, "only to break army horses for riding." True, he was an expert horseman but with a crippled knee, no telling what moment he might ignominiously break his own neck. This thought never occurred to him. Later a message came again from France. "I am no longer in the Remount. I have been assigned to garden work. I am digging spuds to help with the war."

And now I saw little French orphans, babes with soft buckskin moccasins on their tiny feet. Moccasins, that Indian women of America had made for them, with so much loving sympathy for an anguished humanity.

Time and distance were eliminated by the fast succession of pictures crowding before me. The dome of our nation's Capitol appeared. A great senator of Indian blood introduced upon the floor of the United States Senate a resolution that all Indian funds in the United States Treasury be available to our government, if need be, for the prosecution of the war. From coast to coast throughout our broad land not a single voice of the Red Man was raised to protest again it.

America! Home of the Red Man! How dearly the Indian loves you! America! Home of Democracy, when shall the Red Man be emancipated? When shall the Red Man be deemed worthy of full citizenship if not now?

A slight motion of the strange pale-face standing before me attracted my notice. I scanned him closely, to see what part of the dream he was. I wondered if a part of any dream could be cognizant of the rest of the actors, dream fellows, beheld by the dreamer or seer of visions. A pity he could not have seen the pictures that held me spellbound a moment ago. Alas, I did not have the courage to try to put them into words. When at last I spoke, the luster of his eye grew less bright. He was fast losing interest. From the questions with which I plied him, he probably guessed I was a traveling book agent.

Did you ever read a geography? The Red Man is one of the four primary races into which the human family has been divided by scientists. America is the home of the Red Man. Have you read the June *Designer*, 1918, about Indian children in Red Cross work? Have you read the April *National Geographic Magazine*, 1918, in which the Secretary of the Interior, Hon. Franklin K. Lane, has contributed an article entitled, "What is it to be an American?" In the third paragraph of this article we are told "There has been nothing of paternalism in our government." I would like to ask "How does this apply to the Red Men in our midst?"

Slowly shaking his head, the stranger withdrew cautiously, lest he be snared into subscribing for one or all of these publications.

The Coronation of
Chief Powhatan Retold

(Winter 1919)

Mrs. Woodrow Wilson, wife of the President of the United States, is a lineal descendant of Pocahontas. Wide acclaim has been given Mrs. Wilson in Europe where, preliminary to the world's Peace Conference, both she and her distinguished husband have been enthusiastically welcomed and sumptuously banqueted by the royal families.

It is a remarkable coincidence that three centuries ago, Pocahontas was also received in Court by the King and Queen of England. It is recorded in history "that the most flattering marks of attention" were paid to the daughter of Chief Powhatan. Springing from the tribal democracies of the new world, Pocahontas was the first emissary of democratic ideas to caste-ridden Europe. She must have suffered untold anguish when King James was offended with her sweetheart husband, Rolfe, for his presumption in marrying the daughter of a king—a crowned head too!"

Through weary miles of tangled forests of the eastern coast, Captain John Smith with four escorts carried word to Powhatan that new presents for him had arrived from England; and that Captain Newport sent him an invitation to come to Jamestown to receive them.

The stately Indian chief, having just returned from a journey, was very likely reclining upon "his bed of mats, his pillow of dressed skin lying beside him with its brilliant embroidery of shells and beads." Dressed in a handsome fur robe, "as large as an Irish mantell." It was the fall of 1608; and the air was damp and cool. With grave dignity he replied to the messengers—"If your king has sent me presents, I also am a king and this is my land. Here I will stay eight days to receive them." As for the cunning proposal that he join the settlers in a common campaign against another tribe of Indians, he said "I can avenge my own injuries." Proud and sagacious was Powhatan, even Captain John Smith had to admit.

When Jamestown learned that Chief Powhatan would be at home to receive the King's gifts, Captain Newport with fifty men immediately set out to the chief's dwelling. Among the many gifts presented at that memorable time, was a royal crown sent by King James I of England. It was a disappointment to Captain Newport that this unusual present brought to the Indian chief no glad thrills at all. But the faithful subjects of England knew that the old chief was exceedingly whimsical. They thought so because he was more interested in trifling trinkets and bright colored beads which appealed more to the artistic eye of the aborigine. He was grossly ignorant of the world's rank and power associated with particular pieces of the white man's articles of dress and decoration. One time, the chief admired a string of blue beads so much that he bought them from Captain Smith, paying three hundred bushels of corn, every kernel of which was worth more than gold to the hungry colonists.

It was not surprising then that the scarlet robe and royal crown did not happen to please his unspoiled taste. Perhaps brooding over the encroachments of the pale-faces upon his territory might have caused him to question the real significance of these King's garments and crown. To the liberty loving soul of Powhatan, this royal camouflage was no comparison to the gorgeous array of Autumn in that primeval forest where he roamed at will.

However, by dint of persuasion, the coronation day was chosen. When the time came for the performance of the solemn ceremony, the courage of Powhatan failed. Such a parley as was held under those ancient trees can scarcely be imagined. The Indian Chief was incorrigible. It was really laughable, did it not in later years prove to be so tragic. After hours of reassurance that the king's garments would not injure him, he reluctantly permitted himself to be dragged into them. The greatest difficulty was encountered when Powhatan stubbornly refused to kneel to receive the crown, as he was requested.

The patience of his visitors was exhausted. Still they who would move heaven and earth to execute their king's command must find a way to move this American aborigine. They resorted to trickery. "One leaned hard upon his shoulder to make him stoop a little and three stood ready to fix the royal gewgaw on his head." At the signal of a pistol shot, a volley of musketry was fired as a salute.

With a muttered growl of surprise, the warrior chieftain tore himself loose from their hands. His eagle eye flashed the wireless "Are you come to trifle with me and to kill?"

Again Powhatan, now a crowned head, was reassured that all was well. Upon recovering his composure, it is told that he generously gave his old shoes and mantle to Captain Newport for his courtesy.

Letter to the Chiefs and
Headmen of the Tribes[7]
(Winter 1919)

My friends and kinsmen:

This little letter is written to you that each may receive a direct message today. There are two things I wish to bring to your special attention. These are English-speaking and retaining ownership of a portion of our Indian lands.

Since the close of the great war, in which our Indians fought so bravely, there is much talk among our White brothers about the importance of all Americans learning to speak English. There are many languages among the White people just as there are among our different Indian tribes. Plans are being made and our government is supporting this new movement to educate all foreigners who now are American citizens, by the study of the English language.

In all their papers, many of which I read, they are urging the returned soldiers and girl war-workers to go back to the schools. Night schools are opened for the working men and women. No one is ever too old to learn.

Friends, if the White people have found it worth while to do this, isn't it even more worth our while to renew our efforts to speak English? No doubt there have been occasions when you wished you could have expressed your thought in English. Remembering this experience, will you now encourage other Indians to make the effort to learn this language?

Very often I have wished that you could write to me in a language we both would understand perfectly. I could then profit by your advice in many things, and you would know you were not forgotten.

And now, I have a word to say about Indians holding permanently a small portion of their inherited lands. Sometimes I fear they are selling their lands too fast and without consideration for the future children of our race. Indians are an out-of-doors people, and though we may become educated in the White man's way and even acquire money, we cannot really be happy unless we have a small piece of this Out-of-Doors to enjoy as we please. For the sake of our children's children we must hold onto a few acres that they may enjoy it as we have.

Many times as I walk on the paved streets of the city, I long for the open Indian country in which I played as a child. I wonder how our White brothers can be content, being born and bred In-Doors. I understand that it is their fast increasing population that necessitates building houses, larger and higher, to accommodate them. The White man is a wonderful builder of stone houses, which to me are better to look upon from the outside than to live in, as they shut out the sky and sunshine.

I shall be glad to hear from you, should you feel interested in these two things about which I have taken the liberty to write you.[8]

Editorial Comment

(Spring 1919)

The Black Hills Council

With the full Council meeting annually and the Executive Committee thereof convening at more frequent intervals, the Black Hills Council of the Sioux has been established for many years. Intelligent, progressive Indians, realizing the necessity of united efforts, organized this association for the purpose of obtaining an equitable and just settlement of what is known as the Black Hills claim.

In spite of the treaty of 1868,[9] "the cupidity of the white man, lusting for gold in the forbidden country of the Black Hills, prevailed upon the War Department to come to his rescue by instituting war against the peaceful roaming Sioux."

The Black Hills claim, like other Indian claims, is the progeny of broken treaties. Paradoxical as it may seem, the very people standing most in need of the aid of justice and the machinery of law is debarred from the courts of America. Three-fourths of the Indian race being non-citizen, have no legal status, though a race that is good enough to fight and die for world democracy is surely worthy of full American citizenship and the protection of law under our constitution! The Indian's voice will not be heard, however, in the courts of our land until our great government uproots the Bureau System, the love-vine strangling the manhood of the Indian race.

Indian tribes are by express statute excluded from the general jurisdiction of the Court of Claims; and in order to present their grievances, they must first obtain the consent of Congress, of which they are non-constituents. In view of this situation it is quite apparent that the sooner the tribal corrals are thrown open, the sooner the Indian will become Americanized. There need be no fear that he may not measure up to the responsibilities of a citizen. Even after the blighting stagnation of the Indian reservations, the Indian will be equal to his opportunities.

The tenacity with which Indians cling to the belief in the democratic doctrine of justice to all is characteristic of the race. It is illustrated by the Black Hills Council which braved the appalling difficulties it encountered. Representative men chosen by the Council were sent to Washington, D.C., in the hope of gaining the ear of Congress. They stormed the very citadel of the Great Father in Washington. By their untiring work, a number of bills were introduced in Congress from time to time—bills which were ostensibly intended to give jurisdiction to the courts to hear and determine what rights, if any, remain to the Sioux in the Black Hills property.

One after another of these bills failed of passage by Congress, while access to the Court of Claims to all other Americans was comparatively easy, types of men like the I.W.W. and the Bolsheviki not excepted. Small wonder that Immortal Justice must be blindfolded upon her marble pedestal lest her tranquility be marred by the Red Man's dilemma!

The fact remains that the Sioux have an intangible right none the less real and just for the postponed settlement, one that can only materialize in a democratic government, by the aid of the American Congress and the courts.

The council has reached the point in its school of experience where the need of legal advice is recognized. The Indian's view must be presented in due form for the consideration of Congress.

The Sioux Nation, acting through its own association, must avail itself of the aid of recognized competent legal counsel; and this under similar conditions governing such employment by the white man in his business affairs. It is time for the Sioux and their friends to inquire why they have not long ago had an attorney or attorneys of their own choosing employed under such conditions as would insure faithful and effective service.

The history of the attempted legislation in regard to the Black Hills Case, if scrutinized, would develop interesting facts and information for those earnestly interested in the establishment of justice to the Indian.

In this connection, the words of an Indian on the floor of the House of Representatives, at the last session of Congress, may be read with great profit by all Indians and friends of the Indians.

Congressman Hastings, of Oklahoma, is a Cherokee by blood. He with his wife and children are enrolled members of the Cherokee Tribe and allottees with the Cherokee Nation. Mr. Hastings is a lawyer of distinguished ability. At one time covering a number of years, he was the official attorney for the Cherokee Nation. He served under the direction and control of the Commission of Indian Affairs and the Secretary of the Interior.

The occasion for his recent speech, referred to above, was in advocacy for a Bill under consideration, where an attorney was to be provided for the Osages and to be of *their own selection*.

The contention of the Indian Bureau was that if the Osages were to have an attorney, which for years it had been denying them, he should be an attorney virtually chosen by and under the direction of the Indian Bureau.

Mr. Hastings said: "They have certain differences with the department. They cannot be represented up here before the committees of Congress. They cannot send an attorney here; they cannot send their tribal council here. There is no way for them to present their claims to Congress now without the permission of the Secretary of the Interior."

In response to the views of a member of the House, opposing him, Mr. Hastings said, "The gentleman has not had the experience upon these Indian matters that some of the rest of us have had. Personally I have lived under the department every day of my life. We have been under the supervision of the Interior Department down there in Oklahoma always, and if you are going to allow the Secretary of the Interior to pick the attorney, to let him be hand-picked by him, you might as well have none at all, because the attorney then must go down and first get orders from the department and the Commissioner of Indian Affairs, else he will not be employed the next year. His employment depends upon his representing their views and not the views of the Osage Indians."

He made his position clearer still: "Now, I have always contended that these people with these large interests ought to be represented by a high-class attorney, and I believe they ought to have something to say about naming him. Let me say to the gentleman, for years I was attorney for the Cherokee Tribe of Indians, and represented them before committees and before the departments and before the courts here, and I do not believe that any tribal representation ought to be dictated to by the Commissioner of Indian Affairs or the Secretary of the Interior."

After an interruption, Mr. Hastings proceeded: "I will say that all of these tribal attorneys that are now employed where approval has to be made by the Secretary of the Interior they cannot, of course, represent any other views than those entertained by the department. . . ."

What is true of the Osages may apply with equal force to the Sioux. The question arises in our minds,—have not the Sioux already wasted too much time in desultory quest for a plan for adjusting the Black Hills controversy?

Is it not emphatically clear from the words of Congressman Hastings on this subject, that the secret of the Sioux Council's failure or the explanation of the postponement of its desire, lies in the fact that the Indian Bureau has been the chief factor in defeating the Sioux to appoint, employ and retain capable counsel of their own choosing?

Sounds from an Anvil

Before the armistice was signed, a reputable gentleman of the West wrote us relative to a school he was opening for young men. He was prompted to this philanthropic and educational work by letters from his soldier boy overseas who wrote of the constant need for good horseshooers in the field.

The father, owning a well equipped blacksmith shop and

having himself won medals for his own meritorious work in this line, at once offered a course of training in Blacksmithing to the young men of his vicinity, feeling that such knowledge would help to make better soldiers.

He was liberal enough to include in the invitation his Indian neighbors. These Utes living in the mountainous region could always find remunerative work in the mines where there is a demand for blacksmithing, even after the war.

The government school in the western Indian Reservation did not teach blacksmithing, though in the Far East, the Hampton School taught it with amazingly good results.

We are advised the white boys took advantage of this offer of training in the blacksmith shop but the Indian Bureau, for some unknown reason, declined to accept the opportunity for the Ute boys.

The reason would be interesting!

The Ute Grazing Land

In Utah, the Ute Grazing Land of 250,000 acres is in jeopardy.

Scarcely a month had passed after the cessation of the World War when on December 10, 1918, in the United States Senate, a resolution was introduced directing the Secretary of the Interior to report, among other things, "What means may be taken to extinguish the Indian title to said lands; and whether it is convenient and advantageous to add said lands, or any part thereof, to the Uinta National Forest."

To the Indian soldier proudly returning home, this is a cruel unwelcome!

Amid the wails of those mourning for their dead on European battlefields, and Indian widows with their orphaned children comfortless, attempt is made to invade their rights!

During the war, these Utes contributed liberally to the Red Cross work and over subscribed their quota for Liberty Loans. The story is told of a Ute grandmother who subscribed $500.00 and when reminded that she had only $13.00 left, she replied, "That is enough for me!" It is within the memory of this same dear old grandmother that her people suffered the loss of their Colorado homes, large tracts of their lands being then turned into Forest Reserves.

A repetition of this experience by the Utes is unthinkable!

Remarks of Representative Church in a House address recently indicates the game of National Park extensions has reached its limit. More particularly is this true when it involves gross injustice to a people who have proven their loyalty in the war.

The Senate resolution states that the Ute Indians are not making an economic and adequate use of their grazing land; and will not in the future be able to make economic and adequate use of it.

These are strange declarations which in their final analysis, reflect discredit upon the Indian Bureau management of the Ute affairs. It is true that the Indians' herds of cattle, horses and sheep have not been large enough to stock their entire range; and that a part of their grazing land is leased, through the Indian Bureau, to white settlers who find it a profitable business. The Utes have protested in vain again the trespasses of these same white stockmen whom the Bureau continues to favor with leases.

In the United States Treasury are some two million dollars belonging to these Utes. Why have they not been encouraged to purchase cattle for their Grazing Land instead of spending vast sums of money in farming desert lands allotted to them without water?

It remains for the American people to say if "in the future" the Indian Bureau shall continue to hinder the Utes from making the adequate use of their Grazing Land. These Indians are natural stockmen and have long wished to engage in more extensive stock raising.

Were the Indians' dream to come true, the Utes would be *free* to invest their money in live stock, with the hands of the Indian Bureau strictly off!

The Utes would become producers in the beef supply of America.

They would find at last the joy of active participation in an American enterprise!

Editorial Comment

(Summer 1919)

Hope in the Returned Indian Soldier

"Can you tell me why a soldier returned from overseas service is called a hero?" These are the words of an Indian soldier in a recent letter. At once I recalled the ovation to Sergeant York, the Tennessee soldier, whose record of having killed twenty-five Germans and capturing 132 others, has been heralded nation-wide.

The Indian soldier further said,—"Last July, 1918, my brother and I, as doughboys went over to Europe with the Wild West Division. We served at the front. I was in bloody battles on No Man's Land in the Meuse-Argonne Sector. I was wounded in action. After my recovery I joined my division and stayed with them until we sailed for the States after the armistice. Today I am alive!—in good health!—and at home! I do not claim to be a hero but I do call myself a lucky bird!"

The returned soldier is a hero more fortunate perhaps than his brother now sleeping in No Man's Land. Both displayed the same fortitude of mind on the field of action. Chance took one and left the other. This incident of chance in no wise affects the heroic bravery of either.

We quote further from the letter,—"I am glad for the many things I learned while in the army. In my travels with the army I have seen a great world. I did not know till then that I had been living in a reservation wilderness. I have seen how men and women engage in the world's work."

These and other like expressions are upon the lips of our returned Indian soldiers. From the ashes of Indian heroes, dead in foreign battlefields, rises the returned Indian Soldier Disciple! He brings home to his race stories of human enterprise and world activities such as they have never even dreamed. He tells of the many friends he has made during his elbow to elbow comradeship with the white American soldiers. Added to the joy of his return is the new interest in life his graphic recitations inspire.

Even as he talks heroism seems to become contagious! Warm blood tingles! The Indian's self-sacrificing part in the world war is a sublime achievement which tinkling cymbals more or less may not augment or diminish! This demonstration of valor and fortitude reveals inherent in the Indian race a high and noble quality of mind.

The black night of world war has served to bring out the brilliant stars of Indian bravery and heroism. The night revealed their presence in our spiritual firmament. They have always been there. We believe they are eternal. The emergency of war ushered them into a world review.

Now in demobilization our Indians in khaki do not lay aside with their military uniform these telling qualities of heroism which have won so much "undistinguished collective acclaim." They continue to be clothed with that divine courage which some have called "Indian stoicism"; and in their company we realize that each and every one of us possess the attributes of heroism, as our divine heritage!

We are reminded of the words of Carlyle, "If hero means sincere man, why not every one of us be a hero?"

The irksome vacuity of reservation exile may require as much heroism, if not more, to live than it did to die in actual battle. It takes courage to live, sometimes. It takes strength to do one's own thinking. Yet these are our responsibilities, we dare not shirk nor permit another to assume. Of course another cannot exercise for us our discerning powers. We must do that ourselves! In the doing prove our heroism!

Every Indian, who stands firmly on his own feet, for the cause of right justice and freedom, is indeed a hero—a living hero in the skirmishes of daily life!

Gift of Angel DeCora Dietz[10]

This Indian woman, artist and teacher of art, while living won laurels for her race. She loved her people much. Their trials and deferred justice lay upon her heart. Believing that in an organization of Indians lay the means of the Red Man's self-expression and power, she was one of the charter members of the Society of American Indians in 1911.

Throughout the years following, she watched the struggles of this Society. She knew the serious handicaps under which it labored for the lack of sufficient funds. But Angel never spoke of her plan. Only after her untimely death last February was it learned she had in her will bequeathed three thousand ($3,000.00) dollars to carry on the work of the Society of American Indians.

The gift is a sacred trust! Such faith in her own race inspires us to our uttermost effort. Angel DeCora Dietz, living and dying, has left us a noble example of devotion to our people. Let us take heed. Let us prove our worth even as she has done.

An Indian Citizenship Campaign

Our president, Dr. Charles A. Eastman, spent about three months this spring on a lecture campaign in behalf of American citizenship for the Indian. Sacrificing remunerative engagements to give himself up to strenuous public speaking, delivering three and sometimes four addresses in a day.

The echo of his plea reached the nation's capitol. During the debate on the fifteen million dollar Indian Appropriation Bill a newspaper account of Dr. Eastman's Indian citizenship address was read into the Congressional Record. We earnestly hope every member of Congress has read it! Had there been no opposition to the generous estimates the Indian Office made for its own self-preservation this appropriation might easily have been thirty millions.

The Indian race is asking release from the clutches of bureaucracy!

If American audiences are an indication of public sentiment,—and Congress truly represents the people, the Indian's cry must be heard!

The American people still remember how their early ancestors fled from the autocracy of Europe to the open arms of the Red Man a few centuries ago. This memory together with the proud record of the Indian in the world war just closed must move all those whose hearts are not stone.

Our Indian philosopher and lecturer was welcomed everywhere and most cordially entertained by notable men and women prominent in human welfare work. As they believe in Americanizing the foreigner so should they desire the privileges of American citizenship for the native, the aborigine! In Chicago an auxiliary to the Society of American Indians was organized by friends of the Indian for the purpose of uniting their efforts to secure citizenship for the Indian.

Elated by so much encouragement from the American people, Dr. Eastman, with Dr. Carlos Montezuma, left Chicago to visit Indian country. There they were met and ably assisted by our First Vice-President, Rev. Philip Gordon, Dennison Wheelock and others. In the towns close to Indian reservations they again spoke before crowded houses.

Throughout the extended lecture tour of three months, in large cities and small towns of America, all went well until attempt was made to enter an Indian reservation.

Indian Bureau autocracy forbade these educated, leading Indian men to hold any meeting on the Indian reservation! Though the riffraff of the white people from the four corners of the earth may enter Indian lands and homestead them, thus permitting daily contact with the very scum of other races, the educated, refined, and patriotic Indian, teaching the highest ideals of democracy is forbidden to meet with his own race, even for a day!

This is not the democracy for which our soldiers fought and died!

This is race discrimination and akin to the rule of might of the old-world powers!

Congress listened to the reading of Dr. Eastman's address

and printed it in the Congressional Record for the information of all. The Indian Bureau denied the reservation Indians, the people most vitally concerned, the American privilege of listening to these same words and from the lips of one of their own race!

An Indian Praying on the Hilltop
(Spring 1919)

Great Spirit, for the superb gift of individual consciousness, I offer thanks with over-flowing heart! For thy great law, protecting my place in the spaces hung with the myriad stars, sun, moon and earth, I offer thanks with my soul!

Along my trail through the wilderness, dreadful dreams overtake me by night and day; and I fear lest destruction make an end of me. Thy power awakens me! Then, oh then, I rejoice in the spiritual realization that earthly disaster cannot kill my spirit. I thank thee for awakening me!

Poor in a land of plenty; friendless in a den of thieves. Without food and raiment; sick and weary of earth,—these are the terrors of my dreams both night and day. Great Spirit I thank thee for awakening me!

None can rob me of thee! And the gift of conscious life,—in spirit!

While upon the hilltop, I am praying, I feel thy presence near. My strength is renewed like the eagle's. New courage brings its vision. I see the dawn of justice to the Indian, even upon earth; and now, Great Spirit, my heart is full of Joy!

Address by the Secretary-Treasurer, Society of American Indians Annual Convention

(Summer 1919)

My brother officers and brothers and sisters of this great country, members of this organization, it fills my heart with joy to hear these encouraging words from my brothers and as they have spoken of their high regard for an Indian sister I know that it extends to all the Indian women in this country and I hope my brothers that at the next meeting you will invite your wife to come with you and you will invite your sister to come with you because you realize that in the home, in the Indian home, the mother teaches the children these very principles we are talking about—we teach our children as they play about our knees and that is why the Indian woman must come to these gatherings, she must listen with her mind open and her heart open that she may gather the truths to take home to our little ones—they are our future hope. Our children! I have received so much inspiration from the words we have heard this morning—you have all felt the same.

The greatest gift in life is consciousness. Not positions, not the dollar, but that the Almighty Spirit gives us life and we have a rational mind with which to see all the wonders of the universe. And this is true, my brothers and sisters—consciousness above all else. That is the way it should be. Let us cling to that. Let us do the practical way. We have had to change from the old style of hunting, have had to leave the old trails—we can do it. We have the power, we can think. We can be fair. Work is honorable as long as men and women are honest. There is no work that is degrading. It is all honorable. I do not need to repeat that, because Indians know it. Or forefathers knew it was no disgrace to go on the hunt to bring the meat home for the family. It was no disgrace for the mother to prepare the meal. Work is honorable. We must have a work and each day do it to the best of our ability.

God has given you life, he has given you minds to think with and hearts that we may be just to all, that we may be true to all mankind. Then we are true to God—to ourselves. That means each day the simplest things begin from sunrise to sunset, from sunset to sunrise again. The new trails we are hunting. We have come from our homes to this national teepee and we are talking with one another in a different language, but we are all proud of our Indian blood, we are glad we are Indians. We want to teach our children to be proud of their Indian blood.

There is so much good in our people—everyone knows that when we give our word, we keep it. Let us save those wonderful things, the virtues of our race, their honesty, clean living and intelligence. Let us teach our children that their Indian blood stands for the virtues of their race.

Now we are meeting a civilization from a race that came from Europe. We have to meet it each day—there is no dodging, and it is not easy. It is going to take courage; it is going to test your strength. It is going to test your faith in the Greatest of All. It is going to be hard, but let us stand the test, true to the Indian blood. Let us do that. Let us teach our children to be proud of their Indian blood and to stand the test bravely.

We sometimes think we cannot speak the English language well and we cannot talk in the conference. That is not it. You can tell us what is in your heart. Use the words that are put in your mouth. Use the words that come to you, that which is in the heart and mind. We come to commune with our minds, with our hearts. Do not sit back because you think that you cannot speak English well. Let us hear from those who do not speak it at all, they can have interpreters. We want to hear from the minds and hearts of our Indian people. Language is only a convenience, just like a coat is a convenience, and it is not so important as your mind and your heart.

I remember my mother. I was born in a teepee. I loved that life. It was beautiful, more beautiful than I can tell you. But my mother said to me, "You must learn the white man's language so when you grow up you will talk for us and for the Indian and the white man will have a better understanding." I said, "I will." It has not always been easy, but I said, "I am going to do the best I can and then I am going to let the Great Spirit do the rest." Now every one of us can do that. Of course there are things to discourage. We seem to have no money, no friends, and *we have no voice in Congress*. How shall we do this thing? Then I think I have forgotten the most important thing of all, and that is our Maker the Great Spirit because this applies to every day thinking in our homes and wherever we go.

Then let us have level heads, let us not cower. We are men and women with minds and hearts. Why, the Great Almighty made us! We are here like other human beings and there is no reason why we should be afraid to hold up our heads. Let us stand up straight. Let us study conditions; let us give reasons why. And if we fail at the first trial, shall we quit? No, we will try again. You believe in right—then stand for that. The first time you stand for right and it is refused you, shall you quit? Then you do not believe in it. We must continue speaking and claiming our human rights to live on this earth that God has made, so that we may think our thoughts and speak them— that we may have our part in the American life and be as any other human beings are.

These are things it would seem quite unnecessary to make a speech upon, perhaps, but I want to tell of them because they all come back to you. We are rational human beings. Shall we think or shall somebody think of us? We are on this earth to think and do the best we can according to our light. That is our God-given privilege. Well, then, let us think. We have no one else to fear after we are right with God. We get our intelligence from Him, our life, then let us think calmly and reasonably.

There are matters that we do not agree upon and the way to do is to sift them down, thrash them out. And keep thrashing. If you do not do it, who shall do it for you? Every one of us each day must think and act—not only think, but we must act, else we will not get the benefit. We must put our thoughts into practice every day in the most complex business matter, in the most simple home duty. Let us think and act as rational beings, like other peoples on this earth.

This us the thought that I would give to you to take home, not only to my brothers at home, but my sisters. We are rational beings. Let us develop our powers by thinking and acting for ourselves. That is the way we grow. We have been told organization is necessary to bring about results. We have been scattered to the four winds. Are we going to organize? This is a national teepee. We are all coming here to consult together and from these various ideas we want to come to a conclusion. Is that any different from other meetings of American people? All other peoples do the same. They come together. I have been in sessions of Congress when the great men there met together. They will discuss their subjects, some on one side, some on another, both giving soundest arguments. Was it treason for these men to have difference of opinions? It was not treason against the Government. They were representing their people, they were representing the Government, but they had different views and they had the privilege of speaking. Now, I am sure in our humble gathering here, we have that same liberty. We are in America, and we have, each one of us, a right to express our views. We agree on the main thing. We want to form some conclusions. We want the privilege of rational men for, were we idiots or lunatics we would not be here, we would be in some hospital or asylum. But, because we are rational creatures, we have a right to express our thoughts and to try to come to some plan, according to the best of our light. That is our policy.

And, therefore, it is necessary that we organize, that we may act as a body; that we may put our ideas together and choose the best. We must support this organization, we must see that it grows stronger. We will all have a chance to express our opinions and then we will try to use the best. That is our work. Let us all express what seems to us the thing that is needed, and we will assort and choose that which we must strive for at this time.

And to do this, we must have organization. The work of the Society this year has been grinding and constant, early and late. Do you think any one would work, devote himself entirely to a cause—without a salary—if he did not believe in it? Then you know we must all work for this thing—that the American Indian must have a voice. He must say what is in him and by exchanging opinions, we are going to grow. I believe in that and that is why I am working with my brothers and I hope as time goes on, my sisters, Indians, will come to do their part in their own homes. Then they will help us carry on this work as it must be done so that we may succeed.

We have sent out from our office thousands of letters. We have brought our files up to date. We have revised our lists up to date. Our membership is doubled and more than doubled in a year. It means a good deal of work when you send in your name and membership fee. We give you a card and credit you with what you have sent. We write you a letter then we put your name on the mailing list and send it to our publishers so that you will be sure to get our magazine and when you think of 2000 names coming in to be taken care of in that way, you can realize the work. On account of the war conditions, clerks have been almost impossible to get in our office. The Government gives high salaries and our Society cannot compete. Then we, in our office, had to get just here and there any clerk we could find. Sometimes I had a clerk two hours for one evening in the week and if I got a clerk two or three evenings in one week for two or three hours, I thought I was doing well. I need two clerks in the office every day of the year to carry on the Society's work as it should be.

It has been extremely difficult this year, the work has been too hard for one human being as I have only one pair of hands and while I am glad to do this for the Society, it has taken longer time and if your letters do not come to you quickly, it is because I have baskets of letters, all awaiting to be answered. I tell you this so you may know that we are busy every day.

Some of our friends write and ask the Secretary to attend to personal matters and to attend hearings on Indian affairs. This consumes many hours. There is no one to carry on the business at the office while I am away. I must leave the work and make the trip to the Indian Office, or to the Committee hearings, and this consumes strength as well as time. All this is a part of our work so you may understand what I have been doing. I hope there are those among you who will help share this burden, that there will be those among you who will help in some way to lighten the work in our office so that it will not fall upon one individual and upon one pair of hands. These conditions the Society could not help, but I explain this so that you will know the need for assistance and that you will also realize the cause of delayed replies to your letters.

Sometimes we are not successful on our first trip to the Indian office or to the Committee hearings, and have to go again, and then again. So you can see we were busy—the work was overwhelming. But with this heavy burden, I was happy, because I saw that the organization was growing. I did not despair because I felt from year to year, as we grow stronger, we are going to have more workers in the office. We are going to have more workers in the field and we are going to have more publicity and that we will have the help our Society is crying for.

I could not complete September accounts and take care of the conference, so that portion of the year's statement is not ready.

I also have the Treasurer's report of what we received and what we expended. Remember that no officer has received one cent of pay. All the expenditures have been for work, carrying the work in the office and getting out the magazine. I want this clear, so that you will all know, and can tell others that no officer in charge has been paid one cent out of these moneys.

IV

POETRY, PAMPHLETS, ESSAYS, AND SPEECHES

Collected here are a selection of nonfiction and political pieces that Zitkala-Ša published outside of her role as a member of the Society of American Indians. Many of these writings were published in multiple forms, as newspaper articles or pamphlets, and given as speeches. The first selection is among her earliest known writing, the 1896 speech she gave at the Indiana State Oratorical Competition (and the subject of some of her comments in "The School Days of an Indian Girl") while a student at Earlham College. The range of material here exhibits Zitkala-Ša's various oratorical, polemical, and political takes on key issues in Native-white relations of her day: her impassioned defense of Indian dance (written at the height of federal regulations against tribal dance and ritual); her critique of Indian use of peyote; and her prose poem about the Washington Monument. The section ends with a series of pieces that she wrote at the request of California Indians to help their visibility and political viability. Engaging and fresh, they were written serially (and called "chapters") for the *San Francisco Bulletin* in 1922, then reprinted in the *California Indian Herald* as well as being distributed in pamphlet form. These pieces, read alongside the tremendous range of her writing, highlight her wit, compassion, historical insight, and commitment to effecting social change.

Side by Side[1]
(March 1896)

The universe is the product of evolution. An ascending energy pervades all life. By slow degrees nations have risen from the mountain foot of their existence to its summit. In the wild forests of northern Europe two thousand years ago roamed the blue-eyed Teuton. To the lowlands by the northern sea came the war-like Saxon, ere long to begin his bloody conquest of Britain. Yet fierce and barbarous as he was, the irrepressible germ of progress lay deeply implanted in his nature. His descendants have girdled the globe with their possessions. To-day it is no longer a debatable question whether it shall be Anglo-Saxon or Cossack, constitutional law or imperial decree, that is destined to mold the character of governments and to determine the policies of nations.

Out of a people holding tenaciously to the principles of the Great Charter has arisen in America a nation of free men and free institutions. On its shores two oceans lavish the products of the world. Among its rivers, mountains and lakes, in its stately forests and on its broad prairies, like rolling seas of green and gold, millions of toiling sovereigns have established gigantic enterprises, great factories, commercial highways, and have developed fruitful farms and productive mines. The ennobling architecture of its churches, schools, and benevolent institutions; its municipal greatness, keeping pace with social progress; its scholars, statesmen, authors and divines, giving expression and force to the religious and humanitarian zeal of a great people—all these reveal a marvelous progress. Thought is lost in admiration of this matchless scene over which floats in majesty the starry emblem of liberty.

But see! At the bidding of thought the tide of time rolls back four hundred years. The generations of men of all nations, kindreds, and tongues, who have developed this civilization in America, return to the bosom of the old world. Myriad merchantmen, fleets, and armaments shrink and disappear from the ocean. Daring explorers in their frail crafts hie to their havens on the European shore. The fleet of discovery, bearing under the flag of Spain the figure of Columbus, recedes beyond the trackless sea. America is one great wilderness again. Over the trees of the primeval forest curls the smoke of the wigwam. The hills resound with the hunter's shout that dies away with the fleeing deer. On the river glides his light canoe. In the wigwam Laughing Water weaves into moccasins the rainbow-tinted beads. By gleaming council fire brave warriors are stirred by the rude eloquence of their chief. In the evening-glow the eyes of the children brighten as the aged brave tells his fantastic legends. The reverent and poetic natures of these forest children feel the benign influence of the Great Spirit; they hear his voice in the wind; see his frown in the storm cloud; his smile in the sunbeam. Thus in reverential awe the Red Man lived. His was the life that is the common lot of human kind. Bravely did he struggle with famine and disease. He felt his pulses hasten in the joyous freedom of the hunt. Quick to string his bow for vengeance; ready to bury the hatchet or smoke the pipe of peace; never was he first to break a treaty or known to betray a friend with whom he had eaten salt.

The invasion of his broad dominions by a paler race brought no dismay to the hospitable Indian. Samoset voiced the feeling of his people as he stood among the winter-weary Pilgrims and cried "Welcome, Englishmen." Nor did the Indian cling self-ishly to his lands; willingly he divides with Roger Williams and with Penn, who pay him for his own. History bears record to no finer examples of fidelity. To Jesuit, to Quaker, to all who kept their faith with him, his loyalty never failed.

Unfortunately civilization is not an unmixed blessing. Vices begin to creep into his life and deepen the Red Man's degradation. He learns to crave the European liquid fire. Broken treaties shake his faith in the new-comers. Continued aggres-

sions goad him to desperation. The White Man's bullet deci-
mates his tribes and drives him from his home. What if he
fought? His forests were felled; his game frightened away; his
streams of finny shoals usurped. He loved his family and would
defend them. He loved the fair land of which he was rightful
owner. He loved the inheritance of his fathers, their traditions,
their graves; he held them a priceless legacy to be sacredly kept.
He loved his native land. Do you wonder still that in his breast
he should brood revenge, when ruthlessly driven from the temples where he worshipped? Do you wonder still that he skulked
in forest gloom to avenge the desolation of his home? Is patriotism a virtue only in Saxon hearts? Is there no charity to cover
his crouching form as he stealthily opposed his relentless foe?

The charge of cruelty has been brought against the Indian;
but the White Man has been the witness and the judge. Anglo-
Saxon England, with its progressive blood, its long continued
development of freedom and justice, its eight centuries of
Christian training, burned the writhing martyr in the fires of
Kenith field from a sense of duty. In the name of religion and
liberty, the cultured Frenchman, with his inheritance of Roman
justice, ten centuries of Christian ideas, murders his brother on
that awful night of St. Bartholomew, and during the Reign of
Terror swells the Seine with human blood. Let it be remembered, before condemnation is passed upon the Red Man, that,
while he burned and tortured frontiersmen, Puritan Boston
burned witches and hanged Quakers, and the Southern aristo-
crat beat his slaves and set blood hounds on the track of him
who dared aspire to freedom. The barbarous Indian, ignorant
alike of Roman justice, Saxon law, and the Gospel of Christian
brotherhood, in the fury of revenge has brought no greater
stain upon his name than these.

But what have two centuries of contact with the foremost
wave of Anglo-Saxon civilization wrought for him?

> You say they all have passed away,
> That noble race—and brave;
> That their light canoes have vanished
> From off the crested wave:

> That mid the forests where they roamed
> There rings no hunter's shout;
>
> You say their conelike cabins
> That clustered o'er the vale
> Have disappeared—as withered leaves
> Before the autumn's gale.

If in their stead, we have to-day a race of blighted promise, will you spurn them? You, whose sires have permitted the most debasing influences to surround these forest children, brutalizing their nobler instincts until sin and corruption have well nigh swept them from the Earth?

To-day the Indian is pressed almost to the farther sea. Does that sea symbolize his death? Does the narrow territory still left to him typify the last brief day before his place on Earth "shall know him no more forever"? Shall might make right and the fittest alone survive? Oh Love of God and His "Strong Son," thou who liftest up the oppressed and succorest the needy, is thine ear grown heavy that it cannot hear his cry? Is thy arm so shortened, it cannot save? Dost thou not yet enfold him in thy love? Look with compassion down, and with thine almighty power move this nation to the rescue of my race. To take the life of a nation during the slow march of centuries seems not a lighter crime than to crush it instantly with one fatal blow. Our country must not shame her principles by such consummate iniquity. Has the charity which would succor dying Armenia no place for the Indian at home? Has America's first-born forfeited his birthright to her boundless opportunities? No legacy of barbarism can efface the divine image in man. No tardiness in entering the paths of progress can destroy his divinely given capabilities. No lot or circumstance, except of his own choosing, can invalidate his claim to a place in the brotherhood of man or release more fortunate, more enlightened people from the obligation of a brother's keeper. Poets sing of a coming federation of the world, and we applaud. Idealists dream that in this commonwealth of all humanity the divine spark in man shall be the only test of citizenship, and we think of their dream as future history. America entered upon her career of freedom and prosperity with the declaration that "all men are born free and equal." Her prosperity has advanced in proportion as she has preserved to her citizens this birthright of freedom and equality. Aside from the claims of a common humanity, can you as consistent Americans deny equal opportunities with yourselves to an American people in their struggle to rise from ignorance and degradation? The claims of brotherhood, of the love that is due a neighbor-race, and of tardy justice have not been wholly lost on your hearts and consciences.

The plaintive melodies, running from his tired but bravely enduring soul, are heard in heaven. The threatening night of oblivion lifts. The great heart of the nation sways us with the olive branch of peace. Some among the noblest of this country have championed our cause. Within the last two decades a great interest in Indian civilization has been awakened; a beneficent government has organized a successful system of Indian education; training schools and college doors stand open to us. We clasp the warm hand of friendship everywhere. From honest hearts and sincere lips at last we hear the hearty welcome and Godspeed. We come from mountain fastnesses, from cheerless plains, from far-off low-wooded streams, seeking the "White Man's ways." Seeking your skill in industry and in art, seeking labor and honest independence, seeking the treasures of knowledge and wisdom, seeking to comprehend the spirit of your laws and the genius of your noble institutions, seeking by a new birthright to unite with yours our claim to a common country, seeking the Sovereign's crown that we may stand side by side with you in ascribing royal honor to our nation's flag. America, I love thee. "Thy people shall be my people and thy God my God."

A Ballad

(January 1897)

Afar on rolling western lands
   There cluster cone-like cabins white.
There roam the brave, the noble bands,
   A race content with each day's light.

Say not, "This nation has no heart
   In which strong passions may vibrate";
Say not, "Deep grief can play no part."
   For mute long suffering is innate.

Above the village on the plain
   Dark, threatening clouds of brooding woe
Hang like some hovering monster Pain
   With wicked eye on Peace, its foe.

Once e'er Aurora[1] had proclaimed
   Approaching charioteer of Day,
Distress, with frozen heart, controlled
   This village with unbounded sway.

What means this rushing to and fro?
   Sad, anxious faces? Grieving eyes?
Now surging tears brave hearts o'erflow
   In sobs that melt the sterner sighs.

What means the neighing steeds arrayed
 With boughs cut fresh from living green?
A dark foreboding they betrayed
 In pawings fierce and sniffings keen.

Apart from this confusion strayed
 Winona to the watering place,
A spring with mighty rocks part stayed
 Like sacred water in rude vase.

'Tis here her nag with glossy coat,
 The brisk young Wala, loves to graze.
Alert, she hears a low, clear note.
 The call Winona gave always.

Nor long was Wala innocent
 That ills now bowed Winona low.
But see, perchance by fates well sent,
 Comes tall and proud Osseolo.

By grief made bold, Winona shy,
 Half chiding, questioned her heart's king;
Yet even reproach was lost well nigh
 In mingling with the murm'ring spring.

"But stay, Osseolo," she prayed:
 "Did you not hear the angry cry
Of howling wolves that last night stayed
 Within the deep ravines near by?

"Did you not hear the moody owl
 In mournful hoots foreboding ill,
With warnings of the Fate's dark scowl
 That all of yesterday did fill?

"To-day as I my Wala called,
　I roused the sullen, sacred bird,
Which merely sight of me appalled,
　Nor ceased to shriek, in flight e'en heard.

"Osseolo, you dare not go,
　Ambitious though perchance for fame.
Our gods, 'tis clear, are with the foe,
　And wars without our gods bring shame."

In deep, sad tones, like muffled bell,
　The curfew of their love on earth
It seemed, and bitter tears did well
　Within her heart foredoomed to death.

Winona's fear was dreaded fact.
　"My chieftain father," he replied,
"Did ask me as a leader act,
　And I, a loyal son, complied.

" 'Tis thoughts of you shall make me strong.
　Though hard and cruel 'tis to part:
But hark! I bear the farewell song
　Begun, the signal for our start."

Soon Wala bore Osseolo
　Fast o'er receding hill and vale.
Like breathing arrow from the bow
　She urged the space from village wail.

For on that day of rounded moon
　There would be heard a festive strain
Of hostile bands they planned at noon
　To pounce upon and glory gain.

Here too was Judas of this tribe,
  A silent, plotting traitor base,
Whom Jealousy and Hate did bribe
  In hands of foe this plan to place.

Osseolo, though brave and bold,
  Was not prepared to meet his foe
Forearmed with his own plottings sold
  Together with the cruel bow.

Like jungle fight was battle din,
  When elephant and tiger groan.
In bloody conflict one must win,
  'Mid thundering roar and dying moan.

The hoarse uproar of fallen ones
  Was pierced by pain and death-fraught cry
Of wounded horse. The life blood runs
  In streams too strong to ever dry.

Winona is of friend bereaved!
  A crouching, wounded form passed on
To death. But Wala's heart now sheathed
  His cruel sword. The traitor's gone.

Osseolo unconscious lay
  Amid the mass in deeper sleep
Till cooling breath of waning day
  Aroused his senses Death would keep.

Although secure in bands of foe,
  Recovered life brought with it hope
To one whose needed strength did flow
  From thoughts of home with fate to cope.

But clings like poisoned dart, his lot.
   In three days hence a sacrifice
To gods of war he would be brought,
   A future favor to entice.

With gnawing hunger, burning throat,
   And eyes that ached for want of sleep,
O'er him one day and night did float
   Like lingering flights from Fiery Deep.

An eagle from his lofty nest,
   With greedy eye fast on his prey,
Were not more sure his aim to test
   Than that ill-fated, dreaded day.

As now it poises overhead
   The narrow space of two brief nights,
The hope of all escape lies dead,
   Too vivid are funereal rites.

Defeat held every plan for flight,
   Which maddened him with wild despair.
The torture did surpass his might.
   His cup o'erflowed with pain, its care.

The second night dispelled the light;
   With it the captive's reason fled,
Or seemed to flee from frenzied might.
   Osseolo seemed madness-led.

That harsh and empty laugh is his,
   That makes your heart so numb and cold,
Once proud—now reeling judgment's his
   That blinds your eyes with pain untold.

And Rumor soon the story spread.
　　Men did, with knowing faces, nod
In movement slow that plainly said,
　　"Our captive's doomed e'en by a god."

The third and final day was spent
　　In singing loud resounding praise
Of all the gods appeased who sent
　　The sacrifice they soon would raise.

That night, though heaven darkly frowned,
　　And great black clouds did veil her face,
They, reason in their vict'ry drowned,
　　Did boisterous revelry embrace.

And even faithful guards did dare
　　To join the band of braves renowned.
And thus they threw aside all care
　　Of him whom fates, they said, had bound.

But with the rushing, rising tide
　　Of thousand laughing voices rose
The captive's trampled, swollen pride,
　　And bound'ries of his heart o'erflows.

Then passed from out the prison gate
　　A figure proudly straight and tall.
Like spirit for its wand'rings late,
　　It glided past the prison wall.

The evening twilight of next day
　　Found by the spring Winona lone
To bathe with tears the sad moon's ray,
　　To add heart-groans to spring's low moan.

Was it a voice from spirit land
　That called in accents so well known?
Or was it only memory's band
　That led from worded keys the tone?

No more the moonbeams seemed to pine,
　But fell like tiny, downy flakes,
Amid the heart's deep sea of brine,
　And sweetened it e'en as the lakes.

No more is heard the spring's low moan.
　It fell like spray of tinkling bells.
Winona is no more alone,
　And now a joy all grief dispels.

New life for her begins to flow,
　Her heart grows warm and eyes grow bright.
A wilted flower revived can grow!
　Osseolo is back this night.

Iris of Life

(November 1898)

Like tiny drops of crystal rain,
  In every life the moments fall,
To wear away with silent beat,
  The shell of selfishness o'er all.

And every act, not one too small,
  That leaps from out the heart's pure glow,
Like ray of gold sends forth a light,
  While moments into seasons flow.

Athwart the dome, Eternity,
  To Iris grown resplendent, fly
Bright gleams from every noble deed
  Till colors with each other vie.

'Tis glimpses of this grand rainbow,
  Where moments with good deeds unite,
That gladden many weary hearts,
  Inspiring them to seek more Light.

A Protest Against the Abolition
of the Indian Dance[2]
(August 1902)

Almost within a stone's throw from where I sit lies the great
frozen Missouri. Like other reptiles, the low murmuring brown
river sleeps through the winter season underneath its covering
of blue sheening ice.

A man carrying a pail in one hand and an axe in the other
trudges along a narrow footpath leading to the river. Close beside the frozen stream he stands a moment motionless as if
deliberating within himself. Then, leaving his pail upon the
ground, he walks cautiously out upon the glassy surface of the
river. Fearless of the huge sleeper underneath, he swings his axe
like one accustomed to the use of his weapon. Soon with the
handle as a lever he pries up a round cake of ice. Hereupon
great moans and yawnings creak up from some unfathomable
sleep and reverberate along the quiet river bottom. The sleeping
river is disturbed by the mortal's tapping upon its crusty mantle; and—restless—turns, perchance, in its bed, gently sighing in
its long winter sleep.

The man stoops over the black hole he has made in that
pearly river shell and draws up a heavy pail. Apparently satisfied, he turns away into the narrow path by which he came.
Unconscious is he of the river's dream, which he may have disturbed; forgetful, too, of the murmuring water-songs he has not
released through his tiny tapping! The man's small power is
great enough to gain for him his small desire, a pail of winter-
buried water!

Here I should have stopped writing had not the man I saw
retracing safely his footsteps returned—in fancy—possessed
with a strange malady. Under some wild conceit regarding the

force of his pigmy hammer stroke, he labors now to awaken the sleeping old river in midwinter. Vainly he hacks at the edge of acres of ice, while Nature seems to humor the whim by allowing so much as a square inch of the crystal to be broken.

Like our brown river, the soul of the present day Indian is sleeping under the icy crust of a transitional period. A whole race of strangers throng either side of the frozen river, each one tapping the creaking ice with his own particular weapon. While the Dreamer underneath moans in disturbed visions of Hope, these people draw up each his little pail, heavy with self-justification. But where is spring? The river dreams of spring-time, when its rippling songs shall yet flood its rugged banks.

Though I love best to think the river shall in due season rush forth from its icy bondage, I am strongly drawn by an irresistible spirit to wander along the brink. A mist gathers over my sight and the celebrated art galleries of a modern city lure my notice. The geniuses of a cultured nation portray in chiseled stone figures of grace and strength in marvelous imitation of God's own subtle works. Then the inner light, burning underneath the eyelids, dispels the darkness limiting the art ground, and there within the extended walls are the bronzed figures of Indian dancers. Aye, they are greater than the marble tribe, for they are the original works of the Supreme Artist.

As I passed by a man hacking river ice, I heard him hiss—"Immodest; the Indians' nudity in the dance is shockingly immodest!"

"Why! Does he not wear a dress of paint and loin cloth?" I would have asked; but a silence sealed my lips, and I thought: "False modesty would dress the Indian, not for protection from the winter weather, but to put overalls on the soul's improper earthly garment. I wonder how much it would abash God if, for this man's distorted sense, a dress were put on all the marble figures in art museums. It were more plausible—it seems to a looker-on—to build an annex to the "Infirmary for Ill-Humored People" where folk suffering from false senses of pride and of modesty may be properly nursed.

Again a voice speaks, "This dance of the Indian is a relic of barbarism. It must be stopped!" Then hack! hack! hack!—the little man beats the crystal ice. Before me hangs a mist-tapestry. Woven in wonderful living threads is a picture of a brilliantly lighted hall with mirrored walls. Over its polished floor glide whirling couples in pretty rhythm to orchestral music. The daintiness and exquisite web-cloth of the low-necked, sleeveless evening gowns must be so from the imperative need to distract the mind from the steel frames in which fair bodies are painfully corseted. It may be gauze-covered barbarism, for history does tell of the barbaric Teutons and Anglo-Saxons. It may be a martyrdom to some ancient superstition which centuries of civilization and Christianization have not wholly eradicated from the yellow-haired and blue-eyed races.

I do not know what special step might be considered most barbaric. In truth, I would not like to say any graceful movement of the human figure in rhythm to music was ever barbaric. Unless the little man intends to put an end to dances the world over, I fail to see the necessity of checking the Indian dance. If learned scientists advise an occasional relaxation of work or daily routine with such ardor that even the inmates of insane asylums are allowed to dance their dances, then the same logic should hold good elsewhere. The law, at least, should not be partial. If it is right for the insane and idiot to dance, the Indian (who is classed with them) should have the same privilege. The old illiterate Indians, with a past irrevocably dead and no future, have but a few sunny hours between them and the grave.

And this last amusement, their dance, surely is not begrudged them. The young Indian who has been taught to read English has his choice of amusements, and need not attend the old-time one. He might spend a profitable winter evening in a library, if such a provision had not been misplaced among the "castles in Spain." Unfortunately for him, there is not even a bookstore where he might buy his reading matter; and because of the inconvenient place from which I get my writing supply, I myself have at times seriously contemplated writing upon the butcher's brown wrapping-paper. But time and opportunity are within the reach of the Indian youth. With these he may yet make some "vigorous self-recovery" against odd circumstances.

It is not so with the old Indians. The fathers and mothers of our tribe have not such weapons against their adversity. They are old and (I have heard them say of themselves) worthless; but what American would shuffle off an old parent as he would an old garment from the body?

At this moment I turn abruptly away from the voices along the river brink, wishing the river-hackers might first conspire with nature. Here a pony is ready, and soon a gallop over the level lands shall restore to me the sweet sense that God has allotted a place in his vast universe for each of his creatures, both great and small—just as they are.

The Menace of Peyote

(ca. 1916)

Peyote is a certain cactus that grows in the Southwest. Its dried crown is eaten in the crude. Analysis of peyote by renowned scientists and medical authorities shows it to be a powerful narcotic, dangerous and habit-forming. Peyote victims of all ages from the adult to the babe in arms are themselves the sad verification of this analysis.

In the early days of the Montezumas, peyote was classed as an intoxicant and forbidden by law. At that time the railroads were unbuilt and easy transportation from the South to North, East and West was impossible. Only the Indians of northern Mexico used peyote in an annual dance; in which both men and women took part. The Christian church, through its manual of 1760, forbade peyote eating. To-day unscrupulous men are shipping peyote into the United States. "It is a large financial proposition. The peyote is raised and imported for a quarter to one cent each and retails for five cents." (R. D. Hall, of the Commission of Internal Affairs, Y.M.C.A.)

Peyote eating has spread to tribes in Arizona and Oklahoma. It is now used among the tribes between the Rio Grande and the Pacific, up to the Dakotas and even to Wisconsin and Utah, Sioux, Cheyenne, Arapahoe, Osage, Kiowa, Comanche, Omaha, Kickapoo, Winnebago, Utes of the Uncompahgre, Whiteriver, and Uintah tribes. Colorado mothers have been informed that the Colorado boys on the Texas border are using peyote.

"Dry whisky" is the common name for peyote. It is a substitute for liquor and drugs. It is the twin brother of alcoholic beverages and first cousin to habit forming drugs. The National prohibition amendment and Drug Acts of our land will have failed of their purpose unless peyote is restricted by law.

Now, while peyote bills are pending in Congress, is the time for activity. It has been the experience in the past that such bills die in committee. Congress has been misinformed. Peyote has been represented as a sacrament in an Indian religion. "I baptize thee in the name of the Father and Son and Peyote," is the baptismal formula borrowed from the ritual of the Christian church. Twelve feathers dangling from a long staff represent the twelve apostles. This twelve apostles idea is borrowed from the white man's Bible. It is not Indian. Rituals of the church have been borrowed as a cloak to hide under, and to evade the law of morals and decency. Moreover religion is the adoration of the Maker with a rational mind. No one in the state of drunkenness, by whatsoever cause, can be in his rational mind; and he cannot practice religion.

At a recent meeting in Philadelphia, the "City of Brotherly Love," Rev. Dr. Samuel Elliott asked: "But how, if the peyote bean is used as a sacrament, can we succeed before the congressional committee when a bill for prohibiting its use is being considered? Those who promulgate the cult will deny the right of Congress to interfere with religious freedom." Reply was made by William Alexander Brown, vice president of the Indian Rights Association: "If religious bodies used vinous wines in the sacrament to such an extent that the Lord's Supper became an orgy, the Supreme Court could not interfere with their religious rights, but in the transgression of morals and decency the plea of religious liberty cannot prevail."

Men, women and children on Indian reservations attend weekly meetings every Saturday night to eat peyote. It takes all day Sunday to recover somewhat from the drunk. Too often in their midnight debaucheries there is a total abandonment of virtue.

Children of school age are taken out of school in order that they may eat peyote. They are not only permitted but encouraged and sometimes forced to eat it. The result is that these children, being more or less under the pernicious effects of the drug, are not in a responsive condition to justify the

Government's paying salaries to teachers to teach them. Babes in arms are given peyote tea. This indiscriminate use of a powerful narcotic has increased infant mortality. These are crimes committed through ignorance and drunkenness. Dare we uphold these conditions by our own indifference to the moral and physical degeneracy in our midst?

The Senate Committee, on January 30, 1918, reached that particular part of the annual Indian Appropriation bill allowing $150,000 for suppression of the liquor traffic among Indians. It was at this point that I was granted the privilege of addressing the honorable Senators and beseeching them to include the suppression of peyote, together with its twin brother, alcoholic beverage.

Congress is appropriating $150,000 to suppress drunkenness among Indians, that in sobriety the Indians may receive the benefits from the Government schools for which this year the entire appropriation is over $11,000,000. Certainly no amount of money appropriated from the national treasury, or the Indians' own funds held in trust by the Government, would educate or civilize unless the Indian is in his rational mind to meet his part of the obligation. The human system, disabled with dope is no receptacle for the jewels of education and civilization. The Indian is no exception.

The amendment to the Indian bill to include suppression of peyote is subject to a point of order. But what is the letter of the law, when the spirit is lacking?

For the alarming menace of peyote there must be found a remedy and soon. If the cure for snake bite is to kill the snake, then the cure for peyote is to kill its unrestricted distribution to the American nation.

Americanize the First American[3]

(1921)

During two summer moons I followed Indian trails over an undulating prairie. The blue canopy of sky came down and touched the earth with a circular horizon. Within such an enclosure of infinite space, virgin soil appeared like a heaving brown sea, slightly tinged with green—a profoundly silent sea. Far out upon its eternal waves now and then came into sight a lone houseboat of crude logs. A captain on one of these strange crafts wirelessed to me an "S.O.S." My inquiry brought the answer: "Many of these houseboats are set adrift with a funeral pyre for a burial at sea."

In low log huts, adrift upon their reservation containing approximately 3000 square miles, are the souls of 7500 Sioux. So widely scattered are they that time and perseverance were required to make even a limited round of visits in the burning sun and parching wind of midsummer.

Listening one day to a sad story of the influenza epidemic among these Indians two years ago, I closed my eyes and tried to imagine this great wild area held in the frigid embrace of winter. I tried to visualize two Government physicians going forth in a Dakota blizzard to visit the sick and dying Sioux. Had they divided the territory evenly between them, each would have had to traverse 2500 square miles to attend to 3750 Indian people. Could they have traveled like whirlwinds to respond to the cries for help, their scant supply of medicines would have been exhausted far too soon. It would have been a physical impossibility for these two wise men to vie with the wind, so they did not. They received their salary as quickly for treating one Indian as if they had cared for a thousand.

Therefore, the small medical supply was saved and the Indians died unattended.

How bitter is the cold of this frozen landscape where the fires of human compassion is unkindled! It is a tragedy to the American Indian and the fair name of America that the good intentions of a benevolent Government are turned into channels of inefficiency and criminal neglect. Nevertheless, the American Indian is our fellow-man. The time is here when for our own soul's good we must acknowledge him. In the defense of democracy his utter self-sacrifice was unequaled by any other class of Americans. What now does democracy mean to him and his children?

Many Indian children are orphans through the inevitable havoc of war and influenza epidemic. Poor little Indian orphans! Who in this world will love them as did their own fathers and mothers? Indians love their children dearly. Never in all history was there an Indian mother who left her darling in a basket upon a doorstep. Indians do not believe in corporal punishment. They are keenly aware that children are spirits from another realm, come for a brief sojourn on earth. When and where they found this great truth is wrapped in as much mystery as the origin of their race, which ever puzzles thinking men and women of today. If a correction is necessary, they speak quietly and tenderly to the intelligent soul of the child. Appreciation of the spiritual reality of the child places the Indian abreast with the most advanced thought of the age—our age, in which one of the notable signs of progress is the co-ordination of humanitarian and educational organizations for child welfare. It is a wonderful work to inculcate in the world's children today the truths accrued from the ages, that in the near future, when they are grown-up men and women, the world shall reap an ideal harvest. Children are to play, on the world stage, their rôle in solving the riddle of human redemption.

Speaking of the constructive and widespread activities of the Junior Red Cross, Arthur William Dunn, specialist in civic education, said: "The aim is to cultivate not only a broad human sympathy, but also an Americanism with a world perspective."

Among other things, a school of correspondence is started between the children of America, Europe and Asia. Loving the wee folks as I do and concerned for the salvation of my race, I am watching eagerly for the appearance of the Indian child in the world drama.

Where are those bright-eyed, black-haired urchins of the out-of-doors? Where are those children whose fathers won so much acclaim for bravery in the World War now closed?

They are on Indian reservations—small remnants of land not shown on our maps. They are in America, but their environment is radically different from that surrounding other American children. A prolonged wardship, never intended to be permanent, but assumed by our Government as an emergency measure, has had its blighting effect upon the Indian race. Painful discrepancies in the meaning of American freedom to the Indian [have resulted].

These differences prevail not only on one, but on every Indian reservation. Suffice it to say that by a system of solitary isolation from the world the Indians are virtually prisoners of war in America. Treaties with our Government made in good faith by our ancestors are still unfulfilled, while the Indians have never broken a single promise they pledged to the American people. American citizenship is withheld from some three-fourths of the Indians of the United States. On their reservations they are held subservient to political appointees upon whom our American Congress confers discretionary powers. These are unlovely facts, but they are history. Living conditions on the reservations are growing worse. In the fast approach of winter I dread to think of the want and misery the Sioux will suffer on the Pine Ridge Reservation.

Womanhood of America, to you I appeal in behalf of the Red Man and his children. Heed the lonely mariner's signal of distress. Give him those educational advantages pressed with so much enthusiasm upon the foreigner. Revoke the tyrannical powers of Government superintendents over a voiceless people and extend American opportunities to the first American—the Red Man.

Bureaucracy Versus Democracy
(1921)

We have a bureaucracy wheel with a $14,000,000 hub and a rim of autocratic discretionary power. Between the two are the segments suppressing the energies of the Indian people. About 90 years ago the American Congress created the Bureau of Indian Affairs as a temporary measure and it was not intended for a permanent institution. Steadily, through 90 years, the bureau has enlarged itself regardless of the diminishing Indian population, "educated and civilized" all this time.

Official power, official business and official numbers have been augmented, impinging upon the liberty-loving Indians of America a wardship growing more deadly year by year.

Whenever a plea for our human rights is made, this despotic-grown bureaucracy issues contrary arguments through its huge machinery for reasons best known to itself. It silences our inquiring friends by picturing to them the Indians' utter lack of business training and how easily they would fall victims to the wiles of unscrupulous white men were bureau supervision removed from all Indians.

I would suggest that Congress enact more stringent laws to restrain the unscrupulous white men. It is a fallacy in a democratic government to defranchise a law-abiding race that the lawless may enjoy the privileges of citizenship. Further would I suggest that this bureau be relieved of its supervising an orderly people and assigned to the task of restraining the unscrupulous citizens of whatever color who are menacing the liberty and property of the Indians. It is true the Indians lack business training and experience. Therefore, I would suggest business schools for the Indians, together with a voice in the administration of their own affairs, that they may have the opportunity to overcome their ignorance and strengthen their weakness.

We insist upon our recognition by America as really normal and quite worth-while human beings.

We want American citizenship for every Indian born within the territorial limits of the United States.

We want a democracy wheel whose hub shall be an organization of progressive Indian citizens and whose rim shall be the Constitution of your American Government—a wheel whose segments shall become alive with growing community interests and thrift activities of the Indians themselves. Indians require first-hand experience as others do to develop their latent powers. They proved their loyalty to country by their unequaled volunteer service in your army in the World War now closed.

You have enfranchised the black race, and are now actively waging a campaign of Americanization among the foreign-born. Why discriminate against the noble aborigines of America—they who have no other father-motherland? The gospel of humanitarianism, like charity, must begin at home, among home people, and from thence spread out into all the world.

Americanize the first Americans. Give them freedom to do their own thinking; to exercise their judgment; to hold open forums for the expression of their thought, and finally permit them to manage their own personal business. Let no one deprive the American Indians of life, liberty or property without due process of law.

A Dakota Ode to Washington[4]
(1922)

The Mystic Circle

Upon the prairie grass sat aged men and women, in mystic circle, their bronzed faces upturned to the stars. Through many winters their once raven hair was whitened till in the uncertain twilight on the plains it appeared luminous about their heads. White blossoming manhood, white flowering womanhood, these seven Dakotah wicareana and winocrana held secret conclave under the night sky.

Keepers of the sacred eagle mysteries, priest and priestess of the Seven Council Fires of their people, they are sages of that other day when Indian camps vied with huge cloud shadows drifting on the playground of the prairie. To-night they have chosen from out their seven a member of the smallest fire, summoned before them a Yankton Dakotah of the young generation. The spokesman, a veritable grandfather of the federated tribes, addressed her saying: "To-morrow is the day of days. Loyal Americans will gather before a great stone shrine at the Nation's capital. South Dakotans beckon to us, the Dakotah to join them. We accept the gracious invitation of our pale-face brothers. This is brotherhood."

As he momentarily paused, his quiet voice floated out into the eternal spaces among the stars, seemed to echo and reecho against the stillness of the night in the concave sky, "This is brotherhood!" The voice continued, "You are called as our messenger, our interpreter. Are you willing to serve?" Without hesitation the answer came, "I am." The other members of the circle, hitherto silent, responded in approval, "Be it so." "Hecetu." The spokesman said, "You have answered well. Service is the highest privilege."

Together they taught her what to say, placed an eagle plume in her hand. "With this sacred quill write word for word what we have told you here tonight," they commanded. "At dawn start upon the journey to the great stone shrine with our message." In final parting bade her, "Upon the way, keep your own heart warm with love and strong with truth. Lift up your eyes for vision."

Upon the Way

Straight as an arrow flies from a strong bow, sped the Dakotah runner from the hallow'd circle of the starlit prairie. At break of day hastened with the message, speeding faster, ever faster. Upon the way were many relays, from footsore pony to stagecoach plunging over rough country roads, from coach to the iron horse gliding rapidly upon a steel track. The miraculous journey to the Nation's Capital is made in safety. All faithful to her trust, the messenger stands before the monumental shrine of Washington.

The Message

"The day of days is at hand. It is now." These the words from the Seven Council Fires of the Dakotah. "We sing the name of our first President. We call him Washington—Ohitika—undaunted leader of nations crying in the dark. He brought them light from the sky, taught them principles of peace and brotherhood; taught the lisping multitudes to say 'We, the people,' counseled them 'to observe good faith and justice toward all nations.'

"The Dakotah people carol with lusty throats the memorable deeds of Washington. He scanned with eagle eye the hope of a united people and happy; beheld the vision of democratic government. He rose on powerful eagle wings, with unswerving purpose attained to lofty virtues of public service.

"A victory song we sing to the memory of Washington, who

disdained kingship upon a lower realm and preferred to be a servant of the people, who by his life demonstrated only 'Right makes might.' Then over all his glorious achievements upheld our sacred emblem, the eagle, pointing to its meaning in all his noble acts.

"We venerate the memory of our great pale-face brother, Washington, the chiefest among guardians of spiritual fires— liberty and unity. Washington, thrice worthy of the decoration of the eagle plume, for he left the impress of its meaning upon the minds and hearts of all Americans.

"This is our glad song to-day. The eagle represents the conscious spirit of man, soaring into the silent upper air for meditation and spiritual communion, soaring away from the transitory turmoils of the day, into the heights, there gaining wider vision, added strength, and wisdom, there finding the se-cret of joyous being, unburdened from the pettiness of make-beliefs.

"Comrades of the earth, the hope of our humanity lies in the preservation of high ideals, in holding fast to these symbols and precepts bequeathed us through all ages and races of men till we have learned their innermost lesson. It is well that the sa-cred eagle is carved upon America's gold, lest we forget in the heat of world commerce our brotherhood upon earth. It is well that the eagle is engraved upon the buttons and insignia of our brave men, lest we forget in the wild flurry of swift locomotion and radio communication to perfect our relationships, man to man, nation to nation, with justice and mercy.

"Long live the memory of Washington, whose praises we sing this day of days!

"Long live the eagle principles he inculcated in the hearts of the people!

"Then shall come many days of peace, prosperity, and hap-piness!"

California Indian Trails and Prayer Trees[5]
(1922)

Chapter I

Very gladly accepting an invitation extended me by our Indian people of California to visit them this summer, I heard of this ancient practice among them which I tell.

When the big trees of California were saplings, the Indian people here then were crooning soft lullabies to their black-eyed babes. The California Indian mother, ambitious for her darling's future welfare, sought out a young tree, usually a pine tree thriving upon a bare boulder. Gently bending its tender top closely to her, she grafted a very tiny, sacred token of her baby in its topmost shoot. Then, releasing the baby tree, she murmured: "In memory of my beloved child, bear this token up as you reach upward to the stars. I want my child to grow upright and strong along with you through all the seasons."

Perchance some mothers in that early day entrusted the redwood saplings also with this prayer for strength and protection. By the ancient ceremony—the sacred token imbedded in the fiber of the tree, together with the vocalized desire—the Indian prayer became a living part of the tree.

In the forests of pines and big trees stand countless prayer trees, silently bearing the sacred token placed in their keeping by Indian mothers.

A few weeks ago a party of tourists stood under some big trees and exclaimed about their height, their circumference and their reputed age. I ventured the remark: "If only we could understand the language of these big trees we might learn interesting things of the past, the experiences of ancient people now gone away to the unknown."

A kind-faced gentleman with iron-grey hair pleased me greatly with his quick reply: "We are learning. They say, 'Take off your hats.' We obey."

It was then I longed to tell some of the things the big trees in their seeming silence were fairly shouting to me, an Indian woman, but words are stubborn things. They failed to come. The conversation naturally turned into new channels while I stood mute among them. All the while the happy party bubbled over with sparkling words at the feet of the big trees. I gazed at their topmost branches. I listened for the Indian prayers and was thrilled with the feeling that I heard them. It is needless for me to say that these trees are held sacred by our Indian people to this day.

Catastrophe it was when both the big trees and the ancient race of red men fell under the ax of a nineteenth-century invasion. Could their every wound find tongue I am sure not only pebbles but mountains of stone would rise up in protest. No wonder that Mother Earth shook with convulsions upon such a dire calamity befalling her children—the big prayer trees and their little brothers, the Indians.

It is an Indian belief that bad thoughts and deeds of man bring disastrous storms and earthquakes. Before we pass upon this as a superstition of untutored minds, let us recall the learned Thoreau's statement that the greatest of all arts is to affect the quality of the day by our own acts. These ideas are akin, like peas in a pod. Truths are universal. Our discernments grow with keener vision. Truths are ever present for us to see, if we will, whether our eyes are blue, gray, or black.

After those cruel and stormy days we have again a comparative quiet. New laws have sprung up in the tracks of the destroyers to protect, at least, our big trees. When will our hearing become sensitive enough to catch the Indian mother's prayer wafted broadcast by the ancient trees of our American forests?

It might be well for Americans who go to Egypt to see the

sphinx to remember that in America we have a living sphinx in the red man. Our American Indians are descendants from one of the oldest races on the face of the earth. The Indian is older than the sphinx. Through untold centuries the Indian people brought upon their trails many treasures. Notable among them is a little grass from which they developed corn. The red man's gift to civilized man is what the civilized world calls, "Indian corn."

There is a story retold by Dr. Gilmore of North Dakota of an Indian woman gathering corn in her small field. When she started to go, she heard a voice cry out to her, "Oh, do not leave me behind. Take me home with you!" Puzzled to know who was talking to her, she looked about. The voice sounded like a child's. Seeing no one, she started away. Again came the piteous cry, "Please don't leave me behind. Take me with you." The sound seemed to come from among the cornstalks. So she began her search and there found a little nubbin. She picked it up and carried it with the other arm. There were no more cries heard in the harvest field. Indians are appreciative of food given them by Mother Earth and were always careful not to be wasteful.

Every step I take on old Indian trails I feel I am treading on ground made sacred by those who have preceded me. Loving my race as I do, it is difficult to understand why they fared so badly under the foremost democratic government of the world. I used to wonder if it could be the pigment of the skin that was our offense. Yet, in nature, flowers of every hue abound. Sin could not be in color. When I began perusing the papers I was amazed at the crimes committed in large cities, brother against brother. Scarce could I believe the palefaces were killing one another, too. From this I reasoned it was not the Indian's dark skin that had brought on his unspeakable sorrows at the hands of heartless men, money crazed.

According to what might be called Indian psychology, the recent World War, now closed, was a monumental attempt at suicide by the Caucasian race. Our Indian philosophy forbids suicide. It grieved me that in the past my people were ruthlessly slaughtered in the white man's quest for gold. It grieved me no less that the white man's greed for gold, for world power, now turned death dealing bombs and gases upon himself. So much did I admire the white man's artistic talents and mechanical genius it was sad, indeed, to see his powers misused for self-destruction.

To an Indian life is a profound mystery. It is too sacred for us to extinguish it wantonly in ourselves or in others.

Again I reiterate, truths and laws of life are universal. They may be seen by those who have eyes to see. The American Indian is far from being blind.

The very next time you spend your vacation among the redwoods or climb old Indian trails in the Yosemite Valley, take your radio set and "listen in" on the life of the American Indian, past and present. "Live and let live."

Lost Treaties of the California Indians

(1922)

Chapter II

Imagine the pride of those fond California Indian mothers whose prayers for their babes were placed in the redwood forests, when their children did grow up straight and strong through all the seasons. This was the fulfillment of their hearts' desire. It was a proud day, indeed, when a California Indian mother's son, grown tall, walked among his people carrying a quiver made of a bear-cub skin.

This was the great badge of bravery and prowess among the California Indians in those days of yore. Bear-cub skins were costly. It was the fearless man with a trained eye and daring heart who, together with another hunter, sought out a grizzly bear and challenged her to a duel without guns for her cubs. It was a dangerous feat. While the infuriated grizzly stood upon her haunches, angrily parrying from her face the threatening thrusts of her bold antagonist, the second man seized the cubs and made away with them.

Then followed a duel to the death between the grizzly bear and the Indian. Occasionally, the Indian lost the fight and paid for the adventure with his life. Bear-cub skin quivers were, therefore, a badge of a daring and successful fighter. No wonder that the mother's breast filled with pride at sight of her grown-up son walking among the multitude carrying a quiver made of the grizzly bear-cub skin.

Thoroughly trained in self-control, unerring aim, and daunt-less daring, dueling with the grizzlies, the California Indians were not at all disposed to use their powers warring against human beings. They were a friendly people, preferring to live in peace with their fellow beings whenever possible. Every autumn they had their white deer-skin dance, when tribal difficulties were settled by arbitration. The dance was a celebration of their amicable disposal of old grievances.

These and other practices among them demonstrated their great spiritual poise. By these celebrations they varied the routine of daily fishing, hunting, drying of fruits, and gathering into stores quantities of acorns. They were happy people, well fed by nature's lavish supplies spread throughout the State now known as California.

Then one day came white men with hearts inflamed by greed. Suddenly the happy Indian people were threatened with extermination. It was more than seventy years ago when United States soldiers came as messengers to California Indian villages.

These men, in uniforms and brass buttons, brought a most cordial and pressing invitation to the Indian people, asking them to meet the Federal Commission sent from Washington, D.C., to treat with them for their wonderlands.

At the time and place named 400 California Indian chiefs and head men assembled. They were well received and generously feasted. The Indian guests were entertained by the Federal Commission; long were the discussions of the treaties they had drawn up, and now offered for the Indians' signatures. For the promise of moneys, subsistence, clothing, supplies and educational advantages, vast territories were ceded to the government; to the California Indians and their descendents 7,500,000 acres of land with clearly described boundaries were reserved "for ever and ever." Four hundred chiefs and head men representing some 210,000 California Indian people signed with thumb marks and cross the eighteen treaties of 1851 and 1852.

This was at the time of the gold rush in California, which brought hither fortune hunters from every clime. The Indians who signed the treaties particularly asked the Federal Commission how their rights were to be respected by the eager seekers of land and gold. They were presented with copies of the treaties, and told to show these government papers to any white man trespassing upon their lands; that the white men seeing these documents would leave them in peace. The wise men erred on their assumption that bits of paper would be sufficient to safeguard the Indians' rights from invasion. The Federal Commission returned with the treaties to the nation's seat of government. They vanished from the life of the California Indians like the passing of a momentary mirage.

Hordes of lawless gold seekers poured into the undeveloped country. Overnight, like mushrooms, thousands of men carrying guns and picks invaded Indian villages. An old chief, one of the signers of the treaty, tried to protect his people according to the instruction of the Federal Commission. With the great papers in his hand he ran out to meet the raiding party of white men who marched into his village, and offered his precious copy of the newly signed treaties to the leader of the gang. With an oath more vicious than the grizzly bear's growl the white man snatched the papers from the chieftain's hand, glanced at them, then struck a match to them. He hurled the burning scraps of paper against an Indian house, from which started a fire that burned the whole village.

Atrocities of the paleface against the California Indian increased year after year. Lest the Indian people in their extremity might seek to defend their homes and children with arms, as it seemed, a law was passed forbidding the sale of guns or ammunition to any Indian. Betrayed, defenseless, and with their proud hearts breaking, the California Indian became a people "without a country."

The gold mania made white men mad till they forgot their ancestors had fled to America as a refuge from European oppressions and butcheries. In the delirium of the gold fever, white men forgot the human rights of the California Indians. Under the pretext of protecting the white men's interests, they forgot to extend the same American protection to the first Californians. By order of an executive session the United States Senate filed in its archives, to be kept secret fifty years, the California Indian treaties of 1851 and 1852, which a Federal

Commission had labored to secure. Thereafter they were called the "Lost Treaties." The signers of those treaties, with their people, were driven from their ancestral homes into holes in rocks of the mountains for shelter. The anguish of my Indian people neither pen nor tongue can tell.

The California Indians of Today

(1922)

Chapter III

The California Indians dwindled from 210,000 to 20,000 during the siege of seventy cruel winters, repeated evictions and the spread of the white man's diseases among them. They were unable to get away far enough to escape deadly epidemics.

In those dark days of terror and desolation there occasionally appeared splendid men and women of the white people who individually befriended my people. Their compassion shines out brightly against that long night of sorrows. All praise be theirs.

A few years ago the fifty years' secrecy of the "Lost Treaties" expired. Those governmental papers have been found. Will the present day citizen strike a match to them as did the lawless ruffian of the raiding party? Let it not be so. Our national honor is at stake. Time is growing short in which we may redeem the fair name of our government. The people are the government. The Indians of California are greatly diminished in numbers, year after year dying broken hearted.

Today a small remnant of a noble race are bravely struggling for existence. They search the country far and wide for seasonal work, from which they earn a scant living. Those who are crippled, blind, or sick cannot work. They are starving. They die untimely deaths for lack of proper medical care. Their sorrowing relatives are unable to give them adequate relief.

To whom shall the Indians go for succor if not to our beloved America? By a test case in 1917 the State Supreme

Court's decision established the citizenship of the California Indians.

Educational advantages of the public schools will equip them to earn a more comfortable living. Liberal education in American schools will be vital to their future success and happiness as American citizens.

"Could the California Indians keep up with American people if given a chance?" someone asked me. It is my belief they can, if given educational opportunities, and if at all disposed to keep up with the "Joneses." Masses of men speak through the telephone, but it was a genius who first invented it. The educated Indians may install modern conveniences in their homes if they wish to spend their earnings in that way. It will not be difficult for them to equal the average American, under like environment.

During my visit to Lake county a few days ago, I found a hundred or more of my people camped under a grove of trees near a very large bean field.

Indian parents, with their boys and girls and gray-haired grandfathers and grandmothers worked together picking beans.

They told me others were working in hop fields and in fruit-gathering. The Indian people are trying to make the most of the harvest season. After the winter sets in, remunerative occupation will be very scarce. They will return to their humble little dwellings on barren rancherias, there to wait till opening spring offers work again.

Their wages are low and only the utmost economy saves enough money to take them through the winter. Some less successful suffer for food and warm clothing before springtime returns.

Indian children sometimes are kept out of schools for the lack of shoes and suitable clothing requisite for their admittance.

It goes without saying that a people too poor to buy sufficient food or clothing cannot pay for medical aid for their sick.

I hope I have not unduly worried county officials with this long enumeration of the needs of our Indian people to make life more livable for them. It certainly will require money to extend public welfare work to the Indians of California. I would suggest that all Californians support the favorable passage of the jurisdiction bill now pending in Congress, whereby the claims of the California Indians against the federal government may be adjudicated at an early date.

Then there will be no need to send destitute Indians to the almshouses, nor will there be need to make them objects of charity when equitable settlement is made with our California Indians for lands taken from them without remuneration or conquest.

Before we may bestow charity we must first be just.

Heart to Heart Talk

(1922)

My California Kinsmen, I greet you in the words of a famous Kiowa Indian chief: "My heart is filled with joy when I see you as the brooks fill with water when the snow melts in the spring." Since my visit with you about two years ago, I see you often in memory. I recall vividly the earnest meetings we held and the words that were spoken then. Do you, too, remember some of them?

We talked about your Auxiliaries—how they made it possible for you to help one another in your various localities. From this far off distance I hear of your victories along the way, and I rejoice with you. The public school opportunity for our dear children at Upper Lake won by the untiring efforts of Mr. Ethan Anderson and those friends who helped him; and also the victory in a school matter won by Mr. Stephen Knight in Ukiah. These are things important for our future success and happiness as well as the immediate help they bring. Where are our Indian poets and song-makers? They should have made a new song for each of these achievements, naming the men of the Indian Board of Co-operation who together won them. They should have given the words and melody to the people, so that our people might learn to sing them. This is the way our ancestors used to do. It's a good thing to do. While the poets and singers furnish the music, let the rest of us dance!

We are glad the sun shines for us. This earth would be a dreary place were it not for the sunlight and warmth which makes all things live and grow. Every day that you see the sun rise in the sky, you should be encouraged in your work, no matter what obstacles and hindrances appear to be. We have minds, hearts and hands to serve us, to aid us in getting some kind of education, a livelihood, and also enable us to offer a helping hand to one another. What if a mountain stood in your path and it wouldn't move out of your way? Certainly you can go around it, or if thought advisable, tunnel through it with diligent persistent labor.

Indians are sociable people and their devotion to their families and even distant relatives is most remarkable. I was born on the Dakota Plains, and had the privilege of living in the great out-of-doors: and of knowing that an Indian tribe is really a big family circle. Either by marriage, by blood, or by adoption every member of the tribe bore some relationship to the rest. It was considered an honor for a hunter who brought home game to divide it with his neighbors. Especially true was this in times when there was scarcity of food, in times of famine. No real man cared to save himself alone and see the rest of the folks die.

This is a beautiful spirit. It is the very essence of the Sermon on the Mount of which our white brothers talk in their modern churches. Our Indian ancestors cultivated this wonderful spirit when they worshipped in the living temples, those ancient forests Nature took so many centuries to build, and which unfortunately our white brothers destroyed. Later the white man built little tiny houses in which to worship the Great Spirit, and from which to preach brotherly love. The Indian on-looker, still unforgetful of the awe-inspiring majesty of the ancient forests that are no more, is compelled to say in his own tongue, when he refers to present day churches, "little boxes" of God.

We who live today are descendents of an ancient and noble race. We inherit their altruistic spirit and a love for Nature. These are priceless. Add to them what you may of the Twentieth Century advantages in its wide variety of work, and let us preserve the good name of our people.

We need to work together, also, in organizations. This is imperative. You have your Auxiliaries, and already have gained beneficial recognition for our people of California. Keep on with the good work. You are blazing a trail for other Indians to follow. You are not only helping yourselves like real men but also setting an example to others.

Perhaps you have read the joint report of the pitiful conditions of our Oklahoma Indians. I visited them last fall and some other time I may tell you more about it. Just now I want to stress one point—and that is the urgent need of all Indians to organize for their own self-improvement and property protection. Within the last year the Oklahoma Indians have organized an Indian Society. At their first annual convention soon to be held in Tulsa, Oklahoma, I shall tell them of your wonderful Auxiliaries, for I have been honored with an invitation to attend. I know they will be encouraged to learn of your heroic efforts and the many satisfying results which you have won through your organization. I hope you will know each other as Indian organizations.

It is clear to us all that Indians must think and act together. They must insist upon having a voice and a part in all that concerns our welfare in this, our country. We must try to learn new things by keen observation. We all have eyes, and pretty good memories, too. Indians must organize and work together in one powerful unit. Let us help to bear one another's burden in the best way we can. Remember, neither riches nor poverty is sufficient excuse for any man or woman, boy or girl to stop trying to do his or her level best every day of life. Do be loyal to your auxiliary work.

Explanatory Notes

II.

AMERICAN INDIAN STORIES

1. *proud owner of my first diploma:* To the extent that we want to read this story as semiautobiographical, the diploma she refers to here is from White's Manual Institute and the upcoming college career takes place at Earlham College, both in Indiana.
2. *Eastern Indian School:* In Zitkala-Ša's own life she taught at the Carlisle Indian Industrial School in Pennsylvania.
3. *Taku Iyotan Wasaka:* Zitkala-Ša defines this as an "absolute Power" in a footnote to the original text.
4. *The Great Spirit:* The first version of this essay was titled "Why I Am a Pagan" and appeared in the *Atlantic Monthly* in December 1902. "Pagan" was one of Zitkala-Ša's publications that drew a lot of attention, especially from Carlisle's Richard Pratt, who declared her "worse than a pagan." Except for the ending and the title the essays are exactly the same. See Note 7, below, for the original ending.
5. *Stone-Boy:* A popular hero in Sioux stories, he possessed supernatural powers and the ability to transform from stone to human.
6. *"Christian" pugilist:* A reference to the author of an unsigned column that appeared in *The Word Carrier* on February-March 1901, which proclaimed Zitkala-Ša's "The Soft-Hearted Sioux" to be "morally bad," though "written in an easy, engaging style" with a "certain dramatic power."
7. *sweet breathing of flowers:* This was the original penultimate sentence for Zitkala-Ša's version of this essay as "Why I Am a Pagan." The last sentence, which read, "If this is Paganism, then

at present, at least, I am a Pagan," was excised from "The Great Spirit," and the final paragraph we have here was added.

8. *Chief Powhatan:* Powhatan, whose real name was Wahunson-acock, united the tribes to form the Powhatan Confederacy and mediated much early contact with British colonists, especially Captain John Smith. Chief Powhatan lived from 1547 to 1618 and, famously, was the father of Pocahontas. The Pow-hatans had about 12,000 people who lived in a 9,000-square-mile area. See "The Coronation of Chief Powhatan Retold," page 196.

III.

SELECTIONS FROM *AMERICAN* *INDIAN MAGAZINE*

1. *Community Center:* At the Uintah and Ouray Reservation at Fort Duchesne, Utah. Zitkala-Ša's was the first of what the SAI hoped would be a widespread practice among Indian reserva-tions, bringing economic relief as well as social uplift.

2. *The Red Man's America:* A parody on "My Country 'Tis of Thee." In the third stanza, "Lane's Bill" refers to legislation to abolish the Indian Bureau, introduced by Oregon senator Harry Lane, and "Gandy's Bill" refers to legislation introduced by South Dakota representative H. L. Gandy in 1916 to prohibit peyote use.

3. *Chief Ouray:* A famous chief among the Utes. He frequently trav-eled, accompanied by Chipeta, to broker treaties with the U.S. government, securing the reservation land in Utah. Ouray died in 1880; Chipeta lived on in Utah at the Ouray reservation (named after her husband) until 1924.

4. *A Sioux Woman's Love for Her Grandchild:* At the end of this poem Zitkala-Ša notes. "This incident occurred upon the coming of Custer's army, preliminary to the battle known erroneously in history as "Custer's Massacre."

5. *Indian Gifts to Civilized Man:* This article was also published in the *Indian Sentinel,* July 1918, and in *Tomahawk,* July 17, 1919.

6. *The Peace Conference Sitting at Paris:* the Versailles Treaty and

League of Nations were the outcomes of this 1919 conference, which ended the First World War. The United States under Woodrow Wilson's administration had entered the war on the Allied side in April 1917; Germany and the Central Powers surrendered in November 1918.

7. *Letter to the Chiefs and Headmen of the Tribes:* Zitkala-Ša includes the following footnote to this open letter: "Dear Reader into whose hands this letter has fallen, will you do a kind act by reading and explaining it to an Indian who cannot read or speak English?—Editor."

8. *taken the liberty to write you:* This open letter is then signed "Yours for the Indian Cause," as Zitkala-Ša signed all of her letters concerning political advocacy work.

9. *treaty of 1868:* A reference to the Treaty of Laramie, which at one point secured lands known as the Great Sioux Reservation and provided legal recourses to provide Native control over the land.

10. *Angel DeCora Dietz:* The illustrator of *Old Indian Legends.* Like Zitkala-Ša, she taught briefly at the Carlisle school and illustrated other books of the time—notably, Charles Eastman's *Indian Boyhood*—as well as books of her own short stories.

IV.

POETRY, PAMPHLETS, ESSAYS, AND SPEECHES

1. *Side by Side:* The speech that was awarded second place at the Indiana State Oratorical Contest, which Zitkala-Ša writes about in "The School Days of an Indian Girl."

2. *A Protest Against the Abolition of the Indian Dance:* Titled "A Plea for the Indian Dance," this piece also appeared in the *Word-Carrier of Santee Normal Training School* in 1901.

3. *Americanize the First American:* The cover sheet of this pamphlet included a picture of Zitkala-Ša framed by a number of small American flags. The longer title of the piece is "Americanize the First American: A Plan of Regeneration."

4. *A Dakota Ode to Washington:* Zitkala-Ša read this "original prose poem" at a dedication ceremony held on June 22, 1922,

for a memorial stone placed at the Washington Monument in Washington, D.C., by the state of South Dakota.

5. *California Indian Trails and Prayer Trees:* The first of a series of four articles about the California Indians that were published serially, first in the *San Francisco Bulletin* and then in the *California Indian Herald.*